The Darkest Before the Dawn

by

JP Barry

The Nearer the Dawn Saga

The Darkest Before the Dawn

Cover Art by *Lisa Dawn MacDonald*

The Wild Rose Press, Inc.
PO Box 708
Adams Basin, NY 14410-0708
Visit us at www.thewildrosepress.com

Publishing History
First Edition, 2025
Trade Paperback ISBN 978-1-5092-6096-6
Digital ISBN 978-1-5092-6097-3
Previously Published 6/21/2018 MuseItUp

The Nearer the Dawn Saga
Published in the United States of America

Dedication

For my husband & daughter - Everything is limitless, especially you.

Prologue

And So We Continue…

Michael angrily paced his space, anxiously awaiting the arrival of his sons. If his tightly balled fists weren't enough to prove his tragically edgy annoyance, his deeply knit brows and scowl definitely did. As if the events of the evening and the answers The Elders would require weren't enough, he now had to contend with *them*. He was grateful both boys were unharmed, but he was severely irritated over their actions, which had set him over the edge.

Orifiel had specifically been warned to forget about what the stars revealed, but did that happen? No. Michael supposed it could've been worse. Orifiel could've told the Mortal Angel and lost his wings. Thankfully, he did not. Only vague hints were dropped, culminating with Gabriel having contact with the girl—seeing and potentially realizing things he shouldn't. But maybe, *just maybe*, this would turn out to be a good thing. A long overdue war between The Heavens and Hell was on the horizon. It had been for some time now. With Gabriel being a top ranking member of the Angelic Army, the Mortal would be in no danger with him by her side. The girl would feel safe because of the bond and Gabriel would protect her at any cost. There would be immediate trust and loyalty from both sides, but sometimes that sentiment didn't always bode well. Nina Luther and Gabriel were rather stubborn individuals. Additionally, if Gabriel caught wind that Orifiel and the girl had fooled around he'd explode, being unsure of why. The other problem was convincing Gabriel to do a job Orifiel was usually sent to do. He'd have questions. Tons of them. Michael was sure of this, but how would he answer them? How could he tell his eldest son this Mortal was exceptionally important and needed to be kept alive without raising any red flags? That she required his defending because she was more powerful than Raphael and shared a divine tie with Gabriel himself? Michael couldn't, so he prayed Gabriel would follow his lead with blind faith, viewing the situation for face value only.

The Powers That Be do not make mistakes...or do they? Your Lord trusts them. You have to as well. Though you must never forget they encompass no souls. The one Immortal trait which embodies a person's moral and emotional nature, their sense of identity. No inner self means no conscience, which equals trouble—big trouble.

Michael had been in the company of The Thirteen on many occasions. Each visit left him feeling cold, detached, and distant. It would take hours before normalcy and balance within himself returned. At the heart of the matter he truly believed Mortals were merely a game for them, but he dare not ever share these true thoughts with anyone, not even his mate. Michael had to be a spiritual leader, a devout follower. For that was his calling.

Blind faith...what a joke.

Then there was the reveal. In order to clean up

tonight's disaster, he had to show himself to Jack and Ellen Luther—something seriously frowned upon unless absolutely necessary. It had to be done. The Luthers had a right to know exactly what transpired with their daughter, but having to lie and omit truths to Mortals created unsettling sentiments.

"Father?" Gabriel said, entering the space. Orifiel followed close behind.

"Sit," Michael instructed.

Neither Gabriel nor Orifiel sat. They simply stood, not moving an inch.

"Sit." This time Michael spoke considerably louder.

After exchanging a brief glance, the two men followed their father's direction and sat shoulder to shoulder across from where Michael stood.

"*You* are a messenger. An Archangel. You sit in *my* inner circle—one of the Elite Seven. You're third in command in Heaven's Army and our Chief Demonic Assassin. You're a Gate Keeper and hold a sword," Michael spoke while pointing directly at Gabriel. "*You*," his attention turned to Orifiel, "are a Guardian. More specifically a Guardian Angel. You are a protector and my eyes and ears when I'm unavailable. And *I* am a Chief Archangel. The order in this room is Orifiel, Gabriel, and me at the top. So I ask myself, why must I stand here and explain your positions—positions you've held for decades, and why haven't either one of you listened to a damn word I've said these past few months?" His tone was harsh, borderline infuriated.

His sons glanced at one another. Both were aware of why their father was angered, but neither had an answer.

"Well?" Michael pressed.

"I eliminated the demons you ordered hits on,"

Gabriel spoke up. He loved his younger brother and knew whoever spoke first was bound to receive the brunt of Michael's rage. He could handle it. Orifiel was weaker and softer than he was. He felt obligated to protect him.

"*Hits*? I'm not a Mafia Crime Boss, Gabriel. I do not order *hits*. Furthermore, I said to *take care of the situation quickly and quietly*, not make it the final bloody act of a Shakespearian tragedy," Michael yelled. "It's to my understanding you tortured your prey then laughed before ending their suffering. Psychopathic lunatics do that. Not my Chief Assassin."

Michael recognized he was taking more than his current discontentment out on him, but he couldn't help it. Being calm and rational all day was exhausting when you had no one to blow up on. Often Michael felt like screaming. He didn't always have all of the answers. More times than he'd care to admit, he had no idea how to handle various issues. Truth-be-told, over the many centuries he often prayed for the best while making ill informed decisions.

"I did my job, Father. I fulfilled my calling as an *Archangel*. I'm a messenger. I sent a message," Gabriel said rather matter-of-factly.

"This is not a joke. I brought you into this world and I will take you out of it permanently if you don't start listening and do exactly what you're told. You're not a Mortal anymore, Gabriel. Stop behaving like one. Look where it got you on Earth. How many crimes did you commit? How many lies did you tell? How many humans did you hurt—physically and emotionally? How many felons did you protect? Lilith is gone. All of your pent-up fury and wrath is for nothing. Get it through your thick skull. She. Is. Never. Coming. Back. Build a bridge. Move along. I'm sick and tired of defending your irrational, psychotic actions."

Gabriel didn't respond, but rather scowled while shaking his head and turning away from his father. Michael realized a chord had been struck. He instantly felt horrible over his words. He loved his son and often assured him that his Mortal choices were in the past and needed to stay there. That he was a good man and certainly not the reason his mate took off. Michael and Hadreniel swore they'd never give up on Gabriel, especially when he was at his worst. They understood his hurt and how the unspeakable torture ran deep for him— deeper than Gabriel would ever let on.

Painfully Michael watched his son rise and move to an isolated corner of the space, where he stared out into the garden. Michael would address Orifiel then speak candidly with Gabriel later. He'd overstepped a boundary. Yes, there were lines never to be crossed even with your children. Slowly Michael moved to Orifiel's side and sat. He knew his other son was more sensitive. Being his heart still twinged over what transpired with Gabriel, a gentler approach was taken.

"Son," Michael said quietly. "What were you thinking?"

"I'm sorry, Father. I had no idea Gabriel was on Earth. It was to my understanding he was enroute to The Heavens, *not* thirty paces behind me. However, if I'm to be honest, even if I had been aware, I'd have done nothing to stop the moment. They *had* to meet. They *need* each other. Gabriel deserves happiness, as does Nina. They're both miserable and it kills me. Gabriel's pain is external. We all view it on a daily basis. Nina's isn't. Hers is internal which is far worse. I'd forsake my joy for them. No questions asked," Orifiel said. Noticeable traces of agony over Nina's and Gabriel's current states were clearly detected in his tenor.

"I'm aware and agree. They both warrant more than what they're receiving, but this isn't for us to decide. It's up to The Thirteen *and* their plan is already in action for all involved parties. We must not interfere with fate. You already did that by knocking around with Nina. Between that, the subtle hints you've dropped, and *especially* after tonight, the oblivious nature Nina once held will be no longer. Son, I beseech you. Please forget what you saw."

"How? The stars don't lie. Micah confirmed it. She has no idea what the alignment means, but she saw the same patterns as I did. They *have* to know. As for the snogging, I've already expressed my regret to you and her. I swear it will never happen again."

"You must let it all go."

"It's destined to happen regardless of what you say. Why not let nature take its course?"

Michael couldn't fault Orifiel's determination. "Micah concurs?" His voice trailed.

"Aye." Orifiel grinned.

Michael nodded curtly before rising. "Orifiel, I need a moment with your brother."

"Of course." He embraced his father tightly. "I am sorry, Father—not only for tonight, but for all of the times I've disappointed you. I want for you to be proud of me, but more than anything, I want Gabriel to be happy again."

"I *am* proud of you, son, and your brother *will* find happiness," Michael said while pulling away, but still maintaining their closeness. He gently touched the side of his handsome son's beautiful face. "Go find your mother. Allow her to dote on you. She worries."

After Orifiel exited the space, Michael turned his attention back to Gabriel.

"I'm sorry, son." He spoke sympathetically. He placed his hand on Gabriel's right shoulder.

"Apologies are for the weak," he replied absentmindedly.

Emotional and physical contact always broke Gabriel. Even the slightest gesture softened him. This was a useful secret Michael learned from Hadreniel, his mate and Gabriel's adopted mother. Outwardly Gabriel was a beast—arrogant and nasty. Internally he was a damaged soul filled with passion and untapped love.

"No, they're not. A strong man, Mortal or not, knows when he's done wrong and will do or say whatever to make it right."

"What now?" Gabriel asked dismissing the comment, but not moving away from Michael's hold.

"Once Vincent realizes more members of Hell's Army have been destroyed, he's going to strike back, and with a vengeance. We need to remain vigilant. Raphael and I have no set plan of attack at the moment. We must wait and see what transpires."

"What *is* Vincent's next move? Surely you have some idea how your old friend's mind operates."

Michael cringed with sorrow and exasperation at the thought of his and Vincent's past. He knew this war, in part, was his fault. If he'd only done things differently. If he hadn't met with Vincent, alerting him to the presence of the girl and the Lost Soul in Savannah, perhaps this could've been avoided.

"If I had to guess, I'd say he's going to go after the targets from tonight again and won't stop until he traps and tortures the boy and kills the girl."

"Why are we protecting them? Why do we care?"

"The girl is a Mortal Healing Angel. She's almost as powerful as the Angelic version of Raphael. When her soul passes, she'll be stronger than him. She's also a partial seer, though the ability is limited at best. As of right now, she can only see visions pertaining to her and her mate. I'm unsure of how strong this gift will grow. It needs to be monitored and I have to be made aware of any new developments. The boy was a Lost Soul, but after tonight, he's a Mortal Angel as well."

"So what? She's a talented healer which everyone knows healers can't help Demons, and he's a nobody— a common run-of-the-mill Mortal Angel. Why would they want him or to waste their time killing her? There's more to this story. What aren't you telling me?"

"A healer of her strength may be able to cure all, Angelic or Demonic. It's anyone's guess what will transpire when her time comes, but if Vincent finds this bit of information out, we're royally screwed. With her on our side we'll be an unstoppable undefeated force. As for the boy, he's a rare find. He encompasses both good and evil with the potential to become exceedingly forceful if trained properly. Plus, since her seer abilities foresee her and his futures and Vincent's voice can be heard inside of his head, we'll have a direct line into whatever Vincent is plotting."

Gabriel paused, thinking before speaking again. "He's the one who was struck by both sides? The one Orifiel was tailing?"

"Yes. Vincent wed the two tonight. By default, he's part of our tribe now, but I don't trust him. He has both light and dark from within. He's the male version of—"

"My Lilith. Yeah, I know. Orifiel already filled me in. I fought the night Heaven and Hell collided inside of the Lost Soul," Gabriel answered cutting Michael off mid-sentence, turning, and walking back to the farthest corner of the space. After all of these years, he still couldn't come to terms with what happened.

"Have you seen her recently?" Michael inquired cautiously. He knew from time-to-time Gabriel sought Lilith out, watching her from afar. He never stopped his son. Perhaps it was his only way of coping with his loss. On Michael's order Lilith wasn't to be harmed. She meant too much to Gabriel even though Michael thought otherwise. If it were up to him, she'd have been long gone.

"No. Let her rot in Hell for all I care," Gabriel spat.

Michael discerned he was lying but let the topic rest. Lilith had shattered his son's soul, leaving him a broken man. Admitting he still kept tabs on her would make him feel weak, and Gabriel certainly couldn't have that.

"What do you want? Where are you sending me?" Gabriel asked in a tone so flat Michael feared he was close to losing all sense of emotional connection to the Universe. Gabriel ran his hands through his neck length, dark blond hair.

"To follow the girl. You're a skilled fighter, third in command in our army, and a highly trained Demonic assassin. Your name is feared in the Demon world. Alone you've slain at least a thousand of them. I've never seen such talent before. Your Mortal life taught you how to be aware of your surroundings, act quickly, read situations, and assess danger at a moment's notice. That has paid off well. I wouldn't ask if I didn't think you weren't the perfect person for the job."

"How often do you want updates?"

"Every day, several times a day until we know what's going on. This is serious, Gabriel. The girl is in extreme danger if Vincent finds her. He'll not only end her Mortal life but will destroy her soul. If he realizes her healing gift is strong and spares her, she could become our greatest enemy. I need the girl alive or as a true Angel. She's far too valuable to lose." Michael's facial expression and white knuckles caused Gabriel deep concern. The severity of the situation finally struck.

"This is life or death, son."

"The girl, she's the female target from tonight?" Gabriel's body shook at the thought of the creature he'd laid eyes on earlier. He had to confirm this Mortal female they were speaking of was definitely the one he'd met.

"Yes. Is that a problem?"

"Send Orifiel back. I'll do the behind-the-scenes work." Fear and trepidation collided with the sheer thought of being alone in her presence.

"I can't. He's become too attached to her and because of that, there's an emotional investment between them that I'm afraid will cause him to have a lapse in judgement. Again, you're the *only* one skilled enough to complete this mission."

"Is Orifiel involved with her?" Gabriel's tone reflected disbelief, stress, and a strong possessive jealousy.

Instantly Michael knew the spark had been ignited. Though he wanted to know how hot the flame was, he was too afraid to ask.

"Does it matter?"

"Yes."

"Why?"

"Is she involved with Orifiel?" he repeated, choosing to ignore his father's question.

"His feelings for her are that of friendship. You know our laws and rules and are familiar with your brother. I can't risk him doing something stupid because his soul is too caring for his own good."

An involuntary grin came and went across Gabriel's face once Michael clarified the situation.

"Watch her from afar, son. Any sign of trouble you're to alert me and attack. You need to keep her safe, but more importantly, alive. Should her husband turn, you have direct standing orders to do whatever necessary to handle the situation. If you must eliminate him, do it and don't think twice about it. Use discretion and do not engage in combat unless absolutely necessary."

"Aside from the fact that she's a powerful Mortal Angel, healer, partial seer, and married to a Demi-Demon, what else should I know?"

"Here," Michael answered, handing over a folder. "Everything you'll need is in there. Review it and meet me early tomorrow morning. She has a temporary watcher for tonight." He paused, looking deeply into his son's wide, brown eyes.

"You're the only one I trust to handle this. I need you."

Michael's admittance of trust softened Gabriel's almost nonexistent heart. He loved his father and his new Heavenly family. They'd been kind and welcoming, choosing not to judge him based on his sorted past. There was no scrutiny or push to be something he wasn't. They cared about him endlessly no matter what, and there had been many no-matter-what's since his passing.

"Nothing will happen to the girl. You have my

solemn word."

****

Immediately Gabriel returned to his personal space. Upon his arrival he flipped Michael's folder open. Hungrily he tore through the pages until he found what he desired. A picture. Her eyes were incredible, sparkling with pleasure and pain. The instant connection from earlier returned with a vengeance. Oh, how he craved her and didn't know why. From the second they met this uncontrollable desire to grab, kiss, and take her consumed him. He wanted to hold her until the torture within both of their souls left for good, never to return. He *could* make that a reality. Her tan skin glowed in the pale moonlight, while her dirty blonde hair rustled in the careless night's breeze. Plain and simple, she was going to be a troublemaker, but he loved trouble. Couldn't resist it, ever.

"She's beautiful, isn't she?" Orifiel asked.

Gabriel didn't respond. He couldn't stop staring at the photograph. Thoughts of being with, even just around her, raced through his mind awaking and exciting the Mortal from within him.

"Gabriel?"

"Huh?" Gabriel said, finally snapping back to reality.

"Nina Luther? Opinions?" Orifiel questioned.

"Mortal Healing Angel, lives in Savannah, Georgia, student, limited seer, married to a partial Demon," he rattled off desperate to clear his head.

"All true facts, *but* what's your gut saying?" Orifiel pressed. His golden irises danced with curiosity.

"What are you getting at, little Brother?" He knew something was circling inside of Orifiel's brain.

"Just a question." Orifiel shrugged.

Tossing the folder aside, Gabriel stood. "Orifiel, Father suggests that she and you are merely friends, but I have to question if something else is going on. Are you by chance in love with a Mortal who's already been mated with another man?"

"No. Yes, I care deeply for Nina, but I'm certainly not in love with her. Like you said, she's already been paired, and the stars have confirmed it."

"Liar. Try one more time and remember, I can see your soul and read your aura."

"I'm *not* lying," Orifiel protested.

Gabriel looked him dead in the eyes while raising one eyebrow challenging Orifiel's words.

"The sweat rolling down your forehead, lack of eye contact, body language, pulsating aura, and the sliver of your soul that's falling off all tell a considerably different story. I'll rephrase the question, and I expect the truth this time. What's the deal with the girl?"

"I hate your gift." His face dropped. "We shared one moment a few months ago. Nina was upset. I comforted. Her life's tough. The bloke she's with doesn't help the situation much. I love her, but not romantically. Like family. More specifically, like a sister."

"What sort of moment did you share?" Gabriel asked, feeling his heart sink as angry annoyance for his brother rose to the surface.

"I soothed her soul with mine. You know, absorbed her energy."

"That's impossible, Orifiel. The only way you could connect like that would be if you were a true family member, part of her soul circle, or she was your mate, not simply a friend. Are you related?"

"Biologically, no."

"Spiritually?"

"Yes."

"How?"

"It's too detailed, too personal to discuss right now, brother. Please don't make me," he begged. "You have to take good care of her though. Watch her closely. She can be a real pain in the arse at times. She over-thinks everything. It's only because the cards she's been dealt haven't been good ones, but the ones in her hands are played well. Nina tries to be tough, but she isn't. Love and loyalty are her weakness."

Gabriel nodded in agreement. "If she's part of your spiritual family, then she's part of mine."

"I love Nina very much. You will too. May I ask you one last question?"

"Fire away."

"Did you feel or experience anything when you met Nina?" Orifiel probed, holding his breath.

"No," Gabriel replied quickly and flatly. An obvious untruth, but he couldn't exactly put into words what he was thinking and experiencing. Emotions like these were too strong to process, mainly because he refused to acknowledge anything other than nothing. "Is there anything else I should know?"

"Nope."

"Good. Now, go away. I need to review the target and rest before I leave tomorrow. This mission is baptism by fire."

Orifiel made his way to the threshold of Gabriel's space, stopping, then turning to face his brother one last time before the two would be separated for an undetermined amount of time. He hated not being able to be with Gabriel. It'd been far too long since they had the time to piss the night away, but his brother was needed. Nina required his assistance. Her well-being was far more important than the two men catching up.

"You're always so bloody livid. I hate it. You shouldn't be. You're a great man. It's okay to let down your guard and open your heart and mind to new people. Should you feel something, go with it. It *will* be reciprocated. You have my word, and I never go back on that. If you need anything, call to me. I'll be there immediately. Be careful," he said before exiting.

"Orifiel," Gabriel summoned.

"Oi?" he replied, returning to the space.

"You know, right?"

"Know what?" Orifiel queried though he knew exactly what his brother meant.

Rarely did Gabriel admit his feelings. He found it too difficult to express himself. Orifiel was fully aware of this, but at times he thought by making his brother say the phrase it would help him to realize that loving another soul was a good thing.

"I love you, brother," he mumbled, avoiding all eye contact. His actions showed an un-comfortability uttering those three heartbreaking, life ruining words.

"I love you too. No matter what," Orifiel said, immediately taking his leave.

****

Hours before dawn's first light, Gabriel rose and found his father. Michael was still resting with Hadreniel. He hated to bother him, but if he didn't Michael would be angered over him leaving without a proper goodbye. Gabriel wasn't about to add more fuel to his father's already roaring fire.

"Father," he said in a loud whisper.

"Do you have everything you need, son?" Michael answered fully awake. Heavy, dark bags revealed he hadn't slept a wink. His mind was consumed with worry and fear over this assignment. Without a doubt this man spent the entire night changing his mind over whom to send to Earth in place of Gabriel, but ultimately concluded that Gabriel was the only man powerful enough to handle this situation.

"Yes."

"A fully stocked house is awaiting your arrival. In the garage you'll find adequate transportation. On the kitchen table there's a manila envelope containing all of the necessary forms of paperwork and identification necessary to blend in with the Mortals. Several bank accounts and no limit credit cards have been set up in your name. Clothing as well as various other items have been purchased and put away. The Mortal is traveling to New York City today. Micah is making sure the plane is delayed so you can meet her group when they land. Urim will stay with her until they land at Kennedy Airport. A packed bag is in the corner. Make sure you take it before leaving. Your travel itinerary is with the papers I provided you with last night. Are you sure you can handle Mortal life again?"

"I got this," he replied casually, knowing damn well he wasn't certain of this at all.

"Do not let her see you, Gabriel. You are to watch her from afar," he warned.

"I read the file. I know the drill. Stealth mode. Attack and eliminate if necessary. If I get into trouble, call you. This isn't my first day on the job," he snapped.

"Say goodbye to your mother," Michael answered,

ignoring Gabriel's rudeness. It was nerves. The world had changed considerably since Gabriel last roamed it. Though the Angels kept up with the times with respect to technology and fashion, culture shock was inevitable.

Gabriel's demeanor softened as he sat on the edge of the bed beside his mother. Gently he leaned down and kissed her forehead. Hadreniel reached up and caressed the side of his face. Instantly his fingers met hers as his eyelids closed. She adored her son. To her he was perfect and could do no wrong. He was damaged and required her love and support more than anyone in her life.

"Please be careful, my darling," she begged.

"I'm always careful, Mother, *and* I always return home to you." He smiled in an assuring manner.

"You seem different," she replied, grinning.

"How so?"

"Your heart is warmer, fuller. Life has been slightly restored to it."

"That's because I'm sitting next to the most loving woman in the entire Universe." He winked. "I have to go, but come find me every now and again, and call to me. I'm going to miss you. When I return, I'd like to spend some time with you, alone." He embraced her thin frame tightly.

"When you're home, we can do whatever you'd like. Just you and me. I'll check in often, don't worry about that, but calling works both ways, son. I love you eternally. My soul exists entirely for you and your brother, my precious first born."

After a prolonged moment, Gabriel took his leave, descending to Earth, desperate for a glimpse of Nina Luther—the girl who now haunted his every thought.

Let's see how much trouble I can get into this time around as a Mortal.

Chapter 1

Nina

The airport was packed with fellow Savannahians who, much like myself, were trying to escape the monsoon-like weather Georgia was experiencing. I, however, wasn't only looking to escape the depressing rain, I was getting ready to use the birthday gift Chase had given me to go back to New York for a much-needed, long overdue visit.

Don't get me wrong. After two intense years in Savannah, I started to actually like it. Maybe even more than New York, but you'd never hear me admit that out loud to anyone, *ever*. Savannah had been good to me for the most part. If my family never moved, I wouldn't have met Chase—the most important person in my life. Chase James—soul mate, divine destiny, and brand new Mortal Angel. After many sleepless nights, we were finally on the same page.

My best friend, Jules, and her boyfriend, Mark, suggested they join us on the trip to which we happily agreed. For Jules, Mark, and Chase this would be their first time in the city that never sleeps. The four of us made our way through the crowded terminal, finally able to board the plane after an annoying three-hour delay.

"I'm so excited, Nina," Jules exclaimed, snapping a picture of me supervising Chase storing a carry-on bag in the overhead compartment.

"Take another picture of me and I'll hurt you." Jules was way too peppy, and it was way too early. Between her overly cheerful mood, the time, and lack of caffeine I wasn't in the best frame of mind.

"Oh, Nina. Stop being moody. We're on vacation. We're supposed to be having fun. Once we arrive in New York you'll spring back to life."

"Promises, promises," I muttered, slumping into my seat and pulling my hat tightly over my head.

"Come on, baby," Chase whispered.

"Do you have any idea what hour it is? Ass crack of dawn o'clock."

"Take a nap. We have a good two and a half hours before landing." Nudging his shoulder into mine, he reached for my hand, and softly pressed his warm lips to my left ring finger.

There, on that hand, was a reminder of who and what we were to each other. A black, barbed wire band was tattooed on it compliments of Vincent. As of last May, in the Angelic and Demonic world, we were husband and wife, therefore making him, a once Lost Soul, a Mortal Angel by marriage. Chase too wore the same mark of the Devil.

As per my father's wishes when questioned about the matching body art we were to say we suffered a moment of insanity and thought it would be cool to get permanent matching rings. The excuse worked because no one pressed the matter further.

In the *normal* world, which is what I like to refer to it as, I was a second-year student studying pre-med at South University, while Chase was finishing up his first year as a criminal justice major. We were dating and he was living with my family because of the many issues which existed between him and his father. Neither of his parents was aware of his other life, nor did he plan on telling them, ever.

Boy, if they knew the truth about what's been going on lately...

In general, I really couldn't complain about anything in the normal world. Situations had leveled off from earlier in the year. Other than the mood and sense altering ability, being able to slow down time, and incredible strength Chase hadn't developed any additional gifts. He'd been spending quite a bit of time sharpening his skills and learning about Angelic ways. If anything, he'd certainly embraced this new path which I had to give him credit for.

I, on the other hand, treated anyone who mentioned training to a long rant about how a break from my supernatural existence was required. Chase and I barely made it out alive last May. Being regular teenagers was what we should've been focusing on. I wasn't stupid. A war between the Angels and Demons was imminent, Orifiel had said as much, but *when* was a question I did and didn't want to know the answer to. Ignorance is bliss, right?

Three cups of coffee and nearly three and a half hours later—another unfortunate flight delay on the runway prior to takeoff, the four of us were leaving John F. Kennedy Airport and were on our way to the Waldorf Astoria Hotel. The moment my feet stepped out of the limo my nostrils were welcomed home by the familiar elements of the city. My eyes closed as my senses enjoyed the sound of cars rushing by, horns honking, sirens blasting, the clopping of shoes against the pavement, and the smell in the air no words could ever describe. Chase's ability to enhance the experience wasn't necessary. We checked in and settled into our rooms making plans to hit the city in a half hour.

Over the course of the next two weeks we explored Times Square, Rockefeller Center, Wall Street, Little Italy, China Town, Central and Battery Park, St. Patrick's Cathedral, Ellis Island, the Statue of Liberty, various museums, the famous buildings which made up the picturesque skyline, saw two Broadway shows, walked the Brooklyn Bridge, caught a Yankee game, ate in trendy restaurants, and of course shopped. We were so busy time rapidly flew by. On our last night, due to extreme fatigue, we decided to eat dinner at the hotel. To be honest, I wanted to relax in preparation for the flight home while mourning that in twenty-four short hours my life was going to have to go back to being crazy again. The trip was flawless. Nothing went wrong. I was finally able to breathe easy. Initially, part of me expected Vincent to jump out from behind a building or a bush and attack us, but that fear subsided within the first few days. A certain sense of unknown security was felt allowing me to drop my guard.

"This was fun. We should do it again somewhere else," Mark said while we ate.

"Oh, crap. I forgot to call my parents this afternoon." Grabbing my purse from the back of my chair, my fingers dug through its contents for my cell phone. "Damn it. It must be upstairs."

"Do you want me to get it for you, baby? Mine's up there too," Chase questioned.

"Give me your cell, Jules," I said, ignoring Chase. If he didn't have a phone, he was useless.

"Sorry, Nina. My battery died this afternoon. Mark's too."

"*Great.* I'll be back."

Annoyed, I got up from the table and headed to my room. Mumbling grievances while standing in the elevator didn't help alleviate my irritation. However, if we were in any other city talking to myself in angry tones would've been seen as crazy, bizarre behavior, but we were in New York where this was a totally normal, acceptable way of living.

God, it's good to be home.

The painfully slow lift finally made its way to my floor. As I exited, I made sure to avoid the slight ripple in the carpet Chase had been warning me about for the past two weeks. Picking up my foot to step over the area the heel of my shoe got stuck on the fray of my jeans. My body toppled causing me to fall squarely on my hands and knees. Luckily no one was there to witness the embarrassing moment.

Better fix yourself up. Bruises and scrapes on both knees and hands during the height of skirt and short season don't go.

Still fairly confident I was alone, I ran my hands skillfully over my injuries, allowing the radiating warmth to ease the pain. Once the bright light subsided, my limbs painlessly flexed as if nothing happened.

Could you be a bigger klutz?

No sooner did I close the door to my room, a loud knock echoed through the space. A chill shot up my spine. My feet rooted to the spot. My brain couldn't process what to do. Whoever was on the other side of the wall probably saw what went down in the hallway.

Oh my God. Why didn't you wait until you were in

23

the room before healing yourself? What's wrong with you? Now what?

An all on panic attack broke free consuming my entire core.

If you don't move, maybe they'll go away.

Another loud knock assaulted my ears.

Damn it!

Slowly I made my way to the ingress hoping to catch a glimpse of the knocker through the peephole. It was fight or flight time. The problem was, there was nowhere to flee to. Aside from smashing the window and risking severe injury or possibly death from the ten story plus drop, I was screwed. Fighting this out was my only option. The pounding of my heart thumped in my eardrums. My mouth went dry, and my breathing grew labored.

"Nina? It's me."

Jules.

Without thinking, my fingers hastily turned the handle. Grabbing hold of Jules's arm, I yanked her inside.

"What?" I asked in a strange tone. My hands nervously attempted to pull my hair up into a top knot.

"We need to talk. It's kind of serious." Her expression was unreadable. "Are you okay, Nina? You're all pale and sweaty. Plus, you've got this whole edgy, jumpy vibe about you."

Nothing good ever came from a conversation that started with, "*we need to talk.*" Jules knew. She saw me healing myself in the hallway. For a brief moment, dread and relief crashed into each other. Yes, there were rules and regulations about who Mortal Angels could and couldn't tell our secret too, but surely this situation had to fall into some sort of loophole. How could I not tell someone who obviously saw me using my ability? How could I lie my way out of this? Look at what happened when I wasn't upfront with Chase after he saw me heal Tori.

"Okay. Here's the deal. I'm sure you have a lot of questions, but let me explain first. Please don't freak out and run away like Chase did. Five minutes. That's all I need, and you'll understand everything."

"What?"

"I am a Mortal Angel. A Mortal Healing Angel to be exact. I can heal just about any wound or illness with the touch of my hands. I healed Tori the night of the Winter Dance when she and Tim had that big fight. Didn't you find it bizarre how she took one hell of a spill, but had no real damage on her body except a few minor cuts and scrapes? And Chase—he's a Mortal Angel too," I said.

"Huh?" Was all Jules said. Her face scrunched with confusion.

"It sounds weird, I know, but I'm *not* insane. Which is ironic because if I were, that's the only thing I wouldn't be able to heal. I cannot cure mental health issues—maybe Raphael can, but I can't. I honestly have no idea why that's a condition for this gift, but I swear I'm telling you the truth. My entire family are Healing Angels—mother, father, brother, everyone. That's why we move a lot, so no one can catch onto our secret. Look," I continued, picking up a pair of cuticle scissors and making a small cut on my left palm.

Once I was sure she saw the blood, I waved my right hand over the wound allowing the warmth and light to linger a bit longer than usual. Her face still wore no expression.

"You remember Chase's car accident, right? Well, instead of dying he was sent back to Earth to find me because we're soul mates and to choose a proper path. When people die, they go to Purgatory. Sometimes The Powers That Be can't decide which direction, Heaven or Hell, to send someone, so they're given a second chance to either live a good life and go to Heaven, or a bad one and go to Hell. There's a lot more to it, but that's the general idea. People like Chase who are sent back are what we call Lost Souls. The evening of the surprise party you threw me for my birthday, we were married by Vincent, the leader of the Demonic Army, and Chase became a Mortal Angel by default. That's why we have matching ring tattoos. I'm not Immortal. At some point I will die, like you, Mark, and everybody else. We carry out our missions on Earth while Mortals and when we pass, we become Immortal—full-fledged Angels, like Michael, Raphael, and Orifiel, who are the reason we were saved last summer from becoming part of Vincent's army. Chase has powers too. He can change emotions and senses, slow down time, and is freakishly strong. Remember the batting cages?"

"Who's Vincent? Michael? Orifiel? Seriously, what in the world are you talking about, because nothing you're saying is making any sense."

For the next thirty minutes I spoke nonstop while pacing back and forth, telling Jules everything about Angels, Demons, my other life, the extent of my Heavenly gifts, destiny, and why I never told anyone. She was filled in on why Chase broke up with me senior year, the battle the night of the Senior Dinner, about being kidnapped on my birthday, why Chase was really living with my family, the real reason Sean Logan disappeared, and the truth about Bristol, Sean's half-sister. She sat, not moving or speaking, only listening.

"I'm sorry, Jules, but I had to keep all of this a secret. Please understand and promise, swear, you won't tell anyone *ever*," I begged.

"Why are you telling me this now, Nina?"

"What do you mean, why am I telling you now? You saw me in the hallway healing myself. Didn't you?" I stopped moving. Jules remained sitting at the foot of my bed.

"No. I didn't see anything."

"Then why the hell are you here?" My heart sank into my stomach. I could feel every last ounce of blood draining from my face.

"To talk about Mark and me."

"You saw *nothing*?"

"Not a thing."

"Please feel free to run away screaming if you'd like. I'm a freak. I'm painfully aware."

"No, you're not. Good, bad, or indifferent, you're my best friend. I think of you as a sister. I'm not going to lie. What you shared is probably the oddest thing I've ever heard, and I have a lot of questions, but I'd never tell anyone. I believe you and I swear my lips are sealed. For the record—knowing this about you explains a lot. I'd love to discuss your other life with you further, but right now I need to tell you something before I lose my nerve."

"What's going on?"

She took a deep breath, exhaling loudly.

"What, Jules? What is it?"

Sitting beside Jules, I took her hand in mine and

squeezed it gently hoping this would provide her with the necessary courage and strength to say whatever was on her mind. The pained expression on her face made me forget everything that occurred moments earlier. I was worried for her wellbeing. What if this was bad news? What if Jules was sick or worse?

"Jules, if you're ill I can fix it."

"I'm not."

"Are you in trouble?"

"No."

"Pregnant?"

"Seriously? Do I look knocked up?"

"No, but other than being sick, pregnant, or in trouble, I have no idea what could be the matter."

"I'm a lesbian."

"Are you sure?" The question flew out of my mouth without thought.

"Uh yeah, Nina. I'm pretty sure. It's not like I woke up this morning and thought it'd be really cool or trendy to start liking the same sex. I've known for a long time."

"What about Mark?"

"What about Mark? I tried to force myself to be straight and date guys, but I'm tired of lying. Nobody knows but you. I wanted to see how you'd react before going public."

"But you slept with Mark."

"So?"

"You don't look like a lesbian."

"Exactly what do lesbians look like, Nina?"

"I don't know. You don't have short hair or dress in Bohemian style clothing. I've never seen you in a flannel with boots. You've never expressed an interest in woodworking or sports, and you don't look like a guy.

I've also never seen you check out women."

"Can you say *stereotyping*? Forget it. I never should've said anything." She stood.

"Jules, wait."

"You expect me to sit here and listen to you spill your guts about being some kind of Mortal Angel and I'm supposed believe and support you? You sound like and are acting like a completely unhinged person, but never once did I say or do anything to make you feel bad. If anything, when we returned home, I was going to ask if you needed help because that's what friends do. People stay in the closet for years lying to themselves and everyone around them because of narrow-minded people like *you. And* if you even consider telling anyone about this conversation, I can assure you you'll be glad you can heal yourself. Leave me alone, please," she hissed, slamming the door.

I should've chased after her, but I didn't. What would I say? How does one recover from acting like the world's biggest asshole to their best friend? My body slumped on the bed. I was confident I'd just lost my best friend.

****

The flight home and the week following the trip was abysmal. I wanted to call Jules to apologize, but I was too ashamed, and honestly too scared. Currently, part of me thought she might open her mouth to blab my secret all over town. That was an awful feeling. For as long as I'd known Jules she'd never been this upset. After dinner I'd reach out. It didn't matter what it took to get her to listen, she had to. Her presence was missed, and an apology was in order.

"Hey, baby. What're you doing?" Chase asked.

"I was going to call Jules. We haven't spoken in a while."

"I noticed some tension on the plane. What's up?"

"She kind of told me something and I may have told her something, but I reacted like an idiot which resulted in me hurting her feelings." Saying the words out loud that I offended Jules made my already crummy internal emotions grow worse.

"What did you tell her, Nina?"

"Promise you won't get upset."

"I'm going to regret agreeing to this, but sure. I won't get upset."

"I thought she saw me healing myself at the hotel. You weren't there so you have no idea what thoughts raced through my head."

"Did she?" His facial expression reflected a total state of awareness.

"No. I jumped to conclusions. I'd already spilled the beans before I found out that she wanted to talk about something else."

"She's freaked out now?"

"Not exactly. She actually didn't seem disturbed at all. She had more questions about us, but she was more focused on her own issue. She swore she wouldn't say anything, and I believe her."

"Issue? What issue?"

"I can't say."

"Why not?"

"Because I told her I wouldn't."

"Is it serious?" Chase's jade eyes hooded in concern.

"She's not ill or anything like that. Just drop it, okay? You'll find out in time. Or from Mark." I mumbled the last part.

"Is she pregnant?"

"No."

"Sick?"

"I already told you, no."

"In some sort of trouble?"

"No. Stop. I'm *not* going to tell you."

"You can't go around suggesting you know something then expect me to not be curious. Did she come out of the closet or something?" He laughed, but I didn't. My head dropped and my cheeks flushed.

"*No.*" Chase's eyes opened wide.

"Don't you dare say a word to anyone about this, Chase James," I warned. My body stood ramrod straight while my right index finger jammed itself into his rock-hard chest.

"I'm not going to say a word about this to anyone. Does Mark know?" he said, gently removing my finger and kissing it softly.

"No one does except me and now you."

"Listen, baby. I'm not sure how or why you acted in a way you're ashamed of, but honestly? Jules is still Jules. She's still the same person. You probably should apologize or try to make peace. She's always had your back. Remember last year when she stuck up for you by punching me in the stomach? That's not something a lot of people would do. I'm actually really proud of Jules. For as long as I've known her, she's always blended in, never allowing anyone to truly see the amazing person she is. Coming out had to have been hard for her. She's out of her comfort zone."

"You're right. I acted like an ass, and I need to fix this."

"Go over to her house. Talk face to face. Show her

how sorry you are and tell her how much you support and love her."

Saying sorry had nothing to do with her knowing my secret. It had everything to do with me acting like an insensitive, horrible human being. She'd never tell anyone what I said. Jules was the walking talking definition of what friendship was. Glancing at my watch, it was still early enough to head over to her home without disturbing her grandmother, parents, or brother. Since requests for forgiveness and expressing myself accurately with words was never a strong suit of mine, finding an inspirational, '*I'm sorry*' card usually worked best when diffusing situations. After a speedy trip to the drugstore, my BMW slowed to a stop in the Warner Family driveway.

"Hi, Mrs. Warner. Is Jules home?" I asked, knowing she probably was because her car was parked out front.

"Hello, Nina. She's up in her room," her mother replied, ushering me into the house.

Climbing the stairs two by two, my knuckles softly knocked on her bedroom door.

"Yes?" Jules asked.

"It's me," I answered, hesitating before entering.

"What do you want?" she responded firmly.

"To say I'm sorry for acting like the biggest idiot ever. Please forgive me? I totally blew what you shared out of proportion when it was you who should've been bugging out over my secret. Here. This says it much better," I said, handing over the envelope.

"Thanks." She opened it and read the sentiment. "Aw, Nina. This is the sweetest card ever," she managed to get out before her eyes welled with tears.

"I'm proud of you, Jules. It doesn't matter who or

what you are or identify as. It will never matter to me because I will always accept you and respect your happiness. You'll always be my best friend and sister. You should never have to hide what makes you comfortable, especially when you're around me. I really love you and miss our daily chats."

"Thank you for saying that. I would've gotten you a card, but Hallmark doesn't make any, '*so I hear you have supernatural abilities*' ones." She laughed and hugged me tightly.

"How are you doing with all of this?"

"Better now, actually. It was difficult to tell you, but once I spoke the words out loud to someone other than myself, everything seemed okay—not as overwhelming. I haven't told Mark, but my mom knows. She took it fairly well once the initial shock wore off. She wants to see me happy, and she supports me. We're not going to tell my dad yet. Mom said she had to figure out the right words to use, but I think she believes this is some sort of phase. That I'll wake up one day straight again." She paused. "I'm still me, Nina. I'm still the same old Jules."

"I know and when you find a girlfriend you better share all of the details."

"Deal. Enough about me. What about you? How are you doing?"

"I'm doing well."

"That's great, but tell me more about this double life you, Chase, and your family are living. I want to know everything. You said you and Chase are in some sort of danger. I don't want to see anything bad happen to you guys." She dried her eyes.

One deep sigh and several hours later, Jules had been told everything. It felt amazingly freeing to purge to someone other than my family or Chase. Had it not been well past midnight I would've stayed longer. Before leaving we agreed to meet tomorrow to talk some more. Jules seemed fascinated and why shouldn't she be? Curiosity over the unknown was something we were all guilty of. Once we obtain even the slightest bit of insight into life's great mysteries, we can never get enough. Her extreme interest didn't bother me. If anything, it put my worried mind at ease. She understood the severity of this knowledge and swore it would remain between us. At the moment her loyalty was of no consequence. The purge alone was worth the risk.

Chapter 2

Gabriel

I hadn't seen New York since being a Mortal. Traveling back to the city where many years of happy occasions were celebrated was bittersweet. It's funny how nostalgia erases bad memories because there were plenty of those. Thankfully, Micah delayed Nina's plane which made timing my arrival and acclimating to Earth easier. Watching Nina step out of a limousine in front of the Waldorf Astoria Hotel was another story.

This girl obviously comes from a family that has a lot of money. She's definitely spoiled. What nineteen-year-old can afford to stay at one of the most expensive hotels in New York?

My head involuntarily shook. Having to babysit was annoying enough, but having to babysit a rich princess was going to be a true test of my paper-thin patience. She turned. Her face finally came into clear view. Her enchanting eyes closed as a look of pure happiness spread across her lips.

Shit.

Nina was more beautiful than I remembered. Something about her presence awoke a spark deep within me making me feel human again and that was dangerous.

Come on, angel. Open those eyelids so I can see inside of your soul like I did the night we met.

Unfortunately, my desperate desire went unanswered because she slid a pair of heavily tinted sunglasses off of her head and onto her face obscuring any view.

You have a job to do. If you get sidetracked, you'll miss something. Who cares about her? She's a target you're to keep safe. Period. Besides, your body, mind, heart, and soul belong to Lilith. It's Lilith and only Lilith who should be evoking these emotions, not some random nobody.

I followed Nina and her group for the next two weeks shoving her hold out of my head. However, her husband sickened me. In order to obtain a better idea of the situation, my divine gift of aura and soul reading had to be used. You'd be amazed by how much you can learn about a Mortal by knowing how whole their soul is and what color aura they exuded. His Mortal soul was one of the worst I'd ever seen. It was all sorts of torn and distorted. His aura was always some sort of shade of gray. What does all of this equal? Trouble.

One quarter Demonic my ass. Three quarters is more like it.

The girl with Nina proved to be an interesting subject. I noticed her soul immediately. It was perfect. Not a tear or a dent in it; very childlike. Something was up with her though. Her aura pulsated the entire time. Whenever the man she was with tried to touch her, she instantly saddened, and changed directions so he couldn't. It finally dawned on me several days into the trip she was dealing with issues concerning her sexuality and identity. Never-the-less, she was still a good girl in my opinion. The type of person Nina *should* be hanging out with.

The visit to New York was filled with painful and happy recollections. Seeing my old neighborhood when Nina took her group to Little Italy was difficult. Standing in Rockefeller Center proved torturous. I'd take Lilith there every Christmas, then we'd go shopping. The past flooded every ounce of my being choking my heart with horrible aching sensations. Though the outing to Ellis Island was a highlight.

While they browsed the walls filled with the names of immigrants who'd come to this country, I did the same. Seeing my parents' names felt nice, almost like they were with me again. They were in Heaven having passed many years ago, but I never tried finding them. The agony in my mother's face the day she and my father lowered my empty coffin into the ground damn near destroyed me. I couldn't bear to see them after inflicting such hurt.

Moving along...

There was this one moment that captured my total attention. A new memory from the city which would never be forgotten; only safely locked away in the recesses of my mind. After shopping, Nina sat down on the steps of the Columbus Circle Monument. The way the light caught her rounded edges was remarkable. She was beauty personified. Casually she sipped an iced coffee while chatting freely with her girlfriend. Happiness, true joy, radiated from her aura making her appearance even more divine, if that were even possible. The sound of her laugh was unreal. Everything a man could ever wish for or dream of was right there in front of my face. Ready to say screw it and abandon the mission by approaching her, she shrieked. The reason for her panic? A pigeon. A common street pigeon frightened the girl who so boldly and bravely stood up to Vincent twice. Once the girlfriend shooed the bird away, Nina returned to her blissful state, but that wrinkle in time proved I wanted to be the man protecting her. My soul required something inside of Nina's innocent, unconventionally pure being. She could heal me. She could make my anger and pain subside. Forcing myself from the happening was difficult, but necessary. Swearing I wouldn't fall victim again would be damn near impossible.

You have to try, Gabriel. This is a mission not 'The Dating Game.'

Before I knew it, they were sitting in John F. Kennedy Airport waiting to go back to Savannah, something I was less than pleased over. Acclimating to new spaces sucked enough, but now not only did I have to blend in with Mortals in a vastly different era than accustomed to, I'd have to get used to living in Georgia. Being in New York was easier because even though times may have changed, at least I still remembered the lay of the land.

The happy girl exiting the limo two weeks prior had turned into an irritated, wounded, and totally hopeless one. I had no idea why, but her distress bothered me to the point of anger. Her tool of a husband seemed oblivious to the mood shift which added to my infuriation. How could you not realize your wife was depressed? Every single time Lilith suffered a temperament change I was aware, and I did whatever possible to turn her negative into a positive.

Anxiously my foot tapped against the carpeted floor. My hands balled into tight fists. It was almost time to board the damn airplane.

You're dead Gabriel. If the plane crashes nothing will happen. You cannot die twice, dumbass.

I tried to calm down, but I couldn't. Michael wanted me to follow her nonstop, but he'd have to understand getting on any type of aircraft was out of the question. With my bags in hand, barely able to breathe, my legs raced to the first safe place available. The designated outdoor smoking area would shield my body enough to safely morph into my Angelic form unnoticed. Within seconds I landed directly in front of the carriage house Michael had setup for me.

"Couldn't do it, huh?" Michael asked, scaring the shit out of me further.

"No. I'm sorry." Raging panic could be heard in my voice through my tone. My body hunched over as my palms rested on my knees. I had to catch my breath, and the world had to stop spinning.

"Breathe," he instructed, gently patting my upper back.

"What the hell is wrong with me?" I shouted out of frustration.

"There are still times when I, myself, succumb to panic induced Mortal memories. It's okay."

"I'm stronger than this."

"Strength has nothing to do with it. This is on me. I never should've expected you to board a plane," he spoke calmly, moving so we were face to face.

"She'll be okay in the air. I'll go to the airport when the plane lands. I couldn't, Father. After all of this time, I still can't do it." My mind struggled to regain composure. Lilith's screams, her long nails digging into my upper back, passengers shrieking, cabin pressure dropping—it all slammed together causing me to relive my moment of death all over again.

"Breathe, son. It's over now. You didn't fail. Sasha will take your place on the flight," Michael urged, while softly pressing his forehead to mine. His soul began to absorb my grief and terror. Instant balance and peace returned. "Better?" He smiled warmly.

"Yes. Thank you." My vitals returned to a normal, balanced state. Unable to help myself, I embraced him tightly. I felt like a child whose parent just scared away the monsters from under their bed.

"That's my good boy. Go inside. See the house. I'll return in a bit for an update. If you should need me, your mother, brother, uncle, or anyone in between, we're a call away." A muted crack declared his exit.

After a quick visual of the home's exterior, I climbed the whitewashed staircase entering the space.

Pretty nice digs.

The house was decorated in a modern style using dark colors to accent each room. A comfortable looking L-shaped, black leather couch alongside a square, glass coffee table were positioned in front of a fairly decent sized, wall-mounted, flat screen television in the living room. The galley-style kitchen was stocked with everything an Angel could possibly need in case a Demon came knocking. A round, glass table with four, gray clothed, high back chairs sat in the open dining area. Exploring further, there was an office and a nice sized bedroom with an exceedingly comfortable bed. Once I'd reached the bathroom, which was adorned in shades of purple housing dozens of candles, I instantly knew Muriel had accented the space. Everything about the house screamed relaxation.

I had to smile. Since my arrival in Heaven all of the

major Angels treated me like family. Well, maybe not Raphael, but that was a different story for another time. They would've done anything to make me happy, and I honestly loved them deeply for it, though I hadn't always shown it.

Love, now there's a word you shouldn't throw around often, if ever.

The best part of the house? The garage. Parked side by side were a red Nissan sports car and a silver, Hummer pickup truck.

Nice, Michael.

I glanced at the kitchen clock. Nina's flight would be landing shortly. Hopping in the car, it was time to learn the roads of Savannah. I arrived in the nick of time to watch them exit the terminal and get into a Town Car. Nina was safe and so was I.

Chapter 3

Chase

What could I possibly say about life since Nina's birthday other than everything had been going smoothly? My internal balance had been restored and a sense of healthiness had returned. No new gifts emerged and fighting Vincent's mental hold became as routine as breathing. My secret? Nina. Since we'd become husband and wife nothing else mattered. It was my job to love, protect, and cherish her, which I enforced on a daily basis. We were closer than ever; unbreakable.

Her brother, the thorn in my side, met a girl at school causing him to hardly ever be home and for his surly attitude to mellow considerably. Our trip to New York was amazing, even though Jules and Mark tagged along. Steve and his girlfriend were out of town visiting her family, meaning we didn't have to meet up with them while we were in the city. Initially I planned to take my relationship with Nina to the next level, but at the last minute I changed my mind. As much as she wanted to, as did I, Jack's warning about the negative consequences weighed heavily in my brain. Fighting the urge to physically be with Nina grew harder as each day passed. Eventually breaking and giving in would be inevitable. When that time came, I'd be ready to protect her from whatever horrible thing was thrown our way. For the time being, holding her close, allowing nature to take its natural course to an extent, was all that was happening.

Learning about Angels and Demons was the greatest weapon of all. Knowledge is power, right? Strengthening my gifts, research, and working out multiple times a day had become my life. Occasionally I'd visit my mother who still held onto hope I'd move back home. Fat chance. Twice I tried to speak with my father, and twice it ended poorly—very poorly. Though he didn't know exactly who I was, he definitely saw me for the freak I'd become. Yes, I was a freak of nature. I'd come to grips with this bold new world, but deep down in the darkest corner of my mind, my soul repelled the Demonic beast within me. Only one solution to the problem existed. Destroy Vincent. Once he was gone all of my problems would be solved. Nina and I could disappear untouched and unbothered for the rest of our Mortal days. Chasing this dream grew into an obsession and it was the only thing I hungered for. When I finally found him, he'd pay—dearly. Oh yes, there'd be severe acts of vengeance for the damage he caused.

Chapter 4

Gabriel

Nina Luther led a fairly dull life. At times I wondered if one could actually die twice. This time not in a plane crash, but rather from severe boredom. She shopped more than any person should or would ever need to, complained quite often, was very spoiled by everyone (family and friends) who surrounded her, and at times she was angry, though she tried to pretend this wasn't the case. Nina couldn't fool me. Her aura shouted bold, vibrant colors of discontentment even when she was smiling. However, the oddest element was how she hardly ever spent any time with her husband but spent tons of time with the girl from the New York trip.

Every day you could set your watch to the two of them. They'd meet at Nina's house at ten, go to the library, break for lunch at one, coffee to follow, shopped in various locations, went back to the library around three, and arrived at home by five. I wondered if the Mortal friend, who incidentally was named Jules, knew of Nina's Angelic status. After one brief eavesdropping moment my suspicions were confirmed. Michael wasn't going to be happy about this.

One particularly hot afternoon I followed them to their usual coffee spot, sat a few tables behind them, and pretended to read some random magazine. Because of the lack of customers, Jules spotted my presence and quickly noticed my uncontrollable desire to stare at Nina. I couldn't help myself. Lord knows I tried. There was something about her that I couldn't resolve. Aside from the obvious, her stunning beauty, sating the desire to get lost inside of those deep, hazel eyes proved impossible. When a moment alone with them was stolen, my divine gifts ceased to work. Her aura or soul didn't present itself, only our raw emotions did. Nina turned and shot a deviously evil, sexy, provocative smile in my general direction.

Oh, those damn eyes.

I wanted to get up, grab, and throw her on the counter, having my way with that alluring body of hers, but I couldn't and of course I wouldn't dare. Despite common misconceptions pertaining to my personal behaviors, even my Angelic one-night stands were treated with respect and dignity. Besides, my soul belonged to Lilith. Though there had been many women after her, none of them meant anything. They were acts of rage and hurt coupled with my desire to feel wanted. Just because Lilith had betrayed me and didn't love me anymore, didn't mean that I quit loving her. That's all that mattered. Instead, I winked at Nina, making my flirtation painfully obvious. Once we broke stare and reality slapped me in the face, despair and pain filled my hollowed heart. Why? Who knew?

A soft buzzing sound drew my eyes back to the table. I glanced at my cell phone. It alerted me that there was a new message which read,

—*How's it going, brother? How's Nina?*— Orifiel's curious words before leaving Heaven played on a loop inside of my head. He knew something, and I'd be damned if I didn't find out exactly what it was.

Chapter 5

Nina

Over the next few weeks, Jules researched and studied up on Angels and Demons. Every book, article, or internet reference in existence she found, and why wouldn't she? The library and Jules were practically best friends. I found it funny because I always thought she resembled a librarian with her spec-like glasses, chocolate, brown hair which was perpetually tied back into a bun, and sensible style of clothing and shoes, but sitting in the stacks, biting on the end of a pencil really proved my point. As fascinating as some of the information was, boredom had set in.

"Coffee break please?" I begged after being held prisoner in the library for three long hours.

"How can you think of taking a break when there's so much to learn, Nina? How are you going to be able to stay safe and protect Chase and your family if you don't know everything?" Jules asked, peering over her glasses.

"I don't know and honestly, I don't care. I want coffee and a break."

"Fine, but when we're done, we're coming right back here. No sidebar shopping trip today," Jules warned.

An epic eye roll later, the hot air assaulted us the moment we exited the book-filled jail. Running to the car to avoid rain, humidity, and the heat had become part of my normal summer routine. What really aggravated me the most was that by the time the car finally had the opportunity to cool off, it was being parked outside of a local café.

"Do you want to sit inside or outside?" Jules asked innocently.

"Uh duh. Outside of course so we can both die of heat stroke or have our faces melt off," I snapped cynically.

"You don't have to be bitchy. It was only a question. Hey, wait a second." Feverishly her fingers flipped through the black, leather-bound book she'd borrowed from the library.

"What?"

"There are a ton of contradictions in most of these books. For example, some say Angels and Demons don't have actual bodies, but they inhabit the bodies of others, like a possession, but according to you, upon death, if callings are fulfilled, you become an eternal Angel in Heaven or on Earth like your friend Orifiel, *but* this book says the only thing eternal is God. Then it goes on to talk about reproduction. How if an Angel and Demon mate the results could be devastatingly horrible."

"Okay, but from what *I've* learned, and personally I think I'd know a little bit more than those authors because I'm an actual, real-life Mortal Angel, once a Lost Soul chooses to be good, they're rewarded over time, eventually evolving into a Mortal Angel on Earth. My dad doesn't know who in our family the Lost Soul line began with, but someone was, and they lived a Godly life. They were given the ability to heal those in need, then they were led to their soul mate, who possessed the same gift. Their offspring were born with the gift, thusly able to heal others as well. Jules, I'm human. I can die, have sex, and make a baby. How do you think I got here? FedEx? Stork delivery?"

"You're missing the point, like always." She sighed.

"Which is?"

"Chase. You have a clean history. Someone years ago became a Lost Soul, lived a positive life, and was blessed with a special gift from The Heavens. No evil ever tainted the pool. Chase, on the other hand, is both good *and* bad. You can't ever forget that. It's nothing against Chase, I really like him and all, but he was struck by both sides at once and developed light and dark powers. In the Angel/Demon world he might be seen as an equal because Vincent married you, but he's not pure like you. Do you understand?"

"All I heard was you insulting my boyfriend. To be honest, when you decide to get a girlfriend, I'll make sure to reciprocate." Sarcasm was my second language.

"Oh my God, Nina. I'm not trying to offend anyone. This is simple genetics and common sense, something you seem to be lacking at the moment. Think about it like this. Imagine a Caucasian woman and an Asian man. The two have a baby. The child will more than likely take on the appearance of the stronger genes making the child look either more Asian or more Caucasian. Now, let's take it a step further. If you and Chase decide to procreate, your child wouldn't be a full-fledged Angel. He or she, in theory, would be three quarters Angel and one quarter Demon, but maybe not. Perhaps the Demon within takes over and now there's a child roaming the Earth who is evil with Angelic powers. Does that make more sense?"

"Where are we going with this?"

"Let's try this another way. Chase won't sleep with you because he's afraid you might accidently become pregnant, and the result could be the creation of an abomination—a baby who could be the apex of evil and almighty power. See? All that stressing you've been doing about this is for nothing. He loves you and is trying to act responsibly."

Initially I didn't say anything. I sat, sipping my iced coffee, taking it all in. What she said made sense, a little too much actually. Chase did refuse to further our relationship, often growing annoyed or evasive whenever the topic came up. All he'd say was when the time was right, we would because currently he wasn't ready. Chase had conducted his own research and had lengthy discussions with my father about our world, but the issue of sex never once crossed my mind. Here I was but a mere few months ago accusing him of not wanting to be with me because he was sneaking around behind my back with Bristol, when all along he was trying to create a safe environment for us.

"Are you all right, Nina?" Jules inquired.

"Huh? Yeah. Totally fine. Just thinking," I replied, snapping out of my catatonic-like state. "Ready to go?"

"Yeah," she replied with a snicker.

"What? What's so funny?" I looked around trying to catch a glimpse of whatever had amused her.

"The guy over there has been checking you out ever since we got here."

"Whatever."

Even though I had a boyfriend it still felt good to know other guys still looked. In all fairness the guy eyeballing me was *very* attractive. He sat a few tables away sipping coffee and reading a magazine. I couldn't take my eyes off of him and his muscular physique. Because he was seated his height couldn't be gauged, but he was dressed rather fashionably with blond, highlighted hair that was tied back in a ponytail. I wished I could've seen his eyes, but his sunglasses covered them. It didn't matter though because plain and simple he was sexy.

"Earth to Nina," Jules said, grabbing my arm and pulling me up.

"Are you *sure* you're into women because that guy is the perfect specimen of what a man should be. It's a shame to waste him. Maybe give heterosexuality one more try, then tell me *all* of the details?"

She rolled her eyes in response. Quickly I shot a cute, half-smile at my admirer who lowered his glasses slightly and winked. Drunk with flattery I made my way to the car and to the library. Reality struck once Jules placed a mountain of dusty books on the table. Instead of focusing on Jules's task at hand, my inner thoughts reverted back to her comments about Chase. After several long moments of pondering the situation, my brain decided it needed verbal confirmation. Part of me wanted Jules to be wrong, but the other part didn't. If she was right, then she was on to something and could prove to be of great help at a later date.

My parents still had no clue Jules knew who we really were. Chances were they'd take it poorly, ending with us having to move *again*. Keeping that bit of information a secret for the moment being was best. Eventually I'd tell them, but today wasn't that day.

"Hey," I said the moment Chase answered.

"Hey, baby. What's up?" The sound of his voice

made my heart crumble. I found myself falling more in love with him each passing day.

"Nothing much. I'm with Jules. What are you up to?"

"I just finished training with your father. In a few I'll hit the gym. I miss you," he whispered in a sexy tone.

An epic smile grew across my face. "I miss you too. Can I ask you something?"

"Sure."

"It's about being intimate."

"Come on, Nina. Not this again. I already told you, when the time…"

"Is right we will." I finished his thought. "That's not it. Jules seems to think you don't want to because if we accidently get into trouble there could be complications." My words and phrasing were chosen carefully but spoken directly.

"She's partially right. That ideal coupled with the unknowingness of how my Demonic side might respond to physically being with an Angel is concerning." His tone was rather very matter of fact.

"Why didn't you ever share this?" Trying to stifle my annoyance didn't work because it clearly rang loudly in each spoken word. Even the dead could've picked up on it.

"For a lot of reasons. First, I didn't want to scare you. Second, I wasn't one hundred percent sure. Third, we always seem to be dealing with something of greater importance. And, fourth, I was looking for a loophole, a guarantee of sorts. When we do, *and we will*, I want it to be risk-free *and* special."

"You should've said something instead of making me go crazy."

"I was trying to protect us, Nina. You should know by now that you're my everything. I love you beyond measure and I would never do anything to hurt you. I know I've done some shady shit in the past, but I also know I've never given you any reason since then to believe I'd ever do it again. On another note, Mark called. Jules needs to either dump him or tell him what's going on because he's starting to get suspicious. He thinks she's cheating."

"I'll talk to her. How about some alone time tonight?" I asked flirtatiously.

"Sounds like a perfect night," he replied in a deep, low voice.

"I'll be home in a little while. Until then, try not to miss me too much."

"Impossible, baby."

Smiling for a hot second, thanking God for the blessing that was my protective, loyal, wonderful boyfriend, something or rather someone caught my eye. *Him*. The attractive guy from the coffeehouse stood in the foyer of the library staring directly at me. This guy went from sweet to creepy in a matter of seconds. Drawing off of my New York take-charge attitude, I walked past him with my head held high completely ignoring his presence.

"Jules," I hissed, when I returned to the stacks.

"Is everything okay?" she asked, placing a book on the floor.

"The guy from the café is here. He was staring at me outside. Do you think he followed us?"

"Did he say anything?"

"Well, no."

"It's not uncommon for people to get coffee then go

to the library. It's like a million degrees outside. It's nice, cool, quiet, clean, and free in here. Maybe he saw you, recognized you as the pretty girl from before, and was trying to work up the courage to say hi or something."

"It's weird," I said while scanning my surroundings.

"Are you sure you don't recognize him from anywhere? Maybe he's one of the Angels? You said last year Orifiel was sent to watch you and Chase. Perhaps a new Angel was sent to look after you two?"

"I've never seen him in my life. Trust me. I'd definitely remember someone like him."

"All right. It's probably nothing, but I can see you're anxious over this, so let's leave," she said while stacking her books. "Give me a few minutes to check these out, then we're out of here."

Even after I was safely tucked away inside of my home, I continued to keep a watchful eye on occurrences happening outside. Every noise caused me to jump up and race to the window. After a little while I forced myself to calm down. Sometimes coincidences happened and it ended there. Not everything had to qualify as a dramatic moment. This was one such moment.

Refocus the lens.

Chase and I had plans to hang out, something we hadn't done in a while. The earlier we started the better. I loved that Chase lived in my house, but I missed the days when he'd climb the oak tree outside of my bedroom window and sneak in. There's something rather stimulating and intriguing about the forbidden. You'd think since we were under the same roof we'd be joined at the hip, but that wasn't the case. Chase was always working with my father, at the gym or school, studying, with Mark, or running errands. Truthfully, I'd been busy myself, but the current setup sucked.

Shoving the creepy hot guy out of my head, I focused solely on selecting an outfit and getting ready for Chase. Skillfully, I flawlessly applied my makeup and tied my hair up in a clip. More than satisfied with my appearance, it was time to find Chase, who'd be in either my father's office or the kitchen helping my mother. By blood he wasn't her son, but he sure acted like it by helping her out however possible. It was his way of saying thanks for everything from taking him in to supporting our relationship. Besides, eventually one day he would be her son-in-law in both worlds, so it was nice to see they actually liked each other and weren't feigning anything.

"Hey, Mom. Where's Chase?"

"Taking out the trash, honey. Are you two going out or will you be home for dinner?"

"Going out. Probably Gino's."

"How was your day with Jules?"

"Fine. Why?" I asked defensively.

Crap. What if she knows something or Chase blabbed? Stupid guilty conscience.

"No reason. You've been spending a lot of time together. Is everything okay?"

I couldn't accurately read the tone of her question. My next few words had to be executed with an abundance of caution. The stress and guilt over keeping such a large secret weighed heavily on my mind causing me to become borderline paranoid at times.

"She's been dealing with some personal stuff. Nothing serious."

Please, Mom. Let's leave this at that because if you push, you're not going to like what you hear.

Chapter 6

Chase

"What's nothing serious?" I asked, walking to the sink to wash my hands.

"Nothing. Ready?" Nina snapped.

It couldn't have been any more painfully obvious that words of any kind were unwelcome. Why? Who the hell knew, but keeping my mouth shut and not pissing Nina off was key in situations like this.

"We were talking about Jules and her personal problem," Ellen informed.

"Yeah, I'm not going to lie. It kind of caught me off guard," I replied, assuming Nina felt uncomfortable speaking in detail about Jules's choice of intimate partners. She needed to get over it. Jules being a lesbian didn't change the fact she was an amazing person.

"Exactly what caught you off guard, honey?" Ellen pressed.

Damn it. You just opened Pandora's Box, moron.

"Uh, Chase, we really should get going," Nina urged, shooting a weary, disapproving look.

I stood stone-still not knowing what to do next. My instinct kicked in causing me to infuse a light air of confusion and distraction into the space, compliments of my Angelic ability.

Please work.

"Your divine gift is exactly that, Chase. *A gift.* A gift you're to use to help others, *not* to change the subject," Ellen scolded.

Her body was now board straight which revealed her true height. Ellen's face knotted with curiosity and concern. At times flecks of Nina were seen in her mother's physical appearance and expressions, especially when Ellen grew twisted.

"Want to take this one, baby?" Ellen was Nina's parent. By default, Nina had to deal with this. I had my own problems with family. One mother was more than enough.

"It's really not a big deal, Mom. Jules is a lesbian. Happy?" Nina huffed with a great sigh and an exaggerated eye roll.

"Oh," was all Ellen said.

"But wait, Mom. It gets better. She knows about us, all of us, and what we can do. I thought she saw me healing myself when we were in New York. Before you freak out, don't because Jules isn't the type of person to run her mouth. She'll keep this quiet. That's why we've been hanging out so much. She's curious and has questions."

"Jack," her mother called in a choppy voice.

"Jack," she bellowed again after five seconds of silence occurred. This time any trace of color in her face had disappeared.

"What's the matter, Ellen?" Jack asked, entering the kitchen.

"We have to move." Much like her daughter, Ellen had a penchant for the dramatic.

"We don't have to move, Dad. Jules Warner knows about us. I told her a few weeks ago. I never would've except I thought she saw me using my gift. She didn't. I own the fact I jumped the gun. However, she is interested in our world and has been trying to learn about our people," Nina informed calmly.

Before the man spoke, his hands raked through his thinning gray hair. A few specks of light brown still existed up there, but not much. I felt for the guy. His wife, though a good mother and partner, was usually a stone throw away from hysterics, while his daughter made his life less than smooth sailing these past few years. Throw the son and me into the mix and he probably should've been a fulltime resident at an insane asylum.

"All right. Let's all calm down. Nina, you did the right thing. You thought you were found out and did what you had to. *However*, should you ever find yourself faced with a similar situation, wait and see what people actually want before spilling your guts. We're talking about Jules Warner. I really don't think we're going to have any problems or have to move. I'll speak with her myself and try to answer any questions she may have." His tone was even and rational.

"What if she tells her parents or someone like *Victoria Wylie*?" Ellen wasn't buying the 'our secret is still safe' speech.

"I'm sorry. Trust me, the last thing I want is to move again or have any of us exposed. Since we don't possess a time machine, what's done is done," Nina pled.

At that moment I felt awful for her. Without thinking I moved to where she stood, taking her in my arms, and praying my touch could alleviate the emotional turmoil she was experiencing. She made a mistake. Haven't we all? I probably would've reacted similarly had I been in her horribly uncomfortable, high heeled shoes.

"This isn't a big deal. I'll have a little chat with Jules. Our secret will be kept safe. If it's not, we'll deal with the situation accordingly," Jack assured. "Now, let's all relax and try to have a peaceful evening."

Ellen, still wearing a horrified look of unease, nodded. Honestly, I had faith and confidence in Jules. She'd keep her mouth shut. Jack could handle the rest. Besides, if she wanted to blab our secret around town, she already would've. By now we would've all been tarred, feathered, and run out of town. Nina, obviously still bent out of shape over me opening my mouth, remained quiet, but once we were alone, I'd get an ear full.

"Were you shot in the damn neck with a truth serum dart while taking out the trash?" she hissed the second I closed the car door.

Here it comes. Watch your answers. Stay unruffled. Let her know she's right. In a few minutes this will all be a thing of the past.

"Nina, what do you want from me? Your mother made it seem like she already knew. Cut me some slack. Look, it's all out in the open, which is something you should've done the moment we returned from New York. I am very sorry, and you have every right to be pissed off at me."

Translation—I am sorry about what happened earlier and the minuscule role that I played. All I did was out Jules. You, my love, were the one who decided to share all of your hidden truths with Ellen. I would've left it at, 'Jules is gay.'

"I'm not going to argue about this right now,

especially when we spend so little time with each other as it is. Let's try to enjoy the night."

"We can definitely do that."

Whoa. That was way shorter than expected. She mustn't be too terribly upset with me.

Dropping the Jules issue, we had dinner at Gino's, then headed to the beach on Tybee Island. She lay in my arms while the cool night breeze blew strands of her dirty blonde hair everywhere. I remained silent, listening to the waves crashing against the shore, the soft sound of the crickets chirping, and the rhythmical murmur of Nina inhaling and exhaling. After a while I found myself staring at her flawless face. Her eyes were fixated on the crescent moon hanging low in the sky reflecting off of the ocean. One lone, bright star stood beside it. Not being able to stop myself, I turned my body on top of hers, crushing our lips together, running my hands through her thick hair. Accepting my advances, she reciprocated by rolling me over. She was trying to take control, attempting to make a play to convince me to go against my desire to wait. She wasn't going to win. Gently, I flipped her back below me. I had to be in charge for now because Nina possessed the power to make me drop my guard and give into lust. That wasn't going to happen tonight. I wasn't sufficiently prepared, physically or mentally.

"Let's slow down a bit, okay?"

"What if I don't want to?" she challenged, yanking me closer.

"We already had this discussion today, baby." I laughed softly, trying to diffuse her mood.

You have such a thick head, Nina. A very pretty one, but never-the-less, a very thick one.

"Yes, but there are ways to prevent getting pregnant you know."

"True, but pregnancy isn't my only concern. I don't want to chance anything."

"Will there ever be a day when we finally do this? Don't you want to with me?" she said while trying to control her deeply rooted frustrations. If she only knew how hard it was for me, she'd be singing a different tune.

"Come on, Nina. How could you even think that? Touching, kissing, even holding you could drive anyone insane, but if we were to be together sexually, besides the pregnancy thing, it might provoke my Demonic side. I've looked into this. There's a chance the Demon buried within me might take over, conceivably harming, or worse, killing you. There's even a possibility the evil could completely win and change me. You have to understand there aren't too many of my kind. There's no one in our world born into this life the way I was or at least none that is known of. We need to be smart, but I promise, baby, eventually we'll find a safe way to express ourselves."

"We have forever, right?" She forced a fake smile.

"That we do, baby," I answered with a real grin. "Let's go home." I helped her to her feet.

"Oh crap," she exclaimed, grabbing at her throat.

"What's the matter?"

Damn it. Now what?

"My necklace is gone." She panicked, still clutching her neck.

"The one I gave you?"

"Yes."

"Don't worry. We'll find it if it's here," I assured, softly kissing her forehead.

Last Christmas I'd given her a protection amulet. I'd read somewhere about how all Angels wore pendants to cover their cores. It provided me with a small amount of peace because she always had it on. It wasn't the actual metal that would save her, but rather the stone. I searched high and low to find a gem which would allow the strongest amount of security. Finally, a fire red bixbyite placed in the middle of a gold cross surfaced in a new age book shop in town. The woman who sold me the piece suggested it was very rare, and would not only guard Nina's core, but would assist in finding things which were once not visible. Too bad we didn't have the frigging thing to help now. Granted, she didn't deliberately lose the necklace, but the annoyance brewing in my stomach couldn't be helped.

I wandered to the left while she headed right combing the ground. Enhancing my own vision to cut through the dark night and endless sand, I spotted a shadow lurking off in the distance. Making sure to remain still as to not alert the watcher or Nina, I kept my head down and heightened *all* of my senses. After a few moments I could say with certainty the figure was male, short, built, wearing jeans, a fitted, black t-shirt, white running sneakers, a gray, knit skull cap, and definitely watching me and Nina, but he wasn't Vincent.

Screw the necklace. You can always buy another one. Get the hell out of here.

"Found it," Nina called.

"Great. Let's go," I answered curtly, snatching her hand, and pulling her to the car.

Because my senses were still fully charged, my fingers fumbled with my keys. Between the sharp vision and intense sounds and textures, I couldn't focus. Once safely inside, I'd take a second to level out.

"Hey," Nina said, touching my forearm. "Are you okay?"

"Yes. Fine. I just want to go home." I fought to remain balanced as my blood boiled and my heart rate accelerated. Someone was out there observing us, and I wasn't in the mood to find out who or what.

"Are you not feeling well?" She sounded as if she was forcing herself not to panic.

"I feel amazing. I'm a little tired, but totally fine. It's a pretty long ride back. Sorry for cutting the night short, but I'll make it up to you. When everyone goes to bed later, I'll sneak in, okay?"

Please, Nina, get your sexy ass in the car.

Before she could reply, I kissed her hard, swiftly lifting her off of the ground and placing her frame into the passenger seat of my Challenger. Seconds later we were off, and my body, mind, and soul returned to my new version of normal.

Please, dear God, don't let this be the start of something bad. I don't think I can handle much more.

Chapter 7

Nina

As I lay in bed staring at the ceiling waiting for Chase to sneak in, my mind wandered. Something was definitely up. Chase's behavior and actions were off, way off. Though I knew better than to question him, a valuable lesson that was learned from recent experiences, my conscience was painfully aware the time had come to start digging deeper behind his back. How would I accomplish this task? I had no idea, but some plan would be thought up. My heart wanted to believe it was nothing. We all have our off days, but avoidance wasn't the answer. What if he was hearing Vincent's voice again? Or a new ability was emerging? Or the headaches were back?

"Nina? Are you still awake?" Chase whispered.

"Yes." Excitement instantly chased all of my negative thoughts away.

My incredibly sexy, smart, loving, protective, amazing *husband* had made good on his promise. I loved falling asleep beside him every night in New York and missed not being able to make it a regular habit back here in Savannah. Quietly, he crept into my bed, wrapping his strong arms around my waist.

"Hey," he said softly, facing me.

"Hey, yourself."

With one swift motion Chase pulled my hips down the cool sheets, throwing the covers over our heads. His warm breath against my cheeks combined with that wonderfully addictive scent of his consumed every last ounce of my sanity. I needed and wanted this forever.

"Did you enhance your senses?" I asked as a reminder.

The last thing we needed was for my parents to come in unannounced and to see us in bed together. That wouldn't be a good thing especially since they'd been so lenient allowing him to live in their home.

"What do you think?" Even though we were entombed by darkness I could still see him smirking. "What's on your mind?"

For the next few hours, we stayed tucked away under a blanket of security the comforter provided us with, whispering until we both fell asleep. Everything and anything had been discussed in between laughing, joking, and sometimes kissing.

There's nothing wrong with this man, Nina. Nothing at all. If something were up, he wouldn't be acting this way. Potential bad occurrences don't always have to be lurking in the background. I forbid you to ruin this moment.

Scaring the paranoid thoughts away, my eyes shut while my ears listened to the sound of Chase's southern drawl. I adored this man and nothing or no one could ever tear us apart.

Chapter 8

Nina

An unnatural fear and heightened awareness of my surroundings hung heavy for the next few weeks. The feeling couldn't be shaken. Knowing who was around me at any point became a measure of primal safety. I desperately wanted to believe Chase was fine, but a part of me, a part I kept trying to bury under oblivious falsehoods warned and nagged me to keep vigilant. Chase appeared normal and healthy, which calmed some of my unruly tension, but something else began happening. Ever since the night at the beach, visions of the Angel Gabriel presented nightly in the form of dreams. The images were rather comforting and soothing. I felt safe and protected when I'd wake the following morning. His eyes were the only part of him which revealed themselves to me, but that one single feature spoke volumes. Gabriel came across as tortured and pained in a way I'd never experienced, but his aching felt familiar. When I'd gaze into those captivating eyes of his, it was almost as if he was absorbing my problems and stress. Several times I thought to call to Orifiel, but I didn't. Why open a can of worms? If Chase started showing signs of declining physical or mental health I'd reach out, but until then, keeping my mouth shut was best.

What was really creeping me out was this constant sense that I was being followed. Several times the guy from the café and library randomly appeared behind me or off in the distance, but when I'd move to get a better look or if I turned away for even one second, he'd disappear. At first it drove me crazy, but lately I'd been writing it off. If this man had any plans to harm me, he probably already would've done it by now. Perhaps my brain was repelling normalcy by looking for something, *anything*, to be wrong. Because of that, awful suspicions developed within me. Lately, my internal scales only felt right when my balance was off. How screwed up was that? Maybe I thrived on drama? This ridiculous sentiment had to be shed. If it wasn't, I'd be stuck in a never-ending circle of misery, destined to live in a downward spiral for the rest of my Mortal existence. I refused to allow myself to create any more anxiety producing situations or scenarios.

"Hello? Nina?" Jules said, waving her hand in front of my face.

"Huh?" I replied, snapping back to reality.

"Are you feeling okay? We're in a shoe store and you haven't tried on a single pair."

"Yeah. I'm fine."

"Then help me find a pair of sneakers."

"Of course." I followed Jules to the front of the shop. I browsed the displays scanning for boxes in her size.

"These look cute and comfortable. Why don't you try them on?" I said.

My eyes wandered to a figure who was standing across the street, leaning against a building. His rather large biceps were folded tightly against his broad chest.

It was him. An active imagination *wasn't* the culprit this time. This guy *was* following and stalking me, and he wasn't going to get away with it.

"This ends now, you sick freak," I hissed, storming out of the store.

"What's going on?" Jules asked breathlessly, hot on my heels.

Not wanting to lose him in the crowd, my feet kept going.

"Wait up, Nina."

"Remember the guy from the café and library? He's been following me all over town. I'm not dealing with this shit anymore."

If I hadn't been so hell bent on confronting him, I might've noticed I was standing in the middle of the street, seconds away from being struck by a speeding car.

"Nina," Jules shrieked.

My head whipped around as I zeroed in on a rust orange coupe. It sounds easy enough to just move out of the way, but for some reason I couldn't. My body froze, fixed with panic and horror.

You're going to die.

My eyelids shut tightly as I braced for my final Mortal moment.

Chapter 9

Gabriel

"Orifiel," I hissed at the sky outside of my temporary home.

Every night come midnight Michael relieved me of my duties until six in the morning. I needed the break, but leaving the Mortal Angel's space was difficult. There were questions, too many of them actually, which required answers. I thought by hawking the girl more than necessary something would reveal itself, but no. Nothing.

"Brother," Orifiel said, dropping from a high limb of the oak tree beside me.

"You have exactly three seconds to tell me what you know about my connection to the Mortal I'm stuck babysitting," I warned, inching dangerously close.

He didn't speak, but rather backed away.

"Don't make me use torture tactics to bleed the information out of your mouth. Screw with me and you can bet your ass I will not think twice about doing it and will feel no regret. I'm a rather accomplished lunatic in case you haven't heard," I threatened.

"If you tell me what's going on, I *might* be able to help," he replied sheepishly.

He knew everything and damn it, one way or another Orifiel would spill it, but buying into his game might be the best way to extract solid facts. Besides, I really didn't want to hurt him. He was my kid brother, though not biologically, and he was my closest friend. Often Orifiel understood my moods better than the others.

"There's this strong draw. It's all in the eyes. Whenever I look at hers..." The sentence couldn't be finished because there was no way in hell I'd admit to wanting to kiss, hold, and worship Nina in ways no married man should ever.

Orifiel smiled. "Please don't hit me for saying this, but Brother, Lilith is gone. It's been decades. It's time to let her go. It's okay to feel primal urges for other women beyond the scope of a one-night stand." He gently touched my shoulder.

"You know I can't do that. It's not who I am."

"She's the enemy, Gabriel. Lilith sided with *them*. Yes, your soul may be bound to hers, but *she* broke that bond. *Not you.* I shouldn't be saying this, Michael would murder me, but on the mission I literally just finished ten minutes before getting here, Urim and I saw her with Ariel."

I didn't answer. They'd been sent to eliminate Ariel. If my Lilith was present, that meant he had to destroy her as well. That's how orders went. Assassinate the target and anyone else who got in the way. Even with my influential standing orders to the army to never lay a finger on her, if she interfered or posed a threat, the assassin would be left with no other choice. My lungs clenched, not allowing for a single breath to be produced. Lilith and I weren't together. We hadn't been for a very long time, but that didn't mean I stopped loving her or didn't pray for us to be together again. Hope is a funny concept. Even when someone leaves you that weak emotion enters and can't be shed.

"Keep your hair on, Gabriel. I took out Ariel and we let Lilith go. I'd never touch her. None of us ever would. My point wasn't to scare you, but rather to inform you that she and I spoke. She didn't ask for you. All she was concerned about was us sparing her. When I told her that you were the reason I wouldn't hurt her, she laughed, suggesting I was just as pathetic and stupid as you. Gabriel, brother, she doesn't love or give a rat's arse about you. I'm sorry. If there was any hope for her, believe me, I'd be doing whatever possible to save her alongside of you."

Anything he said after assuring me that Lilith was okay fell on deaf ears. The fact that she was safe, still roaming Hell and Earth freely was the *only* thing that mattered.

"You still haven't answered my question about the Mortal," I finally spoke, changing the subject.

"Feeling connected to someone isn't a bad thing. I, myself, felt a bond with Nina. Maybe your heart is ready to open up to someone other than your Angelic family. That's not a crime."

"It's more than that, Orifiel." I paused. "You said she was part of your spiritual family. How?"

"Gabriel, keep doing your job. Everything will fall into place. That's all I know for sure."

"Why won't you tell me the truth?"

"Because sometimes seeing is believing. It's not my story to ruin. I have to return to The Heavens to see our father. I love you, brother. I'm always here should you require me for anything."

"If that was a factual statement, you'd be telling me

everything, not worrying about briefing Father on your mission."

"Why must you make this difficult?"

"I'm not. You are."

Orifiel sighed. "Do you trust me?"

"Yes. Of course. I always have. We've shared foxholes in Hell together. Come on, now."

"Then take this bit of advice. Go with whatever you're feeling."

"Fine." Attempting to keep a normal, flat tone didn't work. Instead, one filled with tension and worry over the unknown came forth.

"Brother," Orifiel said softly, turning, and approaching me, "there is nothing, absolutely nothing, to stress out over. Stop fighting fate." He smiled before disappearing into the starless night sky.

What the hell was that supposed to mean?

****

Orifiel's words and the Mortal Angel's face haunted my every moment and thought, day and night. Sleep became a fictitious notion. Eating? Forget about that. There wasn't time. Honestly, more than anything, going home to The Heavens never to return to the Earth again sounded euphoric. However, abandoning my post was impossible, so I continued following the girl without complaining. I tried to detach myself from the situation, but I fell short many times. It bothered me tremendously whenever Nina and the Demon husband fooled around.

While they were on a date at the beach, he spotted me off in the distance. I was sure of this. His aura showed fear and caution. Luckily, I was able to quietly fall back into the shadows without being identified, but I knew more attentiveness on my part needed to be exercised.

Blending into the current climate and culture on Earth was difficult. A lot had changed. I felt like I stuck out like a sore thumb. Though my clothing, cars, and accessories meshed with the rest of the population, my soul didn't and couldn't. After a while of trying to tail the girl without being seen, I finally gave up. If she saw me, so be it. I didn't care. I'd cross and burn that bridge when the time arose. I wasn't a spy or a detective. Orifiel was, therefore he should've been given this job, not me.

Man, she's pissed off over something today.

Nina stormed out of a shoe store completely unaware of the fact that she had stopped moving in the middle of a busy road. Out of the corner of my eye I saw a speeding car heading straight for her. Dropping the newspaper and coffee I was holding, I flung my body at hers, forcefully shoving us to the ground, and out of harm's way.

"Are you okay?" I asked. Her eyes were firmly shut. Her breathing was labored.

"Am I dead?" she asked, refusing to open her eyelids.

"No. Not today."

"You saved my life," she whispered, slowly coming back to reality.

Her now completely opened irises entranced my core. I couldn't think or speak for a moment. All I could do was obsess over wanting to kiss and hold her slender body.

Snap out of it, Gabriel!

"Something like that. Are you hurt?" It was a stupid question to ask because she was a healer and could cure herself, but I suppose habit caused the query.

"I don't think so. Just a touch embarrassed." She

gradually turned her head looking at the many people who'd stopped to stare.

Getting up and helping her to her feet, I led us to the side of the building I stood by earlier.

"I think it's safe to say no one has ever died from a bruised ego or embarrassment," I joked, which caught me off guard. Kidding around was rather uncharacteristic of my personality, Mortal or Angelic.

"Oh my God. Nina, are you okay?" Her friend, Jules, shook with panic. Jules's pale skin and wide eyes added to her look of sheer terror.

"Yeah," Nina replied, still visibly traumatized from her recent near-death experience.

"Thank you." Jules threw herself in my arms.

Uncomfortable with physical contact, my arms moved mechanically while reciprocating the gesture.

"No worries," I mumbled, praying this girl would release her hold. Nina's glaring added to my uneasiness. After a brief moment, Jules's touch evoked something deep within my soul. For the first time in a long time, I squeezed a stranger in return. Her pure soul and vibrant positive aura found its way inside of me filling a massive void.

"Your soul is so beautiful, powerful, and pure. *Never* allow anyone to ever change that," I whispered in Jules's ear. "I have to go."

Disappear, now. Do not, under any circumstance, look at Nina again.

"Wait," Nina called.

Damn it!

"What's up?" I turned slowly. Nina's aura flashed deep distress. This bothered me tremendously. All of her negative emotions weighed heavily on my shoulders to the extent my back might break under the pressure.

"You've been following me. Why? Who the hell are you?" she demanded. Her hands were firmly placed on her alluring hourglass hips.

"The guy who just saved your life. You're welcome."

She muttered a weak 'thank you' while lowering her head. Nina's aura rapidly shifted to awkwardness.

I cautiously approached her, stopping a few inches away from where she stood. Using my right index finger I softly tilted her chin up. As she leaned into the touch, my stone-cold heart thawed. My intentions weren't to make her feel bad, but rather were a way of pointing out her rudeness. "You're safe and you're welcome. In the future, please watch where you're going, Nina. My reflexes are stellar, and my form is fairly indestructible, but I'd rather not test my limits. Okay?"

Son of a bitch!

I slipped. I didn't mean to say her name, it just happened. No. That's a lie. I wanted to say her name out loud. I longed to call her Nina to her face so not only she'd hear it, but the Universe would as well. Hopefully, she didn't pick up on that.

"How do you know who I am?" She snapped, swatting my hand away, and taking a defensive stance. "Who are you and what do you want? Why are you stalking me? Why are you obsessed with me?" Nina's inner bitch switch had definitely been flipped. Truthfully, this version of her was as ugly as sin.

"Following orders is more like it, so don't flatter yourself. Now, let me get back to doing this painfully boring, mind-numbing job, and you can go back to being an angry, scared, self-centered little girl. Then, when that gets old, you can run into the waiting arms of your husband who will tolerate you and your neurotic complaining and whining, because quite frankly, I can't."

"Just who the hell do you think you're talking to like that? Certainly not me. You must have some set of…"

"Wings? Because if you mean wings, then yes. I have quite a large, lovely pair." I paused, taking a deep breath. "You're adorable when you're irritated, but so stupid at the same damn time. Open your eyes. *Look at me.* How is it that I know exactly who you are, but you have no idea who I am when we've already met, and not that long ago either? I guess you're really that self-involved. I was told you were smart and sharp. That was an obvious lie," I barked.

A sizable chunk of me was insulted. She'd been on my mind since the night of our first encounter. Obviously, the emotional surge I experienced had been one-sided.

"You're an…" Jules began stuttering slightly. A state of absolute wonder spread across her face.

"Angel. Yes."

"He's a liar, Jules. I have no idea who the hell he is," she hissed, taking hold of Jules's right hand.

"Oh really?" I challenged, casually slipping my arm around her waist, and leading us behind the bookstore we stood in front of. Her aura pulsated extreme alarm.

"Relax. If I wanted to hurt you, you'd already be dead," I assured.

"Who sent you?" she asked, still unconvinced.

"Michael. My name is Gabriel. I'm one of the Seven Arcs. *Arc* meaning Archangel. I'm a messenger and a Gate Keeper. My gift is reading souls and auras. I'm third in command in the Angelic Army and Heaven's Chief Demonic Assassin. Yes, I've been following you, but more importantly, I mean no harm. Oh, and Orifiel, my brother, sends his best."

"Orifiel," she screamed.

"Seriously? You're calling for Orifiel? This ought to be rich." I shook my head. "Look," I added.

Before I could prove my Angelic status, Orifiel fell to the ground. With reckless abandon, he raced to Nina's side forgetting all of his training regarding assessing situations first. His bond to this girl was dangerously strong. If her hold over him wasn't in a romantic capacity, I had to question exactly what the connection was. Before speaking, he ensconced his body and wings around her, shielding her against any potential threats.

"She's fine, brother."

"Gabriel?" He spun around.

"Aside from the fact your current actions were careless—I had several opportunities to destroy you *and* her, the target made me. Even though I just saved her Mortal life, Nina still believes I'm evil and has forgotten we've already met," I explained, casually removing my shirt to further prove my point.

How had she left such a lasting impression on me and I none on her? I felt foolish for daydreaming and fantasizing like a lovesick teenager.

Orifiel didn't speak. He removed Nina's sunglasses and positioned her body in front of mine. Slowly, not to scare her anymore then I already had, I allowed my wings to expand from my spine. She didn't speak, only watched. Gently, I took her chin, tilting her face so our eyes met. Before abandoning all irrational hope, my soul demanded one last look.

"I'm not here to cause you any harm, Nina. I'm here to protect you, which I swear I will, and I won't let anything bad happen to you, not now, not ever, but you've got to trust me," I whispered, never wanting to see another thing again except those sweet, hazel irises.

"I trust you," she mumbled, barely.

Nina appeared almost drunk, but she was fully locked and focused on the stare we mutually held. Unhurriedly, our faces inched closer. I had no idea what or who was controlling our actions because the rational being inside of me certainly wasn't. My thoughts were hazy. My brain wasn't working properly. My senses dulled, which in my line of work was an obvious hazard. Vincent, or any other Demon for that matter, could've approached and killed us, and I wouldn't have seen it coming. A curious feeling erupted inside of my chest. I had to have this girl. I could feel her warm breath brush across my lips causing the moment to intensify.

Kiss her…

"You're the most striking Angel I've ever seen," she hummed, reaching around my waist, and softly stroking my wings. The intimacy of her touch sent my sanity into a tailspin.

"Your eyes," I mumbled. "You're a goddess."

She paused, backing away slightly. "Don't go. Please. You have to stay with me always," she begged softly.

I wasn't sure if she was in shock, confused, angry, or relieved, because her tone and aura were all over the place.

"I swear. I'll never leave you," I said, closing the space between us.

In all of the years I spent with Lilith I'd never felt

this type of white hot, burning heat and lustful tension. Nina experienced it too. Her aura piqued a deep shade of crimson. I wanted to see her soul, but I couldn't. Our bodies were too close, therefore obscuring my view. Our gaze never wandered. The focus was intense. Finally, giving up and into my inner Demons, I took her face in my hands. As her lips parted, mine drew nearer.

"Gabriel," she whispered.

Hearing her say my name was the kill shot. All things logical ceased to exist. A soft groan rumbled in my throat as I captured her mouth. Nothing but sweet bliss and perfection was felt.

"Brother," Orifiel's firm voice warned.

Immediately the penetrating brain fog lifted.

What the hell is going on?

We both backed up. The spell had been broken. My classic hardened personality sprung back to life. The cold deadness returned, but a sliver of life craved the moment I just experienced to occur again.

Oh man. You're in trouble, but she's worth it and I have no idea why.

Chapter 10

Nina

"What the hell just happened?" I snapped at no one in particular.

Quickly, a mental recap of the last fifteen minutes went down inside of my head.

Almost got hit by a car.

Was saved by a man I thought to be a stalker.

Creepy, lurker guy turns out to be an Angel—*the* Angel Gabriel.

Then, Orifiel guides me into some sort of weird trance with his brother causing irrational thoughts and planting the desire to cheat on Chase.

"You felt it?" Orifiel asked cautiously.

"Felt what?"

"You're screwing with our heads. Stop it, because if you don't, my next move will be to beat the shit out of you," Gabriel said through gritted teeth.

"That threat is wearing pretty thin these days, brother. I'm not screwing with anything," Orifiel defended.

"I didn't think you were," I said, shooting Gabriel a dirty look.

Orifiel could be trusted, whereas Gabriel...no way in hell. I knew nothing about him aside from the fact that I felt utterly drawn in by him as a whole. Afraid I might reach out and claim Gabriel as mine, I moved beside Orifiel, wrapping my arms around his waist, and holding on tightly.

"Thank you for coming when I called. It means a lot. *You* mean a lot. You always have and you always will."

Maybe appealing to Orifiel's softer side like I had several times in the past would make him open up and spill his secrets. Something was definitely going on, and I needed to know exactly what.

"I'll *always* be there whenever you need me, love." He smiled. "There's nothing to be frightened over. You and Gabriel share a connection. That's a beautiful thing. What you're feeling is a bond."

"What kind of connection?" Though Orifiel's answer was rather vague, and more details were required, something was better than nothing.

"A close one. Let's leave it at that for now."

"Why aren't you watching me like you had been?"

"Michael needed me elsewhere, so he sent Gabriel. You're in good hands. The best, actually. I have to return to The Heavens, but I'll check in on you later. For now, you and Gabriel should take this time to get to know one another better," he said hurriedly, kissing the top of my head, and vanishing almost immediately.

I turned to Gabriel. "What's Orifiel talking about?" I snapped. What happened moments ago could never occur again.

"Damned if I know." Gabriel shrugged.

"Don't lie," I clapped back.

"First of all, don't threaten me. That will end poorly for you. Second of all, I have no reason to lie to anyone. If I knew, I'd speak up. I'm the farthest thing from shy and reserved. Third of all, you've got to trust me or this isn't going to work."

"Fine." For some unbeknownst reason I did trust him, and I believed he'd told me the truth. Whatever Orifiel knew, he hadn't shared with either of us—yet. I made a mental note to hunt him down to extract the information out of him. "Now what?" I suddenly felt panicky.

"You go back to doing you. I'll go back to keeping you safe," he answered.

"Why did Michael send you? Does he know about this *shared connection*?" Maybe Gabriel was clueless, but I was more than sure Michael wasn't. There had to be a reason Michael switched out Orifiel with Gabriel. I wasn't buying the Orifiel had been required elsewhere excuse.

Briefly, he studied the space around my silhouette. "I have no idea what Michael knows. Orders are given by Michael, and we angels follow them without questioning his authority."

"I don't want you watching me. I'd rather Orifiel did the job," I explained.

I felt comfortable with Orifiel and weird around Gabriel. Regret and shame over what transpired before seeped in. That wasn't the case after Orifiel and I shared our moment of indiscretion. The urge to repeat it never occurred, despite how passionate it was. However, the heat, that white hot flame Gabriel and I created was too risky to be around. If left alone, who knew what would happen.

"Sorry. You're out of luck. I can't walk off an assignment, angering Michael, because Orifiel is your favorite. The current setup is what Michael wants. Look, truth be told, you *think* you can handle everything, but you can't. Up until this point you've been one very lucky little girl. With that tiny fact in mind, you need me, but I don't need this. Case closed. No one wants anymore complications." He paused, harshly examining my face. Moving closer his lips stopped a few inches away from my ear. "I won't allow anything of a physical nature to exist between us. I'll do my job. You'll be safe. We'll never become one. Stop thinking otherwise."

"Excuse me?" I snapped, pushing him away. How dare he? I had no idea what occurred moments ago, but I would never deliberately do anything to ruin my relationship with Chase. This guy was a jerk, and totally full of himself.

"Uh, hey," Jules said interrupting our exchanges. Truthfully, I'd become so caught up in myself I forgot she was even there.

"My apologies for our rudeness," Gabriel spoke.

"Don't speak for me," I barked.

"All right. Strike my last statement. I'll rephrase. *I'm* sorry for *my* rudeness." He said while walking to where Jules was.

"It's okay. I get it." Jules grinned.

"Are you all right?" he asked sincerely.

"It's weird seeing all of this play out in real life. I'm not saying that you're weird, because you're not, and I don't want you to think I'm being mean, or judgmental, or anything like that, but…" Jules rambled.

"It's fine. It's a lot for a Mortal to take in, but I'm one of the good guys. I promise. Try to think of Angels like this. We're exactly like you, we just lack a shell—a Mortal body. Our forms are composed of our souls, not our organs. Does that make any sense?"

"It does and I believe you."

"It's okay to ask questions."

"So what? You're a mind reader too?" I quipped.

"No, but like I said before—apparently you weren't listening, I can read auras. Currently, hers is shouting confusion," he replied passive aggressively.

"And what does my *aura* say?" I asked.

A nasty smile spread across his lips—those full, lush, desirable, pink lips. "Well, let's see. It says you're a snotty brat who believes she's a princess and everyone should do what she wants, and they should feel sorry for her because of the crosses she must bear in this lifetime. But I really didn't need to read your aura to figure that out because after following you for a few seconds, I had your number. This is how this situation is going to play out. Go back to being the bitchy prima donna who thinks the sun rises and sets off of her ass, and I'll go back to doing my job. Personally, if I were you, I'd stop nagging my husband. You never know when he might turn— decide to dance with the Devil. Just saying."

"How dare you," I yelled, charging him.

"Stop it," Jules shouted, grabbing hold of my left wrist, and spinning me around to face her. "Only ten minutes ago you two looked like you needed to get a room. Now you're both being obnoxious to one another. Get a grip. Nina, you're frazzled. I have no idea what happened between you and Gabriel, but whatever it was, it wasn't anyone's fault. It was strange to watch. I swear it looked like a possession of some kind. Gabriel, you're making snap judgements off of a person you've never spent any time with. Nina is none of what you've assessed. Truthfully, I think you guys should forget about whatever that was earlier. Start over. Clean slate. After all, you're fighting for the same side. Maybe take

Orifiel's advice and get to know each other better."

I watched Gabriel's stare elude us as he gazed everywhere but at Jules or me. "We need to go."

"Is something the matter?" I asked.

"I'm not sure. I have to get you home. Now. I'll take over from here, Jules," he replied, seizing my arm, and dragging me to the street.

Gabriel led the way to a red, two door car. In uncomfortable silence he drove. Part of me feared him. Part of me loathed him. But part of me desired him. It was the third part which terrified me more than having to endure another encounter with Vincent.

Chapter 11

Chase

"Come home, sweetie. We can work this out. Your father is much calmer and misses you. *I* miss you."

"I'm sorry, Mom. No. The current setup is best," I said softly.

I hated hearing her beg and sob, but there was no feasible way to live there. Aside from the love/hate relationship I shared with my father, my life was too complicated and dangerous. My parents would never understand, nor would I ever wish to put my mother in harm's way. I loved her far too much. Vincent would eventually weaponize that. It couldn't happen. At times, lack of personal, uninterrupted space frustrated me, but the Luther's had become family. Though a deep appreciation existed for them and their generosity, I never felt one hundred percent comfortable in their personal space. I wasn't their son, only their daughter's soul mate which did mean something in our other world, but it didn't bond me to them or vice versa, only Nina.

"You can't stay with Nina's family forever."

"I realize that and have been looking for a place of my own. I've also been going to school, eating right, sleeping well, and for once, I'm happy."

Truth be told, I'd put apartment hunting on hold, but she didn't need to know that. She sighed heavily, then gently touched my hand.

"Promise me that you won't cut me out of your life, sweetheart."

"I haven't yet and never will. I love you."

"I love you too."

"Thanks for dinner, Mom. Same time, same place next week?"

"Of course," she said, pulling me into a tight embrace. "Do you have everything you need? Clothes? Shoes? School books? Money?"

I couldn't help but laugh. "Yeah, Mom. I'm all good." I kissed her cheek and left.

I used to feel bad after our weekly catch-up dinners, but that subsided recently. At some point I would've moved away, it just happened sooner than expected. Not having to deal with her constant neediness and my father's domineering ways was a huge load off of my back, freeing up space to address Vincent, and my growing inner abilities. I drove back to the Luthers' in a fairly decent mood.

Why shouldn't you be content? You have a great girl, a handle on your gifts, no more headaches, Vincent is out of your head, you're back in school, and Jack gave you his blessing to propose to Nina.

After we returned from New York, I'd asked Jack for Nina's hand in marriage. The trip solidified everything. Proposing was the only thing I could think about. Not only would this bold move show Nina my level of dedication, devotion, and love, it would also solve several problems. If I made this Mortal commitment (technically we were already married), we could move into a place of our own where I could protect her and be by her side always.

Jack agreed to the request, but there were conditions. I could propose now, but the actual wedding needed to be placed on hold until we both graduated and until he felt I was capable of handling myself mentally and physically in our supernatural world, especially when it came to sexual matters. Though controlling my inner Demons came easier now, at times apprehension concerning this issue lingered. No one knew for sure what would happen in the future.

I went out that very night and purchased an engagement ring, deciding to wait for the perfect moment. When the time was right, I'd know. According to women, or so I've been told, the proposal and wedding were everything. I wasn't about to give Nina anything less than a picture-perfect moment to remember. The ring was safely hidden in my room in a place where Nina would never find it, even if she snooped all day. Jack must've told Ellen because often I'd catch her smiling at me. One afternoon I approached her and shared the news myself. When I showed her the ring, she seemed thrilled.

A red sports car parked in my designated spot at the Luther's house threw me. I knew their friends' vehicles. This one definitely didn't belong to any of them. Quickly, I made my way to the back door. Deep down nothing warned me that danger was on the horizon, but something felt off. My suspicions were confirmed the moment I saw a strange man sitting at the dinner table next to my wife. Nina's eyes were filled with kindness but laced with pain. She felt deeply for this man. That bothered me. What troubled me even more was her hand, a hand which wore the promise ring I'd given her, was placed on top of his. The Demons I'd been repressing from deep within started coming back to life, rattling mental chains in pursuit of becoming free to wreak havoc on whomever or whatever got in my path.

Keep calm and breathe. Control the urge to harm this guy. He could be a relative or close family friend from out of town. Besides, Nina would never betray or jeopardize what you share.

Nina was a good girl, and I would prove that to the monster who lived inside of me who was now hellbent on being released.

Chapter 12

Gabriel

"Thanks for the ride," Nina said. Her tone sounded insincere.

"No problem" I matched the fakeness.

"See you later?"

"Not if I'm doing my job right and you can stay out of harms' way."

"Fine. Whatever."

Her fingers made their way to the door handle to exit the car, but my hand involuntarily stopped the action.

"What's wrong?" I inquired. Her aura boldly shouted distress and disappointment.

"Nothing."

"It's something. Your aura is suggesting otherwise."

"Oh yeah? What's it saying now?" she snapped sarcastically.

"It says," I began, but I was interrupted by my cell phone ringing. "I have to take this but stay. Please," I added once the screen said the call was from Michael.

Nina couldn't go inside until whatever her problem was had an opportunity to be addressed. She nodded, settling back into the seat. My hand stayed firmly on top of hers.

"Michael."

"I had a very interesting chat with your brother a few

moments ago. He tells me Nina Luther is aware of your presence and you're currently with her."

"True and true. Talk later." I tried to rush him off of the line.

"Damn it, Gabriel. I'm in no mood for your crap right now," Michael hissed.

Michael rarely lost control but based off of this conversation, it seemed like he was dangerously close to his threshold of tolerance. He'd been under tremendous pressure and stress, and now the load became heavier. During situations like this, shutting up and doing as told proved to be the only option.

"My apologies."

"I realize you were placed in a compromising position and commend your quick thinking and actions, but revealing yourself was idiotic. What were you thinking? I specifically said to watch the girl from afar."

"I made a mistake, but I fixed it. Her knowing can only help."

"This is how you're going to proceed. You're to stay glued to that girl's side. I don't care how much she complains or how much you hate it. Go into the Luther home, introduce yourself to her parents—Jack and Ellen, and sugarcoat the current Vincent situation as much as possible. *Do not*, under *any* circumstances, alarm anyone *especially* Chase James. You're also going to hawk the boy. I want to know his every move."

"How do you propose I do that? I only have one set of eyes."

"I don't care how it gets done. That's your problem, not mine. Figure it out. I want detailed daily reports when I relieve you at night. If anything should transpire in between, you're to alert me immediately. And while you're at it, try to get her to tell you if she has any visions. Do I make myself clear?"

"Yes, crystal, Father," I mumbled through gritted teeth.

"That's my good boy. Now go meet the Luthers. I'll see you tonight."

I hated this job and despised my existence when Michael was upset.

"Hey. Is everything okay?" Nina asked, glancing down at my fingers which were making small, gentle circles against her soft skin.

Her once calm aura now shouted concern. Deep concern, for me. My heart involuntarily softened making it hard to pull away.

"Yeah."

"What do we do now, Gabriel?" Nina's entire being radiated defeat.

"Introduce me to your parents. I'll explain why I've been *stalking* their daughter."

She didn't speak, but rather sat stone still staring out of the windshield deep in many thoughts.

"Nina, I swear to you that you're safe. Nothing is going to happen while I'm around. I realize you don't know me, but I'm really good at what I do. Feel free to ask Orifiel for a reference," I added, recapturing her hand, and squeezing it the same way Hadreniel had done for me whenever I felt broken. A weak smile found its way to her blank face. It was enough for her to find the strength and courage to lead the way into her home.

"Ground rules," Nina said harshly once we were standing in the foyer. "If we have to endure each other for an extended period of time, you will respect me and my privacy, and I the same of you. Opinions will be kept to ourselves. We must maintain boundaries or else this won't work. We also must practice transparency and be truthful with the other. Agreed?"

"Agreed."

No nonsense...a sexy quality, Ms. Luther.

Her aura grew dim and dark while her facial expression dropped. Stress. Stress over introducing me to Jack and Ellen Luther.

"Make the introduction and I'll do the rest. Okay? You have to trust me, Nina. I realize that's going to be difficult, but I promise you, I'm on your side and I will always have your back. I'm not an evil person. The Heavens deemed me fit to become an Angel, so how bad could I possibly be?" I said, looking into those beautiful, hazel eyes. The initial shock of their effect had subsided slightly, though her gaze was still a powerful force.

"I don't know why, but I do trust you. Do you trust me?" she whispered.

"Endlessly. Come on. Let's get this over with."

Chapter 13

Nina

"Dad?" I called in no particular direction.

"In here, princess."

I glanced at Gabriel. Inside of my core, a nervous annoyance rattled about, but mostly confusion weighed heavily on everything else. Running up the stairs to my bedroom to seek security from the madness of this world was what I really wanted to do, but what good would that be? Eventually I'd have to face facts and admit this wasn't a nightmare, but rather another crummy reality. Softly, Gabriel laced his fingers with mine and nodded. His big, brown irises were full of warmth and comfort.

"A few seconds ago, you said you trusted me. I need you to do that right now. Can you try, for me, please? Tell them my name and I'll take care of everything else. I swear I'll do my best to make this as quick and painless as possible."

His warm, strong hand continued to squeeze mine. The contact provided me with the nerve to handle this situation head on and not bolt. I paused briefly to touch the side of his face, turning it slightly so our eyes met. His power when we visually connected was an awesome force. I felt a bit creeped out for even thinking this, but with one look our past and futures revealed in total clarity. This time the glance didn't cause a punch-drunk effect, nor did it inspire lustful fantasies. He broke the spell by turning away which was Gabriel's subtle way of informing me that the put up or shut up moment had arrived.

"Hey, Mom. Dad. There's someone I'd like for you to meet," I said nervously while entering the kitchen.

My mother stopped cooking. My father didn't speak. It wasn't until Gabriel removed his hand from mine and opened the initial dialogue the realization they must've thought we were a couple of sorts hit me.

"It's nice to meet you both. I'm Gabriel."

"Hello, Gabriel. I'm Ellen and this is my husband, Jack," my mother stated cautiously. "Nina, Chase will be home any minute. If you need to tell us something, you better do it quickly."

"You have the wrong idea, Ellen. I'm not romantically involved with your daughter. The Chief Archangel Michael, whom I believe you've already met, sent me to watch Nina. After speaking with Nina today, we thought it was best that she introduced us. I will not be in anyone's way. You won't even know I'm here. Michael wishes for someone from our Army, such as myself, to watch over Nina. We have no idea where Vincent is, but as long as there's an observer around, she'll be fine. There's absolutely nothing to worry about and no immediate threat has presented, but it's always better to be safe than sorry."

"You're an Angel?" my father asked.

"Yes. One of the Seven Arcs to be exact," Gabriel said, removing his t-shirt, and revealing a vertical scar about twelve inches long on his spine. His wings grew from the mark, while his olive skin shimmered. After a fleeting moment, his wings retracted causing his skin tone to return to a typical Mortal appearance.

I had to admit, Gabriel had one hell of a killer body. It was leaps and bounds more powerful than Chase's. He had six pack abs, defined pecs, powerfully broad shoulders, deep inguinal creases, and massively thick arms. I wondered if he looked that way before his passing or if when he entered Heaven, he was granted perfect physical form.

"Is Nina in danger?" My mother's entire demeanor changed from inquisitive to panic.

He'd already told her no, but my mother would dwell on this until she had reason to believe otherwise. Right now, it didn't matter what Gabriel said because she was going to panic regardless.

"No, Ellen. She's not. Neither is your family. I've been carefully keeping watch, and I am always in constant communication with Michael. If he didn't think I was skilled enough to guard Nina, he wouldn't have chosen me," he reassured.

"How long have you been following Nina?" my father questioned.

"Since she traveled to New York. My qualifications for this assignment are superior. Briefly, my divine gift is reading souls and auras. I'm third in command in the Angelic Army under Michael and Raphael, and I'm Heaven's Chief Demonic Assassin. I lead an undefeated team of Angels. Everyone in Hell is familiar with my name and reputation, and is aware they should not cross me. The ones who have aren't around any longer to share their stories. Michael can confirm this if need be."

"What exactly are you watching Nina do?" my mother queried.

"Everything. I've been tailing her everywhere.

When Nina's home I guard the perimeter of your house. Michael relieves me for a few hours during the overnight, then I return. Nina is never alone. We work in stealth mode which is why you haven't seen us. Due to uncontrollable circumstances my presence required revealing. Had that not happened, this conversation wouldn't have occurred."

"Uncontrollable circumstances?"

"I was about to get run over by a car, Mom. He pushed me out of the way, saving my life," I spoke up.

"Oh my God, Nina. Are you okay?" she shrilled, rushing to my side, examining every inch of me.

"I'm fine, Mom."

"Gabriel, I don't know how to thank you. Stay for dinner. It's the least we can do."

"I can't, but thanks," he replied.

"No, please. Stay." I fake smiled. Honestly, I had a ton of questions and wanted to explore the effect of his eye contact over my sanity some more.

"All right," he replied with hesitation.

"Do you eat Mortal food?" I blurted out.

"Angels need to eat, sleep, shower, and do all sorts of things Mortals do. Granted, we don't need to eat or sleep as much because technically speaking we're dead, but our bodies require some of our old ways. For example, I still cannot function properly without coffee in the morning. Why that is I have no idea. Didn't Orifiel explain this?"

"No. It never came up."

He responded with a slight frown and a shoulder shrug. Wanting to speak with him in private, I led us to the living room and sat on the couch. He stood in the corner of the space with his arms folded against his broad chest, wearing no expression at all.

"Do you ever miss being a Mortal?"

"I guess, at times. The afterlife didn't exactly turn out the way I'd hoped. Nothing in life or death really ever does I suppose, but I've coped. That's all you can really do, right?"

A full understanding of his attitude presented. I felt sympathy over the disappointment he experienced which was totally relatable. I didn't ask to be a Mortal Angel. There were many days when I wanted out, but much like Gabriel, I've dealt. My existence, thus far, hadn't been a dream come true either. This path had been put upon me and I, too, was learning to manage the ups and downs that went along with it. However, he had me curious. I wanted to know more, but I wasn't sure if I should ask or not. Overstepping boundaries and creating unnecessary tension would stand in the way of being made aware of why I felt so drawn to him.

"Dinner's ready," my mother called.

"Mom, where's Chase?" I asked, taking note of his absence.

"He called a few minutes ago. He decided to have dinner with Blanche, but he'll be back in a little while," she said.

"We're speaking of your husband, Chase James?" Gabriel questioned.

"Yes. No. Yes and no. In your world, yes. In the Mortal world we're too young to be married, so he's just my boyfriend," I answered, not really wanting to discuss myself.

"You're what, nineteen or twenty?" he inquired.

"Nineteen."

"I was about your age when I got married. A little

older, but not by much," he replied.

My heart dropped. I had no idea why it did, but my reaction was involuntary. For some unknown reason it bothered me deeply that Gabriel had a wife.

"I'm not sure what period of time you come from, but today women wait," I snapped.

"Gabriel, if you wouldn't mind, what's your story?" My father cut in, shooting me a wide-eyed look, visually cueing me to keep my attitude in check.

"There's not much to tell. I was born in Manhattan in 1921. When I was five, I became ill with Scarlet Fever. One night I fell unconscious from a high fever. All I remember was waking up and being able to read auras, and a little while later souls. It wasn't until I became an actual Angel that I realized when I was sick, I died and had become a Lost Soul. The woman I fell in love with, my soul mate, was one as well. During times of Angelic and Demonic unrest, Lost Souls are automatically given a sixth sense to guide them. This was why Lilith, my wife, and I were presented with a divine gift immediately after being returned to Earth. One day we boarded an airplane which crashed somewhere over the Atlantic Ocean."

"At least you still have the woman you love by your side for all eternity." I meant every word, wishing the same for myself.

A lifeless smile clung for dear life on his lips. "Yes. Lucky me."

"What are your wife's divine abilities?" my father asked.

"Jack. You've asked enough already," my mother said.

"It's fine. Lilith is what The Heavens refer to as a

Demon Goddess. She encompasses both good and evil, but sways toward the evil."

"Like Chase?"

"To a degree, Jack. Chase isn't a Demon God. That's another story for another time. Though he has both light and dark from within him, he's still a Mortal. He also sides with the Angels, which means he's suppressing his inner Demonic urges. It's a complicated situation to breakdown. I fear my explanation wouldn't do any justice. Michael would be the best person to ask."

"If you're an Angel and she's a Demon, how does that work?" My trust in this man had drastically waned. How could he be on the side of righteousness, but coupled with a Demon?

"It doesn't."

"But you're soul mates," I pressed, unsatisfied with his answer.

"So?"

"You're supposed to be together forever."

He laughed profoundly before speaking again. "I guess Lilith didn't get that memo."

"Are you divorced?"

"No. Divorce is manmade, therefore it doesn't exist in Heaven or Hell. Lilith resides in Hell, and I in The Heavens. We'll always be bonded as mates and I'll always love her, but Angels and Demons don't mix. They never have and they never will. Case closed," he said directly and firmly.

Obviously, I'd struck a chord, but I didn't have time to dwell on it because the backdoor opened and shut, and Chase appeared.

"Hey..." his voice trailed the moment he saw Gabriel.

Chase approached the table. Once he reached me, he kissed me, then he placed both of his hands on my shoulders—a bold declaration of possession.

"Chase, Gabriel, Gabriel, Chase. Gabriel has been assigned to be my Angelic watcher," I explained.

"Why?" Chase demanded.

"Because no one knows where Vincent is or what he's been up to. Michael wanted to take some precautionary measures," Gabriel answered.

"Nina is fine and safe. I'm perfectly capable of protecting what's mine without any help," Chase said flatly.

"No one doubts this, Chase—" Gabriel started.

"Great. Go back to Heaven or wherever."

"I can't do that. I have orders to stay here, and I cannot abandon a position because a Mortal believes they can do a better job."

"At least you realize and acknowledge that I could do it better."

"Chase, outside, now," I said.

The last thing I wanted to deal with tonight was Gabriel and Chase rolling around on the floor trying to kill each other in my mother's perfectly clean, blood-free kitchen.

"What's the problem?" I asked the moment we were alone on the porch.

"Who is this guy? Where the hell did he come from?" He sounded livid.

"I already told you." I kept my tone and mannerisms as calm as possible hoping this sentiment would trickle over onto him.

"I don't like it. I've been taking care of and protecting you just fine. You're *my* wife and *my* responsibility, damn it. *Not his*."

Since our Demonic wedding Chase often referred to me as his wife. At first it seemed weird, but over time I'd become used to hearing it.

"Okay. Slow down for a minute. He's acting on Michael's orders and is only watching me from afar in case all hell breaks loose again. Seriously, Chase, think about it. If we had someone looking out for us in the past, we never would've found ourselves in grave danger, *and* if some serious crap goes down, like a *war*, we'll know about it and will be able to escape together, unharmed. Ignore him. I know you can protect me, but why bother when it's Gabriel's task?" Hopefully this reasoning resonated with him.

"No, Nina. That's *my* job." Chase wasn't going to let this go.

"Look, don't you want me to be happy?"

"Yes. Of course, but what does that have to do with anything?"

"I'd be *a lot* happier if you let this go and allowed Gabriel to stay. I don't need *or* want any additional stress. Haven't we been through enough lately? Please, for me, take a breath and pretend to be nice—like I'm doing," I begged.

"Fine, but the first time *Gabriel* oversteps his boundaries, his ass is mine," he warned.

"Deal." I smiled, embracing him tightly.

Peace had temporarily been restored. That was going to have to be enough for tonight.

Chapter 14

Chase

I kept waiting for summer to end hoping it would take the massive pain in my ass, Gabriel, along with it. No such luck. Nothing happened either. We were all still in the same place as we had been. I foolishly thought the adage 'no news is good news' would hold true, and with that, Michael would tell his loyal watch dog to go home, but he didn't. The most irritating part? The bastard was never more than five feet away from us at any given moment. At first, I tried ignoring him, but how could anyone do that? I couldn't even be affectionate with Nina because his constant looming made her feel ill at ease. The only alone time happened when everyone went to bed. Even then Nina was off limits because her parents were down the hall. The less accessible she became, the more I craved her. I was ready to let my guard down so much so that the first second we found ourselves alone, every intention of breaking my 'no sexual next level rule' would happen.

After a few months, obsessive curiosity over Gabriel haunted me. Who was this guy? Why was he really here? Nina shared his 'woe is me' back story which included how his wife became a Demon, and how she believed his current behaviors were based off of his mourning and anger, but I didn't buy it. He was an asshole, plain and simple. Gabriel wasn't happy, therefore no one else was going to be. I detested the way he treated Nina. To him she was nothing more than an inconvenient damsel in distress. His comments were often rude, but Nina snapped back with her own brand of wit which made me smile. My wife wasn't helpless, stupid, nor in need of anyone's assistance, which was an endearing trait that made her even more desirable.

There were several times it appeared an interaction with Gabriel would end in a fist fight, but tolerance and restraint were utilized. He wasn't worth it mainly because his little game to evoke my Demonic side so he could do what he was really sent to do, destroy me, wasn't going to work. I wasn't an idiot or blind. He was a Demonic Assassin and I was one half Demon. If Michael knew, they all knew. Repressing the inner beast within me proved difficult on a normal basis, but adding a man looking at my wife with lustful yearning made the task damn near impossible.

You will not win, Gabriel.

One night, after everyone went to sleep, I climbed out of my bedroom window. I knew Michael arrived around midnight. Gabriel would leave, returning at six. Often, a husky woman's voice or a man with a thick Irish accent, more than likely this was Raphael, spoke with Michael in Gabriel's absence, but they always stayed off to the far-left side of the house, never moving around much. Once the coast was clear, I followed Gabriel.

He lived about five minutes away in a restored carriage house. I tailed him a few times making sure he went to the same place, then I'd watch him from my car. The man literally did the same thing every single night. He entered the house through the garage, then headed into the main living space. He'd flip the television on, eat something, take a shower, and finally end up in his bedroom, where he'd stare at something on the dresser for a good twenty minutes before lying down. For an alleged badass Angel, his actions proved not so much.

Several days later, my growing obsession had boiled over. This time I plotted a way to break into his house. No one guarded it during the day. Since he was always up Nina's ass, doing so would be too easy. After taking the garage door opener from his unlocked car, I walked right into the house as if I owned the place. The space was small, but how much room did a single guy really need? The house appeared extremely clean, abnormally tidy for a man. Nothing of interest lay around. The main living area was void of papers or clutter. The office had a laptop still in the box on top of a desk, which was also free and clear of anything suspicious, but his bedroom held one interesting bit of personal information. The thing he'd stare at before bed was an old photograph of him and an extremely attractive woman. Carefully, I removed it from the frame flipping it over. "Bello and Lilith, 1940," was written neatly in the upper right-hand corner. Maybe Nina had been right. Perhaps Gabriel still mourned the loss of his soul partner. When I'd broken up with Nina, being nice and friendly with those around me didn't happen.

Driving home I decided to cut Gabriel some slack. However, as much effort was invested in laying off of him, every ounce of him still attempted to show me up, proving he was far superior in every way. I wasn't sure if his actions were in response to gaining Nina's attention, or to show me my place, or a barbaric attempt to hit on Jules.

You're barking up the wrong tree with that girl.

It seemed he and Jules formed some sort of tight relationship. Initially, it appeared perhaps a romantic vibe existed, but as time wore on a more sibling style relationship emerged. Often, and to my great displeasure, I'd find myself out with Nina, *Jules, and him.* Nina rationalized those nights by saying she loved being with Jules and since Gabriel had to be there anyway, why couldn't they join in? I could never think of a valid reason as to why not. This irked me tremendously.

Friday night Nina and I were heading to a driving range for a new, different type of date—one I might actually enjoy. Gabriel and Jules followed in the car behind. No shock there.

Screw this.

My left foot depressed the clutch. The gears chirped causing the car to take off like a bat straight out of Hell. Jules driving her and Gabriel roughly translated to a decent head start. Nearly blind and half dead senior citizens moved faster in cars than Jules—the most cautious driver in the entire state of Georgia. There was no way she'd ever deign to go over the speed limit.

Piss off, Gabriel.

Nina, tremendously turned on by my actions, pounced on me the moment the car parked at the driving range. I wasn't about to complain because for the first time in months we were completely and totally alone. The dire necessity to touch her was finally sated.

Aggressively, I tore at her shirt, pulling it off, and disposing of it somewhere on the backseat. Nothing was done to control my emotions. I didn't give a damn if my inner thoughts projected onto her. The gift could only enhance the moment and mood. Her kisses lingered, tasting sweet and sinfully good while her body felt enticing and forbidden. After a few minutes of experiencing lust in its rawest form, I couldn't take it anymore.

"Let's go somewhere," I panted.

"Where?" she whispered in a melodious voice that was spiked with excitement.

"There's a hotel a few blocks east of here. Is that okay?" I asked, reaching for our shirts, then shoving the keys into the ignition.

"Are you sure you're ready for this?"

"I've never wanted something more, baby. Are *you* sure *you* want this?"

"Trust me, I'm ready. What about Jules and Gabriel?"

"They're not invited."

"Seriously, Chase."

"Who cares? They'll show up, realize we're not here, and will find a way to cope. You'll be with me, baby. You're safe. I'd never allow anything bad to happen to you, *ever*."

Confirmation came in the form of Nina's beaming grin. With that, I slid the gearshift into reverse, backing up. A rearview mirror glimpse caught a figure approaching my car. Sharpening my vision, I assessed it was Jules.

"Damn it," I cursed loudly, slamming my left fist against the steering wheel.

"What? What's wrong?" she asked. Her head darted from side to side.

A rather loud rap on the passenger side window jarred Nina, causing her to retreat into my arms. Her response pleased me. Nina knew and trusted that I'd always protect and provide shelter for her.

"Relax, baby. It's only Jules," I assured, trying to keep the annoyance in my voice to a minimum while rolling down the passenger side window.

"I'm not interrupting anything?" Jules asked. A smirk stretched across her lips.

"Nope. Nothing we won't finish later," I answered.

Gabriel stood across the lot. His arms were folded against his chest as he leaned on Jules's car, hawking the situation. The ass knew exactly what was going on inside of my car and decided it was his call to allow it or to stop it. Yeah, no. I decide what does and doesn't happen. *Not* him. *Never* him.

You may have won the battle, Gabriel, but you will certainly not win the war.

Chapter 15

Gabriel

"Seriously, Jules. A turtle just passed us," I said sarcastically.

She frowned. "She'll be fine for a few minutes. What's got you so unhinged?"

"Nothing."

"Really, Gabriel? I can see right through you. Spill your guts or I'll drive even slower."

"It's nothing, and I highly doubt that's possible."

Playfully, she punched my arm. I feigned pain and laughed. If my Mortal mother were to have had another child, I would've loved to have had a sister like Jules.

"Come on. What's up?"

"This," I mumbled.

I was never the type of man to spill my guts and open up, Mortal or Immortal. I always shouldered my troubles alone, but the current situation had become unnerving. The feelings of desire and closeness that were experienced whenever I looked into Nina's eyes had subsided considerably, but I was still drawn to her in a way that I shouldn't have been. Keeping a sizable distance and putting on a jerk façade had become a way of life. However, my heart craved Nina's touch. To say confusion consumed me would be putting things mildly, and since Orifiel wouldn't provide any answers, frustration ate away at my gut. I held no stake in Nina's life, but yet I needed to protect her far beyond Michael's expectations. Then, there was Chase—whom I loathed. He was the enemy. My deep-seated hatred for him was not only due to his partial Demonic status.

"What do you mean?" Jules asked. Her gaze was firmly on the road ahead. Her hands tightly gripped the wheel at precisely ten and two. Her posture was impeccable.

"Nina puts herself in stupid positions. Take tonight for example. She's speeding off with Chase damn well knowing someone is here to keep watch over her because potential danger lurks. This makes it easy for people, like myself, to look down upon her. But girls like her love to play the role of the victim because of the attention garnered. Up to this point, she's been lucky, but luck runs out, and she's too dumb to understand that."

"Nina can be stubborn at times, but that's part of her charm. I suppose she and Chase wanted a private moment, which with you *always* around is probably hard to come by." Jules's rationalization added more fuel to the already burning fire within me.

"Part of her charm? No. I don't think so. Nina does whatever she wants, says whatever she wants, and does it all with no regard for anyone else's feelings. Then, she will either play the damsel in distress or modern-day Joan of Arc card. When the shit really hits the fan, she'll run to my brother, expecting Orifiel to clean up her mess. Additionally, Nina is the worst kind of tease around. As for Chase and her, she's completely blind to the fact that the hand she holds is the one that's holding her down and back. He's Demonic, Jules. Angels and Demons don't mix. I don't care he's her mate. He's not for her. His soul is horrible. There's more evil in Chase than holy. At some point the devil that resides within his almost blackened heart will surface. When that day comes if he should touch one hair on that girl's head, I'll destroy him with my bare hands, no regrets," I ranted. My fists tightly clenched. The thought of Chase harming Nina was too consuming and painful to think about.

"Can I ask you something *without* getting barked at?" she questioned cautiously.

"I'd never intentionally '*bark*' at you. If I have in the past, I'm sorry," I answered trying to push my emotions away.

"Do you by chance have feelings for Nina?"

"No," I snapped. How dare Jules ask that? Was I that transparent?

Stop it, Gabriel. You're a married man. Nina is a married woman. She's a job. You need to remind yourself of that every second of every damn day. You will not betray Lilith because eventually she will return.

"I think your dislike of Chase and your *non-existent* feelings for Nina are clouding your otherwise good judgment," she said as she pulled into the parking lot.

Her soft nature and desire to see the good in everyone was endearing and aggravating at the same time. She wasn't going to see my point or let me win. It was best to drop it.

"Hey," I said, lightly touching her arm, "what we talk about stays between us. Okay?"

"I would never tell your story to anyone, Gabriel, because it's yours to tell, not mine. *All* of your secrets are safe." She smiled brightly. "Do you think they started?"

"Started what? Having sex? Quite possibly." Pure disgust overtook any positive emotions I may have felt at that moment.

I knew damn well what they were up to. Just because it was dark didn't mean their auras weren't visible. The black car pulsated bright red and orange. The thought of his hands all over her body enraged my core. I had to use every ounce of restraint to stop myself from beating the life out of Chase right then and there.

"No," Jules responded in disbelief, sprinting to the car. A few minutes later she returned snickering.

"What were they doing?" I demanded, grabbing her wrist.

"Fooling around. They weren't doing *that* if that's what you're freaking out over."

"Them engaging in *that* type of behavior would be dangerous and you know it."

"Dangerous for whom? Them or you?" she muttered, walking away, leaving me standing in the lot more confused than when I began this stupid job.

****

Tremendous annoyance lingered for the rest of the evening. Trying not to reveal this weakness, I hung back watching the three of them enjoy themselves, hating every single second of it. My life up to this point was very black and white. Now Nina Luther forced shades of gray to enter it. In absolute revulsion I viewed Chase trying to impress Nina with his Demonic strength, who in turn, seemed aroused by this act. An Angel turned on by a Demon...*sound familiar, Gabriel? Those who live in glasshouses shouldn't throw stones.* I felt as if my head would explode until an epiphany struck.

Nina was me and I, Nina. That was the connection. I was trying to stop her from making the same mistakes I'd made. There wasn't any sort of physical attraction, only empathy. Relief found its way deep within me, making my heart turn cold again; the way it should always be. Nothing or no one could ever provide me with happiness again, unless its name was Lilith.

A small part of my soul still felt ill at ease. I couldn't help thinking how Micah dropped the ball with Nina, Chase, me, and Lilith. Your mate was supposed to bring out the best in you, not the worst. Chase made Nina rude and sarcastic because when she was alone, her soul and aura, though by no means pure, appeared even and somewhat whole. The moment Chase appeared, his spiritual nature shifted her balance. I wondered if I'd suffered from the same.

Finally, hours later, back at my post waiting for Michael to takeover, my thoughts mused. Though I was feeling considerably better about the forced bond with Nina, my hatred for Chase remained. While he slept, I protected his wife, who spent most of her time when he was around acting like I was some sort of low life, uneducated thug.

You're wrong about me, Nina. I'm out here every fucking night shielding you from the horrors of this world—terrifying danger, threats lurking in the shadows waiting to pounce that crave to end your existence, while he's inside sleeping. I'd never let another man tend to my wife, but then again, I never would've put her in danger in the first place.

Chapter 16

Chase

"It's nice Gabriel is taking Jules to the party," Nina said casually while she applied makeup.

The random comment came out of nowhere causing my eyebrow to raise. Why would she care?

"Yeah. He's a real everyday hero. I hope Gabriel realizes he doesn't have a shot in Hell with Jules," I replied arrogantly.

"Be nice, Chase. Yes, he knows. Quite frankly, Gabriel doesn't strike me as the type of guy who'd cheat regardless of what happened in his relationship, which, might I add, was horrible."

The fact that she defended him irritated me to the point of annoyance. I wasn't a blind idiot. Every time they made eye contact a spark formed between them. Subconsciously they felt something deeper for the other, something she and I could never share. The only way to stomp that out would be to sleep with her and pray that everything I'd read about intimacy and soul mates proved true. Apparently, the act set each mate's passion on fire, renewing their bond. However, getting her alone was the problem. I'd decided tonight, no matter what, was the night. We were going to a Halloween party hosted by one of Nina's friends. The house would be packed with people. Keeping constant tabs on Nina in a crowd would be impossible for Gabriel. We'd slip away for an hour or so, but in order for the plan to work, preparations were made well in advance by reserving a room at a nearby hotel. This wasn't how I'd envisioned our first time, but desperate times called for desperate measures.

"You're right. I'm sure Gabriel is a good guy," I managed to choke out.

"Good guy or not, he's an epic pain in the ass. We never have a second to ourselves anymore. It's frustrating. Doesn't he ever go home?"

I smiled.

That's my girl.

She was still committed to me, and me alone. I'd been foolish for thinking otherwise. "Gabriel leaves at midnight, after Michael arrives. He comes back around six. He's living in one of those restored carriage houses about five minutes away from here."

"How do you know that?" She turned to face me.

"I know everything." I winked.

She smirked in response before returning her attention to applying her makeup. Unable to control my impulses, I rose off of the bed and grasped her waist from behind.

"Can I help you?" she purred.

"Kiss me," I whispered, pressing our lips together. Without hesitation I pushed her to the bed, wildly pulling on the belt of her silk robe.

*Forget about tonight...do it now...*a voice from within my brain urged.

Within a matter of a few seconds most of our clothing had hit the floor.

"When did your parents say they'd be back?" I

asked breathlessly.

"Eight," she mumbled in between urgent kisses.

Glancing at the clock on her desk it revealed that we had plenty of time. I didn't feel the need to ask if Nina was okay with what was going on. Her actions were trusted, which clearly spoke volumes. She wanted this as much as I did, but perhaps for different reasons.

Slow down. You're attacking her like a starving wild animal would. This moment should be memorable. Just because you've already done this, remember, Nina hasn't. Keep your emotions in check. Take your time.

"Are you sure this is safe?" she asked. Caution hung from each word.

"Yes. I love you and I don't think we need to wait anymore. It's going to be fine. All known gifts are under control. I'm dead sure nothing bad will happen. I promise, baby," I replied, looking down into her eyes.

After a pregnant pause that seemed to last a lifetime, she nodded in agreement. "Okay."

"Nina," a masculine voice summoned with a rather loud rap on her bedroom door.

"Damn it," she hissed, pushing me off of her. "Yeah?"

"We need to speak. Immediately." Gabriel's tone was flat and hard.

"Is something the matter?"

"Vincent's not outside if that's what you're asking," he answered sarcastically.

"Uh, okay. Give me a second." She frantically threw my clothing at me while trying to dress herself.

"Hey," I said, taking her by the wrist.

"I'm sorry," she mouthed.

"We *will* finish what we started later."

A devious grin spread across her face as she walked to the door, opened it slightly, and exited. I lay on the bed vowing tonight would be the night no matter what Gabriel said or did to stop us from being alone. If there was ever a good reason that warranted using my gift for an evil, self-serving purpose, this was it.

Oh, Gabriel. Enjoy the mind trip I'm going to put you on at the party. You've screwed with the wrong guy.

Chapter 17

Nina

"Hey. What's up?" I asked, forcing myself to act calm while making sure to quickly close the bedroom door. After all, Gabriel was doing his job. Unfortunately, my personal life was part of said job, but the constant intrusions were as aggravating as the thrill which shot up my spine every single time I looked into those deep brown eyes of his. The initial shock had long worn off, but something about them chased all of my sanity away and not in a good way, but rather in a dangerous fashion. Not that I'd admit that to anyone, not even Jules. However, there had been far too many times recently when a strong urge to throw him down and kiss those perpetually stoic lips with the hope that that action might fill his core with happiness and remove his pain for good erupted. Obviously, I'd never commit such an act, but sometimes controlling the desire proved trying. Most days I found him to be a bother and his words to be unkind and cruel.

"Extreme caution must be exercised tonight," he said, looking through the center of my body. He was reading my aura shifts and soul status.

"Uh, okay. Is there any reason why you're saying this?" I pressed, aware there had to be another motive for this chat.

"You'll be in an open area surrounded by people in costume. It'd be easy for a Demon to sneak in unnoticed. I'll be there watching, but you have to remain alert."

"Got it. I'll be on the lookout. I have to finish getting ready. Is there anything else?"

"No," he answered, turned, and walked down the stairs.

Liar!

There was definitely something on his mind other than me being careful tonight.

Whatever. Not my problem.

"What did *he* want?" Chase snapped the moment my feet stepped back inside of my bedroom and the door clicked shut.

"Something about keeping our eyes and ears open tonight because Vincent is still lurking." I really didn't wish to discuss Gabriel. I wanted to revisit what we were doing before his rude interruption.

"My parents won't be home for another half-hour…" I started, wrapping my arms around his perfectly toned waist.

"Later," he whispered, kissing my forehead. "When we don't have to rush."

"I'm going to hold you to that."

"You better."

My love for Chase had grown stronger and deeper. Part of me felt bad for Gabriel. I cringed at the thought of his pain and the torment he clearly still felt over losing his wife. Having to watch Chase and I happy together must've felt like a punch to the gut.

Better you than me, Gabriel. Sorry.

Chapter 18

Gabriel

"Nina?" I asked, knocking on her bedroom door for the second time today. *He* wasn't in there this time because I only saw one aura and soul beating. I'd calmed considerably from before. Controlling the desire to rip Chase off of Nina was challenging. The moment I saw the aura of the room shift I thought I'd lose it, but I had no idea why. After interrupting their intimate moment, I tried to rationalize an Angel and Demon mating was a dangerous situation. Sadly, deep down something else troubled me, but I had no idea what. Jules's sharp remark about whom an intimate encounter between Chase and Nina would harm more still resonated.

The Heavens. That's who!

"Just a second," Nina answered.

One thing I quickly realized about her was that she was never on time. Nina ran at least a half-hour late, which as a Mortal would've unnerved me, but as an Angel where time no longer mattered, who cared?

"Okay. You can come in."

"Are you ready to…?"

My brain shouted to turn around and to not stare, but something bigger, an unstoppable force made me stand stone still taking in her seductiveness.

"I'm sorry. I could've sworn you said come in. I'll

wait in the hall," I managed to say.

She stood in heels, thigh-high stockings, and a white, silk, slip dress. Her body was amazing. Extremely curvaceous and drop dead alluring.

"I *am* ready," she laughed. "I'm an Angel. See?" She turned, showing me the two small wings attached to her back.

I've been in Heaven for a long time, sweetheart, and I have never seen an Angel look like that.

"What? Why are you looking at me like that?" Her flawless face scrunched.

"Like what?"

"Like you're judging me. You've got this know-it-all smirk spread across your face. Stop."

"I'm not judging you at all. I'm reading you, but if that's causing you discomfort, I'll stop. It's an occupational habit."

Her aura kept flashing bright orange. My presence, coupled with the fact that my eyes couldn't stop staring at her had her wishing I'd kiss her. I was ninety percent sure of this. The other ten percent was still sizing the situation up, stuck on her body and its every bow.

"What did you *read*?"

"I'd rather not say."

"Why?" she demanded. Her hands found her hips as a look of defiance and fear lingered in her beautiful, hazel irises.

"Because I'd rather not. Let's go."

"No. Tell me."

Never in all of my years of being able to read auras had I been wrong or afraid to share what I saw, but at that moment, having to admit what I knew scared the shit out of me.

"You're turned on by the fact that I'm turned on by how you look, and because of that, you want me to kiss you." There. I'd said it. It was out in the open. Nina could process it however she felt was necessary.

"So?" she said in a dismissive tone.

"To hell with this," I replied.

Her expression grew curious, but somehow my boldness versus hers left her speechless and breathless. Slowly our eyes met. All rational thought abandoned my soul. Not waiting for the gravitational force controlling us to draw us together, I gave up and in. My next few moves excited her but threw off her internal balance. Taking her by the waist, my hands gently slid up her curves, stopping on her neck. Marveling at her unblemished beauty was easy, but intense. My fingertips lightly stroked the side of her cheek and lips. I could've kissed her, but making the tension which already existed between us reach a feverish pitch of desire was far more important. Nina's body trembled under my touch.

"You're a god" she whispered. Her nervous hands finally explored my body. Nina's featherlight touch drove me to the edge of all reason.

"Which would make you a goddess because *you're mine*, Nina." My tone was soft, but serious. Her long, slender fingers laced through my hair, willing me to make the bolder move to finish what we started. Nina's breathing shallowed as her aura screamed for us to become closer.

You've got nothing to lose, Gabriel. Take her. Lilith is gone. Chase is Demonic. And honestly? They don't matter. What does matters is this beautiful creature standing before you. She wants to show you deep, loving emotion and intimacy, something you haven't experienced in a very long time. If you don't embrace this moment, it's likely to never occur again. This girl is too gorgeous and too forbidden not to taste. She's the living embodiment of sin. Give in. Mark her. Make her yours once and for all.

As I inched closer her cool breath teased my skin which cried out for a release. I had to feel her, all of her without restriction.

"Why do we connect like this?" Nina asked, desperately losing all of her self-control. Our brushing lips created an intense spark of energy which filled my deceased core.

"I have no idea. I wish I did, but I don't."

"This is wrong," she mumbled, continuing to taunt my soul with desire. If she truly believed what we were doing wasn't right, she would've pulled away, but she didn't. If anything, she drew closer. If this girl was waiting for me to stop, she'd be waiting for a long time. It didn't matter what my brain shouted. I needed her.

"Is it?" I whispered.

I continued provoking her, forcing a break, a crumble, a wanton lust to form for me and me alone. Her mouth opened slightly as her hands gripped my biceps as if they were the only object providing her with stability. An explosion of intense energy erupted the moment full contact occurred. Seizing her waist, I lifted her. Her legs wrapped and locked around my torso. Swiping the contents off of her dresser, I placed her on it.

"I love the way you kiss," she moaned, tightening her grasp.

"You're pure sin, Nina. Complete and total sin," I mumbled.

Nina wanted to attack, but I didn't. Slow and

deliberate actions while finding the perfect balance of soft and aggressive was important. She needed to know, by feeling it, that my soul craved only hers. Our kisses were deep. Our caresses were seductive. My tongue traced her lower lip while my teeth carefully scraped the surface of her skin. My fingers never left her face except to pull her closer so she could feel what she was doing to me and experience the power she held.

"Your lips are delicious," I said faintly.

"I want you so badly."

"You already have me."

"Please don't stop."

"Never."

"Swear you'll never leave me."

"I swear. I'd rather lose my soul then ever leave you."

"Gabriel," she moaned weakly.

Her need for this moment was intoxicating.

Imagine if you could always feel like this?

"Ayup." Orifiel's voice spoke out of nowhere.

Instinctively I pulled away shoving Nina behind me in a protective stance.

"Am I interrupting something?"

"No. What? What do you want?" I demanded, making sure Nina's body was still glued to mine.

"Why don't I believe that? Anyway, *you* asked me to check out the space Nina would be in tonight and to secure the perimeter. Well, I did. It's safe. You're welcome. I took the liberty of placing a few others on-site as an added precaution. Again, you're welcome."

I turned to Nina. "Are you okay?"

She nodded.

"I need to speak with my brother alone for a

moment. I'll meet you downstairs. Don't even think about leaving without me," I warned.

"Yeah, sure. Whatever," she said brushing me off.

Her entire attitude shifted in a matter of seconds. She went from boiling hot to icy cold just like that, but I supposed I had as well. The once commanding power that had imprisoned us no longer existed. Rational thoughts returned. I imagined Nina felt free of the hold as well.

"I'd like to speak with him also, but it can wait," she added.

"Call to me." Orifiel kissed her forehead. "I miss our little gabs. By the way, you make a stunning Angel," he said, pulling away slightly. His hands softly ran up and down her arms as his eyes took in her entire body with one swift glance. His aura revealed that sexual intimacy had occurred between them.

"Thank you," she said, embracing him tightly before exiting the room.

Their shared closeness and the possibility that Orifiel had done more with her than soul soothing disturbed me. I wanted to punch him for looking at Nina, never mind touching her. She was meant for my eyes only. *Not* his. *Never* his.

"So what's…" Orifiel began.

I couldn't stop myself from grabbing him by the throat and slamming his body against the wall.

"If you ever look at Nina like that again you won't be around to see the sun rise the next day. Are we clear?" I hissed.

"What the bloody hell?"

"Are. We. Clear?" I said through gritted teeth.

"Aye."

"Cut the crap, *brother*," I warned as I applied more pressure to his neck.

"What are you talking about?" he managed to choke out.

"You know damn good and well what I'm talking about."

"Truly, I have no idea."

"Have you slept with her?" I demanded.

"God no. We messed around *once*. It was just a little innocent snogging. Honestly."

"Develop that," I hissed. The ire inside of my soul had reached its boiling point.

"She wanted an escape from reality. Making out was *her* choice, *not* mine. I may have initially gone along with it, but I stopped it. It meant nothing sexually. I swear."

He spoke the truth. Addressing this annoyance became a sidebar for later.

"Why does that girl affect me the way she does?"

"I don't know."

His aura flashed a muddy gray, a sure sign he was lying.

"Liar," I grunted, squeezing my fingers tighter around his esophagus.

"Fine. Let me go and I'll tell you everything."

Immediately I released my grip. He leaned forward placing his hands on his knees gasping for air. Closing an Angel or Demon's airway doesn't kill them because both can sustain without oxygen. What it does do is paralyze them, acting as a tactic to get a point across.

"Now," I commanded.

"I assume you're familiar with the entire concept of soul mates? How they're born in groups, but only one shares a romantic link to you?"

"Oh, you've got to be kidding me. She's from my soul group?" I laughed to mask my fear and disbelief.

"Not exactly."

"Then what *exactly* is it?" I questioned, unsure of how to feel. A soul bond would explain a lot, but apparently that wasn't the case.

"Okay, well you see, you and Nina…"

"Enough," A sharp, hard, Australian accent warned.

My head snapped back. I found myself standing face to face with Michael.

"Orifiel, go to your post," Michael ordered.

"Yes, Father." He disappeared out of the window faster than a bolt of lightning.

"And you," he began, "you're to never use brute force against anyone who is not a target again, *especially* not your brother. Do you understand me?"

"What's the connection?" I spat, ignoring his warning.

"There is none. Stop questioning the Universe."

"Just because you're skilled enough to conceal your soul and aura doesn't mean I can't see your dishonesty," I challenged.

"The girl is not from your soul pool. Whatever you believe you're experiencing has nothing to do with soul mates but has everything to do with compassion. You feel for the girl. You understand her. She recognizes the pain within you, and vice versa. *That* is how you connect. End of discussion." Michael paused, moving closer to where I stood, and placed his right hand on my left shoulder. "Would I lie to you?"

"No. Never."

"Gabriel, you cannot touch her again. She's not

yours. If you're lonely allow Hadreniel to find you a new partner."

"I'm not lonely and I don't need, nor want, a new mate in my life. I already have a wife whom I love very much, and I always will. Nothing and no one will ever erase or change that. I have to go," I said, leaving him standing in Nina's room, knowing what I'd just said wasn't true. The part about loving Lilith had been, but the part about no one ever changing that wasn't.

I hated when anyone brought up Lilith. She was a third rail issue, but Michael was right. I couldn't touch Nina again. Moments ago, we kissed which could've led to other, more serious actions because neither of us could control ourselves. If Orifiel hadn't barged in...

By the time I'd reached the bottom of the stairs, I'd vowed to fight any hold and to never lay another finger on Nina unless absolutely necessary for safety measures only.

"You look amazing, baby," Chase said.

"Mission accomplished." Nina giggled. "Let's get going so we can finish what we started earlier."

But not ten minutes ago this girl was all over me and now she was flirting with *him*. My heart dropped. A strange sensation consumed every ounce of my being—disappointment and jealousy.

Hell no you don't.

The thought of experiencing manmade Mortal emotions over Nina and Chase hardened me, turning my insides to stone and allowing for hatred to settle in.

Now that's more like it.

"I'll be close behind, but unlike Jules, I can keep up," I warned Chase, who in response approached me aggressively.

Bring it, bitch.

Nina grabbed his arm, mumbling something about me not being worth it.

No, sweetheart. You've got it all wrong. He's the one who's not worth it.

He ranted for a moment spewing a string of muted obscenities based solely at me. Honestly? I could've cared less. As a Mortal I'd dealt with hundreds of assholes just like him, some far worse. Besides, deep down he viewed me as a threat because he was well aware of the fact that a bond existed between Nina and me.

Make one false move, Chase, and I'll send your sorry ass straight to Hell where it belongs.

Chapter 19

Nina

"How are we going to do this?" I asked once we were on the road. I silently prayed that Chase's mood would quickly return to normal.

His deep disdain for Gabriel often created foul temperaments. The slightest look or comment would set him off. He'd try to mask it, but never successfully. To me he was as transparent as tissue paper. Initially, fear that Chase might've seen Gabriel and me carrying on before caused me to suffer deep worry, but after thinking about it, that was impossible. He was downstairs with Jules. Plus, the door to my room was closed. I would've heard it open. However, what happened could *never* happen again. I felt embarrassed and ashamed over my actions. I'd betrayed Chase. The moment shared with Orifiel last year was different because it was innocent. There wasn't any shared physical chemistry, only friendship, but with Gabriel, a different story presented. A raw, unexplainable attraction existed.

Enough, Nina. It was an epic mistake. One that will not be repeated. It isn't your fault, so there's no reason to feel bad. If anything is to be blamed it's that damn connection you and Gabriel share which is what makes you act weird around him. The bond isn't controlled by free will, but rather forced upon both of you by something else. Forget about it. Move forward. There's no sense starting a fight with Chase tonight. If you keep your distance from Gabriel and avoid all eye contact, everything will be fine.

"We make a quick appearance, then an even quicker disappearance." Chase grinned.

He'd relaxed considerably which put my troubled mind at ease. Surely if he'd witnessed anything it would've been brought up by now. His attitude would still be fierce with no desire to be intimate.

"Where're we going to disappear to? How are we going to make an unseen getaway? You realize we're going to be surrounded by a ton of watchdog Angels, right?"

He laughed lightly. "I reserved a hotel room which is about three minutes away from where the party is. Let me worry about our escape."

His take charge attitude was comforting and rather attractive. We made our way into the crowded house making sure to show our faces. After a few minutes I grew anxious. All I wanted to do was leave. I was more than ready to get lost in the fun and romance of our own private evening together.

"When can we go?"

"Soon, baby. I promise," he assured. Staring deeply into his eyes, I was reminded of an hour earlier with Gabriel. That spark, that hold, it didn't exist with Chase. This bothered me enormously. How does one force something powerful when it's not there? Or was it? Maybe we hadn't gotten to that point yet? After all, we were soul mates. Nothing was stronger than that. But, if the captivation existed with Gabriel instantly and hadn't evolved with Chase, was Gabriel something more?

"What's wrong, baby?"

"Nothing." I smiled trying to rid myself of disappointment and Gabriel.

"Are you sure?"

"Yeah. I'm just a little nervous," I lied.

"We don't have to go. If you're not ready that's totally fine. We can wait until you are. No pressure."

"I know. I want to."

"Can I ask you something?"

"Of course. Always."

"Are you ready for us as a couple to be independent. Are you ready to be away from everyone else?"

"Aren't we already?" I replied cautiously. With no idea where this line of questioning would go, my answers had to be as vague as possible until solid ground materialized.

"What I mean is, are you ready for us to experience other aspects of life together, *alone*?"

"Like?"

"Moving out of your parents' house, finding a place to live, and a stronger commitment."

"Stronger than soul mates?" A slight sarcastic snort escaped my mouth.

"Marriage, Nina. Are you ready for Mortal marriage?"

Chase's emerald irises which were once fixed on me, now gazed off at something occurring behind us. Chase moved to the right, sliding my body behind his.

"What's going on?" I asked. Uncertainty wildly tugged at my every emotion. It's amazing how one's elation can go from positive to negative extremes in a matter of a few insignificant seconds.

Without answering, Chase walked to where a crying

Jules stood. Mark was exchanging words with Gabriel. Instantly, the dynamic of the room shifted. Trouble was about to ensue, and it had Chase and Gabriel's names written all over it.

Chapter 20

Chase

"Hey, Mark. What's going on, man?" I asked.

I felt like a pressure cooker. Everything negative stored inside of me had knotted tighter and was ready to explode at any minute. I longed for a release and somehow knew one had been found.

"Little Miss Chaste Perfection over here is a frigging liar," Mark shouted. His body trembled uncontrollably. Usually he was a calm, mellow guy, but right now his tone and actions were off. Way off.

"How so?" I questioned, unsure of exactly what he meant. After all, I'd just entered the conversation and had no idea what had transpired.

"Stop touching her," he ordered, grabbing at Jules's arm, trying to pull her away from Gabriel.

"Mark, seriously. It's not worth it," I rationalized.

"Yeah, it is, Chase." His hands clenched and his face turned beet red.

I began infusing the room with a restorative calm vibe but stopped midway through. Gabriel wasn't my problem. If I couldn't knock the jerk out, Mark certainly could. He didn't have to answer to Nina, whereas I did. The same outcome would occur; I just wouldn't have any blood on my hands.

"It's not what you think," I answered.

The only reason I continued engaging was for Jules's sake, whose tear-soaked face became too painful to view. She was a good girl who didn't deserve to feel bad, especially during such a confusing time. Been there. Still there. Jules, of all people, didn't need to experience heartbreaking grief from anyone.

"Why has he been all over her all night?" Mark had rapidly slipped from sane to crazy.

"You have to trust me. There is *no* chance Jules is attracted to *or* doing anything of a physical nature with this guy." I pointed my left thumb at Gabriel.

Mark mulled the words over before his eyes widened. He'd lost it.

"Take your hands off of her, now," he screamed. His body compressed so tightly he ran the risk of snapping his jaw in two.

"No," Gabriel replied calmly, pushing Jules's body behind his, then approaching Mark. The two men's stares locked in hatred and rage. "Walk away while you still can."

"You don't scare me."

"I'm not trying to, but here's how this is going to play out. You're going to attempt to hit me. I'll dodge. You'll miss. Even if by some stroke of luck, you do make contact with any part of me, your hand will instantly break. Then, I'll be forced to fight back which will result in you ending up in the hospital."

A wicked smile spread across Mark's lips. "I should've known the perfect, flawless Jules Warner was nothing but a lying…"

"Don't," Gabriel warned. His tone was sharp and hard. "If you know what's good for you, you won't finish that sentence."

"Bitch," Mark hissed in spite.

"I warned you. You shouldn't have said that." Gabriel's eyelids narrowed, zeroing in on Mark.

After a few seconds of circling, Gabriel made the first move. He lunged at Mark, shoving him to the ground. For the first time in a long time, my mind operated in a crystal clear fashion. There were no voices, no intense bouts of rage, and no blackout moment. Just a release. I grabbed Gabriel from behind, flipped him, then tightly wrapped my fingers around his throat. It felt good. Damn good. I was finally at peace with the Universe.

Chapter 21

Nina

Terror shook my core once I realized Chase's hands were firmly gripping Gabriel's neck. His hold was so tight his wrists shook, and his knuckles turned white. Gabriel's face didn't show an ounce of fear or distress. Skillfully, he head butted Chase, making full contact with Chase's nose. Bright red blood splattered down Chase's face as his cheekbones instantly swelled. I didn't have to be a healer or someone in the medical field to know his nose was definitely broken. Gabriel had successfully been able to stun Chase long enough to free himself completely, but Chase was quick. With one swift motion, he shoved Gabriel into the wall using the force of ten men. I could've sworn the entire room shook upon impact. Pure evil radiated off of Chase's expression as he stared at Gabriel who appeared to be laughing like a lunatic. Though Chase fought with skill, so did Gabriel. The difference was, Gabriel executed moves like a man with nothing to lose and nothing to live for. That notion in itself was far more petrifying than having to face Vincent again.

"Chase," I yelled.

It felt as if my body and mind were going to explode with anger and hatred. Chase had to release the emotional hold over the room.

His shoulders hunched, rising and falling with each heavy breath. Slowly, he turned his blood-stained face to glare at me. I was scared—legitimately scared of the man I loved. He resembled a Demon with cold, empty, soulless eyes. A chill ran up my spine as the comparison of Chase to a Demon finished forming.

"Please, stop," I barely whispered, cowering, and backing away.

Chase's demeanor softened slightly. My sense of sight and sound had almost returned to a normal state. Aggressively, he grabbed my wrist, pulling me out of the house, and pushing me into the car. The moment we were both safely inside, he turned to face me. Without saying a word, he leaned over and buried his head in my neck. I wasn't sure if the warm wet sensation trickling down my chest was blood from his broken nose or tears. He reminded me of a hurt, lost, scared child. I ran my fingers through his fairly long hair, kissing the top of his head.

"Are you okay?" I asked.

"Yeah," he replied, not moving.

"Are you sure?"

"Yes," he repeated, backing away, and putting the car into drive.

Neither one of us said anything. We sat in silence which frightened me to the core. Chase seemed completely fine, happy in fact, until the Mark/Gabriel argument occurred.

Gabriel!

That son of a bitch ruined my perfect night. Gabriel pushed Chase to his breaking point. He was sent to Earth to help me, not flip my already shaky world upside down. I wanted him gone. I wanted him gone tonight.

"Let me heal you," I said the moment we got home.

Chase couldn't walk into the house looking like this. My parents would flip out and I didn't have the time, want, or desire to deal with their, especially my mother's, brand of insanity. No sooner did the words exit my lips, Gabriel's car pulled up. Throwing the vehicle into park, he jumped out.

"This isn't over, Demon," he threatened, moving rapidly toward us.

"Enough," I demanded.

"This isn't your problem, Nina. This is between your *husband* and me. Now move," he ordered, shoving me out of the way.

"If you *ever* touch her again it will be the last thing you'll ever do," Chase hollered back.

Seconds later the two men were rolling around on the hard, pebble driveway cursing at each other. I wasn't sure if it was adrenaline kicking in or Chase controlling the space, but nothing aside from raw hatred raged in the crisp night's air. Jules froze in place resembling a statue you'd gawk at in a museum. Without a thought I took off running into the house.

"Dad. Dad," I screamed, the moment the front door opened.

"What's wrong, Nina?" I actually heard panic in his voice.

"Chase and Gabriel. They're going to kill each other. You have to stop them. Please."

Swiftly, he raced out the door. "Stop it," he shouted, pulling Gabriel to his feet, making sure to wedge his body between the two men.

Gabriel appeared untouched. He had not suffered a scrape or scratch, which wasn't surprising. True Angels didn't bleed or bruise; only Mortal Angels did. Chase, on the other hand, was a bloody mess. His face looked like he'd been beaten to a swollen pulp. I cringed while assessing the damage, but even through the mutilation, his eyes appeared different. Instead of being vibrant green, they resembled two black marbles. Disdain toward Gabriel overtook every ounce of my being.

"This is ridiculous. Two grown men fighting over what? This nonsense ends right now. Do you understand? For crying out loud you're fighting for the same side. You should be friends," my father yelled.

He hauled Chase under a decorative lamppost. "Several lacerations and contusions, a broken nose, rib, and hand. Who knows what else. Come inside. Let me fix this. We *need* to have a serious talk. Gabriel, go home. We'll talk tomorrow," he stated. My father placed his hand on Chase's shoulder and guided him into the house.

"Jules? Are you okay?" I asked.

"Uh, yeah sure. I better go now," she said. Her voice was choppy and weak.

"Jules." Gabriel chased after her.

The two exchanged a few words before she took off. The fact he made her smile, held her close, and pressed his forehead to hers annoyed the crap out of me. That, on top of the moment we shared before this nightmare began coupled with the fist fight, an internal boiling point was reached, and I was ready to blow.

"You. You ruined what should've been the most memorable night of my life. I hate you and wish you'd go away. You're destroying everything. I don't care if you don't like Chase. Honestly, he's not your concern. Your job is to watch me. Watch *me*, not Chase, or my friends, or family. What's your problem?" I spat.

"Most memorable moment of your life? How pathetic. How stupid do you think I am? I knew what you were up to. There's no way I'm going to let you sneak away and be alone with a Demon. You have no idea how dangerous having sex with him would be. What's worse is that you're standing here defending him when he's the one who was wrong. What happened between Mark and me was our business, *not* his. He had to stick his nose into something that didn't concern him and side with Mark. You remember Mark, right? The one that was treating your supposed best friend like crap? Chase has been itching for a reason to start in with me. Tonight, he finally found a way. But perhaps the most curious part of everything is, if you hate me that much why were you coming on to me before? Why did we practically screw on your dresser?" Gabriel sounded infuriated.

"I was *not* coming on to you. Don't make me vomit. You were taking advantage of whatever the hell weird connection we have, which ends now. I would never, *ever* kiss you on my own free will. You're a disgusting, vile, arrogant, piece of shit," I shrieked out of frustration. My body heaved with anger. "What I do with my life is my business, so butt the hell out. You know something? Back off before this ends badly," I said, shaking my head, hoping he'd go and never return.

"I can't back off, Nina. For the moment you are my life whether *I* like it or not. As for taking advantage of you, I'd never do that regardless of what you may think of me. However, rest assured I'll never fall victim to touching you again. The disgusted sentiment is mutual. Michael sent me here to watch you and trust me, you need all of the help that's available. You think Chase is this great guy, but Nina, he's not."

His voice softened as his eyes filled with sorrow. I refused to look directly into them out of fear over how I'd react.

"Nina, please listen. Souls are small, round balls which hover inside of everyone's core. I can see them. When someone commits a sin, depending upon how awful it is, a piece slips away. It cannot regenerate. When one's soul is completely gone, all that's left is evil in its truest form. Chase's soul is ripping, and I don't mean minor tears. Huge chucks are falling off. Tonight, when he went after me, his soul practically split in half. You've never seen pure evil. I have. Horrible things happen to Mortals and Immortals when they lose their soul. What concerns me the most is his aura. It's black, Nina. *Black* like a *Demon's*. It hasn't changed much since this assignment began. We all have devious moments when our auras turn dark, but usually the person's aura goes back to a lighter color within a short period of time. For example, when we started this conversation, your aura was muddy blue, which means fear and anger for the truth, but now it's back to emerald which shows that you're a healer. You have to believe me. It's hard to fully understand the serious nature of this. I know how powerful love can be. How the heart cannot erase deep love like the love you have for Chase."

"Stop. Enough. I can't stand this life and this damn path that I've been forced to travel down. Being a Mortal Angel has done nothing but cause problems. However, the absolute worst part of this mess is you. I didn't think I was capable of ever hating anyone the way I hate you, but yet here we are," I shouted, storming off into the house.

"Nina," Gabriel called, but I ignored his plea.

Life had been going pretty damn well until *he* showed up. Now everything was turned upside down, inside out, and it wasn't fair. When could Chase and I ride off into the sunset? When could we have our happily ever after? It didn't matter what Gabriel had to say. What did he know? My future with Chase became vibrantly clear right then and there. If we were ever going to have our fairytale ending, we'd have to take matters into our own hands. I'd begin planning our escape. Yes. Running away from this insanity was our only chance at true happiness.

Chapter 22

Chase

"What's going on?" Jack asked, running his therapeutic hands over the various injuries I sustained.

The fact that Jack could instantly heal anyone and make their pain vanish was still an amazing wonder to me. A gift I truly appreciated at the moment. I'd never show it, but the discomfort stabbed and gnawed at my core to the point of unbearable levels.

"It was a stupid move and I'm sorry for disrespecting Nina, Mrs. Luther, you, and your home. You've all been so understanding, supportive, and kind. What I did does not reflect my immense gratitude," I answered once he'd fixed me up.

"So why do it?"

"If you're asking me if I'm hearing Vincent's voice inside of my head again, I'm not. I acted on free will."

"Something had to have triggered such a bold response."

I didn't say anything, but I could feel my face knot with anger.

"Chase, soul mates are forever. I assure you, Nina loves you. *Only* you. Gabriel *cannot*, and will *not*, ever break that."

"They share some sort of weird bond," I said out of frustration.

"Explain."

"I can't, but something is definitely going on," I answered. I was annoyed because I couldn't prove my instinct and raw intuition.

Jack laughed. "Jealousy is a normal part of life. Don't waste your time or energy on it. Take it from a man who's been with his wife for many, many years, and has walked in your shoes. It's not worth the aggravation. Nina only has eyes for you and you for her. There's nothing stronger than true mates."

Perhaps Jack's words held truth. Maybe I'd been acting like an insecure jerk and reading into nothing. I flashed him a half smile and nodded.

"Tomorrow you and Gabriel will hash this out with words and find some common ground. You cannot act this way again with him. Practice restraint. Be the bigger man." He paused. "I'm on your side. I always will be, but since Nina needs protection right now, we all have to deal with the inconveniences which come along with that."

The fact that he sided with me, understood my position, and referred to Gabriel as an inconvenience, eased all of my worries.

"I really am sorry," I said, meaning it.

"It's okay, son. Things like this happen. You're young. You've got a lot of growing to do. When you get to my age you'll view situations differently. However, I do need you to keep your temper in check. He's an Arc and an assassin, Chase, which means he's highly trained and exceptionally powerful. Add that to the fact that he's somewhat unhinged...well, next time you might not be as lucky when you two throw down. Be cool around him. Okay?"

I nodded in agreement before I left his office and headed to Nina's room. Through the bathroom door running water could be heard suggesting she was taking a bath. Tomorrow, after I'd made peace with Gabriel for Jack's sake, I'd sincerely apologize to Nina. She deserved that. I flopped on my bed with an epic yawn. Within seconds my eyes shut giving way to the image of me choking Gabriel and how damn good it felt.

Chapter 23

Gabriel

Anger and remorse were suffocating me as I paced the premises of the Luther house. At two in the morning, Michael arrived. I went home, but I didn't sleep even though physical exhaustion weighed heavily on my body, mind, and soul. How could it not? I'd been surviving off of three hours rest for the past several months. I sat at the dining room table stewing, wide awake.

Why do I care about this girl? She's not mine. Yes, Chase is a total douche bag, but that's not my problem. Nina and he are soul mates, and I cannot interfere with that. It's Lilith. That's the problem. I miss and still love her tremendously. Seeing another couple happy the way we used to be is hard.

Michael is right. There's no deep connection. I feel for Nina. An emotion I'm not comfortable with. I'm envious over what she has. If Chase were a better man, I wouldn't care at all. I'd ignore their love. Because he's not, I'm viewing my own pain in real time and want to save her from eternal heartbreak. It's easy to understand why I'd fabricated some sort of pull. I don't want her to end up miserable, like me. As for craving her physically, she's your type. Nina is curvaceous and full in all of the right places. Plus, it's been a while since you've sexually socialized with a woman. Let this go. View the situation for what it is. A job. Nina is not Lilith, and the inevitable hurt Chase will inflict on her isn't your concern.

If I could only see Lilith, I could remind her of what we shared. I'll give her children. I'll give her hundreds of them if it's still what she wants. I don't care anymore. Once we're back together Michael will see how happy I am, and he will find a way to let her return to The Heavens.

I got up from the table and walked into the bedroom. Grabbing the only picture I had of Lilith and me as Mortals, I sat at the foot of the bed staring at the beautiful woman I once called my wife, longing for her. Even though she left, even though her love for me had faded, mine never did.

Yes. I'll start searching for her. If need be, I'll beg her to love me again. Whatever it takes.

At exactly six I returned to my post.

"Father," I said.

"You look awful, Gabriel. Is everything okay? Should I call for Raphael?" He inquired with deep concern.

"I actually feel pretty damn good." I smiled at the thought of Lilith.

"Leave her alone," Michael warned.

"Leave who alone?"

"Lilith. She's gone and you cannot get her back."

"Says who?" I snapped.

"Says me, Gabriel. I forbid you to go looking for her. Case closed."

"I think it's time my wife and I talked."

"If you can somehow persuade Lilith to have a conversation with you, *and* you can convince her to switch sides again, there's honestly nothing, and I repeat the word *nothing*, I can do to sway The Powers That Be into allowing her back into The Heavens. You'd have to join her in Hell. Do you really want that for yourself? Do you really want to see your mother, brother, and I suffer while mourning your loss? We'd be enemies, son."

"No," I replied weakly. He was right.

"If you're yearning for a mate, allow Micah and Hadreniel to assist you. They'll help you to find an Angel worthy of your devotion and Micah will rewrite your destiny. The Angel Trinity speaks of you often. Perhaps she might be a suitable partner?"

"Whatever." I sighed.

"Gabriel, take a break. I've been working you too hard for far too many hours a day. I'm sorry. I should've been more considerate of your time. Rest. Recharge. I'll call for Orifiel to work shifts for a few weeks. Go back to the house or to The Heavens. If Orifiel needs anything, he'll reach out. We still have no idea where Vincent is so it's important someone still watches over Nina."

"Orifiel can't watch her as well as I can."

"Please, listen and do as I say. Nina will be safe. You need some rest."

"Fine, but I have to speak with Jack before taking off."

"Call to Orifiel when you're ready to leave. I'll inform Hadreniel about Trinity and have her set something up," he said, and left.

A break might not be a bad idea. I could clear my head a little and get some sleep. Maybe Michael's onto something. Perhaps it's time to find a new mate and not just another warm body to rub up against.

The thought caused a shrug. Once I was inside of the

Luther's house, Jack escorted me to his office. Chase was already there. Jack insisted, after a rather long lecture, that we make up and call a truce. Neither one of us wanted to, but for the sake of peace, we did. Ellen wouldn't take no for an answer when it came to staying for breakfast, so I appeased her by having a cup of coffee.

The bittersweet smell of freedom assaulted my nostrils the moment I stepped out of their home. I called to The Heavens for Orifiel and waited for him to arrive.

"Gabriel," he said, once present.

"I assume Michael's filled you in?" I asked.

"Aye."

"Orifiel, watch her like a hawk. Make sure she's safe. The Demon is trying to get into her pants. That cannot happen. Do whatever necessary to stop it. If you need anything or something seems wrong, call me. I haven't decided if I'll be returning to The Heavens or staying here on Earth, but please, find me."

"Gabriel, Nina will be fine," he assured, touching my arm.

"Yeah."

An uneasiness found its way into the pit of my stomach. Moving closer, Orifiel used his gift to dimly illuminate the space surrounding us as he studied my expression. "You're scared."

"Nothing alive or dead scares me."

"Rubbish. It's written all over your face."

"Exhaustion is what's written all over my face. I'll be in touch."

"Don't let fear paralyze you. Sometimes time needs time, brother," Orifiel added before he scaled an oak tree, taking watch, and leaving me alone.

Searing pain seeped into my chest. After a moment,

I realized the internal upheaval wasn't physical, but rather an emotional wound. For some unknown, bizarre reason my heart was breaking again.

Chapter 24

Nina

After the Halloween incident, Gabriel kept such a sizable distance I never saw him around. Honestly, I missed his presence. Badly, actually. A feeling of loss settled into my heart and refused to budge. Whenever I was out, I'd find myself searching for him, but I could never find him. Chase was pleased and more relaxed by Gabriel's absence. The tension he'd been walking around with since Gabriel's arrival had vanished overnight.

November brought chillier weather to Savannah. The days were sunny and crisp, but they could've been dark and rainy for all I cared. The leaves that were left lingering on the trees had finally died, falling to the ground, and littering the pristine streets. Lately, sitting on the window seat in my room, reminiscing about the days when Chase climbed the oak tree outside of my window and spent the night became a habit. It was foolish back then to think better days were ahead. On the outside I feigned happiness, but on the inside, I felt as if I were slowly dying. Gabriel's words on Halloween night had a profound effect on me causing insane worry for Chase. Several days were spent looking into what happened when a person lost their soul. Gabriel was right. It was horrific.

Once Demonic desires overtook a Mortal soul, the person became the apex of pure evil. They were incapable of loving, feeling, or caring. All they could do was hate and destroy, and memories, logic, and perceptions ceased to exist. Physical appearances changed as well. Basically, they became a Demon on Earth. What really drove me over the edge was the part about Lost Souls and Mortal Angels losing their grace. Between the rage coupled with their supernatural abilities, they transformed into more than Demons. They became uncontrollable monsters. I slammed the book shut and hadn't been back to the library since. My mind couldn't cope with any more information.

"Want some company?"

My body instinctively moved back as my brain was forcefully thrown into survival mode. My parents had left for an overnight trip with friends and Chase was helping his mother pull off a destination wedding in Florida. I was alone in the house and presently terrified. Initially, I thought I'd be okay all by myself, I had been in the past, but now I wasn't so sure.

"It's just me. Orifiel."

"Are you trying to make me have a stroke?" I snapped.

"Oh relax, Nina." He laughed. "You said you wanted to talk, but then never called. That was about a month ago." He frowned.

The adrenaline rush continued to course through my veins causing me to throw myself into his arms. My frame shook. My heart pounded. Orifiel held me tightly for a few moments before pulling away and leading us to the bed.

"I didn't mean to cause you such a fright. I thought

you might be lonely seeing how everyone is away for the evening. Ezekiel and Muriel are on watch duty, so I have the night off. I figured we'd catch up, unless you're otherwise engaged."

"Ezekiel? Muriel? Wait. What? You're watching me now? Where's Gabriel?" I demanded.

"We may not be as recklessly aggressive as Gabriel, but we're certainly capable of having your back." He sounded tragically insulted.

"That's not what I meant, Orifiel." I reached out and took his hands in mine. "I know you'd do anything for me."

"Don't you *ever* forget that."

I lay down, pulling his body next to mine. We talked about nothing for hours which felt amazing. Though we hadn't known each other very long, I felt we'd been close friends since the dawn of time. I could speak freely about anything and he listened, interjecting at the right moments, while understanding my fears without judgement. The level of comfort he provided was profoundly soothing. I found it curious every time I mentioned Gabriel's name, he'd either brush the question or comment off or change the subject. Not wanting him to become annoyed and leave, I stopped bringing it up.

"Orifiel?"

"Aye, love," he said. My head was resting on his chest as he absentmindedly twirled strands of my hair between his long fingers.

"If I ask you something, will you promise to give me an honest answer?"

"It depends on what's asked. There are certain things I can't discuss no matter how much I might wish to," he replied cautiously, but he didn't stop playing with my locks.

"Gabriel said something on Halloween night that's been on my mind, a lot."

"Like what?"

"He said Chase's aura is black, like a Demon's, and his soul was close to ripping. Chase seems to be doing okay; he says everything is calm inside of his mind, but what if it's all a lie? I don't want to lose him." More could've been said, but the growing lump inside of my throat didn't allow for another word to slip past.

"Chase is fine."

"Then why would Gabriel say such a thing?"

"Gabriel was mad. Sometimes we say things we shouldn't when we're upset. Heat of the moment and all that. Let it go."

"Is it true?"

"I can't read auras or souls, that's my brother's gift, but I know Gabriel and how he can behave when he's bloody pissed off. He gets nasty and conveys things the wrong way. Listen, if Michael thought Chase were a threat, he would've alerted us and told you. He hasn't, therefore, by logic, Chase is fine. Michael knows all, Nina. I swear he hasn't said one word about Chase, and no one is tailing him."

Orifiel's words consoled me enough to alleviate most of my anxiety. If bad things were on the horizon, Michael definitely would've said or done something, and he never would've allowed Gabriel, his alleged best soldier, to abandon his post, leaving Orifiel in charge.

"Thanks for that. I needed to hear it."

Orifiel turned on his side to face me. His golden eyes wandered around my room before he sighed heavily.

"Listen, love. Many, many years ago something horrifically awful and heartbreaking happened to Gabriel in The Heavens. It was before my time, but it was by no means his fault. Vincent is solely responsible for the occurrence. Since then, he's been a shell of a man. Only time will heal him, but until that day occurs, could you cut him some slack? If not for him, then for me? Please?"

"I'm aware, because you told me about this last year. Vincent screwed him over and that angered him, but exactly what happened?" My curiosity had been piqued.

"When he's ready to share the details with you he will. Some moments in our existence cause wounds so deep it never seems like the injury will close up and heal, but it will. We must be patient and have faith—two things Gabriel sorely lacks. Storytime is over for today. It's nearly three in the morning, Nina. Get some rest."

"Please, stay? I can't sleep," I requested.

"I shouldn't, but I will," he said, maneuvering my body so my head was back resting on his chest again. He gently kissed my forehead. "Close your eyes, love." After a brief pause, he continued. "Shall I compare thee to a summer's day? Thou art more lovely and more temperate. Rough winds do shake the darling buds of May; and summer's lease hath all too short a date."

"You know Shakespeare?" I asked, involuntarily sitting, completely shocked by this fact.

"Aye. Shhh," he informed, pressing an index finger to his lips, and guiding my frame back beside his.

"Sometime too hot the eye of Heaven shines, and often is his gold complexion dimmed; and every fair from fair sometime declines," he recited. The combination of his touch and smooth, deep, English accent forced my eyelids closed. My soul melted into his causing me to drift peacefully away.

"You're one lucky bastard, Gabriel." I heard him whisper moments before exhaustion took over and I couldn't speak another word.

Chapter 25

Chase

"Nina?" I asked, knocking on her opened bedroom door. I'd just arrived home from being in Florida with my mother helping her with some over-the-top, ridiculous wedding. With no real desire to assist her, her guilt pulled me in. Nina seemed all right with it, which was a relief. Perhaps, much like myself, she too craved some time alone.

"Hey." She forced a smile.

"Are you okay?"

"Yeah. What's up? How was the wedding?"

"Long and boring. I'm thrilled it's over." I paused. "Your parents are still gone and won't be back for a little while. We have the house all to ourselves..."

"Let's leave Savannah."

"And go where?"

"I don't care."

"Might I ask, why?"

"I'm scared, Chase. I'm scared of everything lately and I hate feeling like this. We need to go somewhere else. Make a fresh start. Live a life where we're Mortals, *not* Mortal Angels. Where Heaven and Hell doesn't exist."

"Did something happen while I was away that I don't know about?"

"I saw you on Halloween night, Chase. The look in your eyes. You enjoyed what you did and wanted to do it. What went down had nothing to do with your dislike for Gabriel. The explosion you experienced felt good. That's terrifying and what makes it worse is Gabriel said your aura is black—black like a Demon's, and your soul is ripping. That can't happen. If we get out of here it won't." Nina's voice quivered with tears.

"Baby, everything is fine. I swear."

"Orifiel suggested the same thing, but I can't stop obsessing over what Gabriel said."

"He's an idiot. Don't listen to him. If something were the matter, *which it's not*, I'd say something and get help."

Truth be told I did, in fact, feel okay. The rage released on Halloween night was the most human sentiment I'd experienced since all of this began. My primitive, primal instinct to beat the shit out of Gabriel kicked in, just like it would've for any other guy.

"What if you didn't? What if the episode came on so fast you couldn't abstain from harming yourself or others?"

"I'd know, baby. I'm aware of my triggers and what an episode feels like now. You do realize I possess the ability of rational thought, where even at my worst moment I'm still able to console myself, *and* know what's happening, *and* when it's greater than me. I've learned to fight my impulses. What happened last year will never happen again. I'm going to be fine. *We're* going to be fine. I promise."

She produced a weak, phony smile to appease me, but she didn't speak a word because of the dam of tears dangerously close to breaching the surface of her tragically sad eyes. Genuine fear resided inside of her heart.

"Come on," I said, grabbing her hand, and leading the way to my car.

"Where're we going?"

"You'll see."

Five minutes and countless requests for Nina to be patient later, I parked a few blocks away from Gino's. I guided us to a bench and asked her to sit.

"Does this place mean anything to you?" I asked.

"Should it?" she replied confused.

"Do you remember our first date?"

"Of course I do, but what does that have to do with anything?"

"Think about that specific evening for a second."

Her hazel eyes narrowed, darkening with deep thought. "Oh my God," she whispered, grinning brightly.

"When we were sitting on *this* bench *that* night, I fell in love with you. I knew I couldn't live without you because I *didn't want* to live without you. Every time I look at you, I fall madly in love with you all over again. I want to spend forever with you," I said, getting down on bended knee, and taking a ring box out of my jacket pocket. "Marry me, Nina."

Chapter 26

Nina

I sat in shock for a few moments, staring at the amazingly beautiful ring Chase held in the palm of his right hand. Diamonds encrusted a platinum band while an obscenely large, square cut rock rested on top.

Are you ready for this, Nina?

Before any over-analyzing occurred, my brain stopped thinking, and I allowed my heart to do the talking.

"Yes," I answered, throwing myself into his strong, comforting arms.

"This is the way I see it, baby. Plan the wedding of your dreams. While you're doing that, we'll find a place of our own here in town. However, if you still feel moving away from Savannah is what's necessary, we will go after we get married."

"Do my parents know?"

"Yes. I asked your father a while ago, but I didn't tell him when, where, or how I was going to pop the question. He's happy and gave me his blessing, but he insisted we wait to tie the knot until after we've graduated. We're destined to be together and technically speaking we are already married. Now, you have a diamond. It's a little more official in our Mortal world. I wanted you to see and know how committed I am.

Hopefully this will ease some of your worries."

How could a man with a black aura and a torn, almost gone soul act and speak this way? He wouldn't because he couldn't. Gabriel was wrong. Gabriel wanted to start something by stirring up trouble. I'd been stressing out for nothing and felt quite foolish for doing so. By the time we got back to the house, my attitude had done a complete one-hundred-eighty-degree turn. We decided to watch some random movie that was on the television, but we never made it past the opening credits. Much like the night in the car when we were waiting for Jules and Gabriel to show up at the driving range, Chase acted as the aggressor. He pushed my body down on the soft, cool couch. Instantly, I felt he was having a difficult time controlling his abilities. My sense of touch and smell were on fire, but it didn't matter. Wanton lust and desire took over for both of us. I pulled him closer, intertwining our legs, and running my hands through his beautiful, dark locks. I was tugging on the buttons of his shirt when he stopped me.

"Let's go upstairs, baby," he whispered, getting off of me, leaning down, pulling me from the couch, and finally up the stairs.

Slowly, once we were on the bed, my fingers returned to removing his shirt. The ink blue, thin, cotton material pooled on the floor exposing his Adonis-like body. His abs were insanely toned and beyond well defined. His arms were huge and powerful. We kissed as we removed each other's clothing until we were lying under the covers in only our underwear. With care he looked deep into my eyes.

"Are you ready?" he asked, stroking the side of my face.

"Yeah. I think so," I answered nervously.

"Don't be scared, baby."

"You've done this before."

"I've never done this with anyone I truly cared for and loved."

He always knew the right thing to say.

Drawing closer, positioning my body underneath his, I exhaled deeply in anticipation. This already amazing day was about to get even better.

Damn it!

The sound of the garage door going up resembled an unexpected ice-cold shower. Immediately, Chase jumped up, throwing the heap of clothing from the floor onto the bed.

"Shit. I thought we had more time. I'm so sorry, baby."

I panic dressed, hauling ass downstairs while Chase hung back, taking a few minutes to compose himself. I met my parents in the kitchen right as they closed the mudroom door.

"Hey, guys," I practically shouted.

Calm the hell down, Nina! They have no idea what you were doing. By acting all jumpy you're going to sell yourself and Chase out.

"Is everything okay?" My mother's tone was full of suspicion.

Quick! Think of something to say.

"Chase proposed." The sounds shot out of my mouth faster than words were thought of.

"Congratulations, honey. Jack. Did you hear that? Chase asked." My mother threw her arms around me, squeezing my frame tightly, then she inspected the ring. "It's beautiful. Absolutely gorgeous."

"Congratulations, princess," my father said, walking back into the kitchen, and kissing the top of my head. "Where is Chase?"

"Oh, he's upstairs on the phone."

Excellent lie, Nina.

"You're going to wait before setting a date, right?" my mother inquired.

"Yes, we're going to wait. I'm not even sure if we'll *tie the knot* after we finish our undergraduate work, but we *will* be living together by then."

"You already live together, Nina."

"Yeah, Mom, but this is your house. Isn't part of a relationship relying on one another? Let's not even worry about this right now because it's years down the road. Okay? This engagement is probably going to be one of the longest ones in history."

The comment appeased her. Several minutes later, Chase made his way into the kitchen. After a few more congratulatory words, my father suggested we all go out to dinner to celebrate.

"I'd love to, but I want to tell my mother the good news. I'm going to head over there in a few minutes," Chase said.

"That's wonderful. I hope she's doing well and is happy about this. We'll celebrate tomorrow night." My mother smiled warmly.

After Chase left my father convinced me to join them for dinner. I didn't feel like hanging around the house alone or calling Jules, so I agreed.

"How are classes going?" my father asked, after the waitress at Gino's took our order.

"Pretty good. Biology lab isn't as difficult..." My thoughts instantly grew distracted.

Is that Gabriel on the other side of the restaurant?

Craning my neck to get a better view was useless. For the next few minutes, I tried to make a positive identification, but I couldn't.

He hasn't shown himself in weeks and now, all of a sudden, he pops up out of nowhere?

Shifting in my chair, I saw a woman with shoulder-length, dark hair and olive skin come into focus.

Is he on a date?

Curiosity got the better of me. Excusing myself to get a closer look, I walked over to where I thought he sat. It was definitely Gabriel *with* a woman. The two certainly appeared happy. Their heads were close revealing that an intimate connection existed between them. Her hand stroked his while he smiled. I'd never seen him grin before. Hell, I didn't think Gabriel knew how to. He looked amazing. The girl was a dog and one of the worst dressers I'd ever seen. She wore a pair of skinny jeans tucked into tall, black leather boots, with a big, bulky, off-the-shoulder, white sweater.

Unless you're a mounted police officer, wading through crap, or horseback riding you should not be wearing those God-awful boots. You and that style need to go away and never come back.

Were they on a date? Friends? Was she Mortal? An Angel? Was she his wife? I had to find out. He was supposed to be watching me, not having a social life. *I* was his social life. Not some busted, nasty chick.

Chapter 27

Chase

"Are you sure this is what *you* want, dear?"

"Yes, Mom. Nina is what I want," I answered, trying to hide my frustration.

"I've always liked Nina, but this whole living with her family setup, along with you acting strangely, and now this out of nowhere proposal, I can't help but think you're being pressured into something you may not be ready for. You're only twenty years old."

"Age has nothing to do with my decisions and no one is pressuring anyone. I love Nina. She's the one."

"What about Bristol? You said you loved her not that long ago."

"Mom, I love Nina, and *only* Nina. I proposed, and she said yes. I'm going to marry her. Period."

"There's something else going on. I wish you'd tell me. Maybe I could help."

"There's *nothing* else going on. My life in this house came to an end." I partially lied.

There most certainly was something else existing in my world, but I couldn't tell her about it. The part about having to move out was a nice summary of the truth.

"Fine. If this is what you want…"

"Yes, Mom," I said, standing, and kissing the top of her head. "Now, if you're up to it, I'd like to take you out for dinner and *not* talk about this anymore. I'm still, and always will be, your son. I'll always love you and make time for us to catch up."

"What are you going to do about your father?" Her gaze implored that she desired resolution to that situation.

I sighed heavily as I took her to my car. This was going to be a lengthy, tedious night. Perhaps being in a public place might slam a pin in her impending harassment. The only thing making my happiness a known reality was the fact that Nina was back at the house waiting for me. A rare smile spread across my lips as the decision to sneak into her room later, like old times, was made. As long as Nina remained present in my life, everything would always be okay.

Chapter 28

Gabriel

After leaving Nina's house I did nothing but sleep and stare at the four walls that made up my bedroom. The first couple of days were the hardest. I was constantly fighting the urge to run back to The Heavens and straight into Hadreniel's arms. Hadreniel always made sense of any confusion, and because of that, I'd feel better. But, for the moment I was more than sure they all knew something and were keeping it a secret. No one could be trusted. I hated that, but my gut was rarely wrong about situations like this. Hiding and trying to wrap my head around my re-broken heart was the lesser of the two evils. Jules called a few times and had swung by to check-up on me, which was rather endearing and sweet. However, pretending to be okay was a tough act to keep up, but I didn't have to for very long. She saw right through the falsehoods and never pressed me for answers or explanations. Her only request was that I stopped lying to her *and* to myself. Once I allowed myself to be truthful and experience misery in its rawest form, clarity came.

Late one Saturday afternoon, Michael stopped by to inform me that the Angel Trinity had arrived in Savannah earlier that morning to use her divine gift of prophecy to find Vincent. After much persuasion on his part, I begrudgingly made arrangements to take her out on a date later that evening.

Perhaps she and I would work as mates. I doubt it, but maybe. What did I have to lose?

I showered, then threw on a pair of loose-fitting jeans and a snug, black, V-neck t-shirt. By six, Trinity arrived, and we were off to dinner. Having no idea where to go, I spotted a restaurant called 'Gino's.' Several times I'd followed Nina there. How bad could it be?

We chatted about random nothingness, such as how ways on Earth have drastically changed since we were Mortals. Though Trinity came from a slightly younger era than me, for the most part we were from the same time period. While she spoke, I stared at her. She was a pretty Angel with shoulder length, black hair, light blue eyes, olive skin, long legs, an exotic face, and a great body. Based off of her body language she appeared to be physically attracted to me. She kept reaching across the table to hold my hand. I didn't stop her. It had been a while since the willing touch of a female was felt. After a bit, my guard dropped, and the night became enjoyable.

We talked and laughed over the meal. Well, at least my version of laughing these days, which consisted of producing a slight smile accompanied by the appropriate sounds. The minutes did, however, seem to pass quickly.

"Hey, you," a seductive voice said. Fingernails ran across my shoulders causing my body to stiffen.

I turned to find Nina standing behind me.

"Trinity, this is Nina," I answered, automatically watching for Chase.

"*Nina Luther?*" Trinity questioned, raising a severely arched eyebrow.

"Yeah. Why? What's it to you?" Nina snapped,

straightening her frame.

"Nothing. Nothing at all. It's just nice to be able to put a name with a face," Trinity replied casually.

"Is something the matter?" I inquired.

"No. Chase is with his mom and I'm here with my parents. I saw you from across the restaurant looking bored, so I thought I'd say hi."

"Hi," I said.

"Could we speak for a second?" she asked. When I didn't get up, she added, "In private."

"Would you please excuse me for a minute, Trinity?"

"Of course, but don't be too long," she purred, squeezing my forearm.

I followed Nina out of the front doors of Gino's.

"What's up?"

"Where have you been?" she spat.

"Why?" I was confused. She wanted me gone. She said she hated me. Why would she care where I've been?

"Aren't *you* supposed to be watching me?" Her face knotted with ire.

A slight laugh escaped my throat. "Where I am and what I'm doing is none of your concern. Someone is always watching you. If that's what you're worrying about, don't. You're safe and in very capable hands. Michael wouldn't leave you exposed."

"Gabriel," she said sternly. Her hands were firmly attached to her hourglass hips.

"What, Nina? What do you want?" I regretted choosing this place to eat.

"*You* as my watcher. Not some other Angel doing *your* job."

"Well, unfortunately we can't always get what we

want. I take orders from Michael, *not* you. Furthermore, I never was and *never* will be a Guardian. I'm one of the elite Seven Arcs. Babysitting *you* is *well* below my pay grade."

"Look at me," she hissed.

"Why?"

She didn't answer, but rather took hold of my face. Her touch caused an instant irrational spark. All of my inhibitions lowered as desire seeped in.

Nope. This isn't going to happen again. Fight it.

With every ounce of strength inside of my soul I fought the gaze, refusing to allow it to have any effect over me. The initial eye lock was pure torture, but moments later, the pull lessened until only a faint glimmer of need and want existed inside of me.

"It doesn't work anymore. Game over. Take some advice. Run home to your husband and this time, *you* leave *me* the hell alone," I warned, before heading back into the restaurant.

My heart raced. My hands shook. In all of my years spent as a Demonic assassin, I'd never felt an adrenaline surge like this, and I'd been in many dangerous situations.

"Is everything okay?" Trinity asked.

"Yeah. That one's a real pain in the ass. Of all the jobs for Michael to give me, I get guard duty for the world's most self-centered child. I'd sooner prefer an extended stay in Hell then have to endure another second of this shit."

"I read the Luther file the other day. No offense, but she sounds like a heaping bag of crazy and trouble. And the husband? Don't get me started on that mess."

"None taken. He's a real piece of work. I beat the

shit out of that dirtbag Demon a few weeks back. There are no words in the English language to describe how amazing it felt. We've all had enough of their drama. For crying out loud, we're preparing for a war because of them, but they don't care that they're putting not only us in harm's way, but thousands of Angels as well. They're selfish and disgusting people. I cannot wait to pull out of Savannah and to put this crap behind me. Orifiel's got it the worst. He's been on *spoiled brat* watch for a while now. How he tolerates this and doesn't lose his mind is an amazing gift all in itself. Come on, let's get out of here before she decides she *needs* something else," I said, paying the check, and taking her by the hand.

On our way to the door, I ran into Jack, Ellen, and Nina. Something was wrong with Nina. Her aura appeared unstable making it difficult to get a good read on her, but sadness, loss, and tremendous distress were clearly visible. Though tempted to apologize for my unnecessary rudeness, I stopped myself.

Not your circus. Not your monkeys.

After a brief exchange of pleasantries with Jack and Ellen, I made a speedy exit.

"Why would Nina Luther be jealous of me?" Trinity asked while we walked to my car.

"I have no idea what you're talking about."

"Come on, Gabriel. You read auras and souls. Tell me my assessment is wrong."

"I didn't see anything," I replied, opening the passenger side door for her.

"I don't need to possess the gift of prophecy to know something is up with the two of you."

"Trinity, nothing, and I repeat *nothing*, is up. She was a job and now she's not. Kill the conversation," I stated firmly.

After making sure Trinity's drop-off spot was safe, I returned to my house, grateful the day had come to a close.

That was fun, sans the Nina Luther part. I suppose I could see myself with Trinity. If I tried hard enough, it could work.

****

"*Gabriel?*" a voice faintly called while I was lying in bed later that night. I muted the television and sat perfectly still.

"*Gabriel? Get to the Luther's home as soon as possible.*"

"*I'm on my way, Orifiel.*"

I raced outside, morphing into my Angelic form immediately.

"Orifiel," I said once I was on the ground in front of Nina's house.

"They found Vincent. He's hiding in Bonaventure Cemetery. Michael and Raphael are closely watching and will continue to do so until they figure out what his plans are. Michael wants me to return to The Heavens immediately and needs you to take your post back. Nina's in serious danger. Michael insists you're the only one who can keep her safe. He left me with specific instructions that you're to train Nina in combat. She has to know how to fight like us—just in case. Also, be vague with what you tell them. Michael fears Chase will go after Vincent in a fit of stupidity."

"Why does Vincent want Nina? It's Chase who should have the target on his back, *not* her," I choked out. I could feel the world stand still. Nothing but protecting Nina mattered.

"We expected she'd be what Vincent would go after which is why Michael sent you to Earth to watch her back. He's angry with her husband, so he's seeking revenge. What better pain to inflict on Chase than to harm or kill his wife? You know firsthand how he operates. I have to go. Please be careful. Call to any of us should there be any complications, updates, or trouble," he said, preparing for flight. "Chase," he added, pointing to a figure emerging from the Luther house, before vanishing.

Chapter 29

Nina

Still hurt and fuming from my encounter with Gabriel, I reflected over exactly what type of relationship Gabriel and I shared. Initially, the plan was to apologize to him for my previous words and actions, but after leaving me standing outside of the restaurant after acting like an ass, and after overhearing his conversation with Trinity, Gabriel could go to hell.

What's really going on here? Does it matter that Gabriel is no longer hawking your every movement? In all honesty, you wanted Orifiel to do the job in the first place. Now, he is. You're safe.

If it's not protection that's bothering you, are you sure you're not in the slightest way attracted to Gabriel and his tragic backstory, rough sarcastic personality, and soft-hearted nature he tries to hide? Plus, he's drop dead hot, and that heat you two share...it's explosive. Put all of that together and perhaps it's possible? Because if you're not crushing on Gabriel, why care if he's around or not, or whom he's dating?

No. I love Chase, and I would never be drawn to another man. Not now, not ever. But as much as I'd like to forget Halloween night, it still happened.

Blank slate this situation, Nina. Be the bigger person. Go apologize.

Making my way to his table, I overheard him speaking with Trinity about me. His words were sharp and as painful as knives being stabbed multiple times into my back.

Oh my God!

How dare Gabriel blame me for the impending war? How dare *she*, someone who knew nothing about me, comment on my and Chase's characters? And the rest of the Angels? How could they be nice to my face, then talk about me behind my back, *especially* Orifiel? I had to get the hell out of Savannah. Now.

After an extremely uncomfortable exchange of pleasantries in the lobby of Gino's between my parents and Gabriel, intense hurt took hold over my heart. I couldn't think about anything other than obsessing over how the Angels were two-faced liars. To think I thought Orifiel was my friend. I confided in him multiple times, sharing intimate secrets. He probably ran back to them, and they all shared a good laugh at my expense. I wanted to tear Gabriel a new one, then slap the smile right off of Trinity's face, but I felt that battling the growing lump in my throat was more important at the moment.

Chase was at home when we arrived which made some of my bad spirits subside. While waiting patiently for my parents to head upstairs to bed so I could talk to Chase alone, his head shot up as his eyes darted from side to side.

"Chase?" my father questioned.

"Someone's outside," he replied, sprinting out of the back door.

I didn't hear anything, but Chase's sense and emotion altering ability had become such a strong internal gift, his wits were always more sensitive than mine, or anyone else's for that matter. A few minutes later, he reentered the house with Gabriel in tow.

"What's going on?" I asked immediately.

"Gabriel," Chase said, standing behind me, and wrapping his arms tightly around my waist.

Gabriel appeared exhausted. Something was missing from his eyes. The corners of his lips were pointing down in a grimace making his usual full ones resemble two thin, red slits. Even his clothing was out of character. He wore a pair of baggy, gray sweatpants and a fitted, white, tank top undershirt. His hair was pulled up in a messy man bun. If forced to guess, I'd imagine he'd been woken from a deep sleep. I'd only seen him a few hours earlier and he looked fine. His new physical state caused a frenzy of worry inside of me.

"We've been able to locate Vincent," Gabriel started.

"What does he want?" my father pressed.

"Retribution for Chase's actions. He wants Chase to experience pain and misery. Vincent's rage has grown and will continue to do so until we eliminate him. What his plans are, we have no idea, but there's reason to believe Nina is his target."

"Where is he?" Chase asked.

"What are you going to do, Chase? Try and find and destroy him yourself?" Gabriel scoffed.

"If that's the plan, where would one look?" Chase wasn't going to let this go.

"I cannot tell you. Michael won't allow it."

"Why not?"

"Because he knew you'd act like this. Listen, Chase, we may not like each other, but I'm all too familiar with the difficult, delicate nature of this situation. You want to protect Nina. You'd give your life for hers, but be smart, man. Let the Angels handle this one."

Chase didn't respond, but I could hear him swallow hard as he tightened his hold on my hips.

"Where do we go from here?" my father questioned.

"Michael wants Nina to learn how to protect herself."

"I'll teach her," Chase said.

"No offense, but we've thrown down. In The Heavens one of my jobs is to train new army members. I'm a skilled fighter in both worlds. Demons don't fight like Mortals. You're a novice. But feel free to join us during instruction. You may learn a thing or two yourself. Also, Jack, your presence will be required in case Nina gets hurt."

"Of course, Gabriel. Did Michael say anything else?"

"No. As updates come in, he'll let me know, and I'll inform you. Training starts tomorrow morning. I'll return around nine o'clock. Nina, please be ready. High heeled shoes and short skirts are not appropriate attire. I'm sure you've got some kind of workout outfit and a pair of sneakers in your closet. And Chase, show her how to tape her hands. We wouldn't want any broken knuckles now, would we? I hear healing Mortal bones is a bitch," Gabriel said, taking his leave before anyone could respond.

My mother, father, Chase, and I all stood dumbfounded in the kitchen for the next half hour. I wanted to say something. I wanted to tell them that part of me was petrified over this while the other part sought comfort in knowing Vincent had been found, but more than anything, I really wanted to curl up into a ball and cry. I was relieved when my father suggested we go to bed. Lifelessly, I walked up the stairs, making my way down the hall, and to my room.

At least Gabriel is back, and he seems to know what he's doing. After all, he is a Demonic assassin and Vincent is a Demon.

"Hey, baby?" Chase said.

"Yeah," I replied, turning around.

"Don't let this get to you. We had a really great day. There's a lot of planning to do. Start thinking about what kind of wedding you want and where you'd like us to live. Worry about that stuff, not about Vincent, or learning how to fight, which to be honest is a good thing. Everyone should know how to defend themselves. Besides, it'll be fun. We can work out and train together." He paused to read my facial expression. "Nina, they know where Vincent is. I'm sure they're hawking him like crazy. Do you really think they, or I, would let him get close enough to harm you?"

I smiled. "No, you're right."

He leaned forward, kissing me long and passionately.

"Goodnight, baby," he whispered.

For the next several hours, I tossed and turned, unable to clear my mind. Good and bad things raced in and out of my brain. In a desperate attempt to find calm and possibly provoke a vision, something which hadn't happened in a good, long time, the end result came up as pure frustration. Even though the images revealed negative prophecies, at least some sort of idea as to what was coming up around the bend always presented itself. I was furious with myself for not strengthening this ability. Maybe if I'd tried to learn about this power, I might've been able to see what was going on behind the scenes with Vincent and the Angels.

Finally, around half past two in the morning, I gave up on sleep. I got up and crept down the hallway to Chase's room. Cautiously, I opened and shut the door, grateful he'd left his television on or else the room would've been pitch black. He looked peaceful lying there fast asleep. Slowly, I crawled into his bed.

"Nina. What's the matter?" he asked. His body sprang up.

"I couldn't sleep."

"Not feeling well, baby?"

"I feel fine. I wanted to be near you. Please let me stay. I'll wake up early and..."

"Shhh. Lay down."

Within minutes, sleep arrived. My last thoughts were of doing this with Chase every night for all eternity.

What a perfect fairytale that would be.

Chapter 30

Chase

"Let's go for a run," I encouraged Nina.

We'd woken early so she could sneak out of my room unnoticed, and now we had a few hours to kill before Gabriel showed up. Gabriel teaching Nina anything irritated the shit out of me, but I really had no say in the matter. His comment about me watching and learning a thing or two was an obvious jab. I may not have had the formal training he'd been given, but I was far from a novice. Between the Demonic gift of strength and my ability to alter situations, keeping Nina and myself safe wasn't a problem. Plus, my combat ability was fairly comparable to his. On Halloween night I'd been able to hold my own. If he'd been a Mortal his face would've been just as jacked up as mine.

After Gabriel left and we'd gone to bed, I began plotting ways to find Vincent myself. There wasn't any time to wait for the damn Angels to get off of their asses and to make a move. Vincent needed to be gone for good, now. The only way to know where the Angel's located him would be to keep my eyes and ears set to hear and see everything. The Angels convened by the bushes off to the far side of the house every night around midnight. Pressing my ability to full strength, I'd listen to them speaking with crystal clarity. The conversations were usually recaps of the day, instructions for the next, and other boring, non-important topics. Occasionally, they'd discuss random things, but none of which held any interest to me. After a while I stopped paying attention to them, figuring if something serious were to happen, they'd inform at least Jack, who'd fill me in.

I eavesdropped last night, but nothing crucial was said. There'd been no shift change, no visiting Angels, nothing. Gabriel watched the house the entire time. Surely, he'd been relieved at some point, but I'd fallen asleep and had no idea when, what was said, or by whom. I wouldn't be as lax tonight, and I prayed Nina stayed in her own room. It's not that I didn't enjoy having her in my bed, but there were tasks to attend to. Once this shit ended, we'd be able to do that every night for forever, uninterrupted by Vincent or Gabriel.

"Do we have to? If The Powers That Be wanted me to run, they would've provided me with four legs, not two," Nina whined.

"It'll be fun. Come on," I urged, guiding her outside.

After a few minutes of stretching, we took off. Nina ran painfully slow and inconsistently. Her rapid change in pace and need to stop for breaks was worrisome. How was she going to learn to defend herself if she couldn't even jog down the block without gasping for air or getting a cramp? When we finally made it back to the house, she collapsed on the couch clutching the stitch in her side, suggesting she was unsure if she'd ever be able to get up again.

"Sorry for slowing you down," she panted.

"No worries. In time you'll get better." I laughed lightly, handing her a bottle of water.

"Yeah, sure. You're used to running like a racehorse

every morning," she snapped, taking the drink and downing half the bottle in one gulp.

"You ran almost two miles this morning, baby. Not too shabby for a first timer."

"Is that how far we went?" Her eyes widened. She looked like she was about to vomit all over Ellen's pristine sofa.

"You did great."

"I'm starving. Grab me a bagel from the kitchen, please?"

"Nope. You shouldn't work out on a full stomach. It might make you sick. When you're done with Gabriel, I'll get whatever you'd like."

"Seriously?"

"Do you want to throw up?" I challenged.

"No," she answered sullenly.

At precisely nine, Gabriel arrived. He strutted into the house like he owned the place, flashing his overly obnoxious personality, wearing tight-fitting gym clothes.

"You didn't tape her hands," he snapped, turning and exiting the living room.

"What an ass," Nina muttered.

Her negative comment pleased me tremendously.

"Ignore him. He's not worth it."

Chapter 31

Gabriel

"I need to see what you know. Use all of that pent up hatred for me and attack," I ordered.

I had no idea why my words were nasty and cruel, but it felt right. The overwhelming desire to protect this girl had consumed me for the past twenty-four hours. I hated the feeling. Truthfully, I wasn't sure what I was experiencing anymore, but I knew it had to stop. The old Gabriel, the version of me which felt most comfortable, had to return. Acting like a jerk was the only way to achieve that.

Nina mumbled something under her breath, paused for a brief moment, and finally approached me with her fingers pointed at my eyes. I was thrown by her actions and unsure of how to respond.

"What the hell are you doing? What the hell is this?" I asked, imitating her hand gesture while trying to suppress a snicker.

"It's what they told us to do in gym class if we're being attacked. Poke your assailant in the eye, kick them in the groin, smash up their nose, and run away. No good?" she asked innocently.

I could hear Chase holding back a laugh while Jack lowered and shook his head. I stared blankly at Nina. I'd never witnessed her appear this cute before.

Stop it, Gabriel!

"Yeah, no. What do you weigh? A hundred and ten, a hundred and twenty pounds at most? Do you honestly believe a Demon my size or bigger is going to be taken out by some sort of shadow puppet, chicken looking move you learned in a high school physical education class by a woman who probably had no formal training in combat? Is this the only pearl of self-defense knowledge you know?"

"Yup," she replied, sounding rather pissed off.

For the next few hours, I taught her how to throw, land, block, and dodge punches. After a while, Nina started to catch on. She wasn't what I would've considered a quick study, but in time I'd be able to train her up well. Over the years, Michael had given me harder projects to deal with. By noon she appeared tired, hungry, and cranky.

"Are we done now?" she asked, plopping on a kitchen chair.

"For today," I answered, washing my hands, and getting ready to leave.

"We have to do this again tomorrow?" she whined as she slipped an impressive and expensive diamond ring on her left ring finger.

Chase proposed.

"Nina, all we did was learn how to hit and honestly, you're not very good at it. You need to practice every day. Look at Chase. He works with Jack multiple times daily," I said quickly, struggling to maintain my composure.

"Between school and having a personal life, I don't have time for this, Gabriel."

"Two things that won't matter when you're dead,

because you didn't learn how to defend yourself. You're going to have to make time. This is important, Nina. Learn this skill. If you don't, you'll come to regret it. That I can promise you."

"Whatever. So much for fun."

"Would you rather have a social life or no life at all?" I shot back in a tone so harsh and nasty, I surprised myself.

She didn't say anything in response. However, her leer spoke volumes. If looks could murder, I would've been killed all over again.

"Now you're getting it. Use that hatred. It'll come in handy when you're trying to kick the crap out of me." I smiled spitefully.

"I don't hate you."

"Love me, hate me—I could care less, *princess*," I replied, showing her that I didn't give a crap over how she felt.

Nina Luther was a job. As long as I kept telling myself that, all would be well. I returned home, showered, and lay in bed. My body required rest, but I was too charged up to sleep. My thoughts raced. In an attempt to find peace, meditation helped to shift my anxious focus to happier times, allowing for me to stop reeling and to remember Lilith. I adored that woman. She was the only woman I'd ever loved.

You sure about that, Gabriel? Is Lilith really the only one?

My buzzing cell phone on the nightstand pushed my wife away, pulling reality back to the foreground.

"Hey, Jules."

"Hey. I heard you had a hot date the other night," she answered. Her smile conveyed through the receiver.

"Did Nina tell you that?"

"Yeah, that and a bunch of other things."

"Such as?" I pressed.

"I'm not getting in the middle of your lovers' quarrel. Anyway, I need help."

"What's going on?" I sat up, choosing to forget about her sarcastic comment.

"It involves Nina and her seer ability."

"Nope. No way. Sorry. Pick something else. *Anything* else. I'd sooner beat the crap out of another one of your ex's than assist Nina with her visions."

"Please, Gabriel? I have no idea what I'm doing."

"What kind of support does her majesty require?"

"She hasn't had any visions. It's bothering her. She feels like she should be doing more, helping more, and she believes this is the only thing that she can bring to the table to aid the Angels and to make herself useful instead of a drain on The Heavens. Nina thinks the Angels view her as a troublemaker and see her as the real reason all of this began. She's really upset."

"Nina said that?"

"Yes."

"Where'd she get that idea from?"

"Gabriel, if I told you I'd be betraying Nina's confidence. I'm trying to be a good friend."

"What do you want me to do?" I sighed.

"Teach me how to evoke the ability."

"Do I have a choice?" If I didn't help Jules, she'd try to figure out how to do it herself, which could potentially be dangerous. She had me pinned against a wall.

"Not really. Sorry."

"When and where?"

"Twenty minutes. New Age Books."

"I'll meet you there." I said and hung up. I went outside and transformed into my true form. Within seconds, I landed behind the shop.

A bit later, Jules and Nina entered the building.

"*Gabriel*," Nina muttered with an eyeroll.

"Take her to my house. I'll be there in a few minutes," I instructed Jules, ignoring Nina. Reaching into my pants pocket, I pulled out my keys and handed them to Jules.

The bookstore was far too exposed to speak freely. After the two left, I exited through the back entrance, lingering in the alley.

"Michael," I hissed.

"Behind you," he whispered, causing me to practically jump out of my skin.

"What are you doing here?"

"I haven't returned to The Heavens since we've found Vincent. Neither has Raphael. When I'm not watching Vincent, I'm watching you. What are *you* up to?"

"If you've been watching me, then you should already know," I quipped.

Sharply, he slapped the back of my head and shook his.

"Sorry," I muttered, rubbing the area he smacked.

"It's all right to help Nina strengthen her ability, but I *do not* want her to go into a full trance state. She cannot see where Vincent is hiding. Help her relax and fall unconscious but pull out after a few minutes. I'll have Orifiel summon Sasha. He'll be able to assist us better. Do you understand?" Michael instructed.

"Yes. How are things going with Vincent?"

"Not good, son. Don't let Nina out of your sight. She's the object of his desire. If Vincent finds and traps her, he's going to destroy her, and painfully."

"I won't let that happen. My mission is to keep the target free from danger and alive. That's what I fully intend to do."

"You're to take out anyone or anything that gets in the way of that."

"Of course."

"If need be, would you sacrifice your existence for hers?"

"I have to go."

"Gabriel."

"What?"

"Have your feelings for the Mortal changed?" he asked curiously.

"Why?"

"You don't love her, Gabriel. Remember that," he warned.

"I don't love anyone. Isn't that the way you created me?" I asked before morphing and disappearing.

Chapter 32

Nina

"What an ass," I spat the second the backdoor shut.

"He's doing his job, Nina. Gabriel cares about your safety or else he wouldn't be here. It would be a nice change if you acted a touch kinder to him and you tried to understand that he wants to help not only you, but all of us. Think about it," my father spoke calmly. He smiled warmly, patted my shoulder, and left the kitchen.

"Whatever. Am I that big of a bitch, Chase?" I needed validation because deep down I was fully aware that I'd been far worse than a bitch to him.

"No, baby. If Gabriel really does care about your wellbeing, he's got a funny way of showing it. Besides, since he arrived, he's been nothing but a huge pain in the neck. Teaching you how to fight has been the only useful thing he's done." Chase sat at the table finishing his lunch while flipping through a magazine.

"Thanks for siding with me."

"That's what I'm here for. By the way, Jules called."

"What did she want?"

"I don't know."

"What did she say?"

"Nothing."

"Okay, so what you're telling me is, you picked up the phone, said absolutely nothing, but somehow knew it was Jules, who also didn't speak a word. Through telepathy you knew she wanted me to call her back," I recapped sarcastically.

"I said, hello. She said, hello. She asked where you were. I told her. Then, she requested a callback. I said, okay. She said, goodbye. I returned the closing. The call ended," he replied in a mocking manner.

"How did she sound?"

"Like Jules."

"That's not what I meant. Did she sound happy? Sad? Angry? Upset?"

"Baby, I have no idea how she sounded, but here's a thought. Call her back and find out for yourself."

"You see? Now I know why I keep you around, Chase James. You're always full of obvious ideas."

"You're so witty." Chase looked up from his magazine and smirked.

For a brief moment I saw my future with Chase, and it was amazing.

"Where's my phone?" I glanced around the kitchen.

I remembered leaving it on the table this morning, but I was pretty sure when my mother set the table for lunch, she moved it.

"It's on the counter," Chase said, vaguely pointing to his left.

Apparently, looking up was too much to ask for. My eyes surveyed the cluttered countertops.

"I don't see it, Chase. Where?" My patience was rapidly dwindling.

All I wanted to do was to call Jules back and hopefully convince her to help me with some research on strengthening my seer abilities.

"Right there," Chase said, pointing at the counter

again, but this time something interesting occurred.

His eyes were still buried in his magazine, but as his right arm rose, the phone slid across the counter into his hand. Cautiously, he looked up. A wicked smile grew on his face.

"Chase," I started.

"Shhh."

He walked to the counter, placing the phone down in its original spot. Moving back to the table he sat, but this time he didn't lower his head. Instead, his energy was intently focused on the object. Raising his palm in the direction of the phone, the device literally zoomed across the kitchen and straight to him. A loud laugh escaped his throat. His jeweled colored eyes sparkled with fascination.

"What the hell?" I marveled.

"Hold on."

Placing the phone flat on the oak surface of the kitchen table, he stepped away. Forcefully, thrusting his left hand away from his body, the object practically slammed back to the countertop. Filled with wonder, his attention turned on me. Concentrating on my frame, he slowly raised both of his hands. I felt as if someone had lassoed my waist and was aggressively yanking me forward. There was no way I could stop the intense, forward momentum. Seconds later he caught me.

"Dr. Luther," he called.

The sounds of my father's footsteps against the polished floors grew louder until he entered the kitchen.

"Yes, Chase?"

"Watch this," Chase said sounding thrilled over the development of a new ability.

What an unexpected change this was. When he first

started gaining powers, Chase had freaked out, becoming depressed and totally stressed, but now his reaction was completely different. Again, he used the cell phone as a prop. Skillfully, he drew it to his hand, then back to the counter. His grand finale was pulling my father closer.

"Amazing. Have you experienced any symptoms of internal or external distress? Any headaches? Anything at all?" My father's tone instantly laced with concern.

"No. I would've said something. I feel completely fine. I have for a while. No headaches, no voices, no rage, no racing thoughts, and I've been sleeping great without having to take any pills."

"Come to my office. Let's see what the limitations are and if we can possibly strengthen this."

Quickly, Chase kissed the top of my head and followed my father down the hall. Plopping onto a chair, I played with the remainder of Chase's uneaten lunch, gazing at the most beautiful engagement ring in the history of ever.

Maybe we'd have a fall wedding.

The decision to wait until Chase graduated from law school and I finished medical school had already been made, but a girl could plan. Having the ring and knowing that Chase was all in was more than enough. My phone buzzing interrupted my happy musings. Why couldn't I have Chase's retrieval ability? I really didn't feel like moving. Annoyed at having to aggravate my aching muscles, I lumbered to the center island, and hit the talk button.

"Hello?"

"Hey, Nina."

"Hey, Jules. I was just about to call you. Great minds think alike. What's up?"

"Nothing much. I wanted to see how training went."

"Tiring, but fine. My body feels like it's on fire. Gabriel was an epic jerk, but whatever. I can't stand his attitude. I guess his date with *Trinity* last night didn't go so well. Perhaps she didn't put out or turned out to be a lousy lay. Listen, do you have some time to spare today?"

"Sure. What are we doing? And, who's Trinity? I thought Gabriel's soul mate was Lilith?"

"Some ugly bitch Angel who has no sense of style that Gabriel took out on a date. It's not important. Anyway, you know how I have seer-like powers? Well, I was hoping maybe we, who am I kidding, you, could do some research? I'd like to strengthen it, maybe even evoke it a bit."

"Why? Is everything okay?" She sounded concerned.

"Everything is fine. I just haven't had any dreams or visions lately. It's bothering me. Even though the dreams are usually bad, at least it's a heads up. I kind of feel a little defenseless without them."

"Understood, but I'm pretty sure there's something else going on that you're not sharing. I can hear it in your voice."

Since there was no sense denying my current mood, I decided to complain to Jules. Maybe that would help me feel better about what Gabriel had said last night. "I overheard Gabriel saying horrible, hurtful things about me to Trinity. Apparently, the other Angels dislike me as well, and think I do nothing but cause drama and stir up trouble. They blame me for this war that's supposed to go down between the Angels and Demons. That's *not* true. Yes, at times, I can be moody and difficult to deal with, but I thought these people were my friends, for lack of a better term. I feel as if I were stabbed a thousand times in the back by the Universe's holiest people. Maybe if I can help them, they'll see me as someone on their team, not just a liability."

"I'm so sorry, Nina. I don't know what would prompt Gabriel to speak so harshly, or why the other Angels would blame you for things that are beyond your control, but I sincerely hope you realize your worth and value in both worlds and actively choose to ignore their negativity. How about I pick you up in fifteen minutes? We can head over to this new age bookstore I found a few weeks ago? Maybe they'll have something there that can guide us in the right direction."

"Sounds like a plan," I said, running up the stairs to clean up and to change my clothing.

Fifteen minutes to the second, Jules arrived, and we were off to the bookstore. She drove to the outskirts of town, parking at the curb of the tiniest, darkest store I'd ever seen.

"This is the place?"

"Yeah. It looks small, well it is small, but, never-the-less, the books are amazing. You'll never find material like this in the library. There's a huge section on Angels and Demons. I've been spending a lot of time here flipping through books and brushing up on lore."

She pushed the door open. Almost immediately my nostrils were assaulted by the heavy smell of burning incense which also caused my eyes to water.

"You get used to the smell after a few minutes," Jules whispered.

"Let's hope so," I replied, coughing.

"Hello, Jules. Back again so soon? Oh, and I see

you've brought company," a short woman with long, ratty looking, oak colored hair said in a dreamy voice. She looked like a kick-back from the days when hippies walked the Earth.

"Hey, Mara. This is my friend, Nina."

"Hello, Nina. It's nice to meet you. Your other friend is waiting for you in your usual section," Mara said slowly and calmly.

"Other friend?"

"Yeah. Gabriel," Jules said quickly.

"Why?" I demanded.

"He can help more than I can."

"Great," I said, rolling my eyes.

I stood uncomfortably in the corner for a few minutes while they spoke. He and Jules seemed tight which slapped at my annoyance levels. I supposed it was because she was my friend, not his, and he was my watcher, not hers. Moments later, Gabriel walked past me without as much as a word or look and left the store.

"Where are we going?" I asked, following Jules out of the front door.

"Gabriel's house. It's quieter and far more private there."

"How do you know where he lives?" I asked.

"We hang out sometimes. Why? Is that a problem?"

"No, but you two look like you're getting really close."

"We are. He's a great guy." She smiled.

Momentarily, I felt weird. A combination of jealousy and anger mixed inside of me. "I thought you weren't into guys, Jules?"

"I'm not. What does that have to do with anything?" Her tone changed slightly.

"You said you were getting close with him. I figured that meant, you know…"

"Know *what*? Because I hang out with a guy that automatically means we jumped into bed together? We're friends, Nina. He understands me. Actually, he seems to be the only one that does."

"I understand you, Jules." Her accusation was rather insulting.

"No, you don't. Gabriel gets me. When we talk it's on a different level. We connect, *not* physically, but rather spiritually. You have no idea how hard coming out has been. To admit to yourself, to say out loud that you're different, that you're a lesbian, is a difficult thing to do. Trust me. I've been on an emotional rollercoaster these past few years—lying, pretending, hurting Mark. I finally found someone who understands that. Gabriel's got his own skeletons and Demons that he's been fighting. Granted, they're totally different than the ones I've been dealing with, but they're just as taxing."

"Now I feel like a total failure as a friend."

"Nina, this isn't about you or our friendship. I'm going through things you cannot even begin to understand and vice versa. The difference is, you have a support system. I didn't, until Gabriel. I'm not suggesting you're judging me, and I know you're there should I need you, but you're busy dealing with your own drama and don't have time for mine—which is okay. It's called life. I still love you and I still think of you as a sister. Stop worrying that I'm socially dumping you because I'm not. If I was, would I be here right now? No."

"I'm sorry. I know I'm not Gabriel, but if you ever want to talk about what's going on and your struggles,

I'll always make the time."

"That means a lot."

"What are Gabriel's problems?" My deep curiosity required sating.

"That's not for me to say. If Gabriel wants to share his woes with you he will. But Nina, cut him some slack. He might be an Angel, but he still has feelings, *deep* feelings actually," she said with a slight giggle.

"What's that supposed to mean?"

"Nothing. We're here."

She pulled into the driveway of a very pristine carriage house. It was slightly hidden from the road and neighboring homes by a small, wooded area. Savannah was known for these types of structures which were once used to house carriages and horses, but since no one traveled by either anymore, the buildings were converted into really cute, trendy, expensive houses. The one Gabriel lived in was two stories, but from being in a few of these prior to today, the first floor was often a garage.

The house was constructed of white siding and tan bricks. A whitewashed staircase located off to the side allowed for people to bypass the garage entrance and enter in a more central area. Jules and I climbed the stairs and entered. Once the door opened, I peeked around. We stood in a very nicely decorated living room/dining room combination. The deep, rich, crimson-colored walls complimented the dark wood furniture and black and gold leafed curtains. A comfortable looking black, leather sofa was pushed against a wall, while a round, wrought iron and glass topped table with two chairs were set to the right. A tremendous flat screen television hung on the wall adjacent to the sofa. The kitchen was painted mocha and had onyx speckled granite countertops. The tidiness of the house surprised me, especially the kitchen. Most men were sloppy pigs who left pizza boxes, soda cans, and clothing everywhere.

"May I?" I asked Jules, pointing to four closed doors.

"Sure. I don't think Gabriel would mind," Jules responded.

The heel of my shoes clopped against the oak floors. Behind two accordion style doors, a washer and dryer sat. To the left was a bathroom decorated in shades of purple filled with an abundance of scented candles placed around the garden style bathtub and vanity. Quickly, I opened the door to a room which had been painted royal blue. Apparently, he'd set this up as an office. A large desk sat in the middle of the space. The floor to ceiling bookcases were overflowing with books. Had I had more time I would've browsed the shelves, but I wanted to finish looking around before Gabriel returned. I didn't want him to think I'd been snooping, which technically speaking I was. The last door led to his bedroom. A heavy, four post bed leaned up against one of the hunter green walls. Unlike the rest of the house, the curtains were drawn tightly not allowing for any natural light to be present. I flipped the switch nearest the door allowing the dim ceiling light to flood the space. For some reason my body felt the urge to wander further in. I felt drawn to the area. A few books rested on one of the night tables beside the bed. A sheer piece of fabric was strategically hung across the bedposts creating a very romantic look.

Okay. Someone else must've decorated this house because the word whimsical would never be used to describe Gabriel.

His closet door was open, revealing perfectly organized clothing, meticulously hung with care.

I wonder if he'd come over and do the same to my closets.

What really caught my attention was a shiny, silver picture frame on the dresser. I went to it and picked it up. The image was an old black and white one of him standing in extremely dated clothing next to a drop-dead gorgeous woman.

This must be Lilith.

Gabriel appeared vibrant and happy in the photograph. His eyes were bright and content. His smile was wide and genuine. The only difference between Mortal Gabriel and Angel Gabriel was hair length and age. As a Mortal he wore it shorter and appeared several years younger.

Maybe it was my imagination, but Lilith's eyes seemed cold and empty. Jealousy and envy radiated from them. Her smile was fake and forced. Once I placed the picture back down, pity sunk into my heart which stirred up many other strong emotions.

That's the bond. You feel for his past. See? It's as simple as that. Sometimes life doesn't have to be as complicated as you make it.

"Nina? Gabriel's here," Jules called.

Hurriedly, I made my way back into the living area.

"Hey." I tried to sound innocent even though what I'd done wasn't wrong. Jules had given me permission to tour the house, but I felt I caught an intimate glimpse of him which I doubted he wanted. A sudden uncomfortableness around Gabriel consumed me.

"Ready?" he asked.

"Sure," I responded coolly.

"Jules, do me a favor and hang out in the living room. Once I know how to help her, we'll talk about it," he said, leading the way to his bedroom.

"Have you ever done this before?" he asked, closing the door. Moments ago, this space had given off a welcoming, inviting impression, but now, here with Gabriel, it felt awkward and dangerous.

"No."

"Lay down. It'll be more comfortable."

"What are you going to do to me?" I could clearly hear the hesitation in my voice.

"Hopefully, make you see all of the things that your brain wishes to purge. However, in order for this to work, you have to trust me and let go in my presence. I swear that you're safe and will remain that way. I also promise that I'd never do anything shady or dangerous to or with you while you're vulnerable and out of it."

I laid on top of the soft, navy blue and gold down comforter and took a few deep, cleansing breaths. His masculine smell stormed my senses causing my body to sink deeper into the mattress.

"Try and clear your mind. Don't force any of your thoughts away or try to redirect them. Let them play out. Eventually, you'll become tired and the world around you will disappear on its own. Focus on breathing. Feel your body as it is." He paused. "Now I'd like for you to imagine a staircase with ten steps going down. You're on the top step, step ten. You're feeling so relaxed, so calm. Step nine, you're going even deeper, feeling lighter…" Gabriel spoke, but the sound of his voice made me drift off faster than either of us thought.

A cloudy vision instantly appeared. Foggy imagery of a graveyard, big trees, and strange looking tombstones revealed themselves. The only thing clearly presenting itself was Vincent's hard, cold, calculating eyes staring directly into mine and a flash of blinding, red light exploding in my face. My body flung backwards knocking the wind out of me. I struggled to breathe. Gasping for air, my frame shot straight up.

"You're okay, Nina. You're here with me in my bed. Nothing bad exists in this space. I won't allow it to. I promise," Gabriel said in a reassuring manner.

My natural reflexes caused me to throw myself into his arms. I buried my face in his neck as hot tears streamed down my cheeks. The smell of cherry blossoms, lilac, and vanilla invaded my nose the moment we made contact.

"You're safe. I'd never let anything bad happen to you, angel. Not now, not ever. It was only a vision. I've got you. Whatever happened on the other side wasn't today's reality. This moment right here is," he said softly, almost inaudibly, as he stroked my hair while rocking us back and forth.

I held on tight not wanting to let go. After several long moments, he pulled away and gently brushed the tears from my cheeks. His big, brown eyes filled with sympathy and concern.

"I'm sorry. I didn't mean for you to get scared. Evidently your mind wants to purge its secrets. We don't have to do this again and we never have to talk about what happened either," Gabriel said. His tone remorseful.

There were no words, only actions. I tugged him close, curling up on his lap like a scared child seeking protection. Patiently, Gabriel held me securely, resting his head on top of mine. To try to explain the effects of what was happening to me internally would be impossible. However, Gabriel's physical presence consoled me in a way I never experienced. I feared letting go would cause the safety net he'd wrapped me in to vanish, and because of that, the world would spiral out of control. I hated myself for thinking Chase could never provide this level of security. In reality, Gabriel should've pushed me away, but he didn't. I'd treated this man like absolute crap. I was totally undeserving of his genuine expression.

"Is Nina going to be okay, Gabriel?" Jules whispered, popping her head into the room.

"Yes, of course. I don't know what she saw, but whatever happened while she was under caused this. Her aura suggests hurt, fear, sorrow, anger, and a sense of being lost, but more than anything, confusion. Since her soul is wobbling, I can't get an accurate read. Head home. We'll catch up later," he answered, not letting go of me, but dismissing Jules.

"Okay," Jules replied, leaving. Thankfully, she took the hint that he wanted privacy for us.

"You're stronger than this, Nina. Pull out of whatever you're stuck on and come back to me. Seeing you like this is crushing me because I can't do a damn thing about it," he said.

It almost sounded like he was pleading with me, but not in a frustrated way. It was more like my emotions were causing him great pain.

"Please, angel. Please."

A few minutes later, inner calmness found its way inside of my core.

"Feeling better?" Gabriel inquired.

"If you consider feeling stupid and embarrassed

better, than yeah, I'm living the dream," I replied, plucking a tissue from the box by the side of the bed and laughing nervously.

"Why do you feel stupid and embarrassed?"

"For starters, I've pretty much treated you like trash since day one, so I don't deserve your kindness now. Plus, I shouldn't have cried and carried on like that. I'm *not* that kind of girl."

"It's okay to be weak and afraid of the unknown. That's why I'm here." A slight smile flashed across his face. "Neither of us has been that great to the other. We're both to blame. I'm sorry for my part, really. Especially for anything I've said or done that's hurt you," he replied, softly touching the bottom of my chin.

Temporarily, I got lost in the wild, deep sea of his eyes. I'd never noticed the tiny gold flecks that surrounded his irises before. A second later, he broke the hold. My emotions for him faded, but they were still present.

"Want to talk about it?" he asked.

"The vision was foggy. A graveyard appeared with a lot of tombstones. It was nighttime, I think. Vincent entered. There was a flash of blinding red light. My body took a blow. It felt like I was dying. Please, don't let him find me again." Anxiety and panic bubbled over with no way to stop it. My hands shook. My heart rate accelerated. There's always a moment which leads way to an epiphany and mine just occurred. This was real, *not* a dream. An honest life-or-death situation that I stood in the middle of.

"I won't let Vincent hurt you," he said, pulling me back into a firm embrace.

"That's what Orifiel said last year, but yet here we

are. I don't want to do this anymore. Find a way to get me out of this. Please. Orifiel couldn't do it, but I need *you* to."

"That's not possible, but I'll get us through this. Have some faith in me. I've never lied to you, and I never will." He paused. "Let's start over, okay?" he said.

"I heard what you said to Trinity about me." If we were going to put our best foot forward this time around the air had to be cleared.

"It's complicated, Nina."

"Did you mean it? Do the other Angels see me as a troublemaking, pain in the ass? I didn't ask for any of this, Gabriel. At any given moment I swear that I'm doing my best. All I ever wanted was a normal life. I'm sick and tired of trying to be something that I'm not, and I'm beyond terrified of having to face Vincent again because we both know that he's going to find and kill me."

"No, Nina. He won't. You have to believe me. I will do whatever is necessary to keep you safe. As for what I said to Trinity, none of it is true." He sighed. "You have this ability to drive me crazy sometimes. What you said about hating me was totally uncalled for, but I understood why you said it. Tensions were running high that night for all involved parties. My words to Trinity were out of anger. It's not an excuse, but it's the truth. As for the other Angels, they don't see you as a pain in the ass, nor a troublemaker. They all really like you, especially Orifiel. He adores you. Don't worry about Trinity. She doesn't matter. No one asks for this life. Shit happens and we deal with it. If we can find a way to put an end to our sniping everything will get a little easier. All right?"

"Agreed. Can we do this again?"

"We don't have to."

"I want to. Will you help me?"

"Of course."

"Are things with Trinity serious?" If Gabriel planned on being with her, fresh start or not, I was out. Something about that particular Angel irked the shit out of me.

"No," he replied flatly.

Good.

"Why not?" I pressed out of shear curiosity.

He didn't answer with words. His eyes glanced over to the picture of him and Lilith. My heart broke.

"I'm sorry about Lilith," I whispered.

"Don't be. I'm not."

"Do you ever miss her?"

"Every single minute of every single day."

"Do you think you'll ever find another mate?"

Again, no answer. He mumbled something under his breath while trying to cover up his pain and sorrow.

You're not as strong as you lead people to believe.

You're like me in that respect.

Truce.

Chapter 33

Gabriel

I watched Nina's entire being change over the next several weeks. Her combat skills were coming together nicely because she was finally listening to my instructions. Added bonus? Our relationship wasn't as strained. We'd found a harmonious balance.

The afternoon I helped her force a vision was rough. Seeing her panic, hearing her cry, feeling her body shake with fear, tasting her salty tears as they streamed down her face onto my lips, and smelling her perfume on my sheets for days after became consuming. I had to make Nina's pain stop forever. I had to protect her. However, my hands were tied leaving me with only two choices— ignore my feelings for her or give into them and secretly allow myself to fall deeper in love with her. My emotions for her grew on a daily basis. Fighting them wasn't working. It was easier to surrender my heart, but the knowledge that she'd never be mine was torturous. I found myself making any excuse to be at the Luther house because when I was not by Nina's side, I grew lost.

Whenever Chase happened to be near us Nina wasn't as friendly, but when we were alone a different person existed. We worked regularly on strengthening her seer ability. Engaging in that activity meant uninterrupted alone time at my home with her, but it became difficult to pull her from the visions before she saw too much. She thought the internal images hadn't fully developed yet, but I knew better. They were there, dying to pour out, which scared the shit out of me. Eventually an opportunity would arise, the dam would give out, and all hell would break loose.

After weeks of intense training, Nina grew into a formidable opponent. The time had come for her to learn how to fight like a true Angel. After speaking with Michael, who cleared it with Jack, Nina was gifted the ability to use her Angelic energy in combat. She was ready. I, on the other hand, was not.

I was nervous as hell teaching her this particular skill. One false move and she could kill me, but she had to learn this. She tried for two hours to fire a bolt at me, but she couldn't. She could do it, but she didn't want to cause damage to my form. This only made her more endearing to me. I hated having to be the one to strike first, but she needed to know what it felt like. Chase argued endlessly over this, but in the end I won.

Bolt after bolt she blocked the blows while firing back. Finally, I made contact by hitting her in the right leg and taking her down. I felt like the biggest piece of shit for hurting her, but this was what she was up against.

"Again," I ordered, once she'd gotten up and I knew she was okay.

Though visibly tired, Nina had to understand how true combat situations played out. Sustain a blow, get back up, and keep fighting. Chase, evidently, had other plans.

In order to get him to settle down, a humble, yet choke worthy, invitation that he alter Nina's sense of sound and sight was requested. Never in a million years would I ever touch a hair on that girl's head in a malicious fashion. However, several moments later, the strangest sensation overtook me. A force grabbed my waist, pulling my body forward. Resisting it was useless.

The prick bastard has a new ability. Michael's going to love hearing about this.

Chase dragged me to where he stood, dropping the hold only when we were inches apart. I glared at him showing no fear while he went off on me screaming about how Nina was exhausted, and I'd pushed her too far by demanding too much.

"This is what combat is like, Chase. There are no breaks. No rests. It doesn't matter if you're seasoned or not. Learning how to defend yourself when you're down and how to push through the fatigue is something she needs to learn as well. You've fought twice and should be aware of this. What we're doing today is slow motion combat. If she can't handle this, she'll be destroyed out on the battlefield," I informed calmly. Yelling back at him would only end badly, especially for him.

"Chase," Jack said, placing his left hand on his shoulder. His aura revealed a father/son bond existed between the two.

You're in too deep Gabriel. You will lose.

When Michael arrived to relieve me, I told him about Chase's additional gift. He didn't appear too terribly thrilled over it. When he asked how Nina's training went, I complained about Chase's involvement and how this hindrance wasn't allowing for me to teach her properly.

The next day, Michael and Orifiel showed up suggesting they were there so Nina could see how Orifiel and I fought. Chase displayed visible signs of annoyance and quickly left. Jack had been called to work hours earlier due to an emergency, and Ellen was out running various errands. Their absence pleased me. It allowed for a free, uninhibited morning.

Upon Michael's command, Orifiel and I began. It was nice to be able to work off some of my pent-up stress by sparring with another skilled fighter. Much like our drills in The Heavens, Michael sat on the sidelines yelling orders. Allowing Orifiel to take me down and believe that he had won the match was my goal. Letting your opponent think they have the upper hand is a key tactic. Once my body hit the ground, I laid perfectly still.

"Gabriel," Nina shouted.

Out of the corner of my eye, I saw Nina attempt to run over to where I was lying. Michael stopped her, instructing Orifiel to finish the job. The second Orifiel reached me, I kicked his legs out causing him to fall, granting me total control over the situation. Within seconds, I had him pinned and completely done for.

"Very good, Gabriel. Watch your opponent, even when you think you've defeated them, Orifiel. It doesn't matter their size or skill level," Michael said.

"Nice match. Your last punch nailed me. Hurt like a bitch," I said, extending my right hand, and helping him off of the ground.

"I've found that hitting pressure points in a certain order does that. It buys you a few extra minutes to plan your next move," Orifiel replied.

"You'll have to show me."

"Of course."

"We fight in pairs now," Michael announced, then stood. "Orifiel, you're with me. Gabriel, you're with Nina."

Nina grabbed my arm. Her lips pressing against my ear caused a sudden chill to run up my spine. The sound of her voice and breath caressing my skin drove me wild.

"Pairs?" she questioned.

"Yes. Pairs. Us versus them. Don't worry. We got this," I encouraged.

"Watch Orifiel and Gabriel for a moment," Michael began. "See how they utilize everything around them and work off of each other's movements and bodies. They're in sync. Two have become one. They anticipate the other's next move and react accordingly. This only works if one knows their partner well."

Orifiel and I screwed around for a few minutes using basic techniques to show Nina what Michael was talking about. This form of battle couldn't be learned by watching. She had to engage in it and fully trust me for it to be successful.

"Let's commence," Michael said.

Nina was visibly nervous and because of this she started making rookie mistakes. After five minutes, I'd been struck multiple times by both opponents because my focus had been solely set on protecting her. The last blow dealt by Orifiel pelted me square in the gut, causing me to drop to the ground, gasping for air.

"Oh my God. Gabriel. Are you okay?" Nina rushed to my side.

"No. No, I'm not. What the hell are you doing? If this were a real combat situation, we'd both be dead. You'd be on your way to Heaven, and I wouldn't exist anymore. Damn it, Nina. Look alive. Trust me so I can trust you. Use my body as a weapon, not as a shield, and for crying out loud, open your eyes. Asses and elbows. Let's go," I shouted out of frustration.

"I'm sorry," she said regretfully.

"Do it right. There's no time or room for fear when you're fighting."

"Enough, Gabriel. Let's try again." Michael spoke.

"You worry about Orifiel. I'll take Michael," I ordered.

This time, once we started her aura darkened and fired up. In that moment, a switch flipped inside of her brain. Instantly, we became one speaking through actions and eye contact. Within mere seconds, we'd taken both men down. She took a gate chain from the ground and wrapped it around Orifiel's neck. Using my back to gain height, she strangled him while I dealt Michael a knockout blow.

"That's my girl," I said, grabbing her thin waist, and holding her frame dangerously close.

I never wanted to let go, especially after she locked her legs around my hips, tucking her face in my neck.

"That felt amazing." She sounded exhilarated.

Not nearly as amazing as holding you and feeling your heart beat against my chest.

"Excellent work, Nina. Raphael is calling for me, but I'll be back later, Gabriel," Michael said before he morphed and vanished.

"I better go too, but a word, brother?" Orifiel asked.

"Sure. I'll be right back, Nina," I said, finally letting her go.

"What's up, brother?" I questioned.

"Do me a favor and watch your back," he whispered.

I didn't answer, but rather shot him a confused look.

"There's something not right about Chase. He's too possessive of her. It's not natural. I sense more Demon than Angel within his core."

"I'm very well aware of that."

Tell me something I don't already know. For crying out loud, his aura darkens every damn second of every damn day.

"You're entering dangerous waters. You better tread carefully," he warned.

"What's that supposed to mean?"

"I'm not an idiot. I know you well. We're brothers and best mates. You're in love with her."

"Excuse me? Your gift only encompasses all things lost, and I'm certainly not lost. When did you take over for our mother and become the Angel of Love?" I snapped.

"I may not be a Chief Angel like our father or an Archangel like you. I don't hold a fancy sword or have the pleasure and privilege of being a Gate Keeper. I'm only a simple Guardian, but my gift is strong and meaningful. Additionally, I can do something better than you and our father. I can read the stars which is far more powerful than all of your abilities put together. The stars never lie, but you do and will when asked if you're in love with the girl," he hissed nastily. In all of the years that I'd known Orifiel I'd never heard him lose his temperance.

"So what? I love her. I'm truly, madly, deeply in love with Nina Olivia Luther. I'd do anything for her. She's all I ever think about. I want her so bad it hurts. Why does it matter?" Admitting my feelings for Nina proved liberating. The tremendous weight that had been weighing me down magically vanished.

"You know Nina's middle name?" Orifiel raised an eyebrow.

"I know every last detail about her. Favorite color?

Indigo, though most people think it's pink. Favorite scent? Honeysuckle and lilac. Whenever she sees either, she stops and inhales so deeply you can hear her happiness when she exhales. She loves sappy romance novels and horrible chick-flicks. When she's stressed out, she heads straight to the freezer for a pint of whatever type of chocolate ice cream is in there. You can't communicate with her until she's had at least one large cup of coffee—which she likes light and sweet at home, but when she's out she'll either have an iced, hazelnut latte or a green tea lemonade, more lemonade than tea, easy on the ice. Orifiel, brother, ask me anything about her and I can tell you. Favorite book? Movie? Time of day? Season? Sounds and expressions? Her different types of smiles? *Anything*." I sighed. He'd broken me. Even though speaking openly had alleviated some of my frustrations, the truth concerning my feelings left behind an air of defeat. "It doesn't matter. It never will. She'll never be mine, nor will I ever be able to tell her what she means to me. Even if I could, she wouldn't care."

"Don't say that. Soon enough she's going to need you, badly, and you're going to have to use every ounce of love you have for her so you can save her." His tone softened as he squeezed my left forearm.

"Orifiel, what are the stars saying?"

"You and her."

"In what respect?"

"Together."

"In love? Are she and I supposed to become one? What about Chase? What about Lilith?" My thoughts were thrown into overdrive.

"It's complicated."

"Orifiel, I can accept the fact that the situation is complicated, and I can respect you for not divulging too much information probably because our father has advised against it, but please, brother, answer this. Does Nina love me?"

"Her soul does, deeply, but it needs to be woken."

An uncontrollable smile spread across my lips before reality hit, striking my happiness down. "How? How do I wake her soul?"

"I don't know. That's not my department. That's Mother's line of work, but I can snoop around and see if I can find anything out. In the meantime, Gabriel, this conversation never happened. No one can know about it."

"Of course."

"Sasha made contact with me this morning. He's ready to help Nina. He'll meet you at your place in an hour. I've got to go. I'm on watch duty with Raphael and he gets bent out of shape when I'm late. Come to think of it, our uncle is always pissed off over something."

"No truer words have ever been spoken. Is Vincent still hiding?"

"Aye, and we have no idea why. I thought he would've made a move by now."

"Me, too. Keep me posted."

"I always do," he said, and took off.

Chapter 34

Nina

Great tension remained between Chase and Gabriel. I hated not being able to act friendly with Gabriel when Chase was around, but I had no choice because Chase, despite what he may have said, felt threatened by Gabriel. As time drew on, the two had learned how to tolerate one another, which was good enough for now.

"Nina?" Gabriel asked, knocking on my bedroom door. Since our truce our relationship started to resemble what I'd consider a friendship.

"Come in."

Our training sessions were always exhausting but energizing at the same time. Fighting with Gabriel in pairs was amazing. Granted, I could've lived without the yelling, but it was the final piece to our crazy little trust puzzle.

"What are you doing?" he asked, standing stone still, watching my hands work.

"Healing myself. I need another minute." Though my focus had been placed on the task, Gabriel's stare was hard not to notice. "What?" I asked, once I finished.

"I've never seen you this way."

"I'm sorry?"

"You look beautiful in your true form, as does your gift."

A warm, genuine smile formed on my face. "No one's ever said that before."

"Because they don't understand."

"Show me the real you," I requested. For some unknown reason my soul craved a direct connection to his, but only in his God given, natural state.

Slowly, without a word, he removed his shirt exposing a severely chiseled chest. Maintaining eye contact with me, his back arched and his wings grew. There he stood in all of his exquisiteness. His shimmering skin and vulnerability were exposed to only me.

"What are you thinking?" he questioned.

A trance-like state overtook my brain.

"There are no words, Gabriel," I whispered, moving closer to him. "Will my wings look like this?"

"Yes and no. Yours will appear the same, but they'll be smaller to fit your frame and they'll be positioned higher. Male wings rest mid-spine. Female wings rest on the shoulder blades. The difference is because men can remove their shirts in public spaces, while women cannot. All you'll have to do is lower whatever you're wearing a bit."

"May I?" I asked, giving into the urge to touch him.

The request was greeted with a nod. Gently, my fingers ran through his feathers stopping on a tattoo etched on the nape of his neck.

"What's this?"

The marking resembled a cross with Angel wings.

"It's my military rank in The Heavens. Orifiel has one too, as does Michael, Raphael, and many others. The lines beneath it represent the Sword of Michael intertwined with mine."

"Sword?"

"All Arcs have one. When put together, the Seven Swords are united. We're the seven most powerful Angels in existence led by Michael."

"So, you're pretty important in The Heavens?"

"Depends on who you ask." A faint laugh came out of his mouth.

"And this one?" I pointed to the one on his right wrist which was a crescent moon with a star over it. This particular marking drew me in. It felt familiar and comfortable, almost as if I'd seen it somewhere before.

"It's my symbol."

"Symbol?"

"When you're created, The Powers That Be bestow a symbol upon you. When someone passes, their symbol is revealed and tattooed on their wrist. Everyone has a different one, even your mate. Lilith's, for example, is a lily of the valley. However, it's said that if you can find another soul who shares your exact mark, they're your twin flame. Twin flames are one soul split into two beings. Once you meet, your heart becomes theirs. Your souls become one because the two halves have been reunited at last, creating a whole."

"If Chase and I don't share the same mark, is there someone else out there that we belong to?"

"It's a legend. A story told to give the mate-less ones hope. I don't know of anyone who's actually met their twin flame. Not all couples end up like Lilith and I did. Stop worrying about it."

"Do you have any other tattoos?" I asked, because I couldn't allow myself to perseverate on twin flames any further. If I did, I'd only be giving myself something else to stress out over.

He opened his mouth and touched his tongue to his soft palate. A small, black key was etched under his tongue. "It's a gate key. Anyone who has it has the ability to open and close Heaven's gates. Listen," he said, retracting his wings and putting his shirt back on, "there's someone I want you to meet. He can help us with your visions."

"Who is he?" I questioned, trying not to blurt out, "*I only want your help, not someone else's.*"

"The Angel Sasha. His gift is breaking fourth wall dimension."

"What's that supposed to mean?"

"Lots of things, but for the most part, Sasha can travel within different worlds, like dreams or in your case, visions. He's not a seer but possesses the ability to internally view what's inside of Mortal's and Angel's heads. If we want to see what he can do for us, we need to leave now."

"Okay," I replied, skeptical about having a stranger dig around my dormant prophecies.

"Hey," he started, turning my face and establishing eye contact. "I'd never allow anyone to mess with your mind or harm you in any way, *ever*." His expression was serious.

"I know." What else was I supposed to say? Having Sasha invade my dreams, a personal, private space felt violating and something I didn't wish to endure.

"Tell me about Mortal Gabriel," I said, once we were inside of his car, as a means to distract my inner concern over what the Angel Sasha had up his sleeve for me.

"What would you like to know?" he questioned. His eyes never left the road.

"Everything."

"There's really not much to tell. I died fairly young."

"What did you do before the plane crash?"

"I worked."

"Doing?"

"I was a lawyer."

"*Really?*" I was surprised by his answer. Gabriel didn't seem like the lawyerly type, but in all honesty, Gabriel didn't seem like the anything aside from being an Angel type.

"Yeah, pretty wild. I went to school, studied, passed the bar, and went to work. It was a real blast," he said sarcastically.

"What was your specialty?"

"Family law." His answer was curt and sharp. Obviously, this was a sore topic that was not up for discussion.

"What about Lilith? What did she do?"

"When I met her, she was a waitress. After we were married, she was a housewife, which was common for women back then."

"Dumb question—what's the deal with age in Heaven? How come all of the Angels look so young?"

"I'm young because I died young. My looks didn't change all that much. Michael, for example, was ninety-two when he passed away, but he looks like he's in his forties now. When someone crosses over, their lost beautiful youth is restored."

"How will I recognize my grandparents?" His words were terribly fascinating.

"I can't tell you that, but don't worry. You'll have no trouble finding your family and friends," he reassured.

"Out of curiosity, exactly how old are you?"

"I've been an Angel for many decades, but that's not the answer you're looking for. If I were still Mortal, I'd be about a hundred or so. I died in my early forties. It's not something I ever really think about. The truth is, Mortal age doesn't matter. Birthdays and time aren't a big deal in The Heavens the way it is on Earth. How old do I look?"

"Mid-twenties, but that's based solely off of your looks, *not* the way you speak or carry yourself. It's obvious you're not from this generation."

"Thanks, I think."

"Is Gabriel your real name or did you have another name when you were a Mortal?"

"Gabriel has always been my name. Gabriel Moltisanti to be exact, but in Heaven there's no need for surnames."

"You're Italian?"

"When I was alive, yes, but in The Heavens, skin color, gender, heritage, sexual orientation, and surprisingly enough, religion doesn't matter. I can't fault you for seeing the world the way you do, you're still a Mortal. All of the hate and prejudice seen on Earth isn't present in Heaven. You'll understand what I'm saying one day."

"Do you live with your parents and siblings or alone?"

"Are you asking about me or in general?"

"You."

"I exist with my family."

"When I die, will I see you in Heaven?"

"Maybe. What's with all the questions?"

"Curiosity. Plus, I'd really like to get to know you

better. I feel like you know practically everything about me, and I know so little about you. I'm sorry," I replied, insulted over his annoyance.

Reaching over, he took my hand, and placed it on his thigh. "*I'm* sorry. I know you want answers, but some things can't be shared, only experienced when the time is right. The Mortal version of me is long gone. He doesn't exist anymore. It's also uncomfortable to talk about. I live with Michael, Hadreniel, and Orifiel—my Heavenly family, in The Heavens. When your time comes, I'll find you and we can 'hangout.' I'd rather not discuss my past life right now."

"Can I ask you another question *not* about your Mortal days?"

"Shoot," he said.

"What was Michael's last name and what did he do as a Mortal?"

"Norman. Minister."

"Raphael?"

"Reilly. General practitioner of medicine."

"Hadreniel?"

"Martin. Poet. And before you ask, Orifiel's last name was Lori, and I believe you already know his life story. Game over." He smiled.

"What about their mates?"

"Michael and Hadreniel are Heavenly mates, meaning their souls bonded in The Heavens, and Raphael, like Orifiel, doesn't have one."

"Why?"

"I have no idea. I never asked. Maybe their mates haven't been created yet. We're home. Here. I mean, here," he said, ending the conversation.

Once we were inside of his house, a short-built,

slender man in his early twenties was flipping through television stations while lounging on the sofa. His brown hair was styled perfectly, cropped on the sides and longer in the front. His tan skin shimmered slightly while his coffee brown eyes sparkled. He was dressed like he had just jumped off of the pages of a fashion magazine in trendy, well-coupled clothing. Once he realized he wasn't alone, he sprung up full of energy.

"Hey, hey," he cooed.

"Take it down a notch, or a thousand notches, Sasha." Gabriel sighed.

"Never." He flashed a devious smile. "This pretty little thing must be Nina Luther. You know you're gorgeous, right? Love, love, love those shoes." He pulled me into a tight embrace.

"Hi. Thank you," I said cautiously, unsure of how to respond to his cheery attitude.

"Oh relax, pumpkin. I don't bite. Though, I would bite Gabriel if asked," he whispered as he entwined our arms. "The bedroom, Gabriel?"

Without speaking, but rather shaking his head, Gabriel took us to his room. He drew the curtains and dimmed the lights before taking his usual seat on the chair in the corner.

"Guided meditation or forced rest? Dealer's choice," Sasha asked. He took a moment to roll and crack his neck and fingers.

"Guided meditation. It doesn't take long to get her under—maybe a minute or two."

I stood nervously next to the bed playing with my fingernails not knowing what to expect. Sasha seemed to mean no harm, but would his presence in my visions screw with my head, altering, erasing, or jumbling them up? How would I feel upon waking? Would he make the visions more tolerable or worse? Could he manipulate or restrict them so I couldn't see as much?

"Hey," Gabriel said, standing, and taking my hands in his, "there's nothing to worry about. I'll be here the entire time, angel."

"Promise?"

"I swear."

"Sasha will lie next to you. He's going to hold your hand so he can be present in the vision. You will not see or hear him. He will not interfere in any way. Nothing bad is going to happen," Gabriel assured in the softest voice I'd ever heard him use. His tone was rather reassuring.

I took my place on the bed next to Sasha and closed my eyes tightly.

Here goes nothing.

Chapter 35

Gabriel

Once Nina's eyelids shut, I nodded curtly at Sasha. Most times his presence was too much for me. His gift was phenomenal, but his personality was overwhelming. I was serious, whereas he was the farthest thing from it. Sasha handled situations too lightly, often losing himself in other's worlds. It took Orifiel days to find him this time and quite frankly, if I pulled that crap with Michael, he'd tear me a new one.

"Gabriel," Nina shot up in full panic mode.

"I'm right here," I said.

"Can't you join Sasha in the vision?" Her anxiety levels were sky high.

"I can't, but here." I sat on the floor beside her. "Is this better?"

She inhaled deeply. "Yes."

This seemed to relax her a bit.

Slower than normal I guided her surface thoughts away, freeing her subconsciousness, and allowing for her inner secrets to purge themselves. After a few minutes, Sasha's eyes opened. His pupils scanned the room as he spoke. While in his trance he was able to see nothing, but yet everything at the same time.

"Huge wrought iron gates. She's entering the cemetery. We're focusing on tombstones while walking down a paved path. It's night. Very dark. She's not scared, but not comfortable either. She's forcing herself to keep going. We're moving in a definite direction. It's rather cold; freezing, actually. The vision is starting to fade. I'm going to spin her into another realm within this dream." He paused momentarily.

"We're in. I highly doubt she's aware of what happened. Vincent's around. She senses it. He's pulling her body using some kind of mental force, but he's not touching her. There's laughter. Something's very off about Vincent's face and appearance. I can't put my finger on what's different because she's not fully aware of it herself. She isn't focusing the way I'd like her to. I'm going to try to open a new reality. Maybe I'll be able to get a better look. Wait, hold on." Sasha paused for a second time.

"You're carrying her down a hallway. She's knocked out. You both look like you've been through the wringer. Damn it. She's drowning in a pool of ice water. I think she's in a bathtub. I can't see anything, but I can hear your voice. I'm pulling her out before she gets too lost or dies. We obtained enough this time. Fight the urge to shake her awake, Gabriel."

I watched in terror while Sasha's eyes moved faster and faster from side to side. The few seconds it took for him to bring Nina back to reality seemed like an eternity. In those mere moments I was aware of my entire form and every emotion which resided inside of it. Nina sprang up, gasping for breath. I grabbed her frightened body and held it tightly against mine.

"You're fine and safe, angel. I have you and I won't let go," I kept saying over and over. Her long nails dug into my back.

"You altered the vision," she screamed at Sasha, who stood panting in the corner, completely wiped out from the experience.

"No, I didn't. Your initial vision started fading. Your thoughts were manipulated to travel into another world which existed within the original one. If anything, I evoked a dormant prophecy, allowing you to see more of the future."

"There are more?" Nina asked shocked.

"Hundreds, maybe thousands. I have no freaking clue. You're a far more powerful seer than I expected."

"How do you know that?"

"When I was spinning us out of the first vision, at least twenty additional ones came up. I chose one at random."

"Show me," she demanded.

"I can't."

"Why the hell not?"

"Seers are both helpful *and* dangerous. They're helpful to us, but dangerous to themselves, *especially* when that seer is a Mortal. Humans don't realize they cannot alter fate and what's been dictated by The Powers That Be. Very bad things will happen if that should occur. Right now, all you can do is allow your visions to surface when they so desire. Until then, I will not partake in evoking them."

"Gabriel will," she snapped.

"No, he won't. It doesn't matter how much he loves you. Gabriel knows better because he's aware of the consequences."

His declaration of me loving Nina caught me off guard. What the hell did he see when he was inside of her head besides what he stated?

"Fine," she snarled, pushing me aside. "I'll do it myself."

"You can't." Sasha smiled. "Only I can see them and take you there. Like I said, when the time is right, your subconscious mind will purge everything naturally. The way it should be."

Nina stood in the door frame. Her aura screamed frustration. Her facial expressions were hard, but her eyes were filled with tears. A loud, dark wail exited her mouth. Her fists balled tightly by her sides.

"Angel," I started.

"Don't *angel* me," she barked, storming out of the room and out of the house.

"Let her be," Sasha replied.

Nina's distressed emotions had no effect on him. Sasha could've cared less that his words cut her.

"I can't do that," I replied, annoyed by his apathy.

"You left The Heavens a callous man and will return a weak one. It's clay to stone, Gabriel. Not the other way around."

"Screw you, Sasha." I left the room, slamming the door.

"Don't make promises to Nina you cannot keep," he called after me.

I found Nina pacing angrily outside of my house. Without thinking, I approached her which was an epic error because once I was close enough, she began throwing wild punches in my direction. I didn't speak. I simply allowed her to smack me without defending myself. After a few minutes, she grew tired and fell into my arms.

"I'll take you there or at least try to. I don't know how to evoke buried visions, but we'll figure it out," I whispered while I stroked her long, soft hair. The more I caressed her locks, the more the blend of honeysuckle and lilac could be smelled which, in turn, drove me crazy.

"You will?"

"Yes. I'd do anything for you," I said, immediately regretting my choice of words.

Why did you say that?

"Really? Why?" she questioned, pulling away.

"We're friends, aren't we?" I said rushed.

Please end the conversation with that, Nina.

"Yes. We are friends." She smiled. "When can we start?"

"Let some time pass. Allow things to die down a bit. There are rules I must exist by, Nina. If broken, the consequences are severe. Sasha wasn't lying about that fact."

"I respect that. Just don't weasel out on me."

"That won't happen. I better get you home."

"Will we be working with Sasha again?" she asked hesitantly.

"Maybe. That's up to Michael."

"Can I ask you something?"

"Anything. Always."

"What did Sasha mean when he said that you loved me? Do you?" Her wording was direct and confident, but her aura spoke otherwise.

Honestly, I couldn't get an accurate read on her, but I knew this question had to be answered with extreme caution.

"Of course I do. As a friend."

"I love you too." She smiled coyly and squeezed my hand.

Damn it.

My heart skipped a beat once she uttered those three little, life ruining words.

This is bad. This is very bad.

Chapter 36

Chase

Keeping my inner anger in check became harder by the day. I wasn't an idiot. When Nina started becoming secretive about where she was going and what she was doing, I followed her. She and Gabriel would enter his house and spend the better part of two hours together, *alone*. When they would emerge, he'd drive her home. This occurred almost daily for a few weeks. Jealousy consumed me to the point of sneaking around the perimeter of Gabriel's house. After heightening my sense of sound for a few moments I realized this wasn't a social call, but rather Nina attempting to strengthen her seer ability. I'd thought the worst and now felt foolish, especially when Nina had told Jules during a phone conversation that she was doing this for us, because living without me wasn't an option.

Taking some of the bits and pieces that I overheard from various Angel tête–à–têtes, I sat on my bed with a notebook writing down clues they dropped about Vincent's whereabouts. So far all I knew was he was hiding in a cemetery somewhere near or in Savannah. Figuring out which one proved problematic because several existed around town.

"Chase?" Nina asked, lightly knocking on my bedroom door.

"Hey, baby. What's up?" I closed the notebook and shoved it under my bed. If Nina thought she didn't have to share everything with me, why did I have to with her? What's good for the goose is good for the gander. Besides, much like her, I was doing this for us and our future.

"Have you heard from Jules?" she asked concerned.

"No. Why?"

"Gabriel just texted me. Apparently, Jules called him asking him to come over right away, but when he got there, she wasn't home. Her parents don't know of her whereabouts either. I called her a bunch of times, but her phone must be off because it goes straight to voicemail."

"Do you think something's wrong?"

"I don't know. It isn't like Jules to just vanish."

If Jules Warner said she'd be somewhere at a certain time, she was. If even the slightest chance of her being a minute late arose, she'd call.

My body snapped up as my mind instantly flashed to the shoebox inside of my closet. I had to force myself to remain still and not race to it, while keeping control of my inner emotions. If I didn't, Nina would automatically know something was up.

Sean. No. It can't be. You're stretching. He's in Hell somewhere, not on Earth...or is he? He swore he'd make Jules his one day, but did he mean it? You know he meant it. He was obsessed with her. As a Mortal he was always somewhere between weird, antisocial, and creepy. As a Demon, who knew what effect that had? If Sean is behind this, he'd played his cards well, waiting long enough for everyone to forget about him being gone. Out of sight, out of mind. The perfect time to make a surprise comeback is when no one would suspect it. Shit! How the hell am I supposed to stop this?

"Nina," Ellen called.

"Yeah, Mom?"

"You have a call."

"Who is it?" Nina asked.

Please be Jules.

"It's your brother."

Damn!

"Go talk to Steve. I'll drive around and look for Jules. Don't worry. I'll find her," I assured, kissing the top of her head, and ushering her out of the room as fast as possible.

"Where's Jules?" a voice demanded the moment the door clicked shut.

I spun around in primal defense mode only to find Gabriel standing by the window with his arms folded tightly against his chest. A stoic look was etched across his face. He obviously knew Jules was missing and apparently climbed through the open window in stealth mode.

"No idea," I answered truthfully.

"Try again," Gabriel hissed.

"I. Don't. Know." Honestly, I didn't, and I wasn't about to share my suspicions with this asshole either. Whatever the situation, I'd handle it.

"Really." He smirked.

With one sudden movement, he shoved my body against the wall. With the force of a hundred men, his fingers wrapped around my throat and squeezed. Even with my great inner strength there was no way I'd be able to fight his paralyzing grip.

"One more time. Where is Jules? And don't you

dare say you don't know because your Demonic aura says different."

"The closet," I managed to push out.

"Show me," he barked, releasing his grasp.

After finding the shoebox, I handed it over. Quickly, he flipped through everything in it.

"Do you think Sean took Jules?" I asked, trying not to show any emotion.

"I had Ezekiel stop by the Warner house. He sensed a Demonic presence, but he couldn't accurately say whose. With that in mind, and because Sean is a young Demon, we haven't had an opportunity to formally introduce ourselves to him, but yeah, I do."

"So, because a Demon was at Jules's house I'm automatically a part of it and should be blamed for it?" I snapped.

"I don't trust you. I never have and I never will. A hunch suggested Chase James had his hands all over this and surprise, surprise. You do. All bad roads lead back to Demons."

"The feeling of disdain is mutual."

"I could really care less. Now, shut up. Let's go," he ordered.

"What makes you think I'd do anything with you?" I challenged.

"Do you love your wife?"

"What's that got to do with anything?"

"Can't admit that you love her out loud?" He sneered.

"Of course I love my wife."

"Well, she loves Jules, and if something happens to her, your wife will never forgive you *especially* after I show her this box, tell her what you knew, and how *you* weren't willing to help."

"I'll meet you outside," I snarled through gritted teeth.

****

He drove with no noticeable direction for about a half hour before I finally said something. "Do you have any idea where we're going?"

"No, Chase. I thought a leisurely drive through the sticks of backwoods Georgia would help us to bond and to become best friends. Of course I do," he snapped. "Orifiel's been giving me directions the entire time. We're here." He paused, turning, and locking his eyes on me. "Listen, and listen well. You're to stay behind me. Follow my lead. Head down. Protect your core. It's only us in there. No healers. I have no idea how many Demons are around, nor do I know which ones, other than Sean. We're going in blind. If you decide to help your little Demonic friend, I'll kill you and enjoy every moment of it."

"Let's get one thing clear. There may be a piece of Demon inside of me, but I'm the farthest thing from one."

"Prove it," he challenged. "We go in together and come out the same way. I have your back. Don't make me regret saying that."

Gabriel was fast. Within mere seconds, he'd broken into the extensive space in the middle of nowhere like a career criminal. His eyes glanced from side to side. He seemed rather aware of his surroundings, taking in every last detail.

"He's alone," Gabriel mouthed his silent words.

Without warning, he took off running. I caught up in time to see him lunge at Sean, who was seconds away from pressing his lips to Jules's, thusly making her his eternal Demonic mate. The most primal scream fled Gabriel's throat as he tackled Sean to the ground. I wasn't sure what to do other than grab Jules. An evil look danced across Gabriel's face while he strangled whatever existence was left inside of Sean out.

"Beg, bitch. Beg me not to kill you," Gabriel hissed at Sean in the most psychotic tone I'd ever heard.

"Screw. You," Sean choked out.

"Ah. So, you're looking for a little foreplay," Gabriel replied with an evil laugh. Removing his right hand from Sean's throat, he extracted a military style knife from a sheath he had concealed inside of his boot. Running the silver blade up and down Sean's face and neck seemed like a euphoric experience for Gabriel. No fear existed within him. His actions, words, and behaviors were raw and completely unhinged.

"That little pig sticker isn't going to do a damn thing," Sean taunted.

"I know, but I like to play with my prey before I kill it. Tonight, I'm in the mood to cut your tongue out. Any last words?"

"Don't," Jules yelled.

Gabriel froze in position, but his body still dominated Sean's paralyzed frame. When he looked at her, his eyes softened.

"Please, Gabriel. Don't."

"If you ever come back to Earth or harm Jules, Nina, or Chase, I will find, torture, and finish you. Consider this your one and only lucky day, you filthy piece of worthless trash," he spat, slugging Sean's jaw, then slamming his head against the ground so hard I doubted he would ever wake again.

Grabbing Jules's arm, he dragged her to his car.

"Are you hurt?" Gabriel asked.

"No," Jules answered. Though not physically harmed, emotionally the girl was a wreck.

"Take Jules home. Call Nina. Tell her Jules is fine. Do not under any circumstances share with Nina what happened. You're to tell her you found her at the mall, or the library, or wherever is most believable. I don't care."

"Where are you going?" I asked.

"I have to alert Michael. I'll be back soon."

"Gabriel," Jules began. I could hear stifled horror hidden within her otherwise calm words. "What's going on?"

"You're safe. He will never touch you again. That's all you need to know."

"I have a right to know why I was dragged into this," she demanded.

His head lowered as he sighed heavily. "Apparently the Demon made a deal with Vincent for you."

"Oh my God," she whispered. "Sean just grabbed me when I was coming out of the drugstore. I didn't know it was him until he told me. He looks so different."

"I'm sorry this happened to you. We will discuss this later if you'd like, but right now I have to leave for a few minutes. Chase is here and he will protect you. I trust his ability and judgment. He's going to take you home and wait with you until Orifiel arrives. You've met Orifiel. He's a great guy."

"Okay," she whispered weakly.

"Handle this," Gabriel said, tossing me his car keys, and taking off on foot.

I drove Jules home and stayed until Orifiel arrived,

which wasn't very long. Upon returning to the Luther house, Nina seemed relieved and content after I told her that I found Jules at the local pharmacy. I, on the other hand, hated myself for putting Jules in danger. There were at least a hundred other ways, better ways, I should've dealt with what I knew instead of ignoring it.

It's over and done with now. There's no sense in stressing out over the 'should haves' in life. You know better for the future. Be happy things ended well. Next time the bullet might not be as easily dodged.

Though I still despised the shit out of Gabriel, tonight he earned my respect.

Chapter 37

Nina

December break from school had finally arrived, but there was no reprieve from the daily training with Gabriel. Often, when my family was out, he'd bring Michael and Orifiel along. When present, we could fight in pairs or they would demonstrate a variety of difficult moves. Gabriel appeared different when he was in combat mode. He was more focused and intense. I supposed being in his element brought out that flicker of joy I often saw whenever he delivered a kill shot. He'd show no mercy, acting like battling to the death was the only goal, the ultimate reward.

"Move your ass, Gabriel," Michael yelled. "Faster. Stop wasting time. You took Alva down in under forty-five seconds. Rasha and Samael were dealt with at the same time, clocking in less than one minute. Why is it taking longer than five minutes to defeat Orifiel? Fifty Angels in our Army have to die, including you and me both, before Orifiel could obtain a noteworthy rank." He paused. "Nicely done, Orifiel. War and fighting are an art form. Gabriel has no idea how combat requires great skill and finesse. Wear him out. Use his weaknesses to your advantage. You know what they are."

Both men nodded at Michael taking no offense to his words.

"Come on. What are you waiting for, you *dodgy git*?" Orifiel instigated.

"*Succhiami il cazzo*," Gabriel hissed.

"Oh, I see. You want to do this like Mortals. Well then, bring it, *Bello*."

"Don't ever call me that again."

The two men's bodies became tangled as they rolled on the ground literally beating the crap out of one another.

"Gabriel has weaknesses, Orifiel. Capitalize on them," Michael encouraged.

"You're just trying to show off in front of your *girlfriend*," Orifiel provoked.

"She's not my girlfriend, nor is she a weakness, you filthy pig," Gabriel grunted.

"You could have fooled me, and I am not a *pig*. I was a Scotland Yard detective. Get your facts straight, *consigliere*." Orifiel smirked, getting into position to send a bolt in my direction.

Immediately, my defense mode kicked into high gear. Fully prepared to block whatever was thrown my way, Gabriel lunged, shoving me to the ground, covering my body with his. The Earth shook upon impact.

"Are you okay?" he asked. His eyes and hands scanned my body.

"I'm fine. Orifiel didn't make contact."

"You idiot. You stupid, fucking moron. What the hell is your problem?" Gabriel raged at Orifiel once he was back on his feet.

"Weakness," Orifiel replied, stone-faced.

"If you ever pull that shit again, I will end you. I don't care who the fuck you are. Put one finger on that girl and I will hunt you down and hurt you in ways you could never imagine. You'll think your Mortal death was a day at the park. Do you understand me?"

"Like I'd ever do anything to hurt Nina," Orifiel seethed.

"You're injured," Michael casually noted looking at Gabriel's neck while attempting to diffuse the tense situation.

"Fuck off," he replied angrily, disappearing into my house.

Without thinking, I took off after him. I found him by the front door.

"What's going on?" I asked, taking hold of his forearm. "You can't win every time. Besides, these training exercises are for me to see and know what could possibly happen."

He didn't say anything, but rather looked through me.

"Are you seriously angry over what Orifiel said? He was trash talking to get you going, and guess what? He did. Orifiel would never harm me. The move was purely to distract you."

"You don't understand, Nina. There are boundaries and rules which I'm dangerously close to breaking."

"What are you talking about? What boundaries? What rules?"

"Forget it. I can't do this right now. I have to go."

"Michael said you were injured. Let me heal you."

"No."

"What about meeting up with Sasha later? Is that still on?"

"Not today. I'll see you around," he said, rushing off.

I stood in the foyer not knowing what to think.

Could Gabriel really be that big of a sore loser? What a horrible trait. I made my way to the backyard to see if Michael and Orifiel were still there. Michael had apparently left, but Orifiel hung around.

"Do you want to tell me what's going on?" I asked directly.

"Gabriel's having an off day. I wouldn't worry about it."

"But he's hurt."

"Yeah, so? He's also mentally and emotionally damaged, but we still love him anyway," he quipped.

"I'm not joking around. Be serious, Orifiel."

"He's fine, Nina. Raphael will track him down and do the healing thing later. For now, Gabriel is going to be okay."

"Why did you try to hit me?" I questioned, desperate to know if what I'd said to Gabriel before was true, that the rogue bolt had been a distraction tactic.

"Michael said to target Gabriel's weaknesses, so I did," he replied in a cavalier, very non-Orifiel kind of way.

"This attitude you're rocking right now sucks. I'll see you when I see you," I said, turning around.

"Damn it," he said, grabbing my arm. "Open your bloody, beautiful eyes, Nina. You're Gabriel's *ultimate* weakness."

"Lilith is his ultimate weakness," I defended.

"He'd forsake her for you in a heartbeat."

"Don't say that." This situation was becoming far too complicated. I couldn't handle it.

"Why? It's the truth."

"Stop."

"No."

"Gabriel is hurt because of you, *not* me," I said, breaking free from his hold, sprinting into the house, and closing and locking the door behind me.

Do not dwell on this. Grab your keys and go to the mall. Get lost in holiday shopping and the sights and sounds of the season. Forget this morning ever happened.

After scribbling a quick note to my parents, I texted Chase, and took off. Twenty minutes later, I found myself parking my car and climbing the stairs to Gabriel's house not knowing why. All I was sure of was this was the last place I should be.

So much for not obsessing over everything.

"Gabriel," I said the moment he opened the door.

"Nina." He smiled.

Chapter 38

Gabriel

I was shocked to find Nina standing on the other side of the door. I'd left in a rush after acting like such a jerk. I thought for sure she'd hold a grudge for days until something else to be angry over came about.

"I'll call to Sasha in a little while to tell him not to swing by. If that's why you're here, I'm sorry. I'm not in the mood right now."

"That's not why I'm here. You already told me we wouldn't be doing the seer thing today. I wanted to make sure you were okay."

"I'm fine. Raphael healed me about five minutes ago, but thanks for being concerned. Come in." I led her to the couch, motioning for her to sit.

"What's up?"

"Am I a weakness?" she asked bluntly. Her gaze met mine.

"Yes," I whispered, becoming entranced by the way her eyes changed color more than her aura.

"Why?" Her voice softened to an almost inaudible tone.

"You just are," I said, moving dangerously close to where she sat, unaware of why the draw to this beautiful creature was so powerfully strong.

"More than Lilith?"

"Yes."

"What do you see when you look at me?"

"Everything I need and desire. Am I a weakness?"

"Yes."

"More than Chase?"

"Yes, and I don't know why."

"What do *you* see when *you* look at *me*?"

"All the things I want but can't have."

"Tell me, angel, what do you want?" I asked, brushing a loose strand of hair away from her face, and tucking it behind her ear.

"You," she barely murmured, shocked by her own free-flowing answer.

"You already have that. You've always had that, since day one."

With that declaration, her lips touched mine. The most powerful charge surged throughout my soul, awakening emotions, thoughts, and feelings which I hadn't experienced in decades. Pain vanished. Suffering and misery seemed like a distant memory from a long-lost past. I wanted more than the few harmless, innocent pecks she gave me. I needed to take her in my arms and further what we were doing, desperate to see how much stronger Nina could make me. Controlling my inner self proved to be a difficult task.

Finally, Nina broke and made the bolder move. All of my will unraveled. The way she made me feel—alive, almost Mortal again was too good to lose. Rolling her on her back, I climbed on top, pulling her closer with each kiss. Nina's touch drove me insane. The intensity created a fire so out of control, I wasn't sure if it could ever be extinguished. I had no idea how long we carried on for before I lifted her off of the couch. Her legs tightly wrapped around my waist as I made my way to the bedroom, not allowing the kissing to pause, not even for a second. I wasn't sure what would happen once the hold broke. Her soft sounds, long nails clawing into my back—I could barely breathe. There was no way in hell I'd let go of her now. Especially not after this. All things logical flew out the window as clothing carelessly dropped on the floor.

"You're gorgeous," I said in between kisses.

"You're beyond," she replied. The words tripping off of her tongue.

I couldn't help myself from staring at her body. She, Nina Luther, the most beautiful Angel in existence, was here, in my bed, with me.

"Don't stop," she whispered, tugging me back down.

If I hadn't been so caught up in the moment, I would've realized she, like I, was being driven not by free will, but rather by an uncontrollable force.

"Never," I mumbled, knowing this was wrong. We were both married and from vastly different worlds. It could never be. We could never be. "What happens next, angel?"

"Everything, Gabriel. I want you. I want us, and I know you want the same."

"I do," I said, positioning my body so we could become one.

"Knock, knock…oh lord. I'll come back later…much later," Sasha said, taken back by what he'd seen, and stopping us dead in our tracks seconds before Nina and I could never go back to being friends, or whatever the hell we were.

Our shared connection instantly broke. She pushed

me away faster than I could move. She grabbed at her discarded clothing and clutched it tightly against her chest as she retreated to the farthest corner of the room where she stood wiping her lips with the back of her hands as if the thought of what just happened disgusted her.

"I was choking," Nina practically screamed at Sasha. "And, he was helping me," she added, quickly dressing herself.

"All right. So, what you're saying is, Gabriel, in his boxer briefs, was performing the ever so popular, but yet practically unheard of *frontal* Heimlich maneuver on you, while you were in your underwear as well. And this was all happening while you were both lying down in bed? Is that the story you *really* want to stick with? Personally, I would've gone with the I-was-giving-Gabriel-the-kiss-of-life-even-though-he's-been-dead-for-a-billion-years excuse, but that's just me." He shrugged. "Shall we begin?"

"It wasn't like that," Nina snapped.

"Oh, sweetie, I could care less. Calm yourself. Your secret is safe with me. Now, let's get started. I haven't got all day."

Flustered and embarrassed, Nina pushed past Sasha and headed for the bathroom. Once she was out of earshot, I grabbed Sasha's shoulder.

"Erase the memory when you're inside of her head. I know you're not supposed to, but I know you can and will."

"Everyone has moments of indiscretion, Mortal or Immortal. What happened, or at least the few seconds that I saw, seemed like two, mutually consenting adults enjoying each other's company, passion, and bodies.

There's no crime in that. Sure, you're not supposed to share intimacies with a Mortal, but if you don't tell, I won't either."

"If you hadn't arrived, I don't know how far we would've gone. Sasha, please, erase the memory," I pleaded in a tone I hardly ever used.

The look on Nina's face once she realized what had happened disturbed me. I couldn't let her walk around carrying the weight of it on her shoulders. She had other things to worry about. Besides, her reaction reflected a woman who was repulsed by my touch. It reminded me of Lilith toward the end of our time together.

"From the looks of it I'm pretty sure you and Nina would've made the beast with two backs, but if that's what you want, consider it gone. When Nina wakes, she won't remember a thing. She'll think we're here for our session." He paused to study my face. "I'm sorry the desired reaction wasn't received. It hurts, but Mortals are off limits anyway. Consider what happened a stolen, unexpected gift."

"I don't care about me. I only give a damn about Nina and her happiness. She has a mate and a strong, solid chance of experiencing Earthly bliss. That's something I never really had."

"You'll find happiness again, Gabriel. At times it might seem like such an emotion doesn't exist, but it's out there. Things didn't go as planned with Lilith. So what? You'll find someone else. I'm sure of it. You're a good-looking guy. There are many Angels who'd jump at the opportunity to be with you fulltime, not just for one of your standard one-night stands."

"There's this force, Sasha. It keeps drawing us together. That wasn't the first time it's happened."

"You've been fooling around with Nina? I haven't seen that memory play out in her subconscious past."

"Today was the first time I've touched her *like that*. We kissed and screwed around a bit some months back, but before it could turn into anything more, Orifiel arrived. The pull has been there since we met. Orifiel is aware of something Michael refuses to make public. Their lips are sealed. It's driving me crazy."

I had no idea why I shared such an intimate detail of my existence with him. Sasha and I were never what you'd consider close, or even friends for that matter. We hardly worked together, and we never hung out socially. We'd pass each other in The Heavens. That was it.

"But you believe I will? You think I'll tell you what's going on inside of Nina's head, *then* get inside of yours to confirm everything?"

"Yes."

"Oh, pumpkin, you know me too well. I'm going to need a stretch of deep rest to get lost in her thoughts. See if she'll allow me to stay while she sleeps. That should give me enough time to uncover her divine path and plan. I'll need the same from you. We can go from there."

I knew he'd be willing to break the rules. He was a dream junkie who loved getting lost within other people's worlds. The more drama he found, the more inebriated he'd become. Every hidden secret made him stronger. There was no way Sasha could resist such a tempting offer, especially since I agreed to welcome him into my otherwise closed-off world.

"This stays between us, because if it doesn't and Michael finds out, what happened earlier between you and Nina will somehow find its way back into her pretty little head," Sasha warned, then disappeared into the bedroom.

Maybe now I'd get to the bottom of whatever the hell was disrupting my otherwise comfortably miserable existence. It was doubtful, but this plan was better than nothing.

Chapter 39

Nina

"Okay, pumpkin. Lay down and let's get started." Sasha snickered. "I never thought I'd say that to a girl," he added, looking in my direction. "That was a joke. You know, a joke? Something said to be funny? It's funny because I'm gay and like guys and you're a girl."

I didn't know how to react. Who cared if he was gay? Certainly not me. He could've been an androgynous being and it wouldn't have mattered. I'd almost had sex with Gabriel. That disturbed and horrified me to my core. Gabriel, a man who wasn't my mate. A man who caused such internal confusion. Sasha preferring men to women was the least of my worries.

"It's okay to laugh, Nina. Nothing bad happens when you do."

I still couldn't speak. My brain kept replaying the past hour's events. What was I doing? What had I done? Who was I? An anxiety attack immediately struck me. My entire body flushed outwardly with a cold sweat. A tightness in my chest suffocated my lungs. The world detached from reality, allowing the flight side to win the war. Turning for the door, I bolted, but I didn't make it past the hallway because of Gabriel.

"I'm so sorry, angel, but I'm going to right the wrong, okay? Trust me and have faith that I'll fix this. If you run away, I can't do anything to make it better," he whispered.

"Do you not remember what we did?" How could this man be at ease, in control, and relaxed at a time like this?

"It's kind of hard to forget something like that, but panicking will get us nowhere."

"How are you going to make this okay?" I asked, half pushing, half clinging to his torso.

"Never doubt me. If I say I'm going to do something, consider it done," he assured, leading me back to his bed. "Lie down and allow Sasha to do his thing. When you wake, you'll feel amazing. I swear."

"High strung much?" Sasha quipped sarcastically.

"Cut her some slack. Do your job," Gabriel urged.

Sasha took his usual position beside me, intertwining our fingers. "Let's have some fun. Sleep," he said, and with that, my eyelids dropped.

The space faded allowing for a visionless, dreamless, peaceful slumber to blanket my consciousness.

****

"Wake," Sasha instructed.

Slowly my eyes opened. To be honest, that had been the best rest I'd ever had, but it concerned me that not one single vision had occurred.

"There were no dreams. Why?"

"Just because you're a seer doesn't mean you'll see images every time. Even Trinity has blank moments."

"Ugh, Trinity," I mumbled under my breath.

"You don't like her?" Sasha snorted.

"I don't really know her," I said quickly to defuse the situation. I wasn't sure if he and her were friends or not, and I certainly didn't want to make any waves.

"I don't like her much either. She thinks she's so deep and oracle-like, but her head is empty and boring. Yours is way more fascinating."

"Who gives a shit about Trinity? Nina, what happened when you came over here earlier?" Gabriel asked. He came across as anxious and stressed out.

"You let me in, and we talked until Sasha arrived." What an odd question.

"What did we talk about?"

I thought for a few moments, but I couldn't remember a thing about our conversation. "I'm sorry, but I can't recall. Was it important? I know I stopped by unexpectedly because you were injured during our training session. I wanted to heal you, but you said that Raphael already had. You were pissed off that Orifiel had beaten you, but that's all I got."

"Yes, that's exactly what happened. I'm only asking you because sometimes when seers don't experience visions they might suffer a short-term lapse of memory, but you seem okay," he said, seemingly relieved.

"I feel fine actually. That was a great nap. How come you didn't use guided meditation?"

"Rarely do I use meditation when I'm trying to get someone to fall asleep. Over time, I've strengthened my ability to the point where my presence and touch alone can cause a Mortal or Immortal to sleep. Gabriel doesn't possess this gift, which is why he had to find another way to get you to relax. When we started working together, I used Gabriel's method because you were most comfortable with it. I needed you to trust me. Now we know one another. Plus, my way is quicker and easier. Watch," Sasha said. He rose off of the bed and approached Gabriel. As light as a feather, he ran his slim fingers down Gabriel's forehead and over his eyes. "Sleep." He spoke softly.

Instantly, Gabriel's body fell into the armchair he stood in front of.

"See?" Sasha paused. "Wake," he instructed, making the same motion over Gabriel's eyes. Gabriel's figure sprang back to life. "No damage, right, Gabriel?"

"None at all," he replied, forcing a smile.

"My work here is done, for today at least." Sasha yawned while stretching like a cat.

The brief nod exchanged between Gabriel and Sasha suggested something was off which raised a red flag. While I was out perhaps an issue occurred?

What if they stole your visions? What if this whole 'sleep' and 'wake' business is Sasha's way of erasing your memories?

"I can't steal anything from you, sweetie. All of the visions stored inside of you remain in place, but like Gabriel said before, seers draw blanks from time to time. It's no big D," Sasha said.

"You can read minds too?" I snapped.

"No, but I can read people, especially ones I've visited in their sleep. Look, pumpkin, go home. Enjoy the freedom from school. Decorate a tree, hang a stocking, raid the mall, but stop obsessing about this other world. Let the visions come naturally. If you don't, they'll be foggy and nondescript. They'll make no sense. Stop trying to control the gift, because this one you can't. This ability tells *you* what to do, *not* the other way around. There's an attractive man waiting at your house *for you*. Stop wasting time and go be with him. That's what I'd be doing...figuratively *and* literally."

For the first time since meeting him, Sasha actually made sense.

"You're right. Thanks."

"I'm always right, terribly misunderstood, but *always* right," he joked. He proceeded to hug me, then he led us to the front door. "I'll see you after the holidays. Michael requires my presence elsewhere. In the meantime, should you have a vision, tell Gabriel immediately. He'll be able to communicate with me directly." He leaned closer. "Hey, have you and Gabriel ever fooled around beyond that Halloween faux pas? And, chill. I won't tell a soul. There's a code I must live by that's been dictated by The Heavens. Part of it pertains to the total privacy of those I've worked with."

"No. Why?"

"I was just wondering what it would be like to engage in a fling with the gorgeous Archangel." He flashed a bright boyish grin.

"Well, good luck with that because I'm pretty sure he's into girls, not guys."

"A boy can dream, you know." He winked.

As I drove home, Sasha's words resonated. Lately, all I'd been seeing were foggy, random images. The only logical explanation had to be that I'd been forcing them and hyper-focusing too much on them, not allowing for nature to organically take its course. My fear of Vincent had to be pushed aside. Once that happened, perhaps then, crisp, accurate visions would return. The problem? Each vivid dream I had, had Vincent inflicting pain *on me*, destroying everything in his path. Shoving that away and quieting my thoughts was almost impossible, but it had to be done.

By the time I'd parked my car and entered my house,

I promised myself that I'd stop stressing over my gift. I needed to ease up on it and in turn, it would predict the future—I hoped.

Chapter 40

Chase

Even though I fully trusted Nina, her family, and for the most part Gabriel, I'd still find myself sneaking around and digging for anything unusual. I kept a watchful eye on Gabriel, Orifiel, and the other Angels when they were patrolling outside of the house. Though, to the naked eye, my behaviors may have appeared crazy, a small part of me knew something greater than all of us combined was going on. The burning desire to know exactly what consumed me.

At random I'd follow Nina to Gabriel's house for her seer training sessions. Initially, it was only the two of them. However, recently, a new person appeared regularly. This drew me to investigate the situation further. Though Nina had finally shared with me that she was working on strengthening this gift, a part of me still felt ill at ease. Taking my usual spot behind a heavily tree-covered area beside Gabriel's house, I enhanced my sense of sound. Bits and pieces of their conversations allowed for me to realize that this Angel, Sasha, could somehow break into Nina's dreams. He would get Nina to fall asleep, then he'd share what he saw with Gabriel. Often, even with my supersonic hearing abilities, I couldn't make out complete sentences. They had to have been communicating through Angelic telepathy. After a few times of spying, it became evident that this Sasha character was gay, which comforted me enough to end my stalking.

Most days when Nina trained at the house I'd watch because I still didn't like it when Gabriel was around Nina alone. The way he looked at her didn't sit well with me. Sometimes I'd have no choice but to leave the house because of school. Those days worried me the most, causing me to lack concentration. Though I was confident Nina would never touch another guy, something wasn't right between the two of them.

I lay on my bed jotting down notes, frustrated that I wasn't any closer to finding Vincent. I scoped out several smaller neighboring cemeteries, assuming he'd want to hide somewhere out of public view, but I came up empty each time. With no one to ask for help, because no one would provide it, this became a solo mission. Finals forced me to put my personal problems aside. Once the New Year began, I'd pick back up where I'd left off. Perhaps the break would free my mind, allowing for things to gel.

I thought the Jules/Sean situation might cause some sort of negative emotions within me, but it didn't. There should've been some kind of relief or sadness, but it never came. When I arrived home that night, I sat on the steps waiting for Gabriel.

Once he arrived, I didn't say much other than that Jules was okay and Orifiel was with her. However, it was what he offered that provided me with great comfort. He told me to forget about what happened. To not allow it to resonate. Sean being a Demon made him the enemy. The version I'd befriended no longer existed, and never would again. Maybe it was his understanding words, or my own Demonic side, but I hardly thought about that incident, probably because part of me was scared to. I was afraid that the Demon inside of me would slowly start surpassing the Angelic portion, and at some point, would take over completely.

Full blown panic attacks would strike whenever I'd think about myself as a Demon. My palms would sweat. My heart would pound. Invading racing thoughts made me want to scream at the idea of harming someone and the consequences that went along with it. I wanted to lock myself in my room, getting as far away from everyone as possible. I kept rope under my bed in case I had to tie my hands together so I couldn't hurt a soul. Sometimes, I didn't know what to do with myself. The edginess consumed me causing me to suffer from severe manic moments. I'd try to calm down by getting lost in an activity which would force my mind to focus only on that. Sometimes it worked, sometimes it didn't. When it didn't, I'd make myself lie down and breathe. I'd remind myself that this was an anxiety attack, and anxiety was only a series of irrational thoughts, therefore the idea of becoming a Demon was foolish.

For days after, I'd feel shaky and hated being alone with Nina or her family. I was terrified I'd blackout and hurt them. I always pulled through though and I found creative ways to avoid them. School was a good excuse to be alone. They'd think I was studying, not hiding. If I spoke the words out loud, the Luthers would believe I'd gone crazy, or perhaps worse. Don't get me wrong, there were good parts sprinkled in. Once my mind voided the stupid ideas I was totally fine and completely content, but I was always fearful the bad views would return, and tragedy would ensue.

"What are you stressing out about?" Gabriel asked one afternoon as I exited my car.

"Nothing," I replied dismissively. I wasn't in the mood for him or his heaping bag of bullshit.

"Really? I suggest trying again because in case you've forgotten, I can read your aura."

"I'm good. Seriously."

Gabriel examined my face and body for a few seconds before continuing. "You're scared," he said flatly.

"Fine. I'm stressed out and terrified. Happy?" I snapped.

"No. Why?"

I had a choice. Purge my emotions to a man I didn't care much for or keep quiet. Part of me thought talking about the anxiety might help, but the other part disagreed.

"You're having panic attacks, aren't you? Does this have anything to do with Sean?" Gabriel questioned.

"No."

He studied my entire being for a second time. "Your Demonic side won't come out unless you allow it to. You control it, Chase. It does not govern or define you on its own. Everyone has a Demonic component attached to them. I'm a full Angel and there's still evil inside of me. How else could someone explain how I do what I do without regret, remorse, or doubt? A switch doesn't suddenly flip inside of your head that makes the Demon wake and do bad things. It has to be wanted and willed. There's no such thing as a blackout moment where you go nuts and start hurting those around you. From time to time, we all blow our cool. Maybe we throw something, shout, say regrettable things, or punch a wall, but we don't lose our sanity or perception of what's right and wrong. Those dark thoughts in your head, you've put them there and you need to do whatever necessary to erase them. Once you do, you'll be fine.

"I'm a Demonic assassin. I've destroyed thousands of them in unimaginable ways. When I first started, I thought I'd turn into a monster, but I didn't because I control me, and I learned to separate the job from who I am. When I'm on a mission, my focus is on that. When I'm not, my focus is on me. The two worlds never meet. I force myself to forget about my assignments the second they're over. I do know and understand what's going on inside of your head. I've been there. It takes time to find balance and you will, but, Chase, before that can happen you must let it all go. Focus on being a husband, a student, a son, a friend, and stop worrying about your other world. I have your back and I've got you covered."

"What if I lose it one day and the Demonic side takes over? What if I'm not strong enough to keep pushing it back? It's happened, Gabriel. Last year I almost succumbed to it."

"You're not going to and yes, you're strong enough to do anything you put your mind to. After Lilith left me, my entire soul hardened and turned black. I loved her. I still do. Being without her affection is the most painful thing I've ever endured. There were days when all I wanted to do was not exist. Other days, I'd go crazy on anyone around me; it didn't matter who. One night, I lost it, and completely trashed my space. I broke and I'd done nothing to stop it. If anything, I did everything to welcome it. I didn't talk to anyone about what I was experiencing or share that the weight on my shoulders was crushing me, nor did I find a suitable outlet to channel my hatred. When Orifiel entered my space to stop me, I struck him so hard I hurt him, bad. It took Raphael almost three days to heal him. Orifiel forgave me, but I never forgave myself. It was in that moment that I realized what I'd become. I harmed someone I loved, someone who wanted to help me. That was my turning point. I talked to Michael, and he showed me how to turn a negative into a positive. I'd allowed my inner pain to get out of control, but you don't have to. Reach out to whomever, even me. I'll listen and do whatever I can to guide you back to the path you strayed from. Just do something, anything, to get this heaviness off of your back."

"No offense, and I do appreciate what you're trying to do here, but when you were attacking Sean, you looked like an absolute lunatic. Your advice, though rational, is kind of difficult to accept when it's coming from you."

"I'm sure I did. I'm also confident I sounded like one as well. But that's the secret. That's the trick. In those moments when I'm fulfilling my calling, I use all of my pent up fury for good. The world needs to be saved from Demons. When I'm eliminating them, if I happen to be a little too aggressive or allow myself to let loose and enjoy it, who cares? My actions benefit The Heavens and Earth, so why can't I profit from it as well? You could do the same. It works. I promise."

"Why are you telling me this?"

"Because Nina needs and loves you. When someone feels a certain way about another person, that person can't act uncaringly because they're relied heavily upon. It's not a burden, but rather a priceless gift. Lilith desperately wanted something from me. I tried to give it to her, but eventually I gave up for selfish reasons. I regret that decision. However, hiding and feeling scared of being near Nina is only going to drive her away. You don't want that. Happiness is a thing of the past for me, but not for you. Learn from my mistakes."

"I need time away from everyone and everything."

"There's no such thing. You're a husband and have responsibilities. You've got to man up. Face your demons head on."

"Great," I said sarcastically.

Once again, he backed away and thoughtfully assessed my body. "Do you want to call it off with Nina?"

"Who said that? All I said was I needed to take a break from this life."

"You may not be saying the words, but it's what your aura wishes for."

"Fine. I've thought about it."

"Listen really well, Chase. If you dump that girl, it will be the biggest mistake of your Mortal *and* Immortal life. Nina is the entire package—beauty, brains, and then some. She loves you *despite* your soul connection. If she were my mate, I'd never, *ever* let her go. But hey, if you're tossing her aside, I'll gladly take her off of your hands. I can show her how a *real* man behaves when he's faced with adversity."

Getting on my feet, I grabbed hold of the front of his shirt. I was seething with rage, but the urge to strike him was repressed.

"Nina's *mine*, *not* yours, or anyone else's. She'll always be mine. If you ever touch her, I'll destroy you," I warned.

"If you don't dismiss the *best* thing in your world,

you'll never have to worry about me or anyone else. Besides, that quick moment of anger says it all. It should tell you everything you need to know," he spoke calmly, flicking my fists away, and straightening his shirt.

"Son of a bitch," I mumbled. He'd tested me to show me how much of an ass I'd been lately.

"Reality checks are helpful." He smirked.

Though Gabriel didn't possess mindreading skills, the fact that he could see my inner emotions and thoughts shocked me. Aura reading was apparently more powerful and useful than I had initially expected. His arguments were comforting and reassuring. Compared to his existence, mine was pretty damn good. My focus needed to remain on that. Nina and I had to work on being Mortals first, and I had to stop obsessing over our other world. Once that happened, peace would return, and the chance of me living a normal, anxiety free life might be possible.

"Thanks, man. That actually helped."

"Good. I meant what I said. You can always talk to me. What's discussed will remain between us. You have my word that I will do whatever I can to make sure you're okay. I'm not the enemy, Chase. I have no intention of ever hurting you." His smile resembled a small, plastered grin. "You perceive me as the bad guy because we're two alpha males. What you're forgetting is that we're fighting the same war, but for different end games. You, for your future. Me, for revenge."

"Truce?"

He nodded and extended his right hand. Willingly, I accepted his gesture.

"Chase, every day we're invited to start a new chapter. Toss the book you've been writing in. Begin a fresh one. You *and* Nina deserve it."

Chapter 41

Gabriel

As if dealing with my own personal hell wasn't enough, I not only had Michael, but now Jack Luther on my ass. This seemingly boring job had turned into a production. I hated complications, but more than anything, I despised living as a Mortal.

Mortals showed compassion and a range of other emotions on a daily basis, something I wasn't comfortable with. The more time I spent on Earth, the more my old days and ways rose to the surface. Giving a shit about Chase James was a prime example of this.

Perhaps it was the affection stolen from his wife, or the idea of knowing what he was going through mentally, or my brain believing that I was alive again, but I felt obligated to say something to him to alleviate some of his tension. When I finished speaking with Chase, the oddest sensation crept inside of my core. I'd helped him and I didn't even like him—something Mortal Gabriel would've done. Mortal Gabriel was a good man. Archangel Gabriel wasn't. He was a cold, shallow, heartless, emotionless shell of a past life. I liked it that way, but Nina screwed all of that up for me.

Damn it. Forget about the girl. She's married and alive, unlike you who's very much so dead.

Fooling around with Nina had changed everything.

Processing the event and trying to decide if what happened was for the best or not still occurred daily.

"Are you even listening?" Orifiel asked.

"Huh?" I answered, annoyed that I wasn't alone to relive kissing Nina over and over again via an amazing memory. Though Sasha erased the moment for her, it was still active for me. That single chunk of time caused happiness—a Mortal feeling that refused to leave my core. When my eyes closed, her soft skin against my rough hands, the smell of her lilac and honeysuckle shampoo filling my senses as strands of her hair brushed against my face, and the taste of her strawberry lip gloss haunted and teased me to the point of insanity. A spark of life had imbibed my dead soul because of one experience.

"What I said was, Michael said you can return to The Heavens for a while to rest before we go after Vincent. He wants you ready for anything. I'll stay on Earth and watch after Nina." He stared at me. "Where are you?"

"Right here. There's no reason for me to return to The Heavens. I'll be good to go whenever I'm needed."

"Where's your head at, brother? You're off. That's not like you. What are you thinking about?"

"Nothing."

"Liar," he shot back. He moved to the window behind the couch and opened it. A smile spread across his face as he gazed at the stars. "It happened," he whispered in a sing-song style voice.

"What happened?"

"You and Nina," he marveled, still examining the early night sky.

"I don't know what you're talking about."

"Keep lying. That's totally fine. You still have your wings, so you didn't make or profess love to her, but something strong definitely went down between the bonded ones."

"I'm not talking about this," I said quickly, heading for the door.

He seized my wrist and spun me around aggressively. Our eyes locked. Orifiel's normally kind, soft irises were hard and full of tension.

"Tell me what transpired," he demanded.

"Tell me why and I'll share every last detail," I challenged.

"The stars shifted from their original position. Now I can't get an accurate read. I need to know what you did so I can piece it together and try to figure out what's to come," he answered.

"Is Nina in danger?"

I never placed much stock in the stars or their placement, but Orifiel seemed concerned, he was borderline hysterical actually, which manufactured a mutual fear.

"Just tell me. I swear I won't breathe a word of this to our father."

"Nina showed up here, unannounced and uninvited. I let her in. I don't remember exactly how it happened, but we started fooling around. One thing led to another, and we ended up in bed together, only to be interrupted by Sasha. If he didn't walk in when he did, we would've slept together. There's a good chance I would've lost my wings, and it would've been worth it. I had Sasha erase Nina's memory of it. If Nina were questioned about what happened, she'd have no recollection of the incident. The look on her face once she realized what we'd done, coupled with the fact that we're both married drove me to ask Sasha to do it. She seemed disgusted and couldn't get away from me fast enough. It brought back memories of how Lilith did the same thing toward the end of our marriage; like the thought of my touch was repulsive. I didn't want to relive that, especially not with Nina."

A bright smile found its way back to his face. "Nina's happiness means more to you than your own. You didn't want her soul to falter and become consumed with stress. By erasing the time block, her soul regenerated. Celestial balance is off because she doesn't remember. The stars will realign accordingly in time."

"The stars and their placement foretold what Nina and I were going to do?" I scoffed.

"Yes. In the near future, she's going to need you and will lean on you more than anyone in her world. You, and you alone, will breathe life back into Nina two times that I can see now. The stars tell a lot, Gabriel."

"What else do you see?"

His words spiked my curiosity. The thought of Nina and I sharing a closer bond was thrilling, yet nerve-racking in the same breath.

"I don't see anything else, *currently*. The stars need to fall back into proper place, but, Gabriel, whatever you do, do not allow Sasha to erase any more of her memories. If the stars shift too much, they'll cross. No good has ever come of that. Promise me, brother."

"I swear. Did I cause any damage?"

"No. A few movements won't affect much, but constant changes will. So, how was it?" He grinned.

"What do you think?" I smirked. "I've got to go. Jack Luther wants to speak with me. I'll catch you later."

With that I headed over to Nina's house hoping

she'd be home. Spotting her car in the driveway, I smiled.

Jack opened the door and led us to his office.

I stood in front of his desk with my arms tightly folded across my chest. I had no idea what he wanted, but I prayed it wasn't anything serious.

"I hear you're working with Nina on her seer ability. How's that going?"

"Fine, but I think asking her about this would be more beneficial. There's really not much to tell you other than the visions are usually the same, very primitive and nondescriptive. Honestly, I'm not even sure of their accuracy. The only thing causing an eyebrow to raise is the cemetery setting, which is where we've located Vincent. However, our Army is on it and Nina is unaware of that specific detail."

"What does Michael say?"

"Nothing really. Just to keep an eye on Nina. No one can stop the visions, but the environment in which she views them in can be controlled. For now, everything is calm. The Angel Sasha guides her through the dreams, pulling her when he believes she's seeing too much. Nina hasn't asked many questions. She seems to be accepting the images for face value."

"Does Nina know about the connection between Vincent and the cemetery?"

"Like I said before, no. She's more focused on Vincent than the cemetery."

"She's a smart girl and she will start inquiring about it sooner or later. How do we answer her when this occurs?"

"When the time comes, we'll figure it out. There's no sense in stressing out over it now. Vincent hasn't made a move. He's still hiding in the same place. Michael's been watching him closely. If and when Vincent switches things up, we'll know. The entire Army, myself included, is ready to go at a moment's notice. Before I take off, is there anything else?"

"Ellen and I will be going away for the night. We will be coming home tomorrow morning. Should we cancel our plans?"

"Nina is heavily guarded at all times. I assure you that she's safe. Should anything come up, we'll be in touch."

"Thank you," he said, opening the door.

Nina stood at the end of the hallway. Trying to avoid eye contact was a difficult task. My heart raced. My palms grew clammy. The world around me made no sense.

"Are you okay?" she asked.

"Yes. No. I don't know," I stuttered. "Orifiel is going to watch you," I added, bolting for the door.

To my great surprise, I found Orifiel waiting for me on the porch.

"Did the stars tell you to come here?" I snapped.

"No. The fact that I'm your brother, know you well, and love you did. Go home. I've got this."

Pure adrenaline coursed through my empty veins. Pacing, my hands ran constantly through my long hair pulling at it tightly. I wasn't sure what to do or where to go.

"Brother, what's the matter?" Orifiel asked, stopping my motions by taking hold of my shoulders.

"That brief moment of lust, or passion, or whatever the hell it was is screwing with me. I want her. I need her. I have to have her now," I practically shouted.

"Should I call to Father or Raphael?"

"No. Don't. What are they going to do? Nothing. That's what. They'll tell me I'm crazy when I'm not. I swear, brother, I'm not. This is real."

"I believe you. Let's take a breath and slow down. Tell me what you're thinking and feeling. Can we try that?"

"Every ounce of restraint is being drawn upon to not run into that house, drag Nina out of it caveman style, and get high off being intimate again. Orifiel, I *need* to make love to her. You have no idea how good, how alive, she makes me feel, and I'm not talking about in a sexual way either. Without Nina, I'm lost—desperately hopeless. Like a part of me is missing. I was barely able to control myself before tasting her and now that I have, I can't. I'm terrified of what might happen if we're alone again, but I would do anything for it."

"Stop," he ordered, turning in a defensive stance.

I followed his lead and did the same.

"Orifiel?" Nina whispered.

"Aye."

"Can we talk?"

"Can it wait?"

"Yeah, sure. Oh, hey again, Gabriel. I thought you left." Her smile glowed in my direction.

"I can't do this," I said, ripping at my shirt and transforming.

"Are you sure you're okay?" Nina questioned.

"No. I'm not. You're driving me crazy. Go away and stay away," I snapped, taking off, and landing directly on the front steps of my house. Twisting the door handle roughly, the lock snapped in my hand.

"Hello, son. Close the door and sit down. We *need*

to talk," Michael said calmly, glancing up from the book in his hand.

Damn it!

Chapter 42

Nina

"What did I do?" An unnaturally strong desire to cry swept over me.

"Nothing. Absolutely nothing. Gabriel's under a lot of pressure and needs a little break before he loses the plot. It's hard for us Angels to live as Mortals for extended periods of time. He'll be fine and will return shortly. What's up?"

"Loses the plot?"

"Stops acting rationally."

"He seemed mad at me—more than usual."

"He's not. I promise. His soul requires rest. Angels get cranky too."

For the first time I saw Orifiel and Gabriel for what they were; dead. They were so Mortal-like it was difficult to remember they were Angels. For the second time today, this weird surreal feeling overtook my awareness. It felt as if I was an outsider looking in on my own life.

"All right. I hope he feels better soon," I said, turning to head back to the house.

"Hey. You said you wanted to gab. What's up?"

"Should I check on him? If I said or did something, I'd like to apologize. If there's another issue, maybe I could help. Gabriel means a lot to me. If anything were to happen to him…I don't know what I'd do. What if he leaves again? No, he can't. I thought we were okay," I said, speaking my inner monologue aloud.

Something strange occurred at Gabriel's house earlier, but I couldn't remember what. Not being able to recall it was irritating. Being around him would jog my memory. It had to, right?

"My brother is fine. He's a touch stressed out and in desperate need of a kip, but he'll be fine straight away. What's going on with you?"

"Kip?"

"A nap. Go on," he said, his right hand waved the conversation forward.

"My parents are heading out for the night and Chase is staying with his parents."

"Did he move back home?"

"No. Some out of town family is visiting for a few days before Christmas. Blanche begged him to spend some time there so their family will think everything is okay. She sprung it on him last minute. Chase had no choice."

"And? Because that's not the only reason you're out here." Orifiel winked.

"You know how I'm working with Sasha, right?"

"Aye."

"Well, I didn't experience a vision during our last session, and Sasha and Gabriel were acting weird afterwards. I can't remember much of the afternoon after arriving at Gabriel's house to when Sasha put me under. That's a two-hour chunk of missing time."

"Don't stress it. When seers go into a trance and don't experience a vision, short-term memory loss is a very common side effect. Can you remember events that happened after waking and occurrences prior to the lost two hours?"

"Yes."

"You're fine. I'd forget it."

"That's what Gabriel and Sasha said." I smiled, feeling better. Orifiel's validation was just what I needed. "Thanks for saying that. I'm going to head back inside. Is there any way I could persuade you to join me?"

"In a little while." He laughed lightly. "Until then, if something comes up, call to me."

A few hours later, after an epic argument with Chase, who now wasn't coming home for Christmas, I found myself falling asleep while rereading one of my favorite books. Exhaustion due to my consuming inner anger caused the abrupt crash. Sadly, I was no stranger to this concept. Out of necessity I allowed sleep to enter without fighting it only to find myself square in the middle of the cemetery which had been haunting my visions. The images flashed too rapidly to make any sense of, but sounds were clearly heard. My own screaming cut through the dead air, as a feeling of weightlessness swept over my soul. The life inside of me ceased to exist while I gasped for air, struggling to maintain any semblance of composure. The vision was brief but terrifying all the same.

I have to get out of here.

Without thinking, I grabbed a pair of jeans, a sweater, and shoes. As quietly as possible, I climbed out of the window, scaling the tree to the ground, which wasn't nearly as hard as I had expected. Calling Chase, my parents, or running to Orifiel should've been my first line of defense, but listening to reason and logic didn't make any sense. My body knew precisely what it required.

My father moved my car onto the street earlier and I'd been too lazy to move it back to the driveway, so the chance of anyone, Angel or Mortal, hearing it startup was slim to none. Ten minutes later, my desired destination was reached. This was the only place true comfort could be sought, but yet the very same place which could cause the most pain, ruining everything. However, at that moment, I could've cared less.

Chapter 43

Gabriel

"What do I owe the pleasure of this little visit to?"

"Don't be a smart mouth, Gabriel. You know why I'm here," Michael replied coolly.

"I've done a bunch of shady things since our last conversation. You're going to have to be a bit more specific."

"I'm proud of you for making peace with the boy, son. What you did and said is true growth. It profoundly affected Chase. However, I'm less than impressed that you used an unskilled Demi-Demon as backup on a mission and didn't eliminate the target, but I'm sure there were reasons, which I will not question. The Mortal girl is safe. I doubt the Demon Sean wishes to meet with you again. That's all that really matters. I won't press the issue any further because everything was handled quickly and quietly. Lastly, I know what you did with the girl. That will never happen again. I'm not repeating this because we've already had this conversation last October. Do you understand me?"

"Yes. It was an error, but it's been fixed. Please don't ask how."

"I had no intention of asking. I also won't mention the rules pertaining to Angelic and Mortal relationships *or* the ones concerning adultery."

"I'm aware of both, Father, but thanks for the reminder."

"I'm chalking the lack of good judgment up to living as a Mortal for too long. Return to The Heavens for a little while. Once we decide to move in on Vincent, I'll call. Until then, rest. You've earned it."

"I'm fine. I don't know what the hell came over me. Nina is a very attractive, alluring woman. With us working closely, being together so often clouded my better judgement. Lines were blurred. I apologize. It won't be an issue going forward. I intend to continue training and protecting Nina, completing the mission I was sent to do. Once Vincent is handled, I'll return home. How's mother?" I said, changing the topic of conversation because the stinging sensation of lying to Michael's face sickened me.

"Worried. Missing her son. She's working on a few things at the moment. When she's finished, she'll visit."

The thought of someone missing my presence created an involuntary smile. "I'm going to get some sleep. Orifiel is watching Nina tonight. If he needs anything, he knows how to reach me," I said, embracing him, hoping he'd leave. I wasn't in the mood for company, and I didn't want to continue being deceitful.

After Michael left, I showered, and headed to bed. As I aimlessly flipped through several dozen television stations my thoughts swarmed around Nina. It didn't matter what movie played because my focus was nonexistent. The faint smell of her rose shampoo lingered on the pillows driving me insanely crazy with desire.

You can look, but you can't touch. She's off limits. Case closed.

Finally, as I drifted off to sleep, a loud bang at the front door shook me back to reality. Glancing at the clock, it was fairly late. I wasn't expecting anyone. A Demon wouldn't knock, and the Angels would allow themselves in freely. The pounding grew progressively louder with each passing second. Pulling the door open, I was stunned to find Nina standing there, soaking wet from the heavy rain.

Initially, my thoughts suggested this was a dream, until the realization of being awake stated otherwise. Something had to be terribly wrong because Orifiel wasn't around, nor did he notify me of anything amiss. I grabbed her arm, yanked her into the house, and slammed the door shut.

"Where's Orifiel?" I demanded.

"Watching my house because he doesn't know I'm gone," she said, before buckets of tears streamed down her face, which for once wore no makeup.

"What's going on?"

"I had a bad vision. No one's home. I need you." She wept uncontrollably.

I wasn't sure what to say or do. Eventually Nina would provide me with a cue, but until then, standing still worked best.

"Make this better," her voice trembled.

Well, there's your direction. Too bad it's unrealistic.

Asking what was required to make her feel better was the wrong thing to do. That always made Lilith angry. Lilith expected me to have all of the answers all of the time. When I didn't, a war ensued. Quietly, I pulled her close, holding her tightly.

"I'll make it better, angel. I promise," I whispered,

silently kicking myself in the ass for making another assurance that couldn't be kept. "Do you want to talk about it?"

"No."

"Do you want to talk about anything?"

Please say yes, because I'm not sure how to proceed from here. It's been years since I dealt with an emotional woman who relied on me to be her rock so I'm very rusty at it.

"I want to stay here," she said, digging her nails into my back.

"Okay, but don't you think your parents will notice you're gone if they come home early? Don't you think Chase might as well? And, at some point in the near future, Orifiel is going to realize you've given him the slip."

"My parents are gone for the night. They won't be returning until tomorrow morning and Chase is with his *parents.* Why are you trying to get rid of me?" A fresh wave of tears erupted from her eyes while she spoke.

"No. No, I'm not. Stay as long as you want."

Good save, Gabriel. Looks like you still have the ability to fold like a lawn chair when a woman cries.

"Really?" she asked, doe eyed.

"Yes, really," I confirmed, avoiding eye contact out of fear we'd have a replay of the close call from earlier, but this time since no one knew she was here, no one would stop us. I couldn't let that happen; especially since I promised Michael it wouldn't. He let my indiscretion slide and didn't question my tactics with Chase. He trusted me and I would not let him down, not again. Tempting fate wasn't on my "to do" list for tonight. Michael could pull me from Earth if another screw up went down. There was too much at stake to risk anything.

"Lay down with me?" she asked innocently.

"Where?" I replied cautiously.

"In bed," Nina said in a tone suggesting I'd asked the dumbest question ever.

"Why don't I get you some dry clothes?" I said, rushing to my room.

She followed me into my bedroom where she stood by the side of the bed openly removing her sweater and revealing a very tight, formfitting, white tank top underneath.

"Take what you want," I said, exiting as fast as possible.

What the hell?

This had to be a test of will. After a few deep breaths, I reentered the space to find Nina buried under the covers. Stiffly and uncomfortably, I slid my body beside hers, allowing her to position herself around me.

"Are you still upset with me?" she asked. Her voice was laced with exhaustion.

"No. I wasn't earlier either. I'm sorry for acting like a jerk."

"Orifiel said you had a lot going on. Do you want to talk about it? I'm a good listener." She yawned.

The simple fact that Nina offered to listen to my worries melted my heart. No Mortal woman, aside from my mother, had ever done that. Without permission, my body instantly relaxed and coiled tightly around hers.

"I'm good, but thanks. Get some sleep. I'll alert Orifiel."

"Don't. He'll come here and make me go home. Right now, all I want is to be here with you." She paused, burying her head in my neck. Her warm breath danced against my skin driving me wild. "I should be running to Chase, but he's busy dealing with his family. He's always busy dealing with something and he gets annoyed whenever he's bothered with any additional drama."

My once relaxed frame tensed and unwrapped itself from hers. In order to not provoke another bout of crying or cause her to think I was abandoning her, I rolled on my side so we were face to face.

"Spouses are supposed to help each other endure the bad times. It's a vow, or something. When one partner is hurting, it shouldn't matter how much is on the other's plate. I'm sure Chase wouldn't be upset if you reached out to him."

"I can't. Not right now at least. Lately, Chase tends to go to extremes. I don't feel like dealing with his mood swings. He's been closed off, distant, and he's always in his room avoiding me." She moved nearer. "Can I tell you something that stays between us?"

"Sure," I replied hesitantly.

"I love Chase, but most times I don't fully trust him. I think he faults me for what happened to him. More times than not, I walk around fearing he's going to up and leave me because this life became too much for him. That's crazy, right?"

Nina wanted to hear a verbal nod of agreement, but I didn't know Chase well enough to provide that assurance. Though I fully understood the reasons for Chase's withdrawal, it wasn't my place to justify his actions, especially since I was the guy who wanted to steal his wife. However, the emotions Nina experienced were all too familiar. I felt similar ones with Lilith. I never fully trusted her intentions. Often, Lilith blamed me for everything wrong in her world. The difference was, I foolishly believed she'd never leave me.

"I'm not exactly the best person to talk about marital troubles with. My wife and I haven't seen eye-to-eye on anything for many decades, but all relationships should be built on trust. If there's no trust, there's no relationship. Marriage is tough. You have to work on it all the time. How do you think Chase would feel if he knew you were here, in my bed?"

"Probably the same way I felt when I caught him sneaking around and making out with his ex-girlfriend last year, but this is different. I haven't cheated on Chase. Seeking comfort from a friend whom I trust endlessly isn't wrong. It's not like we're attracted to each other."

Her words stung. Though I was happy that Sasha had successfully wiped the memory of us fooling around from her brain, an attraction on my end *did* exist. Evidently, not so much for Nina. She saw me as a protector, a friend, and worse, a brother. What hurt me the most was that she was using *me* to get back at Chase for *his* past indiscretions.

"You and Chase should probably talk about all of this," I said, getting off of the bed.

"Where are you going?"

"Your clothes should be dry. It's time to get you home. I'll keep watch with Orifiel."

"Don't bother." She sprung up and stomped out of the room.

An angry Nina dressed in my clothing made her sexier than I ever imagined. I wanted to grab and take her, claiming her as mine.

"Damn it. Nina," I hissed, chasing after her, and forcing myself to snap back to reality. "You're scared, distraught, and a whole bunch of other things, but I only know that because I can see your inner emotions, which technically is cheating. Chase can't. He doesn't have that advantage. I'm also not Mortal, which means I view situations differently. I'm here for you. I always will be, but sleeping in my bed tonight because a chunk of you is mad at Chase for choosing his parents over you, and don't say you're not pissed off because your aura is screaming it, isn't going to make things better.

"I'm sorry that he cheated on you with his ex-girlfriend. That was very wrong. I can't imagine how awful that must've made you feel, but it's not for me to judge. If you're concerned over the state of your relationship, a dialogue with Chase needs to be opened. If he leaves you, he's an idiot. If you were my partner, I'd never, *ever* do anything to hurt you. If I unintentionally did, I'd fully expect you to call me out on it. I'd rather have a knockdown, drag it out fight, then risk losing your trust."

She didn't respond. Her lovely hazel eyes darkened as her aura pulsed. Tears pooled in her tear ducts, but this time the action of crying was that of a purge. Earlier, her energy indicated upset and stress, but now it seemed as if my words had struck a nerve. All of her destructive emotions came pouring out in a cleansing process. I waited a few seconds to see if she'd throw herself into my arms, but she didn't. Instead, her slender body cowered forward, while her back slid down the wall. Her hands clutched her knees to her chest. Her head lowered. She sobbed steadily and endlessly. I'd never seen such pure emotion from her before. Even though it was a sad one, it was beautiful.

"Come on, angel. Let's go to bed," I whispered, scooping her up, and placing her back on the mattress.

"When I was Mortal I grew up in an environment where boys were to always act like men. We were expected to be strong and unshakable no matter what. I always lived by that unspoken, idiotic rule. Anyway, a few years into our marriage Lilith found out that she was pregnant, but we lost the baby. After leaving the hospital, I went to my mother's house. The moment she opened the door, every single fear, disappointment, sorrow, and uncertainty came out of me. I couldn't stop the grief. It was the first time I cried like that in front of her. As she hugged me she told me that crying cleansed the soul. It washed away the negative so the positive could come to the surface to reveal itself. That's what's happening to you right now." I had no idea why I shared such an intimate detail of my past with her. Truth be told, I hated discussing my Earthly existence, but it just came out.

"I'm so sorry you went through that. I never thought about you having children. How many do you have?" She sniffed.

"I don't have any. Lilith was never able to carry a baby to term."

"I can't see you as a father," Nina replied, studying my face.

"You have a lot of good to look forward to. Stop focusing on the bad. It's tough, but try. Don't hold your emotions back. When you feel them, let it out. If the person you're unloading on acts like a jerk and never talks to you again, they aren't worth it. You dump on me all of the time. I'm still here. Chase will be too," I answered, returning the topic of conversation back to the matter at hand. We were done discussing my Mortal days. I'd already said too much.

"You're right," she whispered, gripping my chest

tightly.

"Get some rest. You'll feel better tomorrow," I assured.

"Promise?"

"Have I ever let you down?"

"Never."

She smiled and closed her eyes. After a few soft sounds, her body became dead weight. I had fully intended on sleeping tonight, but that was out of the question. There'd be no way I'd be able to rest peacefully trapped in this situation. I thought about calling to Orifiel, but stopped myself from doing so. If he was on top of his game like he should've been, he would've seen Nina leave the house. That never would've happened on my watch. I decided to wait and have him realize what had happened before telling him she was safe. This would teach him a lesson. It was the exact same thing Michael would've done to me.

Somewhere between one and two in the morning, I dozed off. Nina's body was still tangled securely around mine. For a hot second I imagined us together doing this every night. Envy and jealousy waged war inside of my head as I forced myself to realize that could never happen because of Chase.

You may not have eternity with Nina, but you had today. Take it and run.

****

"*Gabriel.*" Orifiel's voice frantically screamed within my head, jarring me from the wonderful, deep sleep I'd been enjoying. Nina remained out cold. Our bodies were still twisted into one.

"*Yes?*" I questioned, already aware of why he was so panicked.

"I can't find Nina. Please tell me you know where she is."

"She's in my bed, safe."

"What?"

"After she gave you the slip, she came here. That was several hours ago, Orifiel. You're only realizing this now?"

"She must have snuck out when Ezekiel was briefing me. Please don't tell our father."

"I don't have to. He knows all, sees all, and hears all. I'm sure you'll be dealing with this little screw up tomorrow."

"Don't remind me. Shall I come get her?"

"No. Let her sleep. I'll return her in the morning."

"Please, be careful, Gabriel."

"I haven't touched her. I don't intend to either."

"Are you okay? This has got to be killing you."

"Yes, Orifiel. I'm fine. Better than fine actually. Can I tell you something?"

"Aye."

"This moment I'm living right now is Heaven. The version we know and exist in is nothing compared to this."

"Enjoy it, brother, because once Father is done tearing me a new one, I'm more than sure he'll be heading your way."

"Have you ever loved someone so much that you wanted to keep them hidden from the world? Have them all to yourself?"

"I believe that's called kidnapping."

"The scary thing is, I don't see that as a bad idea."

Chapter 44

Chase

Returning to my parents' house and pretending all was perfect was bittersweet. I missed quite a bit of my old life. Living a few brief moments of it revealed a lost comfort. For three days all I had to be was Chase James, son, not Mortal Angel, part Demon. I refused to use my gifts or think about my other world. I allowed my mother to dote on me and father to ignore me. Guess what? Not a single anxiety attack or moment of panic arose, only a sense of feeling alive and healthy again was had.

I spoke with Nina a few times to make sure everything was okay and to let her know I was thinking about her. Just because I didn't miss all of the craziness, didn't mean I wasn't happy with her. It was the opposite. This short break would end up being a good thing for both of us. People needed to be apart in order to realize what they had. They also required space and privacy. Aside from the one overnight trip to help my mother some months back, we were together all day, every day. No space, solitude, or moments of longing had occurred since then.

Flopping on my bed, I flipped the television on. It felt fantastic being in my bed, in my old room, alone. No one was knocking on the door. No one required anything. Nothing. Not that I wasn't grateful for the accommodations the Luthers had provided, they treated me like a son, but as much as I hated to admit it, I missed home. It wasn't *that* bad here. However, I was in better hands at Nina's house in case something weird came up. My parents never mentioned Nina or the Luthers, nor did my mother extend an invitation for Nina to join us. Over dinner an aunt questioned Nina's whereabouts. For some reason I let it slip we'd become engaged. My father was noticeably annoyed. My mother smiled, quickly adding it would be a long engagement.

Early that morning my mother asked me if I could possibly stay longer due to family members changing their plans. I agreed, but I knew there would be consequences. Nina wasn't going to like this one bit.

Time to pay the piper.

I grabbed my phone and called Nina, fully aware that the conversation was going to be a rough ride.

"Hey, baby," I said.

"Hey," she answered brightly.

"How mad would you be if I said I was staying at my parents' house until the day after Christmas?"

"Why?" Her tone hardened.

"Some family decided to stay longer."

"Fine."

"Come on, baby. I have obligations too. Though my family isn't as close as yours, I still have one. It's only a few more days."

"What if I said no?"

"I'd say you were being selfish."

"Do I really have a choice or are you asking as a formality?" she snapped.

"If you need me to come back, I'll leave, but if you don't, I'm staying." I stood my ground.

"Will we at least see each other for Christmas?"

"Probably not, but we can celebrate the day after."

"So, what you're saying is, we won't be together for the holiday because the people who threw you away are more important than me?"

"Are you being serious, Nina?"

"Whatever." The line went dead.

Initially, I intended to immediately call her back, but I stopped myself from doing so. Giving Nina time to cool down was always best. In a few hours, when the storm calmed, I'd reach out again. Besides, we could never stay mad at each other for very long. I did understand where she was coming from. Being apart for Christmas sucked, but no other choice existed. Inviting her here to this already stretched to the limit environment wasn't a good idea. Tossing my cell phone on the nightstand, I sank into my bed.

I loved Nina, but she had to realize we were partners—equals in the relationship. The longer I tried to justify my actions, the worse I felt until I finally reached for the phone. The truth was, lately I'd been acting like an ass, allowing my inner issues to push Nina away. That wasn't fair to her.

—*"I'm sorry, baby. I love and miss you, badly. I'll make this up to you. I hate when we fight."*—

After hitting send, I waited a few minutes for a response, but it never came. I figured she'd ignore any gesture from me tonight, but she'd call tomorrow. Exhausted, I shut the light. I'd deal with the fallout later. Soaking up all of the alone time possible was far more essential.

Chapter 45

Nina

A chill rattled through my body causing me to pull the covers tighter around my shoulders. An arm coiled around my waist squeezed my hips with the movement. For a moment, I thought the limb belonged to Chase, but then my eyes opened.

"Don't freak out. You came over here last night because you had a vision, and you were upset. We didn't do anything aside from talk. Yes, that's my arm, but it's only there because *you* put it there, and every time I moved away, you'd yank it back. You're actually quite forceful and strong. You've done nothing wrong, and besides Orifiel, no one knows you're here. The next move is yours because your aura is too scattered to get a good read. Honestly, I'm still half asleep. My focus is questionable at best," Gabriel said evenly, in a monotone voice.

The events leading up to this moment were crystal clear. I was pissed at Chase for choosing his family over me. His actions weren't right, nor fair. I didn't care if that sentiment came across as selfish or not. George James was an abusive jerk who thrived on being a bully, and Blanche James was a raging co-dependent. They let him leave and were letting my parents care for him. Granted, my parents were a far better choice not only as more competent, stable people, but as guides and aids for his other life, something his crummy family would never understand. Missing Christmas was the ultimate slap in the face. Even Chase's attitude since being there had changed. I didn't like it one bit. As if arguing with Chase wasn't enough, I'd experienced that horrible vision. Alone and frightened, I sought comfort from Gabriel.

"Can I ask you a question?" I said, lying on my side. His arm was still draped over my waist. I should've moved it, but the contours of his body fit mine so well it felt right.

"Yeah," he mumbled. His voice was heavily laced with sleep.

"When you were a Mortal, who was more important? Your mother or Lilith?"

"They both were, but if you're asking me who I listened to, I listened to my mother until I married Lilith. Wife trumps mother. I had to live with Lilith. I wanted to sleep soundly, not with one eye open."

"If we were married and your mother told you to do something and I said no, you'd listen to me?"

"Yes," he answered, yawning. "Look, forget about whatever Chase did. You lost the battle. Focus on winning the war—the long run. Move on. Not all Mortal men think like I did."

"What if I don't want to?"

"Nothing good will be gained if you keep harping on this. Let it go, angel."

"Why do you call me angel?"

"Because it's better than calling you Demon. If a more detailed answer is required, I'll provide it once I'm fully awake."

"You're a giant jerk," I joked.

"I'm aware. I'll apologize for it later, but right now it's four thirty in the morning. I'd like to get at least one more hour of sleep. Is that okay, or do you want to talk more, or do you want me to take you home?"

"Go back to sleep," I whispered.

"Thank you."

Truthfully, I wanted him to wake up and chat with me. Perhaps do something to make me feel better. Though self-regarding, my thoughts were scattered and tragically unsettled. Lying in a bed other than mine, not knowing what was right or wrong anymore was torturous.

"All right. I'm awake. Speak your mind," Gabriel said, sitting up.

"Go back to sleep."

"Your aura is literally flashing the brightest light ever, so that's not going to happen."

"I don't know what to do, Gabriel," I whispered, afraid if I spoke too loudly, I'd cry.

"Yes, you do. You're overwhelmed. Stop for a second and remember you're a student, healer, daughter, sister, friend, and wife—even though you're mad at your mate. Couples fight. It's healthy. He chose his mother over you. So what? In the grand scheme of life this one fight isn't going to amount to anything except a few days of tense emotions. I used to fight with Lilith. My parents fought. I'm sure yours do too."

"It's more than that. You're oversimplifying it."

"I'm really not. You're complicating it. Two choices exist here. Stay mad at Chase, which will accomplish absolutely nothing, or say screw it, and do your thing while he's away. When Chase returns, show him how much you missed him, but also show him his absence didn't break you. Right now, you're coming across as needy and clingy. Quite frankly, you're neither. Don't ever allow anyone to ruin your happiness. Look at me. I let Lilith do that and I'm miserable."

"What happened between you and her?"

A dark laugh escaped his throat. "The easier question would be what didn't?"

"Tell me about her."

"She's a Demon. That's all anyone needs to know."

"She broke your heart." My soul softened over the visible pain in his eyes.

"I'd rather not discuss my tale of woe right now. Listen, go shower. Your clothes from last night are in the laundry room. I'll make some coffee and breakfast, then I'll take you home."

"Maybe one day you'll see me as a close enough friend to discuss your past with. When that time comes, find me." I smiled and headed to the bathroom.

I was still unsure of how to address the Chase situation, but I did feel heaps better now that I'd righted a wrong. If Chase knew I'd spent the night at Gabriel's house he'd flip out, but maybe if he wasn't too busy playing son-of-the-year that wouldn't have happened.

Serves you right Chase James. Now we're even.

Chapter 46

Gabriel

Things I hated doing—talking about Lilith and my Mortal past. Mortals were always so consumed with needing to know everything about another person. Angels didn't care. Any information we divulged to one another was completely voluntary. I despised everything about my Mortal life, aside from my parents. They were good people whose love was pure and real.

"You can cook too?" Nina asked, sitting at the table.

She looked surreal. Her wet hair hung in loose curls. She wore no makeup, so her natural beauty was clear and present. In the light of day, Nina was a goddess. A goddess I couldn't exist without.

"I can do a lot of things."

"I see that. This is, without a doubt, the best coffee ever. I'd be one happy, well caffeinated girl if I could drink this every morning for the rest of my life and then some."

"Lilith hated the way I made coffee. She always said it was too strong and tasted like mud." *Why did you say that? Quick. Change the subject.* "Listen, Sasha thought spending the entire night with you might give us a better idea of what's going on inside of your head. By watching your REM cycles he'll be able to help you see more clearly. Thoughts?" I asked, hoping she'd focus on this and not my Mortal life comment. Most of what I'd said was a lie, but what was I supposed to say? 'I need Sasha to tell me what's screwing with my brain when it comes to you?' The only way she'd agree to do this was if I made it seem like she had something to gain from this.

"Sure. When?" she answered.

"If your parents agree, we can do it tonight."

She laughed. "I doubt they'll agree."

"They will."

"I think I know Jack and Ellen a little better than you."

"Nina, if I say they will, they will." I hated when people challenged me.

"If you say so," she replied in a sing-song style voice.

"When I prove you wrong, will you stop doubting me?"

"*If* you prove me wrong, which you won't, I'll not only stop doubting you, but I'll let you open up to me about your past too. I want us to be friends, Gabriel. I see you as one, but you don't think of me that way."

Smiling softly, I spoke. "Really? I certainly don't share my bed with my enemies, then make them breakfast the next morning. I don't offer them protection and comfort, and I most definitely do not try to make them feel better at five in the morning when I'm exhausted. Come on. We better go." I tossed the plates in the sink.

"Hey," she hummed, sliding her body in between mine and the dishwasher.

"Hey," I replied, placing my hands on the counter, jailing her with my arms. This action didn't seem to bother her. If anything, her aura remained level and calm, as if this position was a common occurrence between us.

"You should smile more often," she mused.

"Oh yeah? Why's that?"

"Because you have some pretty cute dimples."

"Thanks. I think."

"When was the last time you laughed?" she asked, looking up at me through her long eyelashes.

"Excuse me?" What the hell did laughing, smiling, or dimples have to do with anything?

"When was the last time you let go and laughed until you cried and your stomach hurt?"

"Why does that matter?" Truthfully, I couldn't recall when emotions like that were ever experienced.

"Just curious."

"How about you?" I felt compelled to ask. I'd bet my soul the sound of her unrestraint laughter was unspeakably perfect.

"It's been a while."

Her aura darkened slightly in a mournful way. Absentmindedly, she bit her bottom lip. Her hazel irises were firmly focused on her bare feet. My body remained still. I wasn't sure what my next move should be. I wanted to lift her spirits, but I was far from a humorous person. Even as a Mortal I was always rather serious.

"I want to feel something positive again," she spoke.

"There are a lot of positive things in your life. They may be dormant for the moment, but winter eventually thaws, and spring awakens whatever you believe to be gone," I replied, knowing what I'd said was a bunch of bull. I'd given up on happiness a long time ago, but she required assurances that all hope wasn't lost. I could provide that.

"You know that strange connection we have?"

"Yeah…" my voice trailed in a leading fashion. Our conversation had taken a sharp turn into dangerous terrain.

"What does it do to you?"

"I'm not sure I follow," I questioned knowing damn well what she asked, but treading lightly. One false move, one wrong word and I'd be royally screwed.

"How does it make you feel?"

"It's complicated, but mostly it's confusing."

"Me too," she said, half grinning, but I could tell she wasn't satisfied with my answer.

Tell her what she wants to hear. She won't stop pressing until you do. Besides, maybe you'll feel better after putting everything out there.

"Listen, Nina, if you're asking if it makes me want to experience things I shouldn't, then yes, it does. If you're asking if it makes me question my fidelity to my mate, then again, yes, it does. If you're asking if it makes me want to spend more time with you than is socially acceptable, again, yes. I could go on, but I think you catch my drift. The point is, we're both fully aware of the pull and we don't give into it because we know we can't." I tried to be vague, but direct.

"If you *could* give into the connection, would you?"

"Would you?" No way would I admit that first. The last thing I needed was for Nina to run from the house or feel strange around me. My mission couldn't be compromised. Additionally, Nina couldn't leave my world.

"Honestly?"

"That would be nice," I replied, holding my breath which was stupid. What answer was I expecting? Nina to admit to being in love with me? Her agreeing to abandon everything and run away with me? Fat chance of that ever happening.

"I would and I hate myself for that."

"Don't. As long as we don't do anything stupid, we'll be fine. Besides, the connection isn't nearly as strong as it initially was."

"I suppose."

"Hey," I said, tilting her chin so our eyes met. "See? It's not as powerful," I lied, something I'd been doing a lot of lately. Truthfully, I wasn't looking at her, but rather through her. If I had been, I'd be going crazy with lust.

"Come on, angel. We should go," I urged.

Relief occurred when Nina asked me if I could drive her car back to her house. I'd seen the way she drove. It frightened the crap out of me. How the DMV hadn't revoked her license was beyond me.

I'd barely stopped the vehicle when Nina bolted. My heart dropped once I saw her run into Chase's arms. She clung to him tightly, wrapping her legs around his waist. Her aura grew brighter and happier with each kiss. Anger, rage, and jealousy stormed my core. I'd been used and felt foolish for spending the better part of the night fantasizing about what eternity with her would be like. It gave me hope, especially when she admitted if given the right opportunity she'd give into our connection and explore it further. I should've been smart enough to not allow myself to fall victim to her. Walking past them as if they didn't exist, I entered the house. Sasha had to explore Nina's mind tonight because answers were needed now.

"How can I help you?" Jack asked, taking a seat at the kitchen table.

"Michael believes if the Angel Sasha could see more of Nina's visions, we could guide her third eye better. In order to accomplish this, Sasha would have to spend one night traveling through her subconscious mind. I assure you that he's a good man and a professional when it comes to his gift. I'll be there as well. You're more than welcome to be present to observe or to ask questions. Nina has worked with him before."

"This will help all parties involved in this mess?"

"Yes," I replied.

"Where have you been? No note, cell phone off, nothing," Ellen snapped at Nina the second Nina walked through the back door.

"I ran to the mall to pick up a few last-minute things before it got crazy with Christmas shoppers," she lied. "I'm sorry for not leaving a note, and I forgot to charge my phone last night, but I was with Gabriel which means I was totally safe."

"You expect me to believe that you went shopping dressed like that?" Ellen inquired while surveying Nina's uncharacteristically relaxed attire.

"Jack?" I questioned, not caring about their impending argument, trying to get the focus of conversation back on something far more important. If everyone else standing in that room could have an agenda, why couldn't I?

"As long as it's done here and Nina agrees, we're fine with it."

"Great. I'll call to Sasha and set it up for tonight."

"Didn't Sasha say that he'd be away until the New Year?" Nina questioned.

"I'll return with Sasha later," I replied, ignoring Nina.

Without waiting for a response, because their questions or concerns were of no interest to me, I left. This would happen regardless of whatever hang-ups they might need coddling over. Besides, being in the same room with Nina and Chase became too consuming. The space started closing in on me. I felt suffocated.

Taking my usual post out front, heartache set in. A lump formed in my throat as I watched Nina and Chase's silhouettes through her bedroom window. They moved closer and closer together until they became one.

A single tear formed and rolled off of my cheek, shattering on the cold, hard ground. I hadn't experienced that in decades. At that moment I accepted my place. She used me to seek revenge on Chase. Now that everything had returned to good, she wouldn't need me. I'd be tossed aside until he screwed up again or something spooked her that she didn't want to burden him with.

"I'm sorry," Sasha said softly, approaching me from behind.

"For what?" I snapped.

"You're in love with her and it's not reciprocated. You want to give her the pieces of your crushed heart, but she's not interested. You'll say I don't know what I'm talking about, that she's just a job, but we both know that's not true. I may not possess the gifts that you and the other Angels hold near and dear, but I have eyes and a heart. Most, if not all of you, believe I have a meaningless mission. I hear the hushed whispers and know I'm being made fun of, but I'm not blind. Do you want to know what I think?"

"Sure. Enlighten me," I huffed, not in the mood for any part of this conversation.

"Allow yourself to love Nina. Somewhere in that

experience you'll find what type of love she's capable of giving back."

"What are you doing here?" I asked, changing the subject.

"Oh, you know me. I heard my name being used a bunch of times and had to find out why."

"They agreed to you spending the night. Are you available?"

"Yes. I'll be back at eight. Technically, I'm on assignment at the moment, but the target's brain is fairly blank. There's not much to do other than wait. I told Michael to give me a few more days, then I'll dive back in. When can I wander through your beautiful mind?"

"If I can find Orifiel, now."

Quickly, I called to Orifiel telling him I was exhausted and in dire need of sleep. Thankfully, he arrived a few moments later, swearing he'd keep a better eye on Nina. Neither of us had heard from Michael, which suggested we might be in the clear. Within a half hour of being home, I'd fallen fast asleep.

Good luck decoding nothing, Sasha.

****

"Wake," Sasha commanded.

My eyes opened. My body felt remarkably rested. Glancing at the alarm clock, I'd been out for about seven hours, a record for these past few months.

"So?" I questioned, truly believing he'd seen nothing. My mind was stronger than his. It more than likely ousted any probing into my private memories.

"Mystery solved. I fully understand why you're so damaged."

"What's that supposed to mean?"

"It means an acute comprehension as to why you do,

say, and act the way you do is now known."

"Okay, great. You saw shit. What did you see about Nina? The future? This damn hold she has over me?"

"I had no idea the type of life you lived. You're a good man and were a great husband to a woman who didn't deserve you. I could feel how much you loved and worshiped her. Memories don't lie. Your version may be skewed, but when I'm watching from the sidelines I see everything, truthfully. Stop blaming yourself. You did everything to make Lilith happy. You always found ways around the negative. Yes, you did some unsavory, shady things, but who hasn't? You're letting your Mortal past destroy your Heavenly happiness. I don't understand why."

"All I care about is what you saw pertaining to Nina, not your take on how I ran, and run, my life."

"Look, Gabriel, I'd love to tell you everything, but I can't," he said, raising a hand to stop any interjections. "But, what I can say is there's a bond, a strong one, which burns between you and her, and it will for *all* eternity. Your souls will remain parallel, meaning she'll always be a dominate figure in your Immortal world, and you in her Mortal and Immortal fate. In what capacity? I can't say with one hundred percent certainty. I'm unsure if I'll ever be able to, but I'll know more once I'm inside of Nina's head for longer than an hour."

"Will you tell me the entire story or will you hold back like you're doing now?"

"I'll tell you what I can. What can be gathered from matched images." He paused. "I'm sorry about Lilith."

"Don't be. I'm not."

"Stop. I felt your pain. I saw you lying on the floor of your space crying uncontrollably for her. I viewed the moment your soul hardened and your heart turned to stone. I witnessed how you cope with this loss on a daily basis. Gabriel, your Mortal days were challenging, but you always traveled down the path of good. That man still exists, just without the baggage of a woman who never loved him. There is a person out there who will truly love all of you. I've seen it. Open your mind. Let your heart do the talking."

"I think you've been dream surfing too much. You don't get two God given mates. Only one. I had her and screwed up. Now, she's gone. And, for the record, she did love me. It was me who failed her. If I'd only given her what she wanted we'd be happy. I wouldn't be the person I am today. I'd be in love and enjoying the afterlife, not miserable."

"It wasn't your fault that you couldn't give her children."

"It's more than that."

"It doesn't matter you didn't want offspring. You still tried for her, and you would've been a great father. You hid your own desires to make her happy. Not many spouses would do that. The same applies with your profession. You wanted to be a lawyer; just not one for *la famigliai*. You were an amazing counselor, regardless of what you may believe."

"Enough."

He didn't debate any further. His aura strongly reflected sorrow and pity, which I hated. I didn't want anyone feeling bad for my choices as a Mortal.

"Your greatest weakness is your best strength. Seek solace and comfort from it. Embrace it tightly because in the end, she'll be the last one, the only one, standing beside you. She'll feel your love, experience your disappointment, and pine for you when you're not there. You'll be unbreakable and limitless. What I viewed was absolutely beautiful. I'll see you at Nina's house at eight. Until then, rest and reflect," he said.

"She who? Whom are you speaking of? Lilith? Nina? Hadreniel? Trinity? Who?"

"You already know the answer to that. You're just too afraid to admit it," Sasha replied, before leaving.

For hours Sasha's words haunted me. I tried to distract myself, but I couldn't. Finally, I gave up and called to Orifiel. Peace arrived in the form of sparring out my pent-up anger. The release the physical activity provided me with allowed for the most comfortable version of myself to rise to the surface. Damn, if it didn't feel empowering.

Chapter 47

Chase

After not hearing back from Nina all night, I realized if some sort of effort to see her wasn't made, I'd pay dearly when returning to the Luther house for good. I woke early, made a quick trip to the mall, then headed over to Nina's house. Nina's car was missing, which caused anxious worry to grow inside of the pit of my stomach. My apprehension mounted when Ellen said she hadn't seen Nina all morning, nor had she heard from her. Pacing the driveway while calling her multiple times, I became incensed when her voicemail picked up. She had another half hour before I went looking for her. My gut suggested that she wasn't in any kind of danger, but rather she was acting childish. However, I couldn't be sure. Finally, her car pulled up. The closer it drew, it became evident that she wasn't driving, but rather Gabriel was. Doubt, jealousy, and anger surged through my blood causing it to boil.

The second she got out of her BMW, she threw herself into my arms, apologizing for acting silly. Initially I thought that she'd done something with Gabriel, but once he pushed past us like we didn't exist, I realized nothing went down. If it had, she would've been acting differently; the same way I had after screwing up with Bristol.

Though I was slightly shocked by how easily Jack and Ellen agreed to allow someone to travel through Nina's dreams, it didn't matter because this could work to my advantage. No one would object to her husband being present during the process, and maybe I'd gain knowledge from it as well. I might finally be made aware of Vincent's whereabouts. Switching gears, I quickly called my mother saying I wouldn't be returning tonight, that a situation had come up that couldn't be placed on hold. Begrudgingly, she agreed making me swear that I'd return tomorrow. When I told Nina that I'd stay the night to be there with her and gave her the bracelet I'd picked up, all was forgiven and forgotten. I casually threw in that I'd still be gone for Christmas Eve and Christmas Day, but her attitude was considerably calmer and more understanding this time around. It's amazing how an expensive gift could erase almost anything.

At precisely eight o'clock, Gabriel arrived with Sasha. Nina didn't seem affected by their presence. She appeared to be enjoying the attention which was totally uncharacteristic of her. Usually, she hated being the center of anything. I sat on the desk chair in her room with my arms folded tightly across my chest.

"I'm not going to harm Nina in any way," Sasha said, looking directly at me.

"I didn't say you would, but Nina is *my* wife. I want to be here for this," I responded as nicely as possible.

"Understood," he replied. "But, for this to work, I'll need to touch your wife and rest beside her."

"I'm fine with that." Sasha being in bed with Nina was the last thing on my mind. The man wasn't a threat. Gabriel on the other hand…

Sasha plopped carelessly onto the mattress and

faced me. "This is what usually happens. I'll lie next to Nina holding her hand. Once she's asleep, I'll jump into her subconscious mind viewing her dreams and visions. I've been at this for a long time so I'm fully aware of the difference between a dream and a vision. Usually, I call out what's seen to a viewer, in this case it would be Gabriel, but I won't be doing that tonight. That's only something I do on quick trips, not long journeys. Tonight is a journey. When the images fade, I'll wake her. We've done this before. There's nothing to fear. Any questions, comments, or concerns—just ask."

His desire to inform me and comfort me was a nice change of pace. Often, I felt lied to or told only half truths.

"What's the purpose of this experiment?"

"To see if a longer period of time inside of the visions can guide us better. She may view a detail that we can use as a clue, or she may already know the outcome of a situation which we could then change if it doesn't bode well for us. We all have seer abilities. We all already know our fates. The difference between Nina and the rest of the world is that her brain willingly purges her path which comes out in the form of visions. The average mind doesn't do that, therefore making what Nina can do a true gift. If I were to do this with you, I could dive into the deepest recesses of your mind, catching a glimpse of your destiny. However, this can't be done unless otherwise instructed because that would be an abuse of power. Does any of that make sense?"

"Yes. One other question. With whom do you share this information with once it's obtained?"

"For this, Michael, Raphael, and Gabriel. They're spearheading this mission. I can't share every detail from this assignment with you, but I will let you know the basics, Chase. I wish I could promise you more, but rules are rules. Nothing is worth losing your wings over, ever. I'm only looking at certain, specific surface visions. Detailed instructions for this task have been given to me and will be followed to the letter. I know you love her. How could you not? She's beautiful on so many levels, but we need to make sure she's not only safe, but you are as well. Don't make this amazing girl mate-less at such a young age."

I nodded, wondering if my gift of sense and perception altering could trick him into divulging more information when they woke.

You've got about nine hours to figure it out. It's going to be a long night.

Chapter 48

Nina

"Ready?" Sasha asked.

"As I'll ever be."

We'd done this many times over the past few months, so nerves were no longer a factor. I knew the drill and usually woke feeling like a million bucks. Plus, a good night's sleep to alleviate the toll that Chase's absence had been causing me would only help. I didn't regret spending the night at Gabriel's, but twangs of guilt popped up all day. What made my remorse intensify was Chase's surprise visit, coupled with his admission that me being upset, upset him. To add insult to injury, Chase suggested that he didn't give a damn about how pissed his parents would be by his temporary absence tonight, because being by my side was all that mattered. He did casually throw in that he'd still be with them for the holiday and though that still bothered me, I let it go after he swore he'd be home bright and early the day after Christmas.

We spent the day alone locked away in my bedroom. Lying in his arms and kissing him for hours was Heaven on Earth. Somewhere in between making up and making out, he gave me an early Christmas present—a gorgeous, diamond, tennis bracelet. It wasn't the gift that mattered. I loved it, but it was him chasing after me and trying to right the wrong that caused my emotions to run wild. My happiness meant more to him than his parents, which made me feel important and special for the first time in a long while.

"Stop fighting sleep. Shut off your mind." Sasha sighed.

"I'm not."

"Really, Nina? That's the lie you want to tell?"

"There's like fifty people watching me. That's a lot of pressure," I countered.

"More like four. All you have to do is fall asleep, not recite Hamlet's, *'To be or not to be'* soliloquy in perfect Elizabethan English." Rolling onto his side, Sasha placed his right palm on my forehead. "Sleep," he commanded.

And with that, my consciousness slipped.

Chapter 49

Gabriel

"Rise and shine, Valentine. Wake," Sasha said, poking Nina gently.

She'd been out cold for twelve hours, not moving once. I, on the other hand, spent the entire night pacing while keeping one eye on Chase, who thankfully fell asleep somewhere around midnight. I wanted to be alone with my thoughts, but with Jack and Ellen constantly popping their heads in every hour, it became an impossible task. I tried to assure them that Nina would be fine and to get some rest, but the advice fell on deaf ears. The evening sucked. Having to keep my body and mind in motion and not allow visions of kissing, holding, and waking beside Nina to play out internally was a rather trying experience.

"How did we sleep?" Sasha asked, sitting and stretching like a cat.

"Great, but there weren't any dreams. That's twice now," she replied sounding rather concerned.

"Oh, on the contrary, you did. Multiple clear ones. You just can't remember them. Long slumbers are vastly different from the naps we take. In those you only experience one REM cycle, but when you're out for the night, several occur making it harder to recall every little detail, if any at all."

"What were the visions?"

"The same. Nothing new or exciting."

"Damn. Why can't I see more?"

"Your mind isn't ready to yet. Be patient. The visions will come." Sasha smiled. "Do you remember your dreams every morning?"

"No." She sulked.

"Don't be so hard on yourself, baby," Chase said, wedging his body in between Sasha's and Nina's.

She beamed warmly, pulling him close, and clinging to him the same way she had with me the night prior. My presence was ignored. After a few minutes of watching Chase play husband-of-the-year, Sasha and I took our leave.

"Did you obtain anything of value?" I asked anxiously the moment we stepped outside.

"Oh yeah. Nina's got a lot going on up there."

"Were there any matches between us?"

"Several images were extremely similar."

"I don't have the time or desire to screw around right now, Sasha. I'm exhausted and can't sleep because that girl is in my every thought. Put up or shut up."

"Kitty's got claws," he snapped, grinning. "There's *definitely* a shared destiny line between you and her. A deep one, actually. Considerably stronger than I initially thought. I'm one hundred percent sure it's not a soul mate connection. To be honest, I've never seen anything like it before."

"Destiny line? What other type of connection could she and I share?"

"Destiny line is a term for two souls whose paths will continually cross in life *and* death. From the point of meeting until eternity, your existences will constantly weave in and out. Usually, there's a meaning or a purpose for it, but what that is, I don't know. It's a journey you and she will have to take together. In time, you'll figure it out. As for the type of connection you share, it could be anything. Perhaps you're related in some way? Share a divine purpose? Will carry out a mission together? Again, I have absolutely no clue because I didn't see *that* part. All I saw and felt was uncontrollable love, which could mean or be brought on by anything. We love for many different reasons on different levels."

"So, what you're saying is there's a strong possibility I recently fooled around with and have been having impure thoughts on a regular basis about someone I'm related to?" This suggestion was vomit inducing.

"Seriously, Gabriel? That's all you heard? I said, you *may* be related. But, even if you were, there's several generations of separation. You'd be something like nineteenth cousins, twenty-five times removed."

"You viewed more than what you're telling me. Didn't you?"

He sighed heavily. "Gabriel, let this go. Allow nature to take its course. Stop fighting the Universe and its plans. Like I've said a hundred times now, there's a strong bond, but I've never seen one like it. Because of that, I can't speculate what it may be. I'm not even sure how to describe it to investigate it further. Parts of your suggested futures became visible, but I never hold much truth to those visions. The future is subject to change at the drop of a hat."

"Does she love me, romantically or intimately? Like one would for a mate? That's all I need to know."

"If I tell you no, you'll be heartbroken because you're madly in love with her. If I tell you yes, you'll be frustrated because she's mated with another. Why does it matter? You lose both ways."

"You know how this plays out," I whispered in disbelief.

"Not completely, but I have a general idea. I'm telling you, friend to friend not Angel to Angel, allow things to happen the way they're meant to."

"Does Vincent kill her?" My words shook with terror as I spoke them.

"If I answer that question, I'll lose my wings."

"I can't take this shit anymore. My father, brother, and now you. Everyone knows something and they refuse to share it, but you all expect me to keep doing my job, and never question why this girl is kicking my ass emotionally. This is how I'm playing the game from now on, and you can run back to Michael and tell him because I don't care. I'm done listening. I'm done doing his bidding. I'm leaving to go find and do whatever is necessary to get my mate back."

"You can't do that. Think of the consequences. Besides, who will watch over Nina? Only *you* can finish this job."

"I have and in every scenario I've imagined I end up happy. As for Nina, let Orifiel take a turn at the wheel," I spat, transforming into my true form, and disappearing.

I was done with Savannah, Nina, and being an Angel. Lilith would fix this. She always did. Whatever it took. Lilith was worth it.

Chapter 50

Nina

"I hate this."

"Just because you didn't see anything doesn't mean that your gift is gone. Like Sasha said, allow the visions to come out naturally. Don't force them because they're there. Unfortunately, they're taking their sweet time to come to the surface," Chase rationalized.

"There has to be a way to make them come out faster."

"You know I'm always down to try new things, but I don't think that you should mess around with this one. If you were to find a way who's to say the visions will be accurate?"

He made a good point. I was screwed. There was nothing I could do to help myself purge any faster. What a horrible feeling. My hands were tied. All of the complaining and screaming would accomplish nothing.

"Hey, let's forget about all of this for today. I have to head back to my parent's house, but how about we revisit the past tonight?"

"How so?" My curiosity piqued.

"I'll pick you up at six, take you out, and sneak into your room later tonight." He smiled devilishly.

"You're on."

A surge of excitement struck my soul, making the

long-forgotten sensation of anticipation return.

After Chase left, I flopped on the couch trying to forget about my recent lack of visions. Diving into an old chick flick on television I found myself relaxing and becoming increasingly tired. Closing my eyes, I convinced myself that a quick nap wouldn't be a bad idea. If all went well, maybe I'd need the extra energy later.

My thoughts wandered. I made plans for the perfect wedding while I smiled over the thought of being held in Chase's arms for all eternity. He was drop dead gorgeous. Maybe tonight would be the night we'd become one. Out of nowhere Gabriel came into focus. The random images flying in and out of my brain ceased, only wanting to zoom in on one thing, and that one thing was him. I could feel his strong arms wrapping themselves around me and pulling my body close. Gently, he placed me on a bed in a room which looked vaguely familiar. Lying on my back I looked up into his deep, big, brown eyes. They were wild with passion and intrigue. Slowly he pressed his soft, full lips to mine. The action felt good, dare I say right, making me hold onto the moment for as long as possible. A strange fluttering sensation tore me from Gabriel's security. My eyes snapped open to find hundreds of feathers falling from up above. My hands swatted the fluffs away as something warm and wet covered my face causing the material to stick to my skin.

"No. Buttons, no. You're such a bad boy," my mother scolded.

My body sprung up. Immediately I saw Buttons on my chest. He was licking me in between ripping one of my mother's throw pillows to shreds. Fabric and stuffing flew everywhere.

"Get off," I said annoyed. "Here." I turned to my mother, thrusting the dog at her. "Why is this mongrel here?"

"Your aunt and uncle had to go out of town for a friend's wedding. Jenny dropped him off about an hour ago. Help me clean this mess up please," she said, walking to the kitchen, and putting the dog behind a baby gate. "By the way, what were you dreaming about? You had this big grin on your face."

My cheeks flushed. "I don't remember," I lied.

"Those are usually the best ones." She smiled, studying my face. "Are you okay, honey?"

"I'm not really sure," I said, curling tightly into her arms the moment she sat.

"What's going on?"

"Promise you won't get mad, and I won't get into any trouble?"

"I promise."

The second she agreed, it was okay to speak freely without fear of consequences. We'd traveled down this road many times. If she said she wouldn't get upset, she never did. It was comforting and at times it made it easier to open up.

"Something weird is going on."

"Like?" she questioned, appearing concerned. Worry immediately etched on her face.

"There's this weird thing between me and Gabriel."

"A good weird or a bad weird?"

"When our eyes lock, the world stops. I slept at his house last night." I cringed while professing the truth.

"Slept *how*?"

"In bed with him."

"Was there anything more than just sleeping going on?"

"No. It wasn't like that. Chase pissed me off and you guys weren't home. I acted impulsively."

"Do you have feelings for Gabriel?"

"I have no idea."

"Have you two discussed this matter? Have you acted on it in any way?"

"We kissed, once, a long time ago, but it meant nothing. As for last night, he slept on his side of the bed and I on mine. There's just this strange pull whenever we look at each other. He acknowledges it too. It's honestly the most powerful thing I've ever experienced."

"Is there an attraction?"

"Yes," I whispered, wincing.

"What about Chase?"

"I love him more than anything. He's my soul mate."

"Okay, honey. This will stay between us, and be assured, I'm not upset, but you have to figure this out, soon. You're engaged to your soul mate, but feeling drawn to another man, whom might I add, is not Mortal. You're under a tremendous amount of stress, as is Chase, and maybe Gabriel makes that stress lessen when Chase is busy dealing with his own. It's okay to be friends with Gabriel. You can have a relationship with him without it being anything more than that. It seems like you and he might share a friendship based off of different similarities. He's helping and protecting you through a very difficult time. You're probably helping him deal with an issue he's been wrestling with. As long as no lines are crossed, everything should be fine. It's perfectly normal to find other men aside from your mate attractive.

It's called human nature. However, looking and touching are two different things. Maybe it would be best for now if you and Gabriel didn't hang out as often. Take a little break. See what happens."

"I can't cut Gabriel out."

"I didn't say walk away. Move back a bit. Give the relationship space. Intense situations, like the one we're all in, make people act without thinking. Take this time apart and reflect, remembering Chase is in a tough place too. His actions are being driven by a lot of factors. Before Chase left, we had a long talk. Having to spend time with George and Blanche wasn't something on Chase's list of fun things to do, but in the end, he had no choice. All relationships are filled with having to do things you don't want to while your partner understands, even when they don't."

"When did life get so real and complicated?"

She laughed. "You're growing up. This is all part of the experience. Stan and Mary are coming over for dinner. I better get back in the kitchen. Are you going to join us?"

"No. Chase and I are going out."

"Have fun." She rose. "In case you forgot, my door is always open if you ever need or want to talk."

"Thanks, Mom."

As I stood, gravity pushed my ass back down. My mind drew a blank until a vision of Gabriel on his knees revealed itself. His once beautiful, full, white wings had turned gray and were falling onto the ground. The image vanished, but brief flashes of Lilith and Gabriel searching for her flew in and out of my mind. The episode was quick, but powerful enough to make me jump off of the couch, hop in my car, and race over to his house. He was going after her and she was going to kill him.

Not on my watch, bitch.

Chapter 51

Gabriel

After abruptly leaving Sasha, I headed home, devising a strategy to not only find, but to convince Lilith to come back to me; my beautiful, sweet, Demon goddess. My heart had ached every day since she left me. I was trying to replace our lost love by attempting to give it to someone else, when truthfully no one besides Lilith could ever own my soul. A rather loud rap at the front door echoed throughout the house.

"Thank God you're still here," Nina practically shouted. She looked like a mental institution escapee, complete with wild hair and crazy eyes.

"Are you feeling okay?" I asked cautiously.

"Can I come in?" she asked, speaking rather rapidly.

"Of course."

Nina entered, then slammed the door shut.

"Should I call for Raphael or Michael, Nina?"

"No. No. No," she stammered, pacing in circles. Her nails clawed at her forearms. "I had a vision. Don't go looking for Lilith. She's going to try to kill you. Please. I'm begging you." Tears rolled freely down her cheeks. However, the fact that she saw into my future seemed bizarre. Up until now, Nina's abilities only revealed her fate, no one else's.

"Please, Gabriel. Don't do this. You have no idea

how much I care about, need, and want you around. If this plan is put in motion it would not only hurt you, but me as well. You're too special and important. I can't lose you. I love you," she cried.

By now not only her hands, but her entire body was trembling with fear. The confession of needing, wanting, and loving me broke my soul. This girl's hold consumed every ounce of me. But my mind had already decided on Lilith. Nina wasn't going to stop that from happening. She'd go home tonight to Chase. Who would greet me? No one. I doubted Lilith had it in her to physically harm me in any way, so whatever Nina saw couldn't have been right.

"Nina," I began, pulling her into a tight embrace. I couldn't bear to see her upset and I hoped my touch would sooth her. "Thank you for finding and telling me about the vision, but Lilith is my wife. I love her. We're bonded and have been apart for far too long. It's time we spoke and attempted to work things out. I'm leaving to find her, and I probably won't be returning. I'd like for us to part on good terms with a proper goodbye, not like this."

"No. You're *not* listening. You *can't*," she demanded, pulling away.

"This isn't open for a debate."

"Do you remember what happened in my bedroom on Halloween night? What we said? How we acted?" she asked, sounding odder by the second.

"Yeah. It's kind of hard to forget."

"Have you ever wondered what might've happened if Orifiel hadn't interrupted us? How far we would've gone? The bond we share isn't weakening, Gabriel. It's getting stronger. You know it. We can lie about it all day long, but in the end, something exists between us."

"I will admit that the thought has crossed my mind, but what does that have to do with…"

Chapter 52

Nina

There wasn't any time to think, just act. Yanking Gabriel by the front of his shirt, my lips parted. I had no idea what my end game was. I simply went with what my body desired, somehow knowing this primal, caveman action would prove louder and more powerful than any spoken words. For the first few seconds, only my mouth moved. Gabriel remained stone still with his hands down at his sides. Slowly, his arms found their way around my waist and his lips finally came to life. His firm hold caused my knees to weaken. His kisses were slow, deliberate, and soft. An unexplainable surge found its way into my blood, coursing and pumping an energy like no other. The more Gabriel gave in, the more alive I felt.

"Leave Lilith alone, please," I whispered, backing away slightly.

"I'll do whatever you want. I don't care what has to be done to make it happen. I'd forsake everything for you, Nina. She's not the woman for me. You are. I think about what happened on Halloween night all of the time. You have no idea how badly I want that again. I *need* to be with you on every imaginable level. You taste too good to be forbidden, and I'm tired of denying my feelings for you. You're *my* angel. You're all I want and all I ever dream about. Feel what you're doing to me," he answered breathlessly, closing the gap between us. His thumb traced my jaw while he sealed his body to mine. "Tell me you want the same," he whispered, lightly brushing our lips together.

"What do you think?"

"Say the words, sweetheart."

"You know I do."

"Please, angel. Tell me. Say the words," he practically begged.

"I want this, but more than anything, I want you."

Every ounce of my consciousness painfully knew what we were doing was wrong, but I couldn't stop the forward motion. No moment had ever felt this right. The past, present, and future didn't exist. Nothing did. Nothing mattered. Time stood still. Even though my intended point had been successfully delivered and received—Gabriel wasn't going to search for Lilith, stopping this sinful act would've been a sin in itself. I melted into his arms, allowing him to claim me. Our affections were gentle and easy but filled with longing and need.

"Run away with me, angel. Please. We can leave all of this behind us. We'll start over. I swear I'll take care of you and give you the life you deserve. Our existence could be this moment forever. No more pain. No more suffering." Gabriel's words were barely audible.

"I'd go anywhere with you." My inner desires seamlessly rolled off of my tongue and out of my mouth without hesitation.

A soft moan escaped his lips causing all of my self-control to vanish. Reaching under his shirt I practically tore it off. Our intimacy went from soft and sweet, to passionate and frenzied with no indication of what would happen next, but honestly? I didn't care. My brain had shut off, not allowing for any rational thoughts. Through labored breathing his thick fingers flicked each button of my blouse open. As he attacked my neck with his teeth, I went to work unbuckling his belt.

"I want you, now," I demanded, panting in anticipation.

"Are you sure?"

"Yes."

Pressing my back to the closest wall, he positioned his body around mine. As he adjusted his hips, I felt his heat. In a matter of seconds, we'd hit the point of no return. I'd never craved anything as badly as this moment and experience.

"Gabriel," Orifiel yelled, pounding on the door, instantly causing us to separate and our hold to break.

"Wait. Don't leave. I'll get rid of him," he said, turning to open the front door.

"I'm *really* busy. Go away," he hissed at Orifiel.

"Michael is thirty seconds behind me. He's not happy."

"Son of a bitch."

No sooner did the curse hit the air, than Michael appeared. His normally calm, relaxed face ceased to exist. A hard, angry one hung heavily in its place. His eyes were narrow, creating dark slits.

"Get decent and compose yourselves," he ordered, turning his back, allowing us a moment to straighten our clothing.

"Sit," Michael ordered, slamming the door shut.

We all backed up, quickly finding a seat.

"All three of you better listen, and listen well,

because I'm only going to say this once. Cut the crap," he barked.

"Nina has nothing to do with this," Gabriel informed coolly.

"Really? Because I beg to differ, but we'll circle back to that in a minute," Michael challenged. "Orifiel, you allowed the girl to give you the slip. What would've happened if Vincent found her? He's after her. And don't give me the cock and bull story that you were communicating with the others, because I saw you sleeping on the job while I watched her climb out of the window, get into her car, and come here. You were too busy star gazing, meddling in situations you should be keeping your nose out of."

"They deserve to be happy," Orifiel snapped.

"Leave it alone. Here," Michael shouted, handing Orifiel a piece of paper with blue and green dots on it. Orifiel studied it for a few moments appearing deep in thought. "That's the entire story right there. You neglected to view all of the angles; therefore, you didn't see every side of the star pattern. Your interpretation was right, but how it all ends was wrong. Do you have any idea how serious this is? Return to The Heavens immediately and wait for Raphael's orders, and if I find out you screwed up this bad again, you'll think Hell is a vacation spot. Stop being a bloody shit stirrer."

"Yes, sir," Orifiel whispered, taking off without even a backwards glance or a goodbye.

"You're next." Michael's tone softened slightly when he turned his attention on me. "You have a watcher for a reason. Vincent is that reason because that bastard is dangerous and wants to kill you. No Heaven or Hell, nothing exists kind of dead. For one damn minute stop focusing only on yourself because I've got a news flash for you, little girl—you're not the center of the bloody Universe. Get your—"

"Don't you dare," Gabriel shouted, standing, and shoving me behind him in a defensive manner. "You're to never speak to Nina like that again. She may fear you, but I don't." His eyes widened and his fists balled. For a hot second I thought Gabriel might actually strike Michael.

"And that, right there, leads way to the million-dollar question. What the hell is going on?" Michael laughed darkly.

"Sasha," Gabriel hissed.

"Before we go any further, I have to ask you both a serious question which requires an honest answer. Do you wish to forsake your mates for each other? Because if that's the case, I need to know. We can figure something out before Gabriel loses his wings." His entire demeanor was dead serious.

"No." I liked Gabriel, a lot, and we definitely share a bond with an amazing unexplainable passion, but give up Chase for him? No way.

Gabriel simply looked down.

"Then knock it off. There'll be no more sleepovers, no more working on becoming a stronger seer, no more whispering secrets in the dark, and most definitely no more kissing, touching, or screwing around of any kind unless you're training or in combat, in which case I would dictate the parameters, and said parameters would not include fornicating. You will remind yourselves of your current mates and of the consequences which will be suffered whenever the urge to sin with one another occurs again. I don't care how strong the desire may be, this ends now. Have I made myself clear?"

We both nodded in agreement.

"I take full ownership for what happened today, and I accept whatever the punishment is. Warning and stopping Gabriel was worth it," I said.

"Stopping Gabriel from what?" Michael questioned, sounding rather concerned all of a sudden.

"I had a vision that Gabriel went looking for Lilith. When he found her, she killed him, painfully. That can't happen, mainly because I won't allow it to. What the hell is going on here?" Streams of tears rolled freely down my cheeks.

"Shhh. You did the right thing, angel," Gabriel whispered, turning my body and wrapping his arms around my waist. "Hey," he said, tilting my chin up, "you did what was necessary to defuse a potentially lethal situation. I would've done the same."

"But yet I'm getting my ass handed to me," I snapped.

"Don't listen to Michael. He doesn't understand, he doesn't get what we share, what's here," he murmured. "Please look at me, angel."

Not being able to stop myself, I gazed into those big, brown eyes. My once slack arms coiled around his neck.

"Much better." A smile reached his eyes. "Let me shoulder the burdens—yours and mine, angel. I can handle it. Give me your pain, worry, stress, whatever. Allow me to heal you, instead of the other way around. Being by your side, keeping you safe, that's all that matters. If what happened before caused you any discomfort on any level, we never have to speak of it again. I'll do whatever it takes to make sure we never find ourselves in that position at any other point, *if* that's what you want," he soothed, still holding me close, with his forehead pressed to mine. His words were easy to get lost in as they quieted my troubled soul.

"No words could ever express how I feel about you. I don't want to ever change a moment of anything we've shared. I adore who you are and what you mean to me. Please, don't go. There's so much I want to say, but I can't seem to get out what's in my heart," I said, rubbing my nose gently against his.

It was as if we were lost in a dream. Everything immediately felt off the moment this man was near me, but a good off, a safe and sane off. Physical contact was the kill shot. The urge to kiss him consumed every inch of my soul. Not being able to stop myself, my lips brushed against his, teasing him so he'd break and give into my will. His hands made their way up my sides, stopping at my face. With tremendous care, his fingers traced the contours of my cheeks.

"*My* beautiful angel," Gabriel moaned softly.

"Oh. My. God. You can't stop this," Michael said.

"That's what I've been trying to tell you." Gabriel broke our stare so he could give his full attention to Michael. After an icy exchange, he faced me again. He ran his hands through my hair and gently placed my head on his shoulder. The protective action felt natural and calming to my unnerved form.

"Explain it. Explain what you experience when this happens," Michael demanded, wedging his body between mine and Gabriel's.

"The world shuts off. I can't think. Gabriel is the only thing that matters. Reality slips and my focus only exists for him. This unwavering need to be closer takes over and no matter how close we may be, it's never enough. There's this unrelenting force that controls my actions. I swear we've tried to fight it, but giving into it feels right."

"Gabriel?" Michael inquired.

"Same." He sighed.

"Is there a trigger?" Michael asked.

"Eye contact," Gabriel answered.

"This only happens when you look at each other?"

"Hard eye contact. If we look through or around the other, the effects are still present, but not nearly as strong. When I glance at Gabriel's nose, ear, basically anything other than his eyes, the urges are manageable," I replied, hoping that Michael's next statement would explain everything, providing a reason as to why this kept happening.

Stepping away from us, Michael examined the situation. "Look at each other."

Turning toward Gabriel, our eyes found one another's again. Like the previous times, once we connected the Universe melted away. His pleasure and pain shook my core. Without thinking, I slammed our lips together. The action felt true; natural, like we were meant to be doing this. He welcomed my advance and kissed me back with the fiery passion of a thousand suns.

"Angel," he whispered.

"I need to be one with you," I urged.

Gabriel lifted me off of the ground. My legs instinctively locked around his waist. I could feel the cool wall against my back for the second time today. His hands gripped my upper thighs while his tongue probed deeper into my mouth. My nails dug into his shoulders in hopes that this action wouldn't allow for any separation.

"Tell me you want me. Tell me you only want me and no one else," he demanded.

"I want you and only you more than I crave air to breathe," I declared boldly, yanking his shirt off.

"You're mine—*only mine*. All of you," he growled, tearing at his button fly, lifting my skirt, and picking up where we'd left off before Orifiel and Michael interrupted us.

"Stop." Michael's voice cut through the air. Until that moment, I'd forgotten he was there. Gabriel released our hold and guided my feet to the floor.

"I'm so sorry, Nina. I have no idea what just happened. I'm not trying to confuse you or make you do anything you don't want to. I can't stop myself." Gabriel's voice shook. "If you want me to leave you alone, I will, but you have to tell me. And please know, I'm not like that. I've always respected women. You, or any other woman for that matter, deserve more than a quickie against a wall. I wouldn't even subject a one-night stand to that type of misogynistic treatment. Oh my God. What the hell is wrong with me?"

"Don't leave," I replied. I'd never seen him this nervous before. Quite frankly, it was bothersome.

"I don't want to, but we can't keep doing this. You know as well as I that if we continue hanging around each other we're going to screw up. We'll end up doing something we shouldn't. Hell, we almost did."

"I recognize that and agree, but I can't bear to be without you."

"Avoid eye contact and being alone. That's how we solve this problem. Nina, return home, now. Please," Michael ordered as gently as possible.

Turning to head out, I stopped.

"You're not going to do it, right, Gabriel?" I asked. My gaze focused on the doorknob. A strong pair of hands grasped my shoulders, squeezing them lightly.

"I already told you I wouldn't. When have you known me to lie, especially to you?" Gabriel's cool breath whispered.

"Never," I replied, feeling as if the weight of the world no longer rested on my back.

Not wanting to return home, but rather desiring some alone time, I parked my car a few blocks away and cut the engine. I needed to think. I needed a moment to catch my breath before I was in too deep I'd drown.

Chapter 53

Gabriel

"She's Mortal and mated, two details you must remind yourself of every second of every day, son," Michael said the moment Nina left.

"Really? I didn't realize that. Thanks for the update, but you saw what happens. Maybe if you, Orifiel, or Sasha would tell me what's going on, I could process my emotions better and stop acting on impulsive desire. Just because I'm an Angel doesn't mean I'm no longer a man. Everything down there still works, so when a girl like that, a girl who's so beautiful and feels so right is around me, I'm reminded of my gender every moment until she leaves and then some," I yelled.

"Nothing is going on. I already told you that, as has Sasha. You and she share a destiny line. You understand the other's pain, emotions, and thoughts. That's what I witnessed. Stop believing that it's more, because it's *not*."

"That's a lie. There's something else present. If we only shared a divine path, this feeling wouldn't exist. Allowing myself the right to touch Nina in an intimate fashion or letting her share a bed with me never would've happened. Mortal or Immortal, I'd never betray Lilith. Yes, there was a time when impulsive actions occurred with several dozen unmated Angels, but that was purely out of anger and revenge, and only *after* Lilith left me. This isn't like that. Nina makes me dance on the edge of adultery every time I'm around her."

"Gabriel, you cannot claim her."

"I *need* to have her. This is no longer a want or desire. At times, like now for example, I feel like I'm going to go crazy if I don't kiss her. Whenever there's distance between us, closing the space becomes an obsession," I ranted as I paced the small space.

"Are you going to pursue Lilith?" he asked, ignoring my statement.

"I'm going to *pursue* happiness."

"What exactly does that mean?" he questioned, raising an eyebrow.

"If you can be cryptic, so can I. Since the almighty, Chief Archangel Michael can see all and know all, it shouldn't be too difficult to figure out."

He stood, shaking his head. "We have bigger problems at the moment, Gabriel. This isn't the time to wage war with me."

"Wage war?" I laughed. "You know something, *Father*? When Nina and I were intimate, the time I had Sasha wipe her brain of the incident, and don't play it off like this is new news to you because it's not, that moment has become my most cherished memory not only as an Immortal, but as a Mortal as well. The sad part? Only I can recall it. I can't share it with anyone. I've tried to stay away from her. I've tried to channel the old, bitter Gabriel, but I can't. It's driving me mad. Her skin, touch, sounds, taste, smells—everything about Nina makes no sense. All I can be sure of is that I crave her and require her presence. She sets the Universe on fire. I never felt that with Lilith. However, this little problem can be solved rather easily. Chase needs to go. With him out of the picture, I can have her and figure all of this out."

"Stop. Chase is Nina's mate. I'm sorry, Gabriel, but no. I'd tell you to return to The Heavens, but you won't listen. You have something in your head, and you won't rest until peace for it is found. My answer regarding the connection isn't good enough for you, but in time you'll realize what I've said is the truth—that you should've let it go when the chance presented itself, before it was too late."

"I *need* her. Give Nina to me. I've never asked you or Mother for anything and I have always played by your rules. Let me have the one thing that will provide me with eternal happiness. In exchange, I'll do whatever you want. I swear to you that I'll love Nina forever and do whatever is necessary to make that girl smile all day, every day. She'll never know what it feels like to cry again. Father, allow me the right to give Nina everything and more. I'll keep her safe." I paused, turning to face Michael. "I'd give up my soul for her."

"I'm so sorry, son, but that request is impossible to grant. There are many unmated Angels in The Heavens who I'd be more than happy to re-mate you with."

"You ask so much of me, Michael. I carry out assignments without doubting your leadership, never questioning your orders. Rarely, if ever, have I failed you or an assignment. I, and I alone, am the best assassin in your Army. I'm your fiercest warrior, and you can't do this one thing for me? If you won't give her to me, at least tell me the truth."

"I already have. Again, I'm sorry. More than anything I'd love to see you happy, but I can't do what you're asking."

"What if Chase was gone?"

"What are you plotting?"

"Just answer the damn question," I snapped.

"She'd still be mated to him. Mates are in life *and* death. Nina would always love and mourn for Chase, the same way you do for Lilith."

"Lilith doesn't love me anymore."

"Demons aren't capable of love, Gabriel. Even if Chase gave into his inner Demon and became one of them, Nina would end up like you. You're in a no-win situation. It's time to cut your losses."

Involuntarily I turned and violently punched a hole through the wall. I hadn't felt this much rage and disappointment in decades. At least then I knew why. Now I was clueless.

"Son—" Michael started.

"Go. Just go," I said through gritted teeth.

"I will, but only *after* you tell me what your next move is."

"Nothing. That's my next move. I do absolutely nothing. Like you said, I'm in a no-win situation."

"When this is over, there are several Demons that require elimination. You'll return to your old existence as an assassin, and you will feel better."

"No, I won't."

"You will. That's a direct order."

"When this ends and Nina is safe, I'm out. I don't want to be a Demonic Assassin, nor do I wish to hold any rank in your Army, but more than anything, I don't wish to exist. Find a new bitch. If I can't have what I want, neither will you," I replied coldly, turning, and walking into the bedroom, slamming the door shut.

Chapter 54

Chase

Christmas came and went uneventfully. Pretending to be the good son was exhausting, but honestly, it was a welcomed change of pace. Not once did my brain play games with me. I was stress and freakshow free. No one spoke of Heaven or Hell and I didn't have time to dwell on Vincent, Sean, or any other Demonic thing for that matter. I finally felt mentally strong, which caused me to seriously consider my mother's offer to move back home. Though living at the Luthers was best, the anxiety that I experienced in that house was too much. My thoughts often raced with all sorts of crazy things. Now that I was home, I no longer felt as if I'd lose control and harm those around me. My Demonic side became docile, almost gone. The problem? Jack and Ellen would support the decision, but Nina would go bat crap nuts. Fighting with her right now was out of the question.

I'd become no closer to knowing where Vincent was hiding and quite frankly, I didn't care. Gabriel was right. This wasn't my fight. It was his and the Angelic Army's. For too long an unnatural investment in my other world consumed my life, whereas no one else who shared this double life experienced the same effect. Yes, I wanted to protect Nina, but I missed being normal and having peace of mind. How could I be a good soul mate, providing Nina with everything she deserved if I was constantly riddled with anxiety?

I still had every intention of going through with the marriage when the time was right, and I did want to move in together, but being home made me realize I wasn't ready for any of that. Alone time with Nina still caused me massive amounts of fear and doubt. At least when other people were present, a sense of calmness soothed my worries over having a Demonic blackout. They'd stop me before something terrible happened. When Vincent was gone, completely gone, I'd feel better. At that point we could begin our life together, as one. Until that day came, I needed to find a way to tell her this while not destroying what we shared. Prolonging the 'my parents won't let me leave yet because family is still in town' excuse couldn't go on for much longer. I said I'd return to the Luther's the day after Christmas, but I still hadn't.

Nina seemed okay with the situation but distracted at the same time. We talked on the phone multiple times a day and hung out often, but her mind always seemed elsewhere. When I'd question her, she'd brush the topic off blaming exhaustion as the culprit. I didn't pressure her for an honest answer because I'd bet anything she was still hung up on not having any clear visions, and she was probably trying to force a clear mind to evoke one. She said she wasn't working with Sasha or Gabriel anymore, that they all needed a break, which pleased me, but obviously the lack of her ability frustrated her. The only part of being away from Nina which displeased me was Gabriel and his ever-constant presence. He spent the holiday with the Luthers making friends with Steve, who was elated over my absence. Since Gabriel remained on constant watch outside of the house, Ellen extended an invitation to him. Often, she could be pushy or use guilt as a weapon to get what she wanted. I imagined that was the case with Gabriel. Nina came across as put-out over his presence. Her lack of wanting to discuss the matter proved that she didn't want him there either. I'd decided after the New Year I'd tell Nina I wouldn't be returning. In the meantime, some sort of plan to make my absence not seem like a breakup, but rather a good move for both of us had to be cleverly crafted.

She'll be okay with everything once you explain yourself...not. Who is fooling who now?

Chapter 55

Nina

I was less than impressed when my mother invited Gabriel to spend Christmas with us. There was nothing that could be done to stop it. Her actions were not malicious, but rather a goodwill gesture, which I couldn't fault her for. I was confused and wanted distance from Gabriel. Though missing Chase sucked, the fact he remained at the James's provided a break and gave me some space to figure things out.

"I can leave if you'd like. Coming up with an excuse won't be too terribly difficult," Gabriel said subtly, catching me alone in the kitchen on Christmas day.

"No. Stay," I replied automatically.

Asking him to go would be rude. I didn't want to hurt his feelings any more than I already had.

"Are you sure? Because to be honest, it's a little uncomfortable being here after what happened."

His confession brightened my spirits immediately. He, too, felt awkward about our moment of lust, which was a good sign. We both realized and acknowledged the mistake. Maybe now I'd be able to put it behind me.

"Right?" I smiled.

"It didn't mean anything. We were both rather emotional that day, shared a kiss, and said some unexpected, grossly inappropriate things because it's

343

easy to get caught up in intense situations. Shit happens. No one ever has to know. I'd never say anything to anyone about it, ever. The memory will die with me. Oh, wait. That can't happen because I'm already dead," he joked.

A laugh escaped my throat. An appreciation over him trying to make light of the situation soothed my tense nerves. I kept thinking in terms of me and I, not him or we. He'd betrayed his wife as well, but he was right. The day had been a sensitive one filled with worry over Lilith and losing Gabriel.

"Fair enough," I answered, but something still felt wrong.

"Listen, we know there's some sort of pull between us. If we can ignore it, we'll be fine. Like Michael said, we need to avoid eye contact and being alone together for too long. We're going to be okay. Let's just leave the past in the past. Forget it ever happened."

Heaviness, or maybe it was sadness, entered my heart. Or perhaps it was disappointment. I couldn't be sure. Though we were both bonded to others, knowing Gabriel was attracted to me felt good. If he could nullify the situation that easily, obviously what I'd thought was there wasn't.

"Can I ask you something before we close the book, never to open it again?"

"Of course."

"Was it any good?"

"Was what any good?" Gabriel asked, confused.

"What we did," I said quickly, anticipating a negative response.

"What I said that day may have been wrong, but it was the truth. Come on. Look at you, angel. What do you think? Book closed," he replied, handing me something, exiting the kitchen, and striking up a conversation with Steve and his new girlfriend, Jen.

Gabriel's lack of a direct answer unnerved me, but it was totally appropriate. He no longer wished to discuss the matter or prolong the moment anymore just to feed my ego. Oh well. Case closed.

Once Gabriel left, I looked down at what he'd handed me—a black leatherbound journal. Upon further investigation, I saw that he'd written something on the first page.

"Angel,
It's always darkest before the dawn.
Eternally,
G."

The sentiment couldn't have been any truer. I'd never been much of a writer, but that night and every night since, I've poured my inner emotions freely and without restraint onto the blank pages. It actually helped my jumbled mind find peace. By putting my fears, mistakes, and thoughts down on paper, closure came. I realized everyone, Mortal or not, experienced errors in judgement and were afraid of things. The emotional purge kicked off my healing process, allowing for me to forgive myself for my past transgressions. I had to tell Chase what happened, but now wasn't the time. When the right moment presented, I'd bite the bullet.

The day before New Year's Eve, Tori reached out inviting me and Chase to a party at her house. To my great surprise, Chase didn't moan and groan about it, but rather he jumped at the opportunity. I figured he probably wanted a night away from his parents. He'd been there for over a week and was more than likely ready to come back home. As much as I enjoyed the space, we needed to pick up where we had left off. Since I began writing every night, a more relaxed, healthier approach to situations that annoyed me, like the current Chase situation, came about, and the sensation of missing him terribly bubbled up, leaving a hole inside of my heart which only he could fill.

Chase finished the conversation by saying that he had something important to discuss with me. When I questioned him, he assured me that it was a good, beneficial suggestion for us both. Jules thought he wanted to talk about moving in together. That thought put an instant smile on my face, helping me void myself of Gabriel and the disasters that always seemed to occur when we were alone together.

"I'll be ready in like twenty minutes. I swear," I said to Chase, who was sitting in the living room waiting for me to finish getting made-up for the past forty-five minutes.

"You said that ten minutes ago," he said.

"I know, but you want me to look good, right? Well, that takes time." I smiled, wondering what he wanted to talk about and when he'd do it.

"Whatever you look like in twenty minutes is the way you're going. It's getting late. The point of this party is to bring in the New Year at Tori's house not in your bathroom, and the New Year starts in two and a half hours."

"I'm up here now. I'll make sure she's ready," Jules replied.

"Thank you, Jules. I always liked you best of all Nina's friends."

"Yeah, yeah." She laughed.

I sat on my bathroom floor while Jules made the final touches to my hair.

"I hope you don't mind, but I invited Gabriel."

"Why?" I asked, trying not to sound annoyed or give away the fact that I was trying to avoid him like the plague.

Even though he'd rationalized what happened, I still felt uncomfortable about it. I probably always would. He told me he wanted me and when he questioned if I felt the same way, I stupidly said yes, admitting to many other embarrassing truths as well. Then, to make matters worse, we'd come so close to sleeping together—against a foyer wall. Good God. What the hell was I thinking? I'm with Chase, therefore I'm already spoken for.

"I'm not ready to come out to our friends yet, and I don't have anyone to kiss at midnight. Plus, he'll be outside watching you anyway," she replied casually.

"Makes sense."

"He's going to meet us there. Are you excited to find out what Chase has to say?"

"Very." I paused as my optimistic thoughts turned pessimistic. "You don't think it's something bad, do you?"

"No. Why would you think that?"

"Because I did something wrong," I whispered.

"What kind of wrong are we talking about, Nina?" Her tone turned serious.

"I almost slept with Gabriel. The only reason I did it was to stop him from looking for Lilith. I had a vision, which he appeared in. There wasn't any other choice," I defended.

She stopped fixing my hair and sat in front of me. "What did Gabriel do?"

"He wanted it too. And no, I haven't told Chase about it, but I will."

"How was it?" A slight smile spread across her concerned face.

"I don't want to talk about this anymore."

"You enjoyed it," she said, pondering the thought. "How did you leave off with Gabriel?"

"We agreed to forget about it." I chose to ignore her comment about me enjoying it. For a hot second, I thought about opening up and telling her about the crazy connection he and I shared, but I stopped myself. We didn't have the time, plus I couldn't bring myself to deal with it.

"Now what?"

"Nothing. I'm with Chase. Gabriel and I were overly emotional the day it happened. I was scared for Gabriel and mad at Chase. The two feelings collided, and a lapse of judgment occurred. I love Chase and pray that when I tell him what happened he'll realize that when he made his mistake with Bristol, I forgave him. Hopefully, he'll extend the same one-time free pass," I said, standing.

"There's more to this story, Nina. I've seen the way you and Gabriel look at each other. There's a static electricity in the air when you're in the same room. I can smell the heat which exists only when you're together. I can hear longing for the other in both of your voices. And I can taste the bitterness of your lies when you guys suggest there's nothing going on. I'm not saying you don't love Chase. What I'm saying is, I'm surprised it took this long for you and Gabriel to let your guards down and screw around a bit."

"I'm not doing this right now."

I stood in front of my French dressing mirror,

carefully examining myself. The strapless top was laid back and comfortable, but sexy with its ruche bust, tunic length, and jet-black color. The shirt looked great against the tight, dark washed, boot cut jeans, and black and white, strappy, open toed heels.

Smile and forget about Gabriel because if you don't, you're headed for trouble.

Chapter 56

Chase

Nina was always late. I sat thumbing through a magazine in the living room trying not to show my annoyance. I was already anxious over having to share my intentions to move back home. Having to prolong the argument I knew would ensue raked at my nerves. The sound of her heels against the floor drawing closer caused the beginning of an anxiety attack. My eyes refused to glance anywhere other than down at the pages in front of me. Several deep breaths to calm myself later, she appeared.

"With eight minutes to spare. Impressive. Wow. You look amazing," I marveled, putting the periodical down, and forcing myself to look directly at her.

Nina was beautiful. I had to touch, hold, and kiss her soft lips. A gravitational hold pulled me to her. How could I consider leaving this perfect girl's side? I needed to be with her all of the time. My soul grew stronger easily fighting my unease, while my entire body felt alive and full of energy. It had been a long time since I'd actually seen Nina this way. That one snapshot of time renewed my lost, undying love, and reconfirmed my devotion to her. While standing there I fell in love with her all over again, and it was awesome.

Walking up the steps to Tori's house, I pulled Nina

aside. "Hey. Listen, how about we do the social rounds, then get out of here? Let's bring in the New Year alone."

"Sounds like an amazing plan." She smiled brightly, setting my world on fire. "What did you want to talk about?" Her tone turned uneasy.

My mind drew a blank. There was no way in hell that I was going to tell her what I'd intended to. I didn't feel that way anymore. Being with Nina tonight had changed everything. Maybe it was because I hadn't seen her in so long and missed her, but we couldn't be apart anymore. Not now. Not ever.

"Let's move out of your parents' house and into our own place," I spit out involuntarily.

The rational side of my brain knew damn well I wasn't ready for that, but the irrational part didn't care.

"Yes. Oh my God, yes." She threw herself into my arms and squeezed me tightly.

"Hey, guys? Ready to go in?" Jules asked.

Immediately, I saw Gabriel standing beside her which annoyed me and provided me with an even stronger reason to ditch this party as soon as possible.

"Yup," I said, taking Nina's hand, and holding it firmly.

"Just a little warning, Gabriel. Tori can be a bit…uh…what's the word I'm looking for?" Jules said.

"Tori can be a nosey, manipulative, bossy, materialistic bitch who thinks the world revolves around her. On top of all of that, she sincerely believes she's God's greatest gift to all of womankind. But she's fiercely protective of the people she loves and is sadly rather misguided. When she wants, her good side shines brightly, but she rarely wears that face," I finished for Jules.

351

"Sounds like my wife," Gabriel uttered under his breath.

His statement caused me to snicker. I could see him with a Tori-type woman.

"Hey, y'all," Tori exclaimed in the heaviest southern belle accent I'd ever heard her use. "And who might this be?" she asked, pointing at Gabriel, while batting her long eyelashes like crazy in his direction. If I didn't know any better, I'd think she was suffering a seizure.

"Down girl. That's Gabriel and he's with Jules," I said, walking past her, and dragging Nina along with me. In and out was my goal.

"Hey, man," Tim said, stopping me dead in my tracks.

"What's up?" I asked, gritting my teeth together.

I couldn't stand him and what he stood for. Every time I saw him, I'd relive beating the hell out of him after the Senior Winter Dance and how good it felt.

"Mark and I could use some help moving the upstairs couch."

"Sure," I said, then turned to Nina. "Give me a few minutes. When I'm done, we're out of here." I leaned forward and kissed her lips.

She tasted more desirable than ever. To Hell with the damn anxiety attacks and keeping a distance. Nina was the cure I'd been searching for, only I'd been blinded by stupidity and couldn't see it, until now. Crisis—over.

Chapter 57

Nina

"Hey," Gabriel said, approaching me from behind the moment Chase vanished up the stairs.

"Hey," I mumbled.

"Your aura suggests happiness. I'm glad to see that."

"I am."

Suddenly, I felt funny. Something was off inside of me. The sounds around the space muted and the people in front of me became blurry.

"Are you okay?" Gabriel asked, bracing my shoulders.

"No," I replied in a dreamlike trance.

I felt him support my weight as my body swayed.

"Gabriel, what's happening?" I barely spoke.

"I'm not sure, but I'm here, and I'm not going anywhere either. You'll be okay," he answered through a distorted voice.

Because nothing made sense, I had no idea where he was taking me. The more we moved, a weightlessness and freeness entered my soul. The second my eyes closed, I could clearly see a plaque which read, 'Bonaventure Cemetery.' At a very rapid pace, I moved through the cemetery passing hundreds of tombstones, finally stopping at one resembling an Angel with their wings and head down. A figure was perched on top of it. My focus shifted away from the character and onto a large, red, plastic container with a long, yellow spout sitting by the base of the stone. A noxious odor filled the air. Somehow my mind instantaneously made the connection and identified the smell as gasoline. My thoughts refocused on the figure, which now became crystal clear. Chase. His green eyes were filled with hatred, anger, and rage. Vincent's horrific face flashed in front of me before the vision ended.

Chapter 58

Gabriel

"Nina," I shouted, trying to snap her back to reality.

One minute she was fine, the next she was unconscious. Her dilated eyeballs twitched from left to right, rolling around like marbles. I wasn't sure if Nina required actual medical attention to alleviate her current distress.

"Cemetery. Bonaventure. Chase. Vincent. Gasoline. Angel tombstone."

"Breathe, Nina. Take a few deep breaths and look at me. Focus on only me, nothing else," I said, gripping her shoulders, and trying to force eye contact.

Nina had to slow down, because I needed a hot second to make sense of the situation and her words. Once she said Bonaventure Cemetery, it became evident a clear, complete vision, not just a clip of one like she'd been experiencing, had occurred. Now she knew Vincent's hiding place. As to how Chase tied into this was what I had to figure out.

"What the hell was that?" she shrieked, appearing one hundred percent back to normal again.

"You saw an entire vision, like a true seer would." I kept my tone even, hoping this approach would make her purge everything she witnessed faster.

"Every time Trinity has a vision that happens?"

Obviously, the occurrence had freaked her out.

"No, because Trinity has been at this for decades. You'll learn to control the gift. What did you see?" I had no desire to discuss Trinity or how seers saw the future.

"Vincent is at Bonaventure Cemetery. Chase is going to go after him. He had a gas can with him. There was a huge Angel tombstone. The Angel's wings and head are down, and its body was hunched over. The last thing I can recall was Chase's eyes. They became dark and evil, and his face blended into Vincent's. You know where Vincent is. Am I right? Did I have an accurate vision?"

"Yes, but don't panic. I'll tell Michael and the others what happened. Someone will be assigned to hawk Chase. He's going to be fine, as are you. How are you feeling now?"

"Okay, I guess," she said, but I knew otherwise.

Taking her shaking hands in mine, I held them still. "You did well, Nina. You had a premonition and remembered enough of it to repeat it with precision. Everything is fine. It's over. I promise that you won't spiral out like that the next time this happens because you'll know what to expect."

"Was Sasha blocking my visions?" she demanded, pulling her hands away from mine.

"He was guiding your images," I answered truthfully.

"Why?"

"Because we were afraid you'd see too much and tell Chase, who'd most definitely go after Vincent on his own. We couldn't have that. Our Army is ready to attack at Michael's command, and there's a reason why he hasn't sent us in yet. What that reason is, I have absolutely no idea, but it's not my job to know. My job is to eliminate Vincent and to protect you. Nina, I can't allow anything to happen to you. I gave you my word that I'd never leave your side, and I promised you that I'd keep you safe. I have."

"You lied. You said Sasha was there to help," she hissed. A strong look of betrayal spread across her face causing me to feel like the biggest piece of trash that ever walked the face of the Earth.

"It's not like that," I began, but she wouldn't hear it. Turning around, she stormed off back into the house.

Great. Now what?

Chapter 59

Nina

"Jules," I called.

I was fuming and unable to think straight. I required an outlet to vent to. Never in a million years did I ever think that Gabriel would stab me in the back, but he did. He was no better than anyone else in my life. I wasn't his primary concern. His job and protecting his precious army were. Screw him.

"Hey." Jules turned and smiled. "What's wrong? What did Chase say?" Her happy appearance faded instantly.

"Chase isn't the problem. Gabriel is. I had an all on vision and saw everything. For months he's been having Sasha *guide* my dreams, which apparently is another way of saying that Gabriel had Sasha block them so I couldn't see anything."

"That doesn't sound like Gabriel."

"Stop defending him," I snapped.

"What did you see?"

Quickly, I recanted the event. I had zero desire to tell the story again, but I had no other choice. Anger, betrayal, and sudden exhaustion had imbibed each of my spoken words.

"What are you going to do?" she asked.

"I don't know. Have you seen Chase?" I asked,

realizing he'd been gone for a while.

"You have no idea about what? And Chase left about five minutes ago," Tori, who evidently was now standing beside Jules, said.

"Where did he go?" I panicked.

"How on God's green Earth am I supposed to know that?" She shrugged.

"I have to go," I said, quickly darting for the door.

"Nina," Jules called.

"I have to find Chase."

This horrible feeling that he'd overheard my conversation with Gabriel or Jules sat heavily in the pit of my stomach. If he'd become aware of anything, he'd be halfway to Bonaventure Cemetery by now.

"Take my car," she said, handing over her keys. "You better be careful."

Chapter 60

Chase

"Is Nina not feeling well?" Tori asked the second my feet hit the landing.

"Why?"

Concern immediately consumed my every thought. She seemed fine when we left the house. She hadn't been complaining about feeling ill, and if she wasn't okay, she could simply heal herself. Something was definitely up.

"She was talking to Jules's friend, then she suddenly hunched over in pain. That bulging beast of a sexy man took her out back."

"How long ago was that?"

"Maybe ten minutes?"

Pushing past Tori, I raced out of the back door. My eyes only had to scan the yard for a few seconds before I spotted Nina frantically speaking with Gabriel. Something from deep within me urged me to watch and listen from a distance; that Nina was fine and that this was an argument of sorts. Gluing my body to the side of Tori's house, completely out of eye shot, I heightened my hearing. In the past when using this gift, I had a hard time focusing on specific sounds. I could hear dogs barking or birds chirping from miles around, but now I knew how to tune everything else out.

Clearly, I heard Nina recant a vision she'd just

experienced to Gabriel. The two bickered for several moments about how he'd used Sasha to block her ability, but I could've cared less. Vincent's location and how to end him was no longer a secret. Bonaventure Cemetery and gasoline. Without hesitation, I headed to my car. Tonight would be the night I'd destroyed Vincent and reclaim my freedom once and for all.

Chapter 61

Gabriel

"Nina knows everything, Michael. She had a true, full, seer vision. I couldn't stop it. Even if Sasha were here, it still would've happened."

After Nina stormed off, I called Michael. Nina would never tell Chase what had happened in great detail because she knew he'd go after Vincent and lose. She wasn't about to harm the one thing she loved the most.

"Where is she now?" he asked, slightly concerned.

"We're at some girl's house for a party. I'm outside. Currently, she's pissed off at me."

"Keep a watchful eye out. I doubt she'll do anything or tell her mate, but one can never be too sure. I'll meet with her tomorrow to smooth things over. We pulled out of the cemetery a few days ago. Vincent sensed our Angelic presence. It's almost time to attack. I've been plotting our course and assembling the troops. I doubt he'll move anytime soon because he'll be too afraid we're still close by. How did she handle the vision?"

"She panicked, but recovered once she knew what was going on."

"Good. Go watch her. I'll be in touch later." Hanging up, I reentered the house.

"Gabriel," Jules shouted, grabbing my arm, and pulling me into a bathroom.

Please don't tell me you have another ex whom I have to kick the crap out of because I'm not in the mood right now.

"What's up?"

"Chase left and Nina went after him. I think he might've overheard what you and she were talking about. I'm not sure."

"Shit," I spat, throwing the door open and heading out of the house.

"I'm coming," Jules said, running after me.

"The hell you are. You're staying right here or going home," I ordered. There was no way I was about to take her along to God only knew what kind of situation.

"I don't think so," she challenged.

"I don't have time to argue about this."

"Then don't."

"Damn it, Jules," I hissed.

"You're wasting time."

"Fine, but you better freaking listen to every word I say and follow every single order."

Once we got to my house, I tore through the cabinets for several bottles of holy water, then I went to the garage to load up the Hummer with twenty gallons of gas, hoping that would be enough to take out Vincent and whatever other minions he had hiding in the cemetery along with him. My thoughts raced thinking about how Chase and Nina had no idea what they were up against. Neither was talented or strong enough to take on Vincent and win. Hell, I wasn't sure I was, and I had experience. There was a sizable chance I wouldn't survive this battle. What haunted me the most was the knowledge that neither knew how to fully destroy a Demon. I assumed they would think gasoline was all it took, when in fact it wasn't the only component. Nina saw a gas can, *not* holy water bottles.

Before I shoved the keys into the ignition, I reached for the glove box. My hand searched through its contents before I located my amulet. Hadreniel had given me this particular one. Hanging off of a gold chain was my symbol carved out of obsidian; a star resting on top of a crescent moon. I'd worn this particular charm for every mission I'd ever been on. It had yet to fail me. Roping it around my neck, I took off like a bat straight out of Hell finally arriving at the cemetery. Both Jules and Chase's cars were parked by the front gates.

"You're to stay in this vehicle and not move a muscle. Take my phone and contact Michael. Tell him that I went after Nina and to send backup as fast as possible. I don't care what you hear or see. You're to keep your head and body down until either I or Orifiel come and get you. Do it now," I ordered, locking the doors, then scaling the wrought iron gates.

Perhaps I should've called to Orifiel or any of the other Angels, but I had to find Nina. She was in danger. Screw Chase. I had to protect and keep her alive because Nina was the only thing that was keeping me that way.

Chapter 62

Nina

I ran through the cemetery with no direction. Chase had to be here. My focus zoomed in on a tombstone that resembled the one I'd seen in the vision. As quickly as my legs could carry me, I raced to it.

Yes. This was it.

The vision clearly showed Chase at this specific grave. I closed my eyes trying to evoke the image again. A brief flash revealed Chase sitting on top of a rather large tombstone which looked like a fallen Angel. The gray marble Angel was kneeling on a square base with its head lowered and its wings down. A few feet away an archway led to cloisters. Chase was casually cracking his knuckles and neck. He was preparing to fight. His temperament was calm and fixated, while his gaze darted from side to side surveying the area. The vision ran its course for the second time tonight leaving me standing alone in the dark, muggy cemetery completely lost. Maybe I'd arrived too early, or worse, too late. The all too familiar sensation of panic assaulted me like a smack to the face.

Calm down. You've been through this before and walked away alive. This time will be no different.

But my negative thoughts overpowered my rational ones. In the past I knew where Chase was, but tonight that wasn't the case. Right now, I had no Chase, no Orifiel, and worst of all, no Gabriel to support me. I'd ventured too deep into the cemetery for any of them to find me now. Forcing my body to move, I took off searching the other tombstones. Maybe I was the one in the wrong place? Heavy and thick Spanish moss draped giant, live oak trees making the dense fog hang low destroying any long-range visibility. To my great displeasure, I encountered several other tombs, all which resembled the one from the vision.

Damn it!

I couldn't stop searching. I had to find Chase even though the odds were stacking up against me.

"Nina," a familiar voice yelled.

Frantically, I looked around to find the owner.

Gabriel! He's here.

"Gabriel," I hollered into the night air.

"Where are you?" he shouted.

Before I could respond, my feet became trapped inside a thorny vine. My scream sliced through the thick air as my body hit the ground, hard.

"Nina," Gabriel's distressed voice rang out.

I wanted to call for him, to beg him to find and help me, but I couldn't. My eyes became too focused on the scene playing out in front of me. I'd found Chase. To be more specific, I found Chase and Vincent trying to destroy each other. They were fighting like animals. There was nothing I could do but watch Vincent deal Chase a deadly blow. Freeing my feet from the vines as fast as possible, all lucid reasoning abandoned my brain. If Vincent wanted to kill Chase, he'd have to destroy me as well.

Balling my hands into tight fists, I studied the space.

Surely Vincent knew I was around hiding somewhere, but I prayed my exact coordinates remained a mystery. If that were the case, I had the art of surprise behind this attack, which would end after the first strike. With only one chance to make this happen, it had to work.

"Hey, Vincent," I yelled, shooting a powerful bolt at him the second he turned around.

The blast made contact, hitting him square in the pit of his stomach, forcing his body to fly backwards.

"Nina. Stay where you are," Chase screamed.

"No."

I watched Chase raise one hand and ball the other all while he focused on Vincent, who stumbled to get up. Suddenly, a strong force pushed itself against my chest and legs, not allowing for any forward movement. Chase was using his powers to hold me back.

In vain I fought the grip. I couldn't break free unless he released me. Blue and red streaks continued whipping through the air until Vincent and Chase both attacked at the same time. Their strikes met and both men struggled to not be the first to break the connection. The force holding my body shifted to the right allowing for slight movement again. Chase threw the momentum he had on me at Vincent, knocking him back. Vincent faltered, grabbing onto a thick branch of an oak tree. Pure hatred radiated from Chase's eyes as he fired off one last blue bolt. The strength behind the blow lifted Vincent's body off of the ground, knocking him out cold.

Chase grabbed the gasoline can and ran to where Vincent lifelessly lay. Dousing the man, Chase lit a match. The soulless creature's form quickly engulfed in black and maroon flames. I stood watching not knowing how to react.

"It's over, baby," Chase laughed. "The son of a bitch is gone, and he'll never harm you or bother us again. Rot in Hell, you piece of shit," He spat at Vincent's almost completely burnt corpse. He sounded like an absolute lunatic.

Gray and pink smoke with the pungent smell of death filled the air. The fire and vapor subsided rather quickly, leaving a pile of ashes on the ground.

"Chase," I started, but I couldn't finish my thought.

A strong windstorm swept up dead leaves and dirt into little funnels which danced across the ground.

"Chase," I shrieked.

Heavy thunder with some serious cloud-to-ground lightning rumbled, crashing through the sky. The storm picked up creating sustained gale force hurricane winds. Desperately, I tried to withstand the power and strength of the squalls, but I couldn't. My body was pushed back, eventually stopping after slamming against a tombstone.

Enepsigos!

My eyes frantically scanned from side to side trying to find where the bitch was hiding so I could stop her, but flying Spanish moss and debris made seeing anything impossible. All I could do was brace myself against the stone and weather the storm. The wind finally died down, allowing for natural movement to resume.

"Chase," I yelled, running in the direction of the last place I'd seen him.

"Nina."

I ran blindly toward the sound of his voice, spotting him a few yards away.

"I did this for you, Nina; for us. I love you so much, baby, and now we're free." He moved closer to where I stood.

"Where are Vincent's ashes, Chase?" I panicked. Chase may have burned Vincent's form, but we needed to smother his ashes with holy water. According to what Raphael had told me last year, that was the only way to completely destroy a Demon.

"He's gone, Nina. Who cares?"

Before another word was uttered, one final, powerful gust of frosty air whipped through the night sky. I wanted to push Chase out of the way, but everything happened too quickly. The violent wind swept up Vincent's ashes, shoving them directly at Chase.

"Get down," I yelled.

Chase's body dropped lifelessly to the ground. I took off toward him, but a set of arms locked around my waist, stopping me dead in my tracks.

"You can't save Chase. It's too late," Gabriel said.

His clothing was filthy and ripped to shreds. His skin was crusted with dirt.

"No. It's not. It's never too late. I can heal him. I know I can."

"Vincent's soul found a host. Chase is no longer one of us, Nina. He's one of them," he said, shaking my shoulders roughly. I couldn't believe him. I wouldn't believe him.

"Chase didn't fully kill Vincent. He merely burnt his body. Vincent's evil is still very much alive, and now it's inside of Chase. The only way to destroy the core of a Demon is to drown the ashes in holy water, which Chase didn't do. Chase's soul is completely ripped. I watched it happen. There's nothing left. Please, believe me."

I stood there in a state of complete and total shock staring at Chase's motionless frame.

"Look, Gabriel. He's moving. Chase is moving. He's alive. You need to let me heal him," I said, pointing at Chase's slow stirring form.

"If we don't get out of here right now, we're screwed, Nina. Listen to me. Chase, the Chase you once knew, once loved, no longer exists. His soul is completely gone—lost forever. The moment Vincent's ashes entered his body, the old Chase died, and this new one was born."

Hot angry tears poured down my face. "Kill me then. Please, Gabriel, kill me. I can't live without Chase. I love him so much. I don't think I can handle any of this. Please," I begged, weeping uncontrollably. "This is entirely my fault."

"It's not your fault, but we have to go before we're knee deep in a shit storm that I can't get us out of," Gabriel said, grabbing my right arm and pulling it roughly.

I turned, glancing at Chase one last time. He'd finally made it to his feet. He appeared to be taking in the cemetery in its entirety. His head snapped forward. Our eyes locked. To me, he looked the same, only a little disheveled.

"Chase?" I whispered, praying that Gabriel had been wrong.

He didn't respond. A creepy, eerie, wicked smile danced across his face. His skin tone faded as a slight hint of shimmer developed. I felt myself becoming lightheaded and dizzy. Chase's body was transforming into pure evil right in front of me.

No, this isn't real. This is some sort of weird dream. In a couple of seconds, you're going to wake, and everything will be fine.

I watched his beautiful, jade green eyes roll into the back of his head. When his eyes finally rolled back into place, they were bright red and soulless. The last thing I could remember was Gabriel's arms bracing my body and the sound of objects cracking through the early morning air. Blurry red streaks flashed in front of my face, then nothing.

Darkness had fallen.

A word about the author...

A lifelong storyteller, JP Barry specializes in crafting heart stopping, compelling, unique, emotional page turners for a variety of genres. A New York native, Barry is always on the hunt for ideas for her next novel. When not writing, Barry enjoys spending time with her family.

Thank you for purchasing
this publication of The Wild Rose Press, Inc.

For questions or more information
contact us at
info@thewildrosepress.com.

The Wild Rose Press, Inc.
www.thewildrosepress.com